DOWN
Portal

Glenn Cooper

Down: Portal
Copyright © 2015 by Glenn Cooper

Cover Art and Cover Design by Sherwin Soy
Author photo by Louis Fabian Bachrach
Formatting by Polgarus Studio

Note: American spelling is used throughout
except when referring to specific British places and titles.

1

"Mummy, where are we?"

When he didn't get a reply, four-year-old Sam repeated the question more insistently.

His sister, Belle, a year younger, began to cry.

Their mother, Arabel, didn't have an answer and could only stare in mute shock, for one moment they had been in the canteen at the MAAC supercollider in Dartford, England waiting hopefully to be reunited with Arabel's sister, Emily Loughty, and the next moment they were someplace very different. But the other woman had a sick inkling where they were. Delia May quickly snatched Belle into her arms and whispered for her to be a good girl and try to keep still.

They were inside a small house, not much larger than a garden shed. With its earthen floor, small hearth, a few measly sticks aglow, and a rank game bird hanging on a hook, it was rougher than most garden sheds. Sam began to cough from the smoky atmosphere and Delia urgently shushed him. There were loud voices outside and Delia, holding the little girl, crept to a window covered by unlatched shutters which were clattering in the breeze. She pushed one of the shutters open a few inches and peered out. Even though she thought she understood what was happening, she caught her breath at the sight. There in the middle of a muddy road, a short distance away, was Duck, her young charge for the past month. He was naked and a much larger man she instantly recognized as Brandon

Woodbourne was throttling him. Another young man began beating Woodbourne's back with a club and soon a motley assortment of other men joined in the melee and Woodbourne ran off, cursing and shouting.

Just then Sam noticed the hanging bird, took a step toward it and began to giggle.

"Look, mum. My trousers fell down."

His denim jeans were around his ankles and his underpants, lacking elastic, were about to fall from his waist too.

Arabel felt at her own clothes. Her skirt was loose and zipperless, absent buttons her shirt was half-open, and her bra, missing its hooks was flapping underneath. She finally spoke in a trembling voice. "Please, can you tell me what's happening?"

"We must stay very quiet," Delia said, standing away from the window. "I think we're in the place where your sister's been."

"I don't have any idea what you mean," Arabel said. "I demand to know what's going on. Where's the canteen? Where's the laboratory? Have we been drugged?"

"Keep your voice down," Delia implored, but Arabel would not be mollified.

There was a wooden door secured by a simple wooden latch. Arabel went for it. When Delia tried to stop her she pushed the older woman aside, undid the latch, and flung the door open hard enough that it loudly struck the side of the house.

Arabel stared out in shock. She repeated the same question as her young son, "Where are we?"

Delia roughly pulled her back inside and latched the door. She knew where they were but she couldn't make herself say the word. She couldn't because to say it was to make it real.

She couldn't say, "Hell."

2

John Camp awoke in pain and momentary confusion in a surgical recovery suite at the Royal London Hospital. A rotund male nurse was checking his blood pressure and appeared to aim a chuckle in his direction which confused John even more. As it happened, the nurse had just been told about the curious instructions John had given the surgeons moments before the anesthesia kicked in.

"Make sure you use double or triple the number of stitches as usual," John had told them.

"And why is that?" he had been asked through a surgical mask.

"I can't tell you," John had said. "Just do it. The wound needs to be strong."

"Welcome back," the nurse said.

John blinked. His voice was thin and raspy, his vocal chords like sandpaper. "What's so funny?"

"Funny? Nothing. Nothing at all. The operation's over. You did just fine."

"Operation? Oh yeah, I remember. Fuck." He grimaced.

"Pain?"

John nodded.

"I'll just get you a jab of morphine."

With the narcotic coursing through his system he nodded off and began to dream.

The dream was about Hell.

He was trapped inside a fetid rotting room, pounding on the locked door. Solomon Wisdom was on the other side, telling him he could not let him out. No one could. It was his fate. Then Thomas Cromwell was standing beside him, knee deep in human flesh, informing him that King Henry was very cross with John, very cross indeed.

"Will you repent?" Cromwell asked.

"I repent."

Through the door Wisdom laughed, "Repent all you want. It matters not. What's done is done."

When John awoke again he was in a private room in a ward. The window glowed orange in the sunset. Emily had been waiting by his bed and when she saw his eyes flutter open she tried to envelop one of his large hands with her small one.

"How're you feeling?" she asked.

"Worse than before."

"I talked to your surgeon. They made a good-sized incision to clean out the infection. That drip is your antibiotics, two of them, actually, until they get the culture results from your wound."

"Bad bugs in Hell, I guess," John said, searching for the bed controls.

Emily found the box and raised him up to a more comfortable position.

"Better?"

"Better," he said. He asked for ice chips and she spooned some into his mouth. "What were you up to while I was getting my insides cleaned out?" he asked.

"I was in the lab going over data."

"And?"

"I'm sure Matthew is right. The high collision energies produced strangelets and gravitons in surprising abundance. The interaction between the two must account for the phenomenon."

"Phenomenon. That's one of the greatest euphemisms of all times."

"Well, you know the way we scientists tend to speak."

"Is there a count yet?"

"A count?"

"How many people are missing."

"Four from Dartford. Arabel, the children, and Delia, the MI5 lady. South Ockendon's still a muddle. They haven't caught any of the Hellers who entered there."

He waved off more ice chips. "What a fuck up."

Emily nodded and dabbed at her eyes with a tissue. "I can't bear to think what Arabel and the kids are going through. They must be so scared."

"Dirk isn't a bad kid, relatively speaking. I'm hoping he's helping them. And his brother's got to be there too. Trevor told me Duck bonded with Delia May. She'll know we'll be mounting a rescue effort."

Emily nodded. "I know. I talked to Trevor this afternoon. He also told me he'd been seeing Arabel during the past month."

"Really?"

"Seems he fancies her. He's as worried as I am."

"Well, he's a good man. It wouldn't surprise me if he volunteered for the mission."

Emily crumpled the tissue and put it in her handbag. "I don't want you to go, John."

He stifled an incipient laugh because it hurt too much. "I don't want *you* to go."

"I didn't just have surgery. I don't have a life-threatening infection."

"I'll be okay in a few days. I heal fast. I'm a soldier, Emily. This is what I do. You were amazing. I'm proud of how you were able to survive but you're a scientist. You need to stay here and figure out how to fix the problem. You do what you do best and I'll do what I do best."

"I'm sorry, John, but I'm going. If Arabel, Sam, and Belle hadn't been caught up in this then I would never voluntarily go back. But I won't be put off. You know how stubborn I am. My mind is made up."

"Well, I'm not changing my mind either."

They smiled at each other. It was settled.

The large executive conference room at the Massive Anglo-American Collider at Dartford was filling up for the 8 a.m. meeting. There was no pre-assigned seating and participants instinctively sorted themselves according to their own perceived importance. Leroy Bitterman and Karen Smithwick, the US and UK energy secretaries, took prime chairs at the head of the table. Close to them were Campbell Bates, the FBI director, and George Lawrence, the director general of MI5. Ben Wellington from MI5 sat beside Trevor Jones. Senior scientists at MAAC, including Matthew Coppens and David Laurent, and Stuart Binford, head of the lab's public affairs department, rounded out the assembly. Henry Quint came in and assumed the empty seat at the head had been saved for him. When he approached it, Smithwick waved him off and with his eyes cast downward in embarrassment, he took a chair against the wall.

Ben leaned toward Trevor and said, "Is John Camp being patched into this?"

"I don't think so," Trevor said. "He's having some kind of scan this morning."

"Where's Dr. Loughty?"

Trevor scanned the room. "I'd better find her."

She was at her desk, staring at something.

"Hey there," Trevor said gently, sitting down. "Just wanted to let you know the meeting's starting."

She responded to his attempt at a bright smile with a worn-out sigh. "I lost track of time. I suppose I've gotten out of the habit of clock watching."

"Yeah, I can understand that."

She gave her telephone a weary look. "I was just talking to my parents."

"How'd that go?"

"They're so confused. They're happy I'm all right, of course, but they're devastated that Arabel and the kids have gone missing now."

"What'd you tell them?"

"Am I talking to Trevor, a friend, or Trevor, the deputy-head of security?"

"Friend."

"I strayed from the script. I had to."

"How far did you go?"

"Believe me, I didn't use the word Hell once. I called it another dimension, that MAAC opened a passageway to another dimension. I told them we'd get Arabel, Sam, and Belle back."

"Did they believe you?"

"I don't know. They were too scared to ask a lot of questions."

"Just so you're aware, they signed the Official Secret's Act."

"I know."

"Did you tell them you were going back?"

"Not yet, but I will. I have to."

"We've got to go to the meeting." When he stood, he saw what she'd been staring at. It was the charcoal drawing Caravaggio had sketched of her. "That's a good likeness," he said.

She placed it in her top drawer. "I'm quite fond of it."

The meeting began when Emily and Trevor arrived. Matthew had a seat saved next to him. Emily knew everyone except for the man sitting between Bitterman and Smithwick. He had a pugnacious, florid face, which seemed ballooned owing to an overly tight collar and tie knot. She asked Matthew about him but he didn't know him either.

Trevor was asking the same thing of Ben.

"His name's Trotter. Anthony Trotter. He's MI6. Word is the prime minister wanted him involved. Guess what the lads in MI6 call him?"

"Haven't a clue," Trevor whispered back.

"Pig."

Trevor stifled a laugh. "Can you imagine the stick he got at school?"

At the same time Campbell Bates was asking his counterpart at MI5 what he thought about Trotter's involvement.

Lawrence whispered his answer. "As delighted as you would be if you were made second fiddle to the CIA."

"Shall we begin?" Smithwick asked. "Dr. Bitterman and I will be co-chairing this meeting. We are now twenty-two hours into this present incident. This working group will meet daily to coordinate the response.

The first order of business is introducing Anthony Trotter from the Intelligence Services. Mr. Trotter is the ACSS, the assistant chief of the Secret Service, and is an adviser to the Cabinet's Cobra committee. He will, effective immediately, be taking over operational command of MAAC from Dr. Quint. I think we can all appreciate that the scientific mission of MAAC has taken a back seat to the security issues, which have come to the fore in a most alarming way. Are there any questions?"

Emily raised her hand.

"Please go ahead, Dr. Loughty," Smithwick said.

Emily made no effort to sound diplomatic. She'd been through too much for that. "Do you have any background in science, Mr. Trotter?"

He had been doodling on his pad and looked at her from under his droopy eyelids. "I do not."

"Who here thinks it's a good idea to place a scientific installation in the hands of a non-scientist?" she asked. "Everyone here knows I am beyond livid that Dr. Quint exceeded the energy parameters of Hercules I and we have to deal with the disastrous consequences of that action. But solving our present dilemma will require the best possible scientific management, not a bureaucratic management."

"Might I?" Leroy Bitterman asked.

"Please," Smithwick said.

Bitterman warmly smiled at Emily and said in an avuncular tone, "First, I want to publicly say what I privately told Dr. Loughty yesterday, that I so admire the courage and tenacity she displayed under what must have been the most appalling circumstances. We owe her an enormous debt of gratitude for what she has done and what she has volunteered to do again. I want to assure you, Dr. Loughty, publicly and emphatically, that we will not compromise the scientific integrity of MAAC or diminish the work that needs to be done to solve the most pressing problem we have, namely plugging the inter-dimensional hole once all our people have been rescued. With your input, we will be convening a panel of international experts in particle physics and cosmology to assist the scientific staff at Dartford. Mr. Trotter is an expert in other matters and will not interfere with purely scientific and technical administration. He has the confidence of the US and UK governments in handling the complex security and secrecy issues which have arisen. I hope that addresses your concerns."

Emily returned the smile. "Thank you, Dr. Bitterman. That was very helpful and yes, I have some names I'd like to suggest for this advisory panel."

Smithwick then resumed her control of the meeting and dryly laid out an agenda as if this were a routine session about oil production quotas in the UK's North Sea Economic Zone. Emily found her bloodless demeanor wanting and she squirmed in her seat.

"Hearing no comments on the agenda," Smithwick said, "let's begin with a review of the security response to the present situation. Perhaps Mr. Trotter might lead this discussion."

Trotter cleared his cigar-irritated throat. He was not an imposing man, but he fancied himself Churchillian and to promote this image, he smoked Romeo y Julieta Havanas, the brand favored by the great man himself.

"Thank you, madam secretary. As you are aware, SIS has been asked to take the lead on this and to coordinate the activities of MI5, the military, the Metropolitan Police, and other relevant police and emergency services departments. Why the SIS, which is charged with foreign threats, rather than the domestic MI5 apparatus, you might ask? Well, it is hard to imagine any threat more alien than the one we now face."

Emily cringed at the bizarre attempt at humor. Trotter took the stony silence around the table with the sour expression of a comedian whose joke had just laid an egg.

"In all seriousness," he recovered, "the SIS is particularly well-suited to the task at hand given our analytics, information-processing, and communications capabilities. The PM has confidence in our leadership and we shall not disappoint. As I see it, the highest priority is dealing with the aliens who are at large."

A deep, gravelly voice interrupted Trotter. "We're not talking about Romanians or Chinese, you know. These are people from Hell, for Christ's sake."

With all eyes on Trotter, no one had noticed John Camp limping into the back of the room.

Emily and Trevor jumped up and went to him.

"What are you doing here?" Emily scolded.

"I got tired lying on my duff so I signed myself out."

"You should go back to hospital, guv," Trevor said, supporting him around the waist and helping him over to the only free chair. It was next to Henry Quint who flinched at John's presence. His jaw still ached from their last encounter.

"Not a chance," John said. "There's too much work to do. They shot me up with antibiotics and whatnot. I'll be fine."

Emily couldn't conceal her look of concern and was about to argue with him when Trotter spoke up. "This must be John Camp," he said.

"I am. And you are?"

"Anthony Trotter, SIS. I've been made acting director of this facility."

"You mean Quint's not in charge any more?" John said with a grin.

"That is correct," Trotter said.

"Well, that's a bit of good news."

The comment spawned muffled titters around the table. Quint looked ahead stoically.

Trotter finally addressed John's comment. "We're all aware where these people hail from. What is it they call themselves? Hellers?"

"Some do," John said.

"MI5 has been tasked with leading the charge of rounding up these Hellers. Ben Wellington is the liaison with this committee. Mr. Wellington, could you give us a report?"

Ben had prepared some notes but decided to wing it and closed his leather portfolio. "Let me begin with the easier of the two groups, the men who appeared on site here, within the employee canteen. As you are aware, there are four of them, ranging in biological age from the thirties to the fifties, all of them hailing from the London and Kent areas, with stated dates of death ranging from the fifteenth to the nineteenth centuries. The dominant figure of the group is named Alfred Carpenter who claims he was hanged for various offenses in the early sixteen hundreds. I'd describe him as a thuggish sort with low intellect. He continues to believe, despite our explanations and demonstrations, that he's the subject of some kind of black magic. His companions, particularly the more modern of the group, take their lead from him but once separated, seemed to accept the reality of their situation."

"Are they still in this facility?" the FBI Director asked.

"They are," Ben replied. "Our view is that this is as good a place as any to hold them and offers the best overall security parameters given the alternatives. Previously, we kept the young man, Duck, in the security dormitory …"

"And he escaped," Trotter interrupted.

"While on an authorized outdoors walk in the compound," Ben said. "A regrettable mistake. These men will not have the same opportunity. We are in the process of constructing proper jail cells on the dormitory level that will be ready for occupancy tomorrow. When members of the second group are captured, they will be housed here as well."

"Guantanamo comes to Dartford," Trotter said.

Trevor spoke up. "Is there anything John or Emily can tell us about these four men which might be helpful to their guards?"

"I didn't have much to do with them," John said.

Emily said that she hadn't either.

"When we were waiting on our mark for the MAAC restart, Alfred was something of an alpha dog," John said. "I'd describe him as menacing but he's not the worst of the worst. He wasn't a rover."

"A rover?" Trotter asked. "What is that?"

"They roam the countryside looking for people to take down. They live rough, generally sleep during the day, and get vicious at night. They rob and maim. And if they're hungry, they eat."

"You mean they're cannibals?" Bitterman asked in alarm and befuddlement.

"Yes, sir, that's correct," John said. "They're universally feared, a special breed of evil."

Bitterman muttered something under his breath.

Ben piped up. "This could explain something we discovered this morning on the estate in South Ockendon. It hasn't been circulated yet to the working group because it's too fresh. As you know, we evacuated the estate under the pretext of a terrorist threat with biohazardous material discovered in a house. In methodically working through a house-to-house search we found a murdered couple, an elderly man and woman. They'd been stabbed and hacked to death with kitchen knives and cleavers. And this is the particularly troubling part: there were bite marks on their arms and legs with flesh torn away."

"Good God!" Smithwick exclaimed, momentarily burying her face in her hands.

"Rovers for sure," John said. "Any sign of them?"

"None," Ben said. "We initially established a perimeter with local police now supplemented with units of the 16th Air Assault Brigade from the Colchester Garrison but the horses may have been out of the barn before the perimeter became non-porous."

"Have there been no sightings in the general area?" Trotter asked.

"Nothing definitive," Ben said. "The Essex police have responded to scattered reports within a five-mile radius of the estate of suspicious activity in people's gardens, wheelie bins disturbed, that sort of thing. But no sightings."

"Like I said, they're nocturnal," John said. "They own the night."

"Have we no idea how many of them are extant?" Trotter asked.

John rolled his eyes at the word. Who uses words like extant, he thought?

Emily must have been on the same wavelength because she matched his gesture with her own, an upward curl of her lips.

Ben opened his portfolio. "The best handle on that is the number of people missing from the estate, assuming the previous principal of a one-for-one exchange is still in effect. That task is made difficult by our lack of information on who was present and who was absent from their houses yesterday morning at ten o'clock. We are holding the evacuees, nearly three hundred residents of the estate, in a pavilion at the Colchester Garrison and interviews are in progress but we still do not have an account of the number of missing. Undoubtedly, this will become clearer as the day progresses and I will circulate an update this afternoon."

Trotter began tapping his fingertips together repeatedly. Whether it was a nervous tic or an expression of urgency was unclear to John. "Control of the press will be vital. The previous breach was well disguised, so well in fact that MI6 was kept in the dark, which, I must say, we do not appreciate. This breach is very much larger and less well contained so our challenges will be legion. Who is the press officer?"

Stuart Binford tentatively raised his hand and identified himself.

"Very well, Mr. Binford. Please enlighten us on how you plan to communicate the resolution of breach number one and your approach to breach number two."

Binford sounded hesitant, as if speaking on these matters was above his pay grade. He essentially degraded himself as merely a press flack accustomed to taking his orders from Henry Quint, before giving it the old college try. Breach number one, as Trotter dubbed it, had been described as an armed intruder gaining access to MAAC who kidnapped and killed a journalist and subsequently several members of the public. Clearly, they could not invoke Brandon Woodbourne as the culprit since inconveniently, he'd been dead for almost fifty years. Binford suggested inventing a suspect out of whole cloth and declaring his apprehension and death at the hands of the security services. Could this be accomplished, Binford asked rhetorically?

Trotter shrugged and suggested that, while not a routine matter, he was certain his colleagues at MI6 could manage something like this.

On the larger issue of breach number two, Binford continued, "It seems to me that ascribing the South Ockendon incident to a terror plot involving biological weapons production on a residential housing estate, has been the best possible strategy. The press is, and will continue to be in a feeding frenzy, but I should think we would be able to stonewall them on national security grounds. Small, steady drips of misinformation ought to keep them at bay."

"For how long?" Smithwick asked.

"It's hard for me to say," Binford said. "Undoubtedly the longer it goes on the harder it will be."

"Right," Trotter said, addressing the table. "It seems we have the outlines of a press strategy. I'll have someone at my shop call Mr. Binford and begin working on a detailed implementation plan. Which leads us to the next agenda item. To put it rather unscientifically I'd call it plugging the hole."

Emily bristled visibly. Her voice cracking, she said, "I don't think that plugging the hole, as you call it, is the next item at all. The next item must be organizing a rescue effort for the people who've been transported to a very dangerous and terrifying place."

Bitterman was about to answer her but Trotter cut him off. "I appreciate that you've been through the ringer, Dr. Loughty, and I also appreciate that your sister, niece, and nephew have been caught up in this business, and for that very reason, I think you need to recuse yourself from this discussion."

She flew out of her chair in a rage. "I beg your pardon?"

John also tried to stand but caught himself and slumped back down in pain. "Are you out of your mind?" he said, pointing a finger at Trotter. "Dr. Loughty is the most qualified person in the room—no scratch that, on the planet—to understand the things these people are going through and the scientific issues involved in bringing them home and making MAAC safe."

Bitterman raised his hands in an effort to tamp down emotions. "Please, everyone, I'm sure Mr. Trotter isn't suggesting that a rescue effort is a low priority."

"I'm sorry," Trotter said coldly, "that's exactly what I'm suggesting. As I've said, I'm not a scientist but I am blessed with an abundance of common sense. And that has led me to the conclusion that this channel, or passageway to this other dimension has widened. Initially it encompassed Dartford only. Now South Ockendon is involved. With every restart of the collider it seems that the risk only increases. Therefore I believe our foremost priority must be to plug the hole and my unscientific mind tells me the best way to do that is to shut down MAAC once and for all."

Emily shouted back, "I'm not going to sit here and listen to this nonsense and furthermore …"

John gently jumped in. "Emily, let me. Please. They're just going to keep invoking your so-called conflict of interests. So let me say this. In war, you don't leave one of your men behind on the battlefield. Make no mistake of it. This is a war. And the people who are lost on the battlefield are innocent men, women and children. I've volunteered to go back. Emily has volunteered. Trevor Jones has volunteered. We're willing to put our lives on the line and you people should have the courage to back us to the hilt."

"That's very well said, Mr. Camp," Bitterman said. "You have my backing and you have the backing of the US government."

"With all due respect, Mr. Secretary," Trotter said, "it is British soil that has been invaded by these beings and it is British citizens who've been killed. If this were happening in Washington or New York, I venture to say your position would be the same as mine."

Bitterman leaned back in his chair and took a deep breath. "All right, fair point. Let me put it to the experts then. Do you agree that each restart of MAAC increases the instability of the connection between our universe and this parallel universe?"

John watched Emily silently struggle with the question and shift in her chair but Quint jumped the queue and answered before her.

"The answer is undoubtedly yes," Quint said. "The intense collision energy we're achieving at our maximum power of 30 TeV is producing gravitons and strangelets in abundance. These particles are combining in some undetermined way to pierce the veil of our universe and create a connection across the multiverse to another dimensional state. That seems clear. While we don't understand the phenomenon yet, successive high-energy collisions seem to be causing these graviton-strangelet complexes to propagate and now we have two nodes of connectivity along the MAAC tunnel. Each additional restart would, in my estimation, increase the risk of additional nodes forming at any place along the track of the tunnels, that is, at any place encircling greater London."

Bitterman pointed to Matthew Coppens and asked for his opinion. Avoiding Emily's hard stare, Matthew reluctantly agreed with Quint. David Laurence was next and he also concurred.

"I don't want to put you on the spot, Dr. Loughty," Bitterman said, "but you are the scientific director and you are in charge of the Hercules project. Your objective assessment carries a lot of weight with me."

She sighed heavily and said, "I'd like to study the data further but I don't necessarily disagree with my colleagues. That said, I believe we have to approach the problem at hand with a risk-mitigation strategy."

"What would that look like?" Bitterman asked.

"Over the past six weeks, there were six power-ups of the collider. The first was when I was transported, the second transported John, three through five were fruitless and the sixth, yesterday, returned us but transported others at two locales or nodes, to use Dr. Quint's terminology. The rationale for four weekly restarts during John's mission to find me was sensible on the face of it. He didn't know how long it would take to locate me and absent a way of communicating with the lab, he was given four weekly windows of opportunity. I would suggest that to mitigate against further field instabilities we limit ourselves to one restart as soon as practically possible to transport the rescue party and one and only one restart to return as many rescuers and victims as possible, trading them for all the Hellers you've been able to capture."

Bates, the FBI director asked, "How long would we give you to accomplish your mission?"

Emily asked John what he thought.

"I'd say a month," he answered. "If all the missing are still in Britannia that's one thing, but if some of them have been shipped off to Europa that's something else again. We're going to have to know the identities and backgrounds of the South Ockendon people to have any prayer of finding them."

"And when would you propose to leave?" Smithwick asked.

"As soon as possible," John said. "The longer we wait the greater the chance of dispersion of our people to the continent."

Sir George Lawrence, the director general of MI5 asked, "Why the continent? Why can't we assume they'll stay put where they emerged?"

Emily answered, "It's because the flesh peddlers prey upon new arrivals, assess their value, and sell them to the highest bidder. There is no more exotic and valuable arrival as a live person, particularly a live woman, and some of the highest bidders are in Europa, as they call it."

"Good heavens," Sir George gasped. "Ghastly."

"I think we're getting off topic," Trotter said, trying to reassert himself.

"I don't think we're off topic at all," Bitterman said, cutting him off with a time-out hand sign. "The ultimate decision on restarts will rest on the shoulders of two men who are not in the room, the president of the United States and the prime minister of Great Britain. Assuming we go with the very sensible risk-mitigation strategy that has been proposed, I know how I'll be advising the president. I won't presume how Secretary Smithwick will be advising the prime minister. But I'd challenge Mr. Camp on the one-week timetable for the departure of the rescue team. There is much to do. We have to compile a dossier on the South Ockendon missing. We have to do a comprehensive debrief of Mr. Camp and Dr. Loughty so we can better understand the capabilities of our adversaries. We need to plan how to best equip our rescue team to deal with the challenges they'll be facing. And last and by far not the least, we need to give Mr. Camp time to recover from his surgery and for Dr. Loughty to weigh in on Mr. Trotter's hole-plugging scenarios."

John insisted he'd be well enough recovered in a week and Emily said she'd also be prepared to go in a week's time.

"I'm ready when they're ready," Trevor said.

Ben politely raised his hand to speak. "How are the three of you planning on handling the geographical challenges of two groups of innocents, one in Dartford, the other in South Ockendon, or whatever it's called in Hell?"

John said it was a going to be a tough challenge and he'd been giving it some thought. "Best case scenario, we find Arabel, her children, and Delia May quickly, stash them in a safe house with one of us as a guard. Then the other two would make their way to the South Ockendon location, find the missing and bring them back to Dartford for the extraction."

"I can't begin to tell you how many things could go wrong," Ben said.

"I hear you and I don't disagree. It's going to be a fly by the seat of your pants operation."

"Have you considered a larger rescue party?" Ben asked.

John smiled. "Volunteering?"

Ben looked down sheepishly. "Not exactly."

"Given the time frame to departure, the dangers involved, the secrecy, the operational skills needed, I think we're lucky to have three ready and able volunteers."

Bitterman thanked them for the discussion and said, "Hearing no objections to the plan put forward by Dr. Loughty and Mr. Camp, I believe we're ready to seek the approval for a MAAC restart in one week's time."

Trotter muttered loudly enough for some in the room to hear, "And here I thought I was in charge."

"The only ones in charge, as you put it, are the president and the prime minister," Bitterman said considerably louder. "The rest of us are but humble advisors. Now one last thing. I'm quite sure that you will ignore me, Mr. Camp, so I'd like to suggest that Dr. Loughty pull rank and order you to get back to the hospital to get well enough for the challenges you'll be facing next week."

"Thank you, Dr. Bitterman," Emily said, smiling at John. "That is precisely what I shall do."

3

The men in the middle of the road stopped what they were doing, stared at the open door, then began pointing at Arabel and shouting excitedly.

"Look! A woman!" one of them yelled.

"In Albert's house," said another.

"What's happened to Albert and his lot?" yet another said.

Arabel disappeared back inside the house, the door slamming behind her.

The men surged toward the house and Delia, watching from the window, cast about for something to fend them off. Her eyes settled on a firewood axe by the hearth and she seized it. She stepped out, holding the axe in both hands as one might hold a rifle.

"Stay back!" she warned.

The group of men pulled up short. "She's a plump 'un," one of them said.

"Looks good enough for me," a man said with a leer.

Another replied, "I likes the young 'un better."

Then the nearest to Delia sniffed the air. "It's another live one, ain't it? What the devil is going on 'round here?"

A voice rang out from behind the men. "Delia? Is that you?"

She loudly replied, "I'm afraid it is, Duck."

The young man, absent his red nylon Liverpool tracksuit, ran past the others and threw his arms around her waist.

"Naked as the day you were born," she sighed. Clad mainly in her sensible cotton and cashmere, Delia's clothes had come through largely intact.

"I can't believe you're here," he said. "You weren't in the big room when I left. Made me sad but now I'm 'appy."

"I wish I could say the same. Are these men going to hurt me and my friends?"

"Not with old Duck around. Not a chance." He let go of her and turned to the villagers. "This 'ere's my Delia. She was right good to me on Earth and I'm fixin' to be right good to 'er in Down. So back away and go about your business."

Dirk came forward and stared.

Delia looked him over and said, "You must be Dirk. Your brother's told me so much about you."

"Thanks for looking after 'im," Dirk said, "but I confess, me 'ead's swimming. First John and Emily disappearing like, then Duck coming 'ome, now more live 'uns. I believe I need a strong brew."

Duck said. "Who's the moll who stuck 'er 'ead out—she's a rum-doxy, all right."

"Rum-doxy?" Delia asked, finally letting the heavy axe drag against the ground. "I swear I can't understand half the things you say."

"Pretty," Duck said. "Pretty and fair."

"Did you say that John Camp and Emily Loughty were just here?" Delia asked Dirk.

"They was and now they're not," Dirk said. "This 'ere village must be under a spell."

Arabel was listening from inside the house. She told the children not to move and took a few steps out. Her mouth was bone dry. "Emily was here? Jesus, I don't even know where here is."

"She was 'ere in Down, all right," Dirk said.

"Down?"

"It's what we call it," Duck said. "Delia'll tell you."

"I'll explain it all to you soon," Delia said.

"Is she all right? Is Emily all right?" Arabel asked.

"Right as rain, she was," Dirk said. "You know of her?"

"She's my sister."

Dirk scrutinized her. "There's a resemblance. Pleased to make your acquaintance though I don't believe you'll be pleased to make mine. Duck's my brother. I can't say that John Camp was right as rain. He was poorly from a gash."

"Well, thank God they made it back," Delia said.

Dirk took a step toward the house. "You said you 'ad friends. Is there more of you?"

"There are two others," Delia said, "and you must promise me you will treat them very, very gently."

"Yeah, all right. Delicate creatures, are they?"

"Yes they are. They're young children. A boy and a girl."

"Little 'uns?" Dirk said. "'Ere?"

"I'm afraid so. Now, I'll go back inside and prepare them the best I can but in the meanwhile I would very much appreciate it, Duck, if you could find some clothes."

"What, you don't want 'em seeing 'is sugar-stick and nutmegs?" Dirk laughed.

"No, I most certainly do not. Give us a few minutes."

Delia went back inside and sat Arabel down on a rickety chair. Sam and Belle were in a dark corner playing with a pile of firewood kindling and Delia spoke low so they couldn't hear what she had to say. At first Arabel wouldn't or couldn't believe her but after a few minutes of patient telling, it dawned on her that neither she nor Delia had gone mad. MAAC had first thrust Emily across an invisible boundary separating the world as they knew it into another world, and now they were there too.

In Hell.

She began to cry but Delia told her she must stop. Stop and be strong. For the children.

"We will certainly face things we're not suited for," she said. "We will be scared. We will be horrified. We will despair. But know this, young lady.

Your sister and her colleagues will have already begun working on a rescue plan. Do you know John Camp?"

"I've heard all about him," Arabel said, "but we've not met yet."

"Well, John went through to find your sister. It seems he succeeded. He did it once and he'll do it again. We must stay resolute for our sakes and the sakes of the children. We will get through this."

"How can you be so strong?"

"I'm not as strong as I'm sounding right now. In fact I'm surprising myself. I work for MI5 but I'm not an operative, I'm a researcher. I sit at a desk with a computer. I was plucked from my cubicle to babysit Duck. He popped out when John Camp passed over. But I am a tough old bag, as some of the youngsters in my division refer to me. My toughness comes from my life. My only child died at Sam's age. My husband left me. I carried on."

"My husband died too," Arabel said softly.

"Then I expect you're tough too. Come on. Let's be tough together. Let's go outside and face this strange new world with brave faces, shall we?"

It took longer than Delia would have liked for the four of them to cross the muddy road. Over the decades and centuries, the village men had seen the odd woman arrive before. With Emily, they had even seen a live woman, so Arabel and Delia were a spectacle but not *the* spectacle. That distinction went to Sam and Belle because none of them had ever laid eyes on a child in Hell. The men were quiet and standoffish at first sight, confining themselves to staring and sniffing, but soon they sought to block their way and some of them reached out to touch the children, perhaps not believing their eyes.

"Leave 'em be, let 'em pass," Duck insisted. Dirk had given Duck his spare pair of breeches and, though shirtless, Delia was happier about his attire.

"Just look straight ahead, children," Delia said, trying to take her own advice, "and keep holding hands with mummy. They're just curious. You see, they've never seen two lovelier tykes."

"They smell bad," Sam said. "And they're dirty."

"Be polite," Delia scolded. "We're visitors."

Arabel did not speak a single word, her face frozen in fear. She clasped her children's hands as firmly as she could without causing pain.

When their progress came to a complete halt, Dirk came to the rescue with his club, threatening to bash his neighbors the way he'd lit into Woodbourne. The throng parted allowing them to thread the gauntlet but Sam slowed them down twice, first when his shoes, missing their Velcro, came off in the sucking mud, and second, just yards from Dirk and Duck's house when he stopped to ask a man why he was crying.

The fellow, gaunt and sallow, wiped at the tears running into his scraggly beard and said, "It's been so long I'd forgotten what children looked like …"

Inside the brothers' cottage, the children played with a magpie feather on Dirk's bed and Delia gave in and decided to join the lads in a mug of beer. Arabel sat mutely at the table, occasionally glancing over her shoulder at the kids while Delia fired off questions.

"Will we be safe in here?" she asked.

"Why, we won't hurt you," Dirk said, appearing hurt by the question.

"I don't mean you, I mean the men outside. Will they try to break in?"

"Can't say for sure," Dirk said. "The worse 'uns, Albert and his maties, well, they've vanished, perhaps to the place you've just come from. A few of the others might get bold, owing to the sudden appearance of pretty ladies."

"I can see the issue with Arabel but I doubt I'll make the blood run hot," Delia said with a chortle.

To her amusement Dirk said, "You're not so bad."

"I'm old enough to be your mum, if not your gran."

"Not to fret," Duck said. "I'll do the sleeping in shifts with me brother and between us, we'll keep an eye on the ruffians. The little 'uns can have one bed and the ladies can have the other. We'll kip by the fire."

Delia thanked them. "I think we should just stay right here, indoors. It's a bit cramped but it's safest. They'll be working on a rescue and this is where they'll come."

"Who'll come?" Dirk asked.

"I don't know about Emily, as she's had her own ordeal, but I imagine John Camp will be one of them."

"'e weren't too lively when he left 'ere this morn," Dirk said.

"How bad was he?"

"Well, 'e was feverish and weak. He got run through, 'e did, by a rover knife."

"Well in that case, perhaps they'll send someone else," Delia said. "But thank God he and Dr. Loughty were retrieved." She knew about rovers from conversations with Duck at MAAC and she asked, "Do we have to worry about rovers here?"

"Everyone worries about them," Dirk said, "but we've not 'ad a problem with 'em 'ere of late, 'ave we, Duck?"

"Not for a long while," Duck said, looking around the meager cottage. "Slim pickings 'ere, I suppose, compared to other villages."

They were all startled when Arabel spoke for the first time. "When? When will they come for us?"

"I don't know, my dear," Delia said gently. "I expect they'll want to do some preparation and planning. If I know the powers that be, there will be hoops to jump through, but come they will. When John went for Emily, it was a week after she disappeared. So, maybe we'll have to soldier on for a week."

"I don't think I can stay here that long," Arabel said weakly. "We'll want to go home very much sooner."

"The sooner the better," Delia said, touching her arm.

In a tiny voice, Belle announced she was thirsty.

"Do you have any water?" Delia asked.

Dirk pointed to a wooden pail by the hearth.

"Is it clean?"

"It's not muddy," Dirk said.

Delia inspected it and cupped some into her palm. "Tastes all right."

Belle said she preferred juice but Delia cleaned out a wooden mug the best she could and offered it up. The girl thumbed her nose at it and commenced whining. Arabel began to apologize to the girl that there wasn't any nice juice about but Delia cut her off with a calculated demonstration of tough love.

"She'll drink when she's thirsty enough. She's going to have to quickly adapt to survive. We all will."

They heard a horse whinny and clop off through the mud. Dirk opened the door to have a look.

"What was that?" Duck asked.

"Someone's rode off."

"Anything to worry about?" Delia asked.

"Doubt it," Dirk said. "Comings and goings, is all."

The day dragged on.

For Delia, the first order of business was further explaining their predicament to Arabel who grasped they were in a strange land, but was unprepared for just how strange it was. Notions of Heaven and Hell existed in Arabel's religious ethos in a soft-focused way. This Hell was far removed from the fire and brimstone construct in her mind. What little she had seen of it was grimy and gritty, primitive and bleak. With Arabel lying on one of the beds, Delia left it to Duck and his brother to tell the rest, urging them to speak in hushed tones to spare the children. Using their own short lives as illustration, the murder they had done, their hangings, they explained the sad consequence of their actions. The eternal suffering. The interminable afterlife. The impossibility of salvation or deliverance. The absence of children, of procreation. The lawlessness and danger of the countryside, especially at night when the rovers were about. The pathetic, feudal subsistence of the people and the power and cruelty of the crown. With each revelation, Arabel seemed to become smaller, her shoulders drooping, her knees pulling more tightly to her chest. When she could bear to hear no more, she turned away, facing the splintery wallboards, and let the conversation pass over her.

Delia seemed to find strength by doing what she did best as an analyst—gathering facts. She interrogated the brothers to fill in as much detail as possible about their new environs. She had gained a good amount of intelligence about their world during her month babysitting and questioning Duck but now she attempted to learn the minutiae of village life. She sought the stories of each resident of Dartford and their personalities. She learned about the sources of food, water, and firewood. She asked about nearby villages and towns, about dangers from outsiders and within. She wanted to know more about the king's soldiers and the dreaded rovers.

The children weren't hungry enough to eat anything from Dirk's stewpot but eventually they both got thirsty enough to drink the water. By evening, they had stopped complaining about being taken out behind the cottage to go to the bathroom in the weeds. They even seemed to enjoy the adventure of camping rough, as Delia put it to them.

Arabel finally pulled herself from the brink of catatonia and absorbed herself cutting strips from a ratty deerskin and fashioning them into belts, laces, and straps to correct everyone's wardrobe deficiencies. Delia sacrificed a cardigan sleeve, stuffed it with grass and tied it off with hide to make a dubious-looking doll for Belle. Duck, seeing jealousy from Sam take hold, whittled a small boat from a piece of firewood and told the boy that if it rained in the night they'd find a puddle and set it afloat in the morning.

When it was time to put the children to bed they complained about the lumpiness of the mattress and the sharp hay poking through but before long they were sound asleep.

When it was dark Arabel and Delia crammed onto the other narrow mattress and they too dozed off.

Left on their own, the brothers sat by the fire, drinking and whispering.

"I'm right happy you got to meet Delia," Duck said to Dirk. "I mean I would've told you all 'bout 'er and all but I never could have painted the right picture. She 'elped me get through my spell there. She was kind to me, very kind indeed. At first I had a good fright at all the strange things, though I did get more than accustomed to the excellent grub and the soft bed and the fancy clothes and the cartoon vids, which I must tell you about, and the things what you sit upon to crap. There was only one thing I missed."

"What was that?" Dirk asked.

"Why it were you, you old sod. I missed you something awful."

Dirk beamed and poured his brother more beer. "Well, you got me back and I got you back too."

Dirk took the first watch but it had been an exhausting day and his resolve was limited. Soon enough he was snoring away beside Duck. There was no warning when the door burst open and soldiers with torches crammed inside.

Delia was the first to wake and she shouted out in alarm rousting Arabel and the brothers but there was nothing anyone could do but cower.

The soldiers stared at the beds and began murmuring in amazement.

The last to enter the hut was the man who had cried at the sight of the children and it was clear enough he had been the one who rode off in search of a reward.

"I told you it was so, I told you," the man said to the captain of the guard. "There's the living women and there's the children. I still can't believe my eyes. Children."

"I swear I'll have your 'ead on a spit," Duck hissed at the man. "It'll be just desserts for treachery."

"I want protection for what I done," the man told the captain. "Arrest the brothers. Don't let them return to the village."

The captain tossed a couple of coins at the man and told him to protect himself. The coins bounced off his chest. He stooped to gather them up and ran out into the night.

Delia and Arabel stood protectively in front of the children's bed. Sam and Belle were still sound asleep under an animal skin.

"Please leave them be," Duck implored.

Dirk saw him glancing at the fire poker and warned him off. "Duck. Don't. I only just got you back. I need you to stay with me. Understand?"

"I'm sorry, Delia," Duck said mournfully. "You'll 'ave to go with them."

"Come along," the captain said. "Wake the little ones and bring 'em along or we will."

Arabel couldn't hold it back. She began to cry.

"Where are you taking us?" Delia demanded.

"Don't be asking questions," the captain warned.

"I know where you're going," Dirk said. "It's to …"

"Not another word," the captain said. "Or you'll be finding yourself in a rotting room missing large bits of your body."

By the light of the torches Delia searched Duck's face. He seemed to be struggling to find something to say that wasn't going to land them all in greater peril but he wasn't finding the words. Finally he pushed forward, saying he wanted to give Delia a good-bye kiss. Before a soldier pulled him away and tossed him to the floor he managed to whisper in her ear, "I know where they'll take you. When they come, I'll tell them where you are. You can count on good old Duck."

4

A hospital room was an unusual venue for a strategy meeting but all the participants acknowledged there was no such thing as a conventional place to plan a journey to Hell. John took the meeting sitting in a recliner hooked up to his IV antibiotics. Emily and Trevor sat on the bed. Ben Wellington pulled up a visitor's chair.

John had spent the opening minutes listening to Trevor vouch for Ben as a "good bloke" and "one of us" and learning how they had tracked and captured Brandon Woodbourne. But he wasn't going to automatically warm to the fellow on a testimonial. He didn't like the public schoolboy types who ascended the ranks of the British security services. He'd met a boatload of them when he headed up security at the US Embassy in London. If an operative wasn't a dyed-in-the-wool soldier, he had trouble getting John's respect. But despite this he quickly warmed to Ben. He found him smart and straightforward, lacking the dreaded air of superiority and omniscience that, as far as he was concerned, permeated the ranks of MI5 and MI6.

"You'll do," John finally said with a thumbs-up.

"That's a relief," Ben said, mock-wiping sweat from his brow. "I feel rather sheepish that the three of you are heroically volunteering for this mission and I'll be staying behind minding the store. If it weren't for my wife and children …"

"No excuses necessary," John said. "Someone's got to round up the

Hellers. I don't trust Trotter to do it."

"He seemed awful," Emily said.

"Slimy bastard," John agreed.

"Want to know his nickname?" Trevor asked.

Ben lightly protested that he'd told Trevor in confidence but Trevor brushed him off with a laugh and revealed it.

"Perfect," Emily giggled. "Fits like a glove."

Reaching for a pad he'd been scribbling on, John launched into the planning. "Okay, I've been thinking about things we can do to get prepared. We need currency, something of value to trade for. Information, cooperation, you name it. We know we can't bring metal or synthetics with us. All we have is what we can carry in our heads."

"Fortunately, John possessed quite a handy knowledge of metallurgy and munitions," Emily said.

"How'd that work out?" Trevor asked.

"Whatever knowledge I had was good for barter," John said. "I remembered how to design a nineteenth-century cannon which outperformed the ones they had. I remembered that Swedish iron ore made the best steel. I jerry-rigged hand grenades to detonate with a flint striker. It was enough to give us leverage here and there. But with preparation we can do a lot better."

Ben shook his head in confusion. "I spent much of last night watching the tapes from the debriefing interviews the two of you did yesterday. It's too fantastic for words—really hard to get one's mind around all the implications. But here's one thing I'm struggling to understand: why is the technology there so primitive? Moderns are flooding in all the time bringing knowledge of modern technology with them you would think."

John and Emily exchanged glances before she handed him the honors.

"Here's the thing," John said. "Everyone who's wound up in Hell for the last hundred years or more understands the modernity they don't have. They know they don't have an electric grid or the light bulb. They know they don't have large-scale steam engines let alone the internal combustion engine. They know they don't have repeating or semi-automatic rifles or machine guns. They know they don't have plastics or synthetic materials, medicines, antibiotics. The problem for these individuals and for the collective society is that people know what's not there but they don't have the knowledge to bring these things into existence. Think about it. People who do things bad enough to punch a ticket to Hell generally aren't the scientists, the engineers, the inventors, the creative thinkers and doers on Earth. I'm sure there're exceptions but there isn't a critical mass to move the technology needle. That's why they're mired in medieval technology."

"I think that's absolutely right," Emily said. "In my interview yesterday I spent a lot of time describing my interactions with that loathsome character, Heinrich Himmler, who was quite obsessed with, as John put it, moving the technology needle. His goal in death as in life was military domination. He salivated at the thought of having the atomic bomb but seemingly had little insight into the hundreds of thousands of technology building blocks which had to be put in place before nuclear fission was doable."

"The other problem they have," John added, "is that each country operates like a feudal state with a privileged few on the top and the rest just trying to survive as serfs or slaves. There's an absence of hope, there's no children-are-our-future mentality. It's a completely barren environment for innovation and enterprise."

Ben nodded. "You both talked about this Garibaldi as being a different sort of leader."

"He is," John said. "Very different, a man with the unusual capacity to see light in a dark place. But who knows if he has any chance? The odds are stacked against him."

"So what kinds of ideas do you have, guv?" Trevor asked.

John pointed to his laptop on the bedside table. "I'm doing research in a bunch of areas, you know, practical improvements to weapons that don't involve huge advances in underlying technologies. Things we can implement quickly and trade for the assistance we're probably going to need to find our people."

Emily screwed up her nose in disgust. "I'm sorry, John, but what you're offering is a way to help them destroy each other more efficiently. Why don't we bring them things to help them elevate themselves? Loftier things?"

"Like what?" he asked.

"I don't know. Literature, poetry, religion."

He laughed. "Well, if you can memorize the Bible between now and next week then go ahead. You can dictate it when you get there."

She blinked a few times, something she did when an interesting idea flooded her mind. "Why don't we just bring books? My Caravaggio sketch made it through. Why not books?"

John was about to say something snarky about Caravaggio's infatuation with her but he caught himself. "What are books made of?"

Ben volunteered the obvious—paper and ink.

"I know that," John said quickly. "I mean what's the paper made of? What's the ink made of? Are they natural materials? Do they contain synthetic additives?"

Emily rose energetically to get John's laptop and started searching. The others let her work in silence scanning articles for a few minutes before she said with disappointment, "It appears that paper and ink manufacturers use a witch's brew of synthetic additives. Let me narrow the search parameters a bit." She typed, read, and finally said, "Who knew? It seems there's a whole world of all-natural, vegetable-based inks for commercial printing and additive-free paper products—and for real tree huggers, paperless paper made from cotton, bamboo or even stone."

"What about the book you buy in a regular bookstore?" John asked.

"It seems most of them have additives somewhere in the manufacturing," she answered.

"Are there any all-natural printers in the UK who can make books?" John asked, leaning forward, painfully testing the limits of his stitches.

She trolled around for another minute and replied, "Seems so. Special-order type of work. Most of them do work for green companies but we could make a few calls I suppose."

"So you think you could carry books across?" Ben asked.

"If they're all-natural, I don't see why not," John said.

"All right then, which books?" Trevor asked.

John and Emily looked at each other and laughed.

"I guess she's going to be favoring books on how to reach out and touch someone and I'll be going for books on reaching out and crushing someone. Let's make our own lists and narrow them down to just a few. We can't take a whole library. We're going to have to travel fast and light."

"I'll have my research people find a printing company that can securely and quickly do a job for us," Ben offered.

John raised another of his agenda items. "Trevor, tell me about any unconventional weapons experience you might have."

"How do you mean unconventional?"

"Hand-to-hand fighting, knives, swords, axes, bow and arrow, that kind of unconventional."

Trevor shrugged. "I mean we had a bit of close quarter combat practice in the army though I probably did more of that in the police. I can probably get by in a pinch. Swords, axes—you must be joking."

"Believe me, where we're going it's no joke. A week isn't much time but I'd suggest finding you an instructor for some intensive training. Anyone have a recommendation."

"Funnily enough," Ben said, "the chap we use at MI5 for unconventional fighting skills is a bit of a celebrity. Ever hear of Brian Kilmeade?"

"The guy who does a medieval weapons show on the tele?" Trevor asked.

"The very one."

"Is he any good?" John asked.

"I've heard good things," Ben said. "I'll make a call to see if we can get him."

"Okay, last item," John said. "From what I saw on the battlefield in France, King Henry survived. If he made it, my guess is he'd be sailing back to Brittania to regroup. If that's the case we're probably going to have to deal with him again. I need to know more about him to understand which buttons to push and which ones to avoid. I need a resource."

Emily sounded skeptical. "I take your point, John, but he was alive for what—fifty or sixty years?—and dead for over five hundred. That experience must have shaped him more than his brief spell on Earth."

"Maybe," John said, "but your personality gets set early on and I don't think you shed it so easily. He was the big dog on the porch before and he's still the big dog. I'm just looking for an edge."

"I can have our researchers send over a selected number of biographies," Ben offered.

"I don't have time to read," John said. "I need to spend a few hours with an historian who knows Henry intimately, really understands the man."

Ben shook his head. "I'm struggling to imagine how MI5 would describe this assignment to an historian."

"How about tying him up under the Official Secrets Act just in case and I'll bullshit him as best I can," John said.

"All right. I'll identify the best Henry authority in England and run the idea up the flagpole."

A nurse came in, removed his spent antibiotics bag, and reminded John that it was time for his dental appointment. When she left John asked Trevor if he had any fillings or crowns.

"Why do you ask?"

"Synthetics. Your fillings won't be there on the other side. I had a big issue with one of my teeth. I'm getting a root canal or an extraction today."

"Yeah, I've got a couple."

"Make sure you've got room on your dance card to visit a dentist before we're off."

"What do I tell the dentist?"

"That you're off to someplace really remote for a very long time and won't have any access to medics or dentists."

"Got it. What about you?" Trevor asked Emily. "How were your pearly whites?"

John grinned and answered for her. "Miss Perfect never had any cavities, did she?"

Emily heard a knock on her office door and looked up. Henry Quint came in with a hat-in-hand kind of a look and asked if she had a minute. She coolly pointed at a chair.

"I know what you think of me," he said.

"Do you? I wonder if you have any idea?"

"I thought I was doing the right thing for the good of the project by exceeding the energy protocols. If it's any consolation, I've been tortured over the problems I created. I'm sorry, but you must realize that we would have taken the collider up to 30 TeV eventually."

"Would we? My firm belief is that strangelet production is not an all-or-none phenomenon. I strongly suspect we would have seen a correlation with higher collision energies and as a result we would have been warned off going to thirty."

"Maybe yes, maybe no. Pushing the boundaries of science has always been risky. Once the atom was split we could never go back. It was up to society to decide how we used the technology."

Her voice rose. "So far we've been able to control that particular genie. I'm not nearly as confident we can wrestle this one back into the bottle."

"I didn't come here to argue."

"Why did you come?"

"As you're aware, my role has been considerably diminished. They're keeping me around only to make sure I don't go off the reservation. My one real task is to convene a panel of scientists to help us determine how to eradicate the extra-dimensional nodes. I'd like to show you my preliminary list."

She took the paper and read it. "It's a good group," she said. "My only suggestions would be to add Anton Meissner from MIT and Greta Velling from Berlin."

"Good ideas."

"I only wish ..." She paused, blinked, and seemed to lose her train of thought.

"Wish what?"

"That we could ask Paul Loomis. His papers on strangelets are still the best work ever done."

"Well we can't, can we?"

She burned him with her fiery eyes.

"You must really hate me," he said, reaching for the paper and rising.

"Put it this way, if John hadn't punched you silly, I would have."

Cameron Loughty put down his pipe to answer the front doorbell.

"Are you expecting someone?" he asked his wife.

"What?"

He hadn't realized she had gone upstairs so he tried again louder.

She shouted down the stairs, "No. Who is it?"

"I'll be sure to let you know once I've got the door," he yelled back.

Their house was a comfortable Georgian in the Newington district of Edinburgh, an easy walk to the university where Cameron had taught engineering until retirement. He opened the door a cautious crack, then wider at the benign sight of a slight young man with a full mop of hair and a messenger bag across his shoulder.

"Yes?"

"Is this Professor Loughty?" the young man asked.

"It is."

"My name is Giles Farmer. I wonder if I might have a word with you about your daughter, Emily?"

Cameron became instantly cross. "Who did you say you were?"

"Giles Farmer. I'm a blogger."

Cameron leaned in, distrustful of his hearing. "A logger? You seem quite small for that kind of work."

"No, a blogger. I write about physics on the web."

"I see. And are you a colleague or an acquaintance of my daughter?"

"Not exactly, you see ..."

"I'm sorry. I have nothing to say."

"I won't take but a minute. I came all the way from London to talk to you."

"You might have phoned first."

"I can't tell you how many times I tried."

"We don't generally answer the phone unless we recognize the number. What is it you want?"

"I write about the potential dangers of high-energy colliders like the MAAC in Dartford. When they had their incident last month I emailed and rang your daughter countless times but they kept telling me she was unavailable. Yesterday I tried again because I heard from people who monitor the greater London power grid that there'd been another brief MAAC start-up. Thing is, she answered her phone straight away but hung up on me when I told her who it was."

"I am about to do the equivalent with this door."

"What's so funny about it is that she and I've spoken on many occasions in the past and though we've never met in person she's always been friendly, very collegial. I know she respects at least some of my reporting. I read physics at university. The information blackout from MAAC is deeply disturbing and now this. I was hoping …"

"Look, we've been told not to talk to anyone about Emily or about the collider so I'm going to have to go now."

The professor firmly shut the door but through it he heard the young man calling out, "Who told you not to talk about MAAC? What are they trying to hide?"

5

Two constables from the Essex Police Firearms Unit stood outside the detached house in relaxed postures. The police armed response vehicle turned the corner and drove down the deserted road that bisected the now-evacuated South Ockendon estate. When the large van pulled up near them their sergeant hopped out. The droning traffic from the nearby M25 forced him to raise his voice.

"What's the hold-up?"

"You do realize we've searched this one twice," one of the constables said.

"Well, search it again," the sergeant said. "I have my orders and you have yours, all right?"

The other constable said, "I've asked before but do we have any further information on who exactly we're looking for?"

"I only know what I've been told and I've been told fuck all. Just search this one and the next three on the west side of the road then report back. Clear every room, every cupboard, every closet."

A camouflaged Land Rover came into view followed by a parade of them progressing slowly down the road.

"I still don't know what the bloody army's doing here?" the first constable asked. "And why they're putting out all this nonsense about bioterror while we're prancing about without protective gear?"

The sergeant seemed thoroughly disgusted by the situation. "Stop asking questions and start searching."

The front door was unlocked, the way the police had left it after their last sweep. After announcing their presence with a perfunctory, "armed police," the two men entered and started with the formal sitting room, their fingers resting above the trigger guards of their short-barreled rifles. The only place to hide was behind a sofa, which they eliminated with a glance.

"Kitchen," one of them said.

There were plates on the table with a two-day-old, hastily abandoned lunch. They opened and closed the pantry and broom closets before progressing to the powder room, downstairs closet, and then the small den where the curtains were drawn.

One of the constables switched on the overhead light and pointed to some empty bags of crisps and chocolate bar wrappers on the floor by a chair.

"Was this mess here last time?"

"Couldn't say."

"Me neither. These houses are all looking the same by now. Upstairs then."

The master bedroom was en suite with fitted wardrobes along an entire wall.

The bed was unmade.

One of the officers sniffed and wrinkled his nose. "Smell that?"

"Yeah. Bloody pong. Maybe they left their moggy behind and it croaked."

He opened the nearest wardrobe door while the other constable knelt and peered under the bed.

The kitchen knife swung into the meat of his shoulder an inch clear of his bulletproof vest.

He shouted in pain and fear and squeezed off a 9mm round wide of the mark.

His partner sprang up and confronted the wild-eyed young man wielding a bloody knife.

"Drop the weapon now!" he shouted.

The man sprang out of the wardrobe. The officer fired once, striking him below the diaphragm but he kept coming. Rather than finishing him off with a chest or head shot he rammed the steel stock of his assault rifle into his forehead, dropping him like a stone.

"All right, mate?" he called to his partner who sat on the bed, pressing his free hand against his bleeding shoulder.

"Yeah, get me a towel or something and call for an ambulance before both of us bleed out. Christ. It wasn't a dead cat was it? He's the one who smells to high heaven."

"Is he out of surgery yet?" Ben asked an MI5 agent who was staking out the waiting area across from the recovery room.

"A few minutes ago."

"And?"

"The doctor told me he's in serious condition but he'll live which is ..."

The young man caught himself and was about to say something but Ben, who was within earshot, stopped him. There were a few people across the lounge on a vigil for a family member.

"Hold the thought, all right?" Ben said.

He knew what his colleague was thinking.

How can he live when he's already dead?

The consultant surgeon, a Mr. Perkins, was aware of two oddities about his patient, Mr. X, beyond the fact that he had been shot by armed police. The first was that he had been told the security services "owned" the case. The second was that despite a thorough antiseptic scrub before and after surgery, his body smelled of decay. With a combination of irritation and curiosity he agreed to meet with Ben in his office.

The surgeon, a take-charge type, immediately asked Ben, "What's this all about?"

Ben answered his question with another. "What was the nature of her injuries, doctor?"

"I can only give out his condition to immediate family. I don't suppose you're a member of his family."

"I am not."

"Then I believe we're finished."

"Is he conscious?"

"He is not yet conscious. Now we're finished."

"Hardly. This is a special situation involving national security interests," Ben said evenly. "Let me tell you what's going to happen. First, you're going to give me a report on his condition and prognosis. Then you're going to have him transferred to a private room before he is able to communicate with anyone. Neither you nor any personnel from the hospital will see him again. He will be quarantined with armed guards outside his door. A team of MI5 doctors and nurses will be arriving any time now. You will brief them on the work you performed. They will exclusively take over his care until he is ready to be discharged into our waiting arms. Is all of that perfectly clear?"

"Who do you think you are? Get out of my office!" the surgeon fumed. "The next person I'll be calling is our chief executive who'll be barring you and your lot from the premises."

Ben took a letter from his breast pocket and handed it over. "This is for you," he said. As the doctor was ripping it open, Ben continued, "This is jointly signed by the home secretary and the secretary of state for health. It lays out what I just said with considerably more legalese. If this matter were not so urgent I would have been more pleasant. I am not, by nature, an abrasive person. But I'm afraid this is what must happen."

The surgeon sat behind his desk to finish reading the letter. When he was done he looked up and asked, "Who the hell is he anyway?"

"He is a very great threat to this country, that's who he is."

"He's where?" John asked, arching his eyebrows.

"Four floors below us in the recovery room," Ben said with a deliberate deadpan. "I had him taken to this hospital so I could kill two birds with one stone."

"Very funny."

"He'll be moved very shortly to a room on the sixth floor. When he's able to talk I'd like you to assist in his interrogation."

"Do you know anything about him?"

"Other than his aroma, no. He's thin, not much flesh on his bones at all, bad teeth, patchy hair, bad skin. All signs of malnutrition I'm told. He's young, not much more than a teenager. Beyond that, he knew how to handle a knife. That's it."

"Most of them are like that, the ones who live outside the palaces. It's a very harsh environment. They get pretty beat-up looking."

"Probably not much different to your average peasant in the middle ages."

"Except that some of them have been at it for hundreds of years. So he's the first one captured."

Ben nodded. "That's right. He was hiding right there under our noses in one of the vacated houses on the estate. We've had all the houses searched yet again but it looks like the rest of them have slipped the noose. If Brandon Woodbourne's behavior is instructive then the rest of them could be holding hostages in homes or in abandoned buildings anywhere within an indeterminate radius."

John held his tender flank in anticipation of coughing. "If they carjacked someone or if they're modern enough to know how to drive they could be anywhere in England by now."

"Have you seen the way the media is handling the story?"

"I've watched a little TV, yeah."

"Then you'll know that some cracks have begun to appear in our story of a terror cell and bioterror hazard on the estate. Despite our information blackout and no-fly zone above the estate, journos have been using Google street view and tax rolls to place names and faces with every quarantined house and they've gleefully broadcast the details. Every single family has been there for a good while and there haven't been any renters. They've tracked down several evacuees whom we've put up in hotels who've said there was nothing suspicious in the neighborhood until approximately 10 a.m. when a number of dirty and smelly men and women began running through the estate, threatening them, forcing their way into homes, and stealing whatever they could get their hands on. That was, of course, before the local police arrived and well before tactical units came onto the estate. So how that squares with a raid on a terror cell is very much in question."

"You've made your bed," John said. "You've got to stick with the story. What's the latest on figuring out how many are missing?"

"We're increasingly sure there are eight unaccounted for. There was a medical doctor and his domestic partner, an architect. Next door to them were four builders who were doing a renovation project along with a female council employee performing an electrical inspection. Then there was a stay-at-home mum in a third house next door to that."

"Which means eight Hellers if the one-for-one rule is still in effect."

"That's our working assumption. With one in custody that leaves seven unaccounted for."

"Seven extremely dangerous people," John said grimly.

"I assure you, I won't rest until they are all apprehended," Ben said.

John gave Ben a look that intended to say, I know you'll do your best. Then he sighed and said, "I don't know who I'm more afraid for, the people who cross paths with the Hellers here or the twelve poor souls from Dartford and South Ockendon who woke up this morning to another day in Hell."

6

There were eight of them dispersed in three groups in the middle of a featureless, grassy meadow. In the first group were two men, both about forty. Twenty yards away were four more men, ranging in age from twenty to sixty with a woman in her fifties. A further twenty yards away from those five was a lone woman in her thirties.

It was a gray, windy day and the tall grasses made waves of green and yellow. A dense wood was off in the distance several hundred yards away. A single hawk on the prowl circled high above. No one spoke but all of them, except one, behaved almost identically. With blank, open-mouthed expressions they pirouetted, tamping down circles of grass as they looked for the houses and roads that had been there only a moment earlier. The one outlier was the oldest man in the middle group who, with a terrible cry, crumpled to the grass.

One of the two men in the first group asked his companion, "Martin, what's happening, what in God's name is happening?"

"I've absolutely no idea, Tony."

Martin was tall and handsome with an erect posture that came from years of practicing his hobby of ballroom dancing. Tony was shorter, more muscular, and far more volatile.

Tony began to hyperventilate. "Are we dead?"

To Martin, the idea wasn't as ludicrous as it sounded so he did what any man of science might do. He checked his pulse at the neck. It was faster than usual but it was very much there. "Of course we're not dead. Take it easy, you'll make yourself ill."

Tony bent down, hands on knees, to counter a mounting faintness. It was then he realized his Lycra cycling shorts were gone and his underpants were precariously loose.

"What happened to my shorts?" he whispered.

Martin had fared better. His khakis were in place although his zipper was not, and his oxford shirt was buttonless. An insect lighted on his ear and when he brushed it away he noticed his ear stud was gone.

"Our missing house and missing neighborhood are more of an issue than your missing shorts," he said. "Come on, let's speak to the others."

The second group stood their ground as Tony and Martin approached. The biggest man, with bib overalls, half-falling down over an enormous gut pointed at them and shouted, "Here, you two, don't come no closer!"

"Why not?" Martin called back.

"'Cause we don't know who you are or what your intentions may be."

"I'm Martin Hardcastle from number fourteen and this is Tony Krause. Our intentions are to find out what just happened to us."

"You're from number fourteen?" the man asked.

"I can't actually point to the house as confirmation but that's where we're from."

"We was working on number sixteen," the man said.

"Ah, the builders. We've been hearing your racket for the last week."

"Come on then," the man said, waving them forward. "I'm Jack. It's my renovations company. These are my lads and that's my dad," he said, pointing to the older man on the ground, wincing in pain.

The sturdy, middle-aged woman blinked rapidly, as if she was the only one who thought proper introductions seemed absurd under the circumstances, but she capitulated. "I'm Alice Hart. I'm from the council, the electricals inspector."

"How do they look?" Martin asked.

"How does what look?"

"The electricals." When no one saw the humor, he apologized and they hurriedly queried one another as to what was going on.

"There's got to be a rational explanation," Tony said.

"Aliens," Jack's youngest son said. "Alien abduction. There's all sorts of stuff like that on YouTube."

The stray woman slowly approached.

"Isn't that Tracy from number eighteen?" Tony asked.

The woman had dark hair and a paper-white complexion. She was barefoot and clutched a terry-cloth robe to her throat to cover her nakedness. When she got within a few yards she stopped. They saw she was crying.

"Now, now, love, I'm Alice. Come over. We're all friends here. We're just trying to figure out what's happened to us."

"Hello, Tracy," Martin said. "It's Dr. Hardcastle from number fourteen. It'll be all right. There's got to be an explanation."

"What kind of doctor are you?" Jack asked.

"Medical doctor."

"Can you see what's ailing my dad?"

He kneeled beside the man and asked what the problem was.

"My hip," the man groaned.

"I see. Is the discomfort sudden?"

"Yes it's sudden," he said intemperately. "It's been right as rain ever since my surgery."

"I see. Surgery for what?"

"To replace my hip, of course. Two years back."

"May I?" Martin asked, laying him down on his back and palpating the right side of his pelvis, then the left. "What kind of hip joint did they use?"

"Titanium."

Martin sat him back up, stood and muttered to himself.

"What is it then?" Jack asked.

"His artificial hip isn't there."

"What do you mean, not there?" Jack's older boy asked.

"Not there, like all of our zippers not being there. Like our buttons not being there. Like my ear stud and wristwatch not being there."

The older man wasn't done with his complaints. "All my bridgework's gone," he said pointing to the gaps in his teeth.

"I've got holes in my teeth as well," Jack said. "And my watch is missing too."

"The one mum gave you?" his younger son asked, suddenly patting his back pocket. "Hey, my wallet's gone."

"I've got mine," Martin said, checking. He pulled out the leather wallet that was otherwise empty, the credit cards and money gone. "What was yours made of?"

"Nylon I suppose," the other man said.

Tony began to hyperventilate again. "This is too weird. It's too much."

"Where are my children?" Tracy said numbly.

"Were they in the house?" Alice asked.

"No, they were at school."

"Well, that's a good thing. I'm sure they're safe at school then."

"What if I never see them again?" she said.

"You mustn't talk like that," Alice countered. "We'll work this out and get back to where we're supposed to be."

"Maybe we're being punked," Jack's youngest said. "Like for a TV show or a film."

His brother rolled his eyes. "I thought you were just proposing abduction by aliens."

"You can't fault me for laying out all the possibilities. No one else is coming up with anything better, are they?"

"Well it's a stupid idea. Even David Copperfield can't make a whole housing estate vanish."

"Could we have been drugged?" Tony asked in between rapid breaths.

"You mean something that would give a collective hallucination?" Martin asked. "There's no such drug I'm aware of."

"Maybe it's something the army's working on. Some secret shit they're testing on us," Jack's youngest said.

Martin nodded at the young man. "You seem to have the most active imagination among us. Keep the ideas coming. What's your name?"

"Charlie."

His older brother volunteered his name too. "I'm Eddie."

Martin shook their hands. "This hyperventilating man is Tony. That only leaves our patient."

"Jack Senior," the man on the ground croaked.

"Well," Martin said. "I doubt we'll get answers standing in the middle of this field. Perhaps we should split into two lots. One to stay with Jack Senior and the other to try to find help."

Jack bunched and rolled his overalls until they were tight enough to stay up on around his waist. "I reckon we ought to stay together."

"I can shift granddad piggyback," Charlie said.

"Right," Martin said, tacitly assuming leadership. "All that's left is for us to pick a direction. Since I believe we're facing where the street used to be, that way is east. We've got meadowland to the east, west, and south. Forest to the north. Any suggestions?"

No one spoke.

"Hang on a minute," Martin said. Something had caught his eye and he headed out on his own for several yards before returning to the group and declaring, "The grass is beaten down here. There's a path leading toward the trees. I think we should head north to the tree line. Perhaps we'll find help in that direction."

They began to walk.

The temperature was mild, the air heavy with moisture and before they made it to the trees it began to drizzle which made them determined to seek cover. Upon entering the forest, the dense canopy filtered much of the gentle rain, leaving them in fairly dry semi-darkness. Although Tracy was barefoot the soil was soft and a thick layer of rotting leaves provided further cushion. Charlie off-loaded Jack Senior to the ground and stretched his shoulders.

"Where to?" Tony asked.

Martin told them to wait while he did a quick reconnoiter and disappeared into the thicket. Several anxious minutes passed before he returned and announced he had found a trail.

"At least I think it's a trail," he said. "I didn't make out any footprints but it does seem like it's seen some traffic."

Eddie took the next shift carrying his grandfather. They followed Martin to the narrow trail where the leaves did seem stamped into the soil. With the young men sharing the burden of Jack Senior, they carried on for over an hour, all the while second-guessing whether they had done the right thing going into the woods.

"I don't understand how everything we know has just vanished," Jack said. "I feel like I'm dreaming."

"I didn't feel too brilliant this morning," Alice said. "I had a bit of a throat and almost called in sick but I knew I had the inspection today so I soldiered on. Worse decision I ever made."

"Maybe we're the lucky ones," Eddie said.

"How do you mean?" Charlie asked.

"Maybe we're the only ones left in the world. Maybe everyone else is dead and gone and we're the survivors."

Tracy began to weep. "My children. Are you saying they're dead?"

Alice jumped in protectively. "Don't be talking rubbish. Of course they're not dead. No one's dead."

"Yeah, shut your gob," Jack said, scolding his son. "Don't be a prat. Can't you see the woman is delicate?"

Martin stopped and cupped his ear. "Do you hear that?"

"Hear what?" Tony asked.

"Running water."

A hundred yards on, the trail ended at a shallow stream with flowing, clear water. Martin knelt on the bank and cupped some into his hands. After a taste he declared it perfectly fine and all of them drank. While they rested Martin sloshed through the stream and found the trail continuing on. On his return he prompted a discussion about going forward versus reversing course. No one had the inclination to backtrack but Martin made it known he wanted decisions to be democratic.

"I've no desire to be decider-in-chief," he said.

"I'd rather you than my brother," Eddie said. "With his ideas about aliens and TV shows he'll have us barking at the moon. You're a doctor. You're educated."

"Tony's an architect," Martin said. "He went to better schools than me."

"Maybe but he's not what I'd call rock-solid," Jack said. "I'll go with you, doctor."

"By all means, listen to Martin," Tony said with no trace of resentment. "I've got no idea what to do. Absolutely none at all. God, I'm dying for a cup of tea."

"Right," Martin said, accepting the leadership mantle. "Onward and upward."

Eddie helped Jack Senior onto Charlie's back and walking single file, they began to ford the stream.

There was a high-pitched noise, as if a large insect had flitted by.

Then another.

Then one more, but this time the noise ended with a dull thud and a low groan.

Jack Senior let go of his grip around Charlie's neck and splashed into the stream. The clear water began running red.

"Granddad!" Charlie screamed.

Martin turned to see the old man lying face down, a long arrow buried in his back. The doctor's survival instincts were stronger than his healing ones.

"Run," he screamed to the rest of them. "Run for your lives!"

7

The car was far too small for the seven of them but comfort wasn't high on their list of concerns. The only thing that soothed the men's jangled nerves was the darkness.

The darkness was their friend. After all, they ruled the night, at least in their world.

The two women took no such solace.

The driver was the least afraid of the men. Operating a car was an experience he never imagined he'd have again, and after twenty miles on the motorway he relaxed enough to begin to enjoy it. The cars of his day had been more basic, but not so different. There was a gas pedal, a brake, a clutch pedal, a shifter. What else did he need? He tried to ignore the bright, confusing digital displays. The petrol tank was reading full, not that any of them knew how far they were going. He had five pilfered twenty-pound notes in his pocket and he found it somewhat comforting and surprising that Elizabeth's portrait was still on the bills. With a hundred quid he reckoned he could buy enough petrol to take them to John O'Groats plus all the steaks and beer they could eat. Maybe later he'd try and figure out how to make the radio work. He didn't need to look for a map in the glove box because there was one on the dashboard with a moving circle that he reckoned was their car. What a marvel! What other wondrous things were there to be discovered? And this too: what kind of a car name was Hyundai?

The man beside him in the front passenger seat couldn't bear to look out the windscreen or the side windows. Talley fixed his eyes on his lap and planted his feet beside the bloody knives on the floor. He spoke through gritted teeth.

"Where's the bottle?"

From the back seat Barrow said, "I got it."

"Pass it over."

Talley went for a cork but he remembered his mistake and fumbled with the screw top, an invention centuries off when last he drank from a bottle.

"This grog's not half bad. What's it called again?"

The driver, Lucas Hathaway, told him it was called Scotch whiskey.

"The grub's good here too," Barrow said, recounting their feast in the last house they had invaded. After murdering a family in Upminster they had raided the pantry and eaten enough to make their sides split. "So good and plentiful there's hardly no need to cannie."

That provoked guffaws. They were cannies all right. They'd eat whatever they could forage at night—horses, pigs, humans, it made no difference.

"We'll go all fat and lazy, we will." That opinion came from the cramped cargo space in the SUV, from a man called Chambers who was crammed beside another filthy brute named Youngblood.

A lively banter ensued about the seemingly bountiful victuals on Earth. This was proving to be a more compelling subject than trying to fathom the reason they had suddenly found themselves back among the living.

For the first time in hours one of the two women in the back seat spoke. Cristine, in her thirties, was in the middle, next to Barrow. Beside her was Molly, in her forties. Both were scared and haggard.

"Please let us go," Cristine said. "You don't need us. We'll only slow you down."

The women had left the village of South Ockendon to fetch water from the nearby creek on that fateful morning two days ago, though it now seemed very far off. Mid-morning was the safest time of day. They had made the journey through the woods countless times in the thirty years they had been in Hell and had rarely encountered anyone other than a fellow villager bathing or watering a horse. On that morning their long streak of luck ran out. Talley and his band of rovers were passing through the woods after foraging near the village in the night. Talley spotted them first and seeing they were alone, lit after them. Hathaway and the others followed, chasing them from the woods into the clearing.

In the middle of a meadow the six men caught up with them and with Hathaway in particular baying for blood, the rovers were about to commit rape and worse when suddenly they weren't in the meadow but inside a large, strange house, filled with objects and furnishings that the women and Hathaway recognized, but the others did not.

"I'm offended you don't favor our company," Talley said.

"We don't keep company with rovers," Molly said.

"Well maybe you should," Barrow said. "Real men, we are, not soft farmers like the lot in your village."

"Real men that murder and eat human flesh," Molly said.

"Don't provoke them," Cristine whispered.

But Talley repeated, "That's right, don't provoke us. No telling what we might do."

Hathaway found that hysterically funny.

But Cristine persisted. "I'm begging you to pull off the motorway at the next junction and let us off."

"And what would you do?" Talley asked. "You've got nowhere to go. This isn't your place no more. You've got more in common with the likes of us than the likes of them. You're evil beasts. We're evil beasts."

"Evil and fetching," Youngblood said, reaching over the seat to paw at Molly's breasts.

She bit his dirty forearm. He yelped and withdrew it to the laughter of the other men.

Talley turned to her. "You're a flesh eater as well it seems. So don't be acting all high and mighty. You'll stay with us. As long as there's food aplenty you won't be eaten but believe you me we will lie with you whenever we damn well please."

"It pleases me now," Youngblood moaned.

"There's no room for that in this moving crate," Chambers said.

"I claim first fuck for her that bit me," Youngblood said, sucking at his bleeding arm.

"She's mine," Hathaway said. "I've been waiting too long."

"If Jason were here, he'd split your head," Christine said.

"Well he's not here," Hathaway replied. "He's about as far away as you can get."

Hathaway drove on. There were signs for Cambridge but he had no interest. Nottingham was his destination. That was his city. He associated London with death because that's where he had died. Nottingham was where he had lived, and lived well as a real up-and-comer, a one-man crime wave. He had left the city as a twenty-year-old in 1969 for the greener pastures of London. His parents would be long dead. His sister was considerably older than him and had been sickly. She must be dead too. But his younger brother, well, he could still be alive and kicking. It was worth the investigation. No one else had a destination to offer. The other men had been dead for hundreds of years and they were utterly lost. And he wasn't asking the women for suggestions.

Hathaway kept to the left, allowing faster cars to pass and when they did he snuck a glance at the other drivers. He wondered what they'd think, what they'd do if they knew that the silver car in the slow lane carried Hellers.

Talley nodded off.

He was scared of Talley. They all were. He lorded over the band with an iron fist. He decided who they would attack and when. He allocated the booty among them, food and women, by his own capricious rules. He decided who could join their gang and who would be kicked out, and by that he meant, who would be roasted and eaten like any other victim. Hathaway was still a new boy, always tested, often victimized. But in the strange circumstances in which they now found themselves, the power had tilted in his direction. He knew the year on Earth; he'd seen the wall calendar in one of the houses. For him it was the near future, strange but recognizable. For Talley and the others it was inconceivably foreign. To survive here, they'd need more than handiness with knives. They'd need him.

He looked in the rearview mirror. Barrow had nodded off too, his block of a head bouncing against Molly's shoulder. The two women were alert and scared.

"Unbelievable," he said with a quick turn of his head toward them.

"You talking to us?" Cristine said. She had long ago trimmed her hair to a mannish length. Because she used pieces of flint for the job, the cut was irregular and spiky but she was still vaguely attractive, despite the punishments of village life.

"Yeah."

"What's unbelievable?" Molly asked.

"All of this. Being back on Earth. Unbelievable, don't you think?"

Christine seethed at him. "First you want to butcher us, now you want to be all matey?"

"Survival of the fittest. That's what I had to deal with. We all had to make our way. Hell's a tough old place."

"So you're a regular Charles Darwin now, not a filthy rover," Christine said.

"I'm not apologizing for what I've become. You think Jason and Colin would have opened their arms and invited me into the village?"

Christine's reply was blunt. "Fuck off, Lucas."

Talley stirred. "Yeah, fuck off, Lucas," he said mockingly.

Molly spoke up in her thin voice. She was small and blonde though her hair was so dirty she looked like a brunette. She had been pretty once. Now she was all sinew and gristle. "I think it's unbelievable too."

"Don't speak to him," Christine said.

Hathaway smiled. He had someone to talk to. "I mean, once you get over the shock of landing in Hell, well, you accept it, don't you? At least I did. But you figure you've booked a single, not a return journey."

"I thought I'd go to Hell for what I done," Molly said. "But I never thought I'd come back."

"Exactly my point," Hathaway said. There was a long silence before Hathaway filled it. "I wonder if we're meant to do something?"

"How do you mean?" Molly asked.

"You know. Maybe we've been given a second chance, like a test, and maybe we're meant to be judged."

"Well you've flunked the test, you wanker," Cristine said. "We've been back for two days and how many people have you killed so far?"

"None. The others did the killing."

Youngblood had been listening from the rear. "I killed three of 'em," he said proudly. "When you stab 'em here they die. There's little suffering. I like it better when they stay alive, suffering."

"'Course you do, you fucking sadist," Cristine said. "As for you, Lucas, I saw you eat a hunk of bloody flesh not ten minutes after we arrived. Still think you've got a passing mark?"

"I was hungry. I hadn't eaten for three days," he said defensively.

"Spoken like a right cannibal," Cristine said, spitting out the word. "Oh sorry, cannie. Sounds so much better that way, don't it?"

"You know, Cristine, I don't give a flying fuck what you think of me. After I've fucked you good I'm going to let all the lads have their way with you and then I'm going to kill you again."

They drove in silence for several miles. Talley fell asleep. So did the other men.

Molly asked, "Where are we going?"

"Nottingham," Hathaway answered.

"Why?"

"I'm from there."

The brake lights of the cars in front of them lit up revealing a minor tailback forming at a road works. Hathaway slowed to keep his distance. He tensed but relaxed when he saw cars a quarter mile ahead picking up speed again.

Cristine gently scratched Molly's arm with one of her long fingernails and pointed toward the verge. Molly seemed to understand. The car was going no more than ten miles per hour but was starting to accelerate. When Cristine pulled the handle and pushed the door open she flung herself out and rolled on the asphalt before landing on the grass. Molly followed and the two of them, scraped and bleeding ran into the woods beside the motorway.

"Shit!" Hathaway shouted.

Youngblood asked groggily, "Should I go after them?"

The driver behind them was honking. Hathaway didn't know if he wanted him to speed up or whether he had seen the women spill out. Either way he didn't want to chance it. He accelerated and pulled into the middle lane to pick up more speed.

"For fuck's sake," Hathaway shouted. "You fucking idiot. You let them get away!"

"Don't be so hard on Barrow," Talley said. "He does the best he can with the brains he's got."

"I was only having a kip like you was," Barrow moaned.

"Enjoy it?"

"What?"

"Your kip?"

"It were all right."

"Lean over so I can tell you something."

Barrow did as he was told.

"Have a longer one, then."

Talley slashed at Barrow's throat with a kitchen knife and with his free hand pushed him back to keep the spurting blood off his new clothes.

"Good," Hathaway said. "Fucking useless idiot he always was."

Youngblood climbed over and sat beside Barrow's lifeless body.

"Check him," Talley ordered. "See if he's well and truly dead."

"Seems so," Youngblood said, poking hard at his body.

"Then it's not like it is in Hell," Hathaway said. "Seems we can die all over again."

"Barrow's probably back there now, wondering what the blazes happened to him," Chambers said from the back.

Youngblood soon disregarded the corpse and was cooing in pleasure, bouncing his rump on the soft seat. "Pity about the molls. Here I was, looking forward to a good shag with the fair-haired one."

Talley finally forced himself to look through the window into a car they were passing. The driver was a young woman, her face briefly visible in the glow of her instrument panel.

"Plenty of others about," he said, wetting his dry lips with his long, lizard-like tongue. "No shortage of molls in these parts."

8

Ben accompanied John to the young Heller's room. A phalanx of MI5 guards patrolled the corridor. All other patients and hospital personnel had been removed from the ward. In the room next door, video and audio monitors had been set up and John stopped there first to get a measure of the fellow.

As the MI5 medic explained to him, the young man was now in stable condition after undergoing abdominal surgery to remove the bullet and re-route part of his intestines. He wasn't yet eating, he had a nasogastric tube draining his stomach secretions, but he was able to talk. Though he was in four-point restraints he had been sedated to keep him from thrashing about, but for the sake of this interview the sedation had been weaned.

"What's his name?" John asked.

"I didn't ask," the doctor said.

"Well, I guess I know a good place to start."

He entered the room on his own. The young man tugged at his arm restraints and watched him warily. John decided to pull up a chair to seem less menacing.

"My name's John," he said.

The young man was silent.

"What's your name?"

Again, no response, just a piercing stare from eyes so dark they looked like small, black stones. He'd been cleansed along the way, his long brown hair washed, his grimy skin scrubbed. He looked to be in his twenties, not a bad-looking kid. He smelled like a Heller but John was used to the odor by now. He wouldn't be wrinkling his nose like everyone else.

"I'm not going to hurt you. I'm here to help you. I'm going to answer the questions I know you have. You'll be wanting to know where you are, how you got here, what happened to your friends, what that thing is doing in your nose. I've got all the answers. Do you want those answers?"

The kid remained mute.

"Okay, tell you what. I'll just talk for a while and you can join in when you like. I'm not like all the other people you've seen since you arrived here. You want to know why I'm different? It's because I just came from where you're from. Yeah, I was there. I was in Hell. I spent a month there. Even with that tube in your nose, I know you can smell me. You know I'm alive. But I crossed over and I crossed back. I'd like to explain it to you, how I crossed, how you crossed. It'll be easier for me if you tell me when you died."

John thought his demeanor had shifted from fear to puzzlement.

"Okay, twentieth century? Eighteen hundreds? Seven..."

He nodded.

"Eighteen hundreds?"

Another nod.

"Toward the end of the eighteen hundreds?"

An emphatic nod.

"All right. Good. Here goes."

John launched into a stylized explanation of MAAC, portraying it as a giant steam engine, something he thought the kid might understand. The steam engine was so large and powerful that it ripped a connection between the two worlds. This world was far into the future, filled with amazing inventions. He would be safe here. He'd have every luxury. All he needed to do was answer a few questions about the people who came over with him.

John stopped talking when it looked like the kid was going to open his mouth.

"How come I got shot then if it's so bloody safe?"

"My understanding is that you stabbed one of the policemen. That's why."

"Didn't look like no bobbies."

"Like I said, a lot of things are different here. Will you tell me your name now?"

"Mitchum."

"Is that your first name or last?"

"First name is Michael."

"What do you prefer I call you?"

"Mitchum."

"Okay, fine. Pleased to meet you, Mr. Mitchum."

"Just Mitchum'll do. What's this in me nose?"

"It's a tube the surgeon put there until you're healed and can eat. They took a bullet out of your stomach."

"Hurts."

"I'll tell them. They can give you something for the pain."

"Why am I tied down?"

"To make sure you don't pull out your tube or mess up your wound. You've got stitches. Want to see mine?" He lifted his shirt and showed off his flank. "Want to know what happened to me?"

Mitchum nodded.

"I got stabbed by a rover. I'll bet you're one of them. You're a rover, aren't you?"

"What if I am?"

"You are who you are," John said. "I'll make no judgments about how someone in your shoes chooses to survive."

"How'd you know what I was?"

"In one of the houses you ran into after you arrived, the people were carved up pretty good. Some flesh was missing. Rover work."

"So what? We're hungry, we eat. Cannie food's as good as any."

John hid his revulsion. "Cannie. I didn't know that word."

"It's not like when you're living, is it? The rules is different."

"That they are. So tell me, Mitchum, are you the boss man?"

"Me? You must be joking. It's Talley. He's the boss of us."

"All right, Talley. He's the boss. How many in your gang?"

"There's six of us."

John looked perplexed. "Six?"

"Yeah, that's right."

"Not eight?"

"Six."

"But there were eight of you all together."

"You mean the two molls?"

"What's a moll?"

"You know, a lady."

"There were two women? Why were they there?"

"We was chasing them, weren't we? Almost had them when everything went mad."

"Who were they?"

"They was from the village, out gathering water. Hathaway knew them, always went on about them."

"Who's Hathaway?"

"One of us."

"All right, keep going."

"We was happening by, looking for a place to sleep in the wood. Got caught out in the morning. We don't like moving about during the day."

"And you saw the women and you chased after them."

"Yeah."

"And what would you have done to them if you'd have caught them?"

Mitchum sniggered. "Fucked them good and carved them I expect. We was awful hungry."

John clenched a fist behind his back. "All right, I hear you. Tell me this—and you're doing great—were any of the other rovers recent arrivals in Hell."

"How do you mean, recent?"

"I don't know. Last twenty, thirty, forty years, something like that."

"Hathaway's recent."

"How recent?"

"Couldn't say exactly. He was always going on about the strange things he had, like picture boxes in houses, flying machines."

"I see. Do you recall where he said he lived when he was alive?"

He went quiet, thinking. "London."

"Which part of London?"

"Don't know. He never talked about London much."

"Where did he talk about?"

"Nottingham. That's what he talked about. He was from there. Talked about it all the time till Talley told him to shut his gob about it."

"Nottingham. Okay. When you landed here inside a house were the two women with you?"

He nodded.

"Then what happened?"

"The house was empty. No people about. Talley saw there were people outside another house, two men and a woman. We grabbed them, pulled them inside."

"Then what happened?"

"Youngblood found a knife and carved the men, then the woman. Then we had some victuals."

"Cannie food."

"Yeah, that's right."

"And the two women you came with. Where were they?"

"With us. Barrow and Chambers were sitting on them, by manner of speaking."

"How'd you get separated from the rest of them?"

"I wandered up the stairs to have a look about and must've dozed off on one of the soft beds up there. When I woke up, everyone was gone."

"The two women also?"

"Yeah, the whole lot of them."

"And then?"

"I hid in a wardrobe until the bobbies arrived. Then I woke up here."

"Okay, Mitchum, you've been very helpful."

"What's to come of me? When do I get the luxuries you spoke of?"

John dropped all pretenses and his face hardened. He had extracted every useful morsel this animal had to offer. "Here's what's going to happen to you. You'll be treated better than you've got a right to be treated, a damned sight better than you would have treated those two women. When you're healed you'll be locked in a cage so you can't hurt anyone and as soon as we can, we're going to ship you back to Hell."

If someone had set out to design the ideal medieval fighter, the result would have been a man who looked very much like Brian Kilmeade. Everything about him was optimized for speed, power, and efficiency. He was no giant. His body was hard and compact with a low center of gravity that made him difficult to knock down. His legs were squat and thick, his arms, prodigious, his shaved head and muscular neck projected an air of menace, that is until he decided to ruin his hard-man image by sporting an impish smile. He was also aerobically fit, a marathon runner who had set records in over-fifty brackets. He liked to preach, "If you get winded before the other chap, you will be killed, no matter how good your skills."

Trevor helped him wheel trunks of gear into the MAAC recreation center but before opening any, he sat Brian down for what he knew would be an awkward conversation.

"First off," Trevor said, "I'm a big fan of your show."

It was true. *Brian Kilmeade: Fighting Man* was one of his favorite TV programs.

A northern accent resonated from Brian's barrel chest. "That's very nice of you to say, but I'm keen to hear the second-off part."

"Yeah, I'm sure. This has got to be a bit out of the ordinary."

"You think? I get contacted by the MI5 to do a consult at a high-energy physics lab that's been in the news because of the break-in last month, I get offered a king's ransom to drop everything and show up at twenty-four-hours notice with all of my kit, then get stitched up by the Official Secrets Act—no, that's more than out of the ordinary, mate. It's bonkers."

Trevor hunted for the right words. "This is going to be frustrating for you but even with your signature on the gag order, I'm not going to be able to tell you what this is all in aid of."

"Bloody marvelous. The only good bit is that I can't even tell my agent I was even here, so no commission for good old Ronnie-Ten-Percent."

"Silver lining," Trevor said, grinning.

"Why don't you tell me what you can tell me then let's get on with it, shall we?"

Trevor produced a list, prepared by John, of the weapons for which he needed skills training. Brian read it and shook his head. "Two-handed broadsword, Roman short sword, saber, dagger, axe, longbow, crossbow, spear, pike, mace, flint-lock pistol, black-powder musket. You've got to be joking."

"No joke. You got all of that with you?"

"Pretty much. How much time do you have to master what it's taken me a lifetime to learn?"

"Four days."

He snorted. "Four days. Sure. No sweat. And you can't even tell me what you need these mad skills for?"

"Sorry, no."

"And what's your background, son?"

"Police, army, combat tours in Afghanistan, private security."

"You mean to say the police and the army aren't schooling the lads on sword play these days?"

"I must've slept in those mornings."

Brian popped the latches on one of the equipment trunks and said, "Well, let's get a move-on," he sighed. "*Tempus fugit* and all that. I hope you're as fit as you look for I am about to run you ragged, son."

John heard a light tapping at the door to his hospital room and told the visitor to enter. Malcolm Gough, Professor of History, was a very tall beanpole, nearly a foot taller than John but half the weight. He was one of the youngest professors at Cambridge, a prodigy with the complexion of a beaker of cream and delicate, almost feminine features. John had seen his photo attached to the curriculum vitae Ben had sent over but he was unprepared for the man's height.

"Is this Mr. Camp?" he asked, towering over John's lounge chair.

"It is. Thanks for coming on short notice, Professor."

"Of course. Your colleague, Mr. Wellington, was good enough to send a car for me all the way from Cambridge. The train wouldn't have been a problem."

"Well, I'm glad you could make it."

Malcolm folded himself into a chair, his eyes wandering from the bag of antibiotics running into John's arm to a copy of his book, *The Life and Times of Henry VIII*, on the bed stand.

"If you have my book, I'm not sure why you need me."

"I wish I had time to read it, but I'm on a short timetable."

"I must admit, I've never been asked to sign the Official Secrets Act before talking about Tudor England. I am intrigued. My curiosity has been piqued."

"You're going to hate me for saying this, but I'm afraid I'm not going to be able to tell you why I want to know about Henry."

"This is quite fantastic. Mr. Wellington said I couldn't even talk to my wife about this trip."

"That's right."

"He did say you were a history buff."

"Military history mainly."

"Have you studied formally?"

"That's a nice way of asking if I'm educated. I was at West Point."

"I see. And what is it you would like to know about King Henry?"

"His personality. What makes him tick?"

"Made him tick. He's quite dead, you know."

"Sorry. Made him tick. What made him happy, made him angry? What kind of people did he like, what kind did he hate? Did he see through flattery? How did people manage to influence him? Who did he trust and how did someone earn that trust? Who did he admire? What did he think of Thomas Cromwell and vice versa? I need him profiled. I need to get inside his head."

Malcolm nervously worked the knuckles of his long, bony hands. "I admit to being rather dazed and confused by your questions."

"Seems to me they're on the straightforward side."

"Only if Henry were a living, breathing man with whom you wished to have dealings of some sort."

"I'd like us to get beyond my motivations."

"Put yourself in my shoes, Mr. Camp."

"Are you a drinking man, Professor?"

"I've been known to hoist a glass."

"And are you patriotic?"

"I'm fond of my country, yes."

"Well, how about this? One day, I'd like nothing better than to invite you to a nice long drinking session to talk all about my interest in Henry but it's not going to be today. Today is the day you're going to exercise your duty as a patriot, for Queen and country, and tell me everything you know about Henry, the man."

Emily's thumb was getting sore pushing the reverse and play buttons on the remote control. She was sitting between Matthew Coppens and David Laurent reviewing all the video recordings of the MAAC restarts, particularly the one that had brought her home.

"What do you make of it?"

She was referring to the alternating cycles of Duck and Woodbourne switching dimensions with her and John, before Trevor and Ben dove into the field and tackled them to safety.

David shrugged and said that in his view it was obvious. The energy fields were getting increasingly unstable.

Emily, always data driven, asked to see the plots. David had them on his tablet.

She flipped through several screens and had only one word: "Wow."

The strangelet production on the last restart had risen logarithmically.

"What about the gravitons?" she asked.

David tapped on another file. "The sample size is small so it's not at five sigma but the trend is the same. Big rise in gravitons too."

"But why South Ockendon? What's going on there?" she asked.

Again David answered. Matthew was silent, his expression stony. "Well, there's a magnet there. There could be some interaction we don't understand between the strangelet-graviton complex and the magnetic fields."

She shook her head. "God, I hope you're wrong. We have magnets ringing the entire city of London. Matthew, you've been awfully quiet. What do you think?"

The simple question seemed to crumble his defenses and he began to blubber pathetically.

She asked what was wrong but she knew the answer.

"I'm so sorry, Emily. This was all my fault."

A hand on his shoulder only seemed to make him more miserable.

"Look, I don't blame you," she said, looking him squarely in the eyes. He and his wife were devoted to their autistic son who was finally improving in a specialist school near the lab. If he had lost his job, it would have been devastating for them. "I blame Quint. You were worried about your position. You were worried about your family. He bullied you and you were vulnerable. I know how he can be."

"I should have told you. It was a betrayal."

"Yes, you should have done that," David said coldly.

"Guys, I don't want to spend another second talking about the past," she insisted. "Right now we need you, Matthew. I need you. When I go back, you're going to be in charge of the collider. You have to get your head in the game."

Matthew slowly nodded and wiped his face with his hand. "All right. Thank you. I was so worried about you and so terribly guilty. I was overjoyed you came back and now I'm beside myself you're going again. If anything were to happen to you I don't know what I'd do."

"I'll be fine. John and Trevor will be there to protect me. I'll come home again and I'll bring my family back."

"You're stronger than I am."

"Don't underestimate yourself," she said. "You held things together for a month. I talked to people. You were magnificent."

David tapped the table impatiently. "Yes, we were all magnifique, me including."

With that, the mood lightened, but only for a moment.

"We need to talk about the elephant in the room," Emily said.

Unburdened, Matthew became engaged. "You're right. There's every reason to believe that each restart has the potential to propagate additional nodes." It was Quint's term; they almost hated using it but it was apt.

"But we have a minimum of two more actuations," David said. "One to send you over again and one to bring you back."

"The only thing we can do is power down as rapidly as possible after the transfer," Matthew said.

"You'll need to have your finger on the button then," Emily said.

Matthew said he could do better. "I've been thinking about this. In the best of circumstances it would take me the better part of a second, maybe two, to react to the situation and switch off the collider. I can write a program to integrate the video capture and auto-initiate the power-down the instant you disappear. It might reduce the reaction time to a few milliseconds and every millisecond saved might mean less field instability."

"Brilliant," she said, "Do it. Now both of you: while I'm away, it will be vitally important to work with the new advisory committee to deal with worst-case scenarios. You'll have access to the best and the brightest minds in physics."

The two men nodded. No one wanted to say it out loud but they knew what she was saying.

They needed to come up with ways to plug the infernal holes for good if the situation got out of hand.

Ben pulled his government Jaguar into a visitor space outside the low, 1980s manufacturing complex. The drab industrial park was on the outskirts of Birmingham, off the Middle Ring Road. Rocketing along at almost 100 mph he had made excellent time from London even counting the time it had taken to squash a speeding ticket with his ministry credentials.

The managing director of Midlands Green Printing, Ltd, met him at the reception and brought him back to his office. Simeon Locke had the right kind of look for environmental trade shows, Ben supposed, with a tied-back ponytail, long sideburns, and a thin leather vest over an open-collared shirt.

Locke seemed impressed with Ben's business card and made some awkward small talk about never wanting to be on the wrong side of the security services.

"So, very intrigued by your call, Ben. Can I call you Ben?"

"You may, indeed."

"I imagine you lot have established vendors for your printing needs. Is there some government initiative I'm unaware of that requires a certain percentage of green product?"

"Probably not a bad idea but no, this is a one-off."

"All right. Which services were you interested in?"

"We need 100% natural paper and 100% natural ink. No synthetics. Not a trace."

"We can do that, Ben. That's our Rain Forest line. Like the name?"

"Yes, it speaks volumes."

"We can do a variety of paper stocks, matte only, of course, given the synthetic-free process. And we can do a lovely palette of colors, all with natural vegetable-based inks. No surfactants, no extraneous substances. Pure vegetable extracts."

"Thin paper to reduce weight and black ink. And some kind of light, protective cover, also synthetic-free."

Locke looked up from his notes. "I see. Not a problem. We can work with you on designs. Are we talking about training manuals, reference materials?"

"No, books."

"All right. Again, not a problem. Bound books, is that correct?"

"Yes. The binding material must also be all-natural."

"Of course. Natural glues, pure cotton thread for the oversewing. How many books will you be printing?"

"Six."

"I see. Six books. And how many copies of each?"

"Two."

Locke thrust his head forward like an ostrich that had just extracted it from a hole to have a look around. "I'm sorry, did you say, two?"

"That's right. Two copies of six books." He reached into his briefcase and placed them on Locke's desk. "These six."

Locke inspected them, his mouth partly agape. The gap grew wider when Ben added that he needed them in forty-eight hours.

"That's quite impossible, Ben. First of all, we don't take jobs that small, whoever the client might be, and second, that's not in any way a realistic timeframe, even presuming you had the Word files for these texts."

"No files. The pages would need to be scanned."

Locke looked flabbergasted. "I'd like to be helpful to the MI5, given the excellent work you do, but even if I could accept this work, which I can't, my next production slot is in two week's time, so I don't believe we're going to find a way to do business. I might be able to call around and find you one or two green artisans who might take on this kind of small assignment but I'm sure it would take any of them several weeks at best."

Ben smiled. "No, we've decided your company is the best one for us, Simeon."

"Look here, this isn't some kind of communist state where the government decides something and a company kowtows. The last I checked my firm was in the private sector."

"You are absolutely correct. Spot on. And my colleagues at Inland Revenue tell me your turnover last year was 674,900 pounds and 16 pence."

"Is it legal for them to divulge that? We're a private company."

"Yes, perfectly legal, with the court order we obtained."

"On what grounds? My solicitor will be most interested in hearing about any alleged grounds," he said, spittle flying from the corners of his mouth. "We are a law-abiding company."

"I've no doubt you are. We needed to know your turnover in order to take full advantage of incentives. And in that spirit, I can offer you this if you can fulfill our order to our exact specifications and timetable."

From his breast pocket he pulled out a Treasury check and handed it across the desk.

Locke glanced at the check, shook his head as if something in his brain wasn't working and looked at it again. His chair was a recliner and he took full advantage of the feature.

"One million pounds," he said quietly.

"Twelve books, two days, one million in sterling," Ben said briskly. "Now, five of the books are clearly in the public domain but one is not. We don't have time to get the customary permissions so I have a letter here from the Ministry of Justice, fully indemnifying you for any costs and damages which might result from copyright breach, which, I must say, is unlikely to occur since you and all your workmen will have to sign the Official Secrets Act. No one will know about your work. So, Simeon, will you be able to satisfy this order?"

The printer reached over the desk to extend a hand. "Ben, it will be a pleasure doing business with you. Welcome to the Midlands Green Printing family."

9

John wandered around his flat in a mild daze. Trevor had driven him back from the hospital and had left him there to run off to his final dental appointment.

He had only been away for just over a month but he felt like someone coming back to tour an old domicile decades later. There were his books, his clothes, his lager-stocked fridge, his dirty dishes in the sink, his ridiculous mound of mail pushed through the slot as he'd forgotten to suspend delivery, but everything seemed oddly detached from memory. He sank into the sofa and had to think for a moment to recall his email password. At the sight of hundreds of unopened messages he closed the laptop.

He was on his second beer when the entry doorbell sounded and he buzzed in his visitor.

Emily had a carrier bag with Indian take-away and a six-pack of lager.

Peering into his fridge she said that bringing him beer was like bringing coals to Newcastle.

"You can never have too much money or too many beers," he said, wincing when he sat again.

"Are you done with your antibiotics?" she asked, placing the tubs of food on his coffee table.

"A few days of pills to finish before we're off."

"And your stitches?"

"Too soon. They want them in for another week."

"Will they make it through?"

"They're silk so they should be okay. You might have to do the honors on the other side."

"I'm not squeamish."

"So I noticed. You saw enough blood and gore over there for a lifetime."

She sat beside him and fixed him a plate but he wanted to talk first.

"Do you know how many times I thought about seeing you here again during those long, dark nights a million miles away?"

"Me too," she said, resting her head on his shoulder. "We had some good times here."

"It wasn't just the good times, though they were very, very good. I wanted to erase the memory of the one bad time."

Emily laughed and did her broadest American imitation of the seminude femme fatale she'd happened upon that night: "Hi. I'm Darlene. I'm an old friend of John's."

"Ouch. Too perfect. I hope you still believe me that I was never ..."

"Yes! I believe you."

"Good. I want to be sure that particular dragon's been slayed."

She kissed him and said, "Dead and buried."

"Good. Wait for me here. Don't go. I'll bring Arabel and the kids back."

"Who'll remove your stitches?" she asked lightly.

"Trevor's learning how to use a knife."

She turned serious. "I can't bear thinking about where they are, how they're holding up."

"Dirk probably has them safely inside his house, waiting for us to come and get them."

"God, I hope so. If that's the case we'll have to lie low for a month before the next restart."

"Beats every other alternative. So what do you say? Trevor and I will bring them back and you can do what you do best: the science."

She raised her voice. "Please don't ask me again. I'm going. It's nonnegotiable."

"Okay, you win," and changing the subject, he asked, "Can you stay the night?"

"Yes. But we can't have a lie in. Too much to do."

"And that troll Trotter's called another meeting for nine. Did you notice he had a shoulder holster under his perfectly tailored suit jacket?"

"Are you sure?"

"Believe me, I'm sure. What kind of insecure jackass comes packing to a meeting in a lab?"

"James Bond carried a gun, didn't he?"

"One, he was fictional. Two, his character was a real spy, not some desk-monkey like Trotter. Anyway, you know what they say?"

"What do they say?"

"Big gun, little dick."

She pushed him. "Don't be so crude."

"I apologize unreservedly."

"Good." Then she whispered in his ear, "You must have had the tiniest gun in the army."

The MAAC restart was a day and a half away. John was in the lab, going through his pre-campaign checklist when he decided to take a break and amble over to see how Trevor was getting on. One of the security men told him he was over at the recreation center doing some training but when John got there, the gymnasium was filling up with tables, computer terminals and a spaghetti-tangle of cables. He remembered that a decision had been taken to minimize the chance of collateral damage by moving the control room operations and personnel to another building, and the recreation center was filling the bill.

"Have you seen Trevor Jones?" he asked one of the techs.

"We booted him out. I think they went to the tennis court."

The afternoon was warm. Pale, spring leaves shaded the courts. As John got closer he heard the cracks of polypropylene training swords striking each other repeatedly. Trevor and Brian were going at it near the service line of the court unaware he was watching even as he leaned against the fence.

Brian abruptly switched tactics, landing a stinging blow to Trevor's upper arm then, when Trevor was distracted by the pain, he thrust into his gut, declaring him as good as dead.

"Never stop, never stop, never stop! You've got to keep going through the pain. That was a love tap. No blood, no exposed muscle, no severed nerves. Even then you've got to keep defending and attacking or you're going to be a grim statistic."

"Gotcha," Trevor said, dejected.

"Now mind you, unless you're swinging a broadsword from horseback I don't ever recommend going to battle with a free hand. You should always have a second sword or a shield in your non-dominant hand, all right? And your shield's going to be as much an offensive weapon as a defensive weapon. We'll do some shield work next."

Trevor noticed John and welcomed the excuse to take a break.

"So this is the boss man," Brian said, beckoning John to come inside the court. "Heard a lot about you, mate."

John ambled in and was soon chatting away with Brian as if he'd known him for years. He liked the man's big, open smile and his quick wit and told him he was a fan of his TV shows.

"Trevor tells me you're quite handy with medieval weaponry," Brian said.

"Not like you, but I can hold my own."

"Care for a tumble?" Brian said, tossing him a practice sword.

"I'll have to pass," John said. "I'm just out of the hospital." He lifted up his shirt to display his wound.

Brian whistled. "How'd you get that, if you don't mind my asking?"

"A knife, about half the length of that sword of yours."

"You don't say."

John grunted. "You should have seen the other guy."

"Must've missed the news report on the incident."

"Didn't make the news." John was keen to change the subject. "So how's our student doing?"

"He's a quick study, a capable young fellow."

"That's the first compliment this week," Trevor said.

"You're cheeky enough without a big head."

"So rate him for me on various skills," John said.

"Full marks on black-powder firearms. Not terrible on long and crossbows, though we weren't able to do any distance work. We haven't gotten to spears and pikes. Maybe later today. His swordsmanship, well, I wouldn't call it passable yet. Let's see …"

"Tell him about the horses," Trevor said. "Go on, have a laugh."

Brian cast his eyes heavenward. "Oh Gawd! We went riding at a stable last evening. Bloody disaster. Didn't know the mane from the tail. I'll be charitable. He stayed on the saddle. Barely."

John patted Trevor on the back. "Nice work, buddy. Brian, you've got him for today and tomorrow. Don't go easy on him. His life may depend on it."

The comment drained off any levity in the air.

"Take a break," Brian told Trevor. "I want to have a word with the boss man."

The two men left the tennis court and strolled the grounds, John towering over him and bending slightly to hear him over the rustling trees.

"You know, John, I was never in the military like you and Trevor."

"You didn't miss much. It's highly overrated."

"I'm not sure I agree with you. You lads have character. Gobs of it. I've spent years teaching poncy actors how to fake their ways through fighting scenes and I'd trade the lot of them for one of you. You're the genuine article, mate."

"How'd you get into your line of work, Brian?"

"I grew up on a farm in Northumberland so I was good at riding from a young age. One fine day I saw some jousters at a country fair and thought it looked like mad fun so I applied myself to learning the skills. That led to an interest in armor and from there I followed my nose. I fell in with various re-enactor types and then, when I was in my thirties, I discovered the holy of holies. Some bloke from the BBC actually gave me a paycheck to do some work on a men-in-tights show. The rest is history. I've been mucking about in Hollywood for over twenty years and well, you've seen my own shows on the tele. Ancient soldiering's been very good for yours truly."

"That's quite a story."

"Not a fraction as good as yours."

"How do you mean?"

"Well, contrary to prevailing opinion, I'm not a stupid man."

"Didn't for a minute think you were."

"Apparently you haven't spoken to my ex-wives. Here's the thing, John. The Internet's been buzzing with all manner of conspiracy theories about your MAAC and though I'm not, as a rule, big into the rantings of my fellow netizens, since they're usually a fat load of bollocks. But I'm not inclined to reject one particular line of thought, purveyed by an alleged loony named Farmer."

"Never heard of him. His line of thought?"

"All right, follow along with me. A month ago with trumpets blaring and press releases flying about, you lot fire up your multi-billion-pound gizmo intended to unlock the secrets of the cosmos and what not. But what happens? You immediately shut it down and put out some half-baked tale about an armed intruder who proceeds to go on a killing spree in the general environs, a story that's gone remarkably quiet given its sensational nature. Now, I've seen your security around here and it's very comprehensive. You're crawling with armed lads, Trevor's a good man, and I suspect you're a very competent boss man, so a major security breach? It's possible but not so very likely, in my humble opinion. Then, a week ago, amidst reports of a power dip in the south's electricity grid, which can indicate collider activity, so I'm led to understand, there's this very curious incident in South Ockendon, all mysterious and shrouded in secrecy, with everyone hiding behind terrorism this and biohazard that. Thing is, South Ockendon's right over the collider tunnels, isn't it? Coincidence? Maybe. Then yours truly gets stitched up by the Official Secrets Act and gets paid a boatload of cash to teach a highly competent modern warrior, one Trevor Jones, to be a slightly competent ancient warrior and I'm given less than a week to make that happen. And finally I meet the boss man who's nursing a fresh knife wound."

"Where's this taking you, Brian?" John asked with a crooked smile.

"It's taking me here: I think you lot have stirred up a shit storm. I think you've got a very naughty supercollider. I think you've gone and poked a hole in our nice, tidy universe and have yourself a wormhole or what have you, into another dimension. And that dimension's got a decidedly ancient tilt. I think that you've been there. I think you've got an urgent need to go back. I think Trevor's going with you and you need to improve his chances of surviving. And since tomorrow's my last day of hire, I think you're going in two days' time."

John arched his brow. "You've got quite the imagination, Brian, I'll give you that."

"I do actually but this isn't all in my mind. I know I'm right. I'd bet my ex's alimony checks on it."

John pointed over at Trevor, knees up to his chest, sitting on the tennis court. "I think he's ready for you."

Brian ignored him and jabbed a finger into John's chest, once for each word. "Take me with you."

"What?"

"You heard me. Take me along. Whoever you're bringing, whatever your mission, your odds are going to be better if I'm there. There isn't an ancient weapon system I'm not expert in. And I'm not just a warrior, I'm a craftsman. I can make bows and arrows, I can forge and shape a sword, I can fight on land, sea, and horseback. I can do miracles with black powder. I'm fit and I'm strong and I'm mentally tough. You're not going to find a better man for the job."

"Look, Brian ..."

"I know what you're going to say so hear me out. I'm unattached and my three ex-wives are only going to miss my money. I've got no kids, at least none that I'll admit to. I've lived my entire life fantasizing about the past. I'm convinced I was born hundreds of years too late. I want this, John. I want it so bad I can taste it. You'll be happy to have me, I'm sure of it. With your wound, you're not going to be at full strength. Trevor'll do you proud, but he's not going to be able to hold his own against experienced swordsmen. I'm sure the decision's not going to be up to you alone. I expect all manner of government departments will have their fingers in the pie. Argue my case, John. Do it for me and do it for your mission. I want to go. I've got to go."

There was no appetite for a press conference but the government decided they couldn't dodge the media forever. It had been six days since the incident at South Ockendon. The housing estate was still cordoned off and the residents had not been allowed to return. Reports were circulating of missing persons—a crew of builders, last seen at the estate, a council worker, a doctor, an architect, a mother whose child had been at school that day. All the while the police and security services had remained mum.

Ben Wellington had not been pleased to learn that the powers had designated him as chief spokesman for the press event. When he protested, his chief, Sir George, had asked him, "Can you dance, Ben?"

"Dance? Yes, I've been known to take to the floor once lubricated."

"Then get out there and dance your tail off. You have a reputation as a clever boy. Be clever."

Flanked by senior members of the Metropolitan Police he peered at the sea of faces in the auditorium at New Scotland Yard and waited for the press secretary to give him the sign to begin. Then, leaning into the bank of microphones he introduced himself and said he had a statement to make.

The statement unleashed a collective groan through the press corps who anticipated that he would effectively deliver an apologia that all that followed was going to be a colossal waste of time, that because of security concerns and the need to protect an ongoing investigation, few definitive answers were going to be forthcoming. And that is exactly what he did. That didn't stop the questions from flying and Ben, true to his word, sidestepped all of them except for the one that terminated the briefing.

What was the nature of the biological agent found on the estate?

We're not commenting on that at this time.

Is the public at risk?

The risk has been contained.

Where were the missing residents of the estate?

We're not commenting on missing persons reports.

Are the missing residents in quarantine because of exposure to a biological agent?

Again, no comment.

Family and friends of the missing are saying they've been asked to avoid speaking to the media. Is that true?

I wouldn't want to contradict their statements.

Had any terror suspects been apprehended? Were any on the run?

I'm not at liberty to say.

Has any foreign or domestic terror group claimed responsibility?

Not to our knowledge.

And so it went for almost half an hour. Ben had been avoiding one questioner because there was something about him that made him uneasy. He seemed out of place. He was younger than the rest, awfully fresh-faced and earnest-looking for a member of Fleet Street or the broadcast corps. And something about his expression told Ben he wasn't going through the motions like the others, that he really cared about the truth. He called on a fellow a row behind him but the young man seized on the ambiguity and stood.

"Not you," Ben said. "Behind you, in the brown jacket."

"I'll be quick," the young man said, unyielding. "Why is there no one here from the Massive Anglo-American Collider?"

"I'm sorry," Ben said, his pulse quickening. "Who did you say you were and who are you with?"

"Giles Farmer. I write for *Bad Collisions*. It's a blog about the dangers of supercolliders."

"Well, Mr. Farmer, you seem to have wandered into the wrong press conference."

"Don't think so, actually. Five weeks ago there was a well-publicized start-up of the MAAC, followed by an intruder report and a shutdown. Less publicized were five weekly Thames-region power-grid perturbations, consistent with quiet restarts. The last one, six days ago coincided perfectly with your incident at South Ockendon, which is directly above one of the MAAC super-magnets. So, again, why is no one here from MAAC to answer questions? I would like to be able to speak to Dr. Emily Loughty, the research director."

Ben waited a moment to ensure his tone didn't channel his inner turmoil. "As I said, this is a press conference concerning a terror incident at South Ockendon so I have no idea what you're talking about."

With that, the press secretary for the Met announced that the news conference was at an end. Ben left the auditorium for a room behind the stage where Anthony Trotter was lurking watching on a monitor.

"That went well, except for the last question," Trotter said.

"Clever chap," Ben said, draining a bottle of water. "He seems to have connected a good number of dots."

"We'll want to keep tabs on Giles Farmer," Trotter said. "I'll have a team put on him."

"I think we have more urgent business than doing surveillance on a blogger. Besides he's domestic which puts him under the jurisdiction of MI5 not MI6."

"You've got your head in the sand, Ben. This nation is facing an unprecedented threat. The prime minister and his cabinet have appointed me acting director of MAAC, and in that capacity, everything is under my jurisdiction."

10

Solomon Wisdom was at a loss for words. Caffrey, his stout and ever-ready manservant, had fetched him from his study to alert him to the arrival of "more special new 'uns" so he was primed for the possibility of live souls of the same ilk as John Camp and Emily Loughty.

But the sight of children was almost too much for him.

On their journey from Dartford, Sam and Belle had been scared of the horses at first, but after a while they began to enjoy bouncing around in their saddles. Sam had even found his tongue, turning to the captain of the guard who held the reins with one hand and Sam with the other.

"Did you know the horse smells better than you?"

Sam hadn't understood the answer. "That's 'cause he's very much alive and I'm very much dead."

Arabel and Delia had been considerably more frightened and uncomfortable, crammed onto saddles with filthy soldiers. Arabel's rider seemed as scared of her as she was of him and had left her alone, but Delia's, an older fellow with yellow teeth, had become randy. She kept removing his creeping hand from her bosom.

Delia was prepared for the geographical similarities of Hell but the wildness of the countryside was hard to reconcile with the cityscape she knew. Yet as a Londoner, the snaking contours of the Thames were familiar and when Wisdom's mansion house came into view, she recognized the hill. They were in the geographical equivalent of Greenwich.

When he appeared at the door of his grand house, Wisdom's skeletal frame, black frock coat, and dour expression scared Belle and Sam. They cowered behind their mother.

Wisdom finally found enough voice to utter a single word. "Children."

After tossing the soldiers an unusually heavy purse, he instructed Caffrey to bring the visitors to the dining room and have the cook prepare food. Then he disappeared into his study to compose his thoughts. He would defer customary pleasantries and introductions for now. Word would spread fast and he had important decisions to make.

In his chamber he paced and talked aloud as if the only counsel worth receiving was from himself.

"This is an opportunity of grand scale, Solomon, grand scale. Another such opportunity may never present itself. Two live women and two live children! To augment the profit your execution must be flawless. Think, think! Who are the best buyers and how many lots shall I offer? Two lots, I should think. Deal the children to one buyer, the women to another. King Henry has not yet returned from his misadventure in Francia. Perhaps, when he does, he will want the children as a distraction or as a gift for his Queen. I think he will pay well. As for the women, King Pedro of Iberia, I should think. The Iberian ambassador was up in arms, most unhappy he did not get a chance to bid on Emily Loughty. So, let us give him a chance to open wide his purse of gold. And perhaps there are other bidders lurking about the court. A grand scale, I say. An opportunity of grand scale indeed."

He summoned Caffrey, gave him instructions, then breezed into his dining room, prepared for a robust charm offensive calculated to put his guests at ease. Delia and Arabel had been gazing out the windows at the sloping meadows behind the house and the children were playing under the table.

"I do apologize for the lack of a proper greeting. I had some minor business to attend to and now you shall have my full attention and hospitality. I am your host, Solomon Wisdom, and I bid you welcome to my humble abode."

Delia replied, puffing herself up and delivering the strongest rebuke she could muster. In his interviews Duck had said he thought Emily had been taken from Dartford to a "flesh trader" but he hadn't mentioned a name. "I don't know who you are, Mr. Wisdom, but we are not chattel to be bought and sold. I demand you have us taken back to Dartford immediately."

His artificial smile faded. "Bought and sold? My dear woman, why do you make such an accusation?"

"You gave those men a bag of coins. What else clinks like that?"

"That was only some small payment for their troubles. They bring all new arrivals in the area to me for—a welcome. I am told people are appreciative of the information I am able to impart. I do it as a service to my fellow man. I have been among the fortunate few in this unfortunate land and it is charity at work, nothing more, nothing less."

"You must think I was born yesterday," Delia said.

"I have no idea when you were born, my good woman."

"So you'll send us back to Dartford?"

"Of course. Anywhere you wish to go. But first, I insist you share my table. You must be hungry and thirsty after your long journey."

From under the table, Sam asked for a lemon squash.

"We'll eat with you," Delia said, "then we want to go."

"Anything you wish. Ah, I hear footsteps. The feast cometh."

His heavyset housekeeper and cook, her white hair up in a kerchief came in looking about, sniffing, and carrying a large tray. She'd been told there were live children in the house and only when she put the tray on the trestled table did she see Sam poking his head out from under it.

At the sight of him she began to cry.

"Now stop that," Wisdom said sternly, "and fetch the drink. The women will have wine. I really don't know what the children shall have. What do children drink?"

Arabel spoke for the first time. "Is there any fruit juice?"

"I'm afraid we have no such thing," he answered.

"Water then, if it's clean," Arabel said.

Belle appeared and the cook was overcome with another wave of emotion.

"Why are you crying?" Sam demanded.

"Because you are both so lovely and precious," she answered.

Sam had already lost interest in her tears and was staring at her face full of moles. "Why do you have so many black spots on your face?"

Arabel tried to hush him but the cook laughed it off and said, "They are my beauty marks and as you can see I am beautiful indeed, my dear."

Seated at the table, Wisdom personally carved the joint of meat and allocated a few root vegetables to each plate before saying, "Let us eat and let us talk."

"Are you going to say grace?" Sam asked.

"We don't do that here," Wisdom said. "I doubt I can even remember the words."

In a clear voice Arabel said, "Dear Lord, for what we are about to receive, we offer our thanks and gratitude."

"Ah, it conjures memories," Wisdom said, stuffing his mouth with mutton. After a few chews and a swallow, he said, "Now, let me see if you are aware of your rather fantastic circumstances."

"We know where we are," Delia said. She tried the wine, seemed to like it and had some more.

"I see, excellent. Well, the Hell you see is quite different from the Hell we are all taught to fear on Earth."

"Please don't use the H word in front of the children," Arabel whispered.

"Why not?" Wisdom asked.

"I don't want to frighten them. I've told them we've entered a make-believe world from one of their story books."

"I see. What shall I call it then?"

"Anything but that." She carried on, cutting the meat into small pieces for the kids.

"All right, I shall call it by the name the simple folk use. Down. Will that suffice?"

"Thank you, yes."

"Well then, Down is quite different …"

"I know all about it," Delia said, "and I've told Arabel."

"Then I am relieved of a long exposition which I have delivered countless times."

"I've got a question, though," Delia said, her speech slightly slurred by the wine. "How come you're not the least bit curious about us? Leads me to wonder if you haven't seen living people here in the past. The very recent past."

"Indeed I have. The very recent past, just as you suggest. I had the pleasure of briefly entertaining two singular individuals, a woman, Emily Loughty, and a man, John Camp. Given the circumstances of their arrival, I would not be at all surprised if you did not know of them."

"Emily's my sister," Arabel said softly.

"I see a resemblance," he said. "I was told of some great, infernal machine in your time which has opened a channel of sorts between our two worlds. I imagine the four of you must have become ensnared by the teeth and gears of the machine and spit asunder."

"Something like that," Delia said.

"Are you two ladies scientists like Miss Emily?"

"Hardly," Arabel said. "She's the brain in the family. I'm just a mother."

"A difficult enough profession if I recall. And you, Miss Delia?"

"I'm not a scientist either. I'm a spy."

Wisdom lowered his utensils in astonishment. "A spy you say? I was in disbelief that a woman could be a scientist and now I am in disbelief that a woman could be a spy. I am glad I did not live in your time. I would have felt quite off my balance. Are you a spy in the employ of the crown?"

"That's right."

"And whom are you spying upon?"

She started on her next glass of wine. "Right now I'm spying on you."

After a pregnant pause, he looked down his long nose and burst into raucous high-pitched laughter that frightened Belle and set her off into a fit of tears.

Young Charlie, consumed by fear, set the pace, sprinting ahead of the pack. His brother, Eddie, was next, followed by Martin and Tony, the two women, and finally, Jack, whose heavy gut and thick legs made him the least well-suited for speeding through a forest. Martin looked over his shoulder and seeing Jack falling behind called for the sons to help their father along.

Charlie was too scared to slow down but Eddie answered the call and fell back, but before he could reach the portly man Martin heard a cry and slowed.

"Don't stop!" Tony screamed, one hand holding up his sagging boxers. "Stay with me!"

Torn by indecision, Martin picked up the pace again and kept moving forward.

Eddie reached his father who was lying on his side, his heavy body molding the organic forest floor. Blood was oozing around the arrow embedded in his thigh.

"Dad! Come on, I'll help you up," his son said.

Another arrow whizzed overhead.

"I've had it, boy. Save yourself."

"No. I won't leave you."

"I said go! Mind your father. You're the boss now, all right? Look after Charlie and tell your mother I love her. Now go, for fuck's sake!"

Tears streaming, Eddie rose from his father's side and took off running.

Soon he and the others heard a blood-curdling scream and Jack was gone. His severed head was kicked into the bushes as if it were as cheap a thing as an old football. The rovers quickly stripped him of his overalls and work boots then resumed their hunt for the others.

Despite being partially blinded by his tears, Eddie surged ahead of Martin and Tony and called out to his brother, "Charlie, Charlie, where are you?"

Martin could no longer see Alice and Tracy behind him. Despite Tony's protestations, he refused to leave them to the same fate as Jack Senior and

Jack. He stopped and reversed direction, calling for them to hurry along.

Soon, he understood why they had fallen behind. Tracy had stepped on a sharp branch and had punctured her bare foot. Alice was doing her best to move her along but the young mother was hobbled and crying in pain and fear. Just as Martin caught up to them he saw the rovers coming fast, crashing through the woods. There were at least four of them. Three were brandishing long, curved knives and one had a bow. On a full run, the archer nocked an arrow and began to draw the string. Though he was at least thirty yards away, Martin felt the archer's cold eyes upon him. He wondered what it would feel like to be shot by an arrow. It was the kind of cool, dispassionate thinking for which Tony often derided him.

Boom. Boom.

The deafening blasts rang out in rapid succession.

The arrow sailed high and wide of its mark. The archer dropped his bow and clutched his bleeding chest before dropping to his knees.

One of the rovers cursed and grabbed his gunshot arm then shouted at his comrades. They left the fallen archer behind, turned tail and disappeared into a thicket.

Two riflemen stepped from behind a pair of large trees, not ten yards from where Martin, Alice, and Tracy stood in shock.

They were in their forties, clean-shaven, dressed almost identically in dirty-white and threadbare Oxford shirts, rough, cloth jackets, ancient-looking hide leggings, and worn, modern shoes laced-up with rawhide. Their rifles were muzzleloaders. One of them re-loaded and tamped the powder while the other, the taller of the two spoke.

"You're safe now. They won't be coming back."

The riflemen slowly approached and Martin inserted himself between them and the women. "Who are you?" he asked, finding his voice.

The taller man responded incredulously, "The more interesting question is who the hell are you?" Before Martin could say anything, he told his partner, "Do you smell 'em, Murph?"

Murphy sniffed like a bloodhound and swore a low oath. "For Christ sakes, Jason. What gives?"

Rix, the taller man, said, "We'll find out soon enough. Call your mates back so we can deal with the lot of you."

"Why should we trust you?" Martin asked.

"'Cause we just saved your bacon?" Murphy said. "Good enough reason?"

Tracy sank to the ground, too overwhelmed to do anything but sob. Rix propped his musket against a tree and dropped to his haunches beside her. "Look, luv, I'm guessing you're having the worst day of your life, and I'd emphasize the word, life, because I can't explain it but I don't reckon you're dead. But you're safe now. Me and Murphy'll see to that."

Tracy flinched at his odor but his benign eyes seemed to soothe her. "Thank you."

"What's your name, then?" Rix asked her.

"Tracy."

He lifted his head to the other woman. "And you?"

"I'm Alice."

"Will you tell us where we are and what's happening to us?" Martin asked.

"We will," Murphy said. "But first we need to get you lot back to our village."

Persuaded, Martin cupped his mouth and shouted, "Tony! Everyone! Come back. We've found help. It's safe."

Delia was the first to wake the next morning. Arabel was in the adjoining bed with the children, all of them in dreamy repose. She wished she could have escaped into sleep longer herself but she was wide awake, her skin prickling from the coarse bedding. After a check for bedbug bites she got up and discreetly used the chamber pot in the corner then looked out the window. From the top floor of Wisdom's mansion house the muddy Thames looked like a brown snake, frozen in curved locomotion. Wisdom's barge was tied to its moorings. It hadn't been there when they rode past the day before. It had arrived from London earlier, carrying a party of visitors.

On the deck tiny figures made the casting motions of fishermen.

The door to their room had a heavy iron latch that she tried to lift. It wouldn't budge. Her blood boiled at their imprisonment. If it hadn't been for the sleeping children she would have banged the oaken door and hollered so she checked herself and merely seethed.

Under the circumstances she was glad to have something to occupy herself. Before retiring for the night she had asked the white-haired cook for some sewing materials to alter their clothes to deal with the absence of elastic, zippers and buttons. Sitting back on her bed she took stock of what she had to work with—an iron needle with a large eye, heavy thread, assorted lengths of hemp, and a pile of wooden buttons. She picked up Sam's denims first and began to sew a button.

In the dining room Solomon Wisdom sat in his customary place munching on cold meat and bread and washing it down with ale while two groups of men huddled in their respective corners, whispering in their native languages.

Growing impatient, he called out to the two men to his left, "Come now, Prince Heirax, I haven't all day."

Heirax, the Macedonian ambassador to King Henry's court, raised a finger and exchanged one more word with his colleague, a nobleman named Stolos.

"My offer is for all four of them," Heirax announced. "One thousand five hundred crowns."

Wisdom theatrically arched his eyebrows and addressed the three men to his right, "Gentlemen, do you wish to raise your bid?"

Navarro, the Iberian ambassador was rail-thin and feverish from a lingering bout of dysentery. The Macedonian bid seemed to stress his frail constitution and his retainers, de Zurita and Manrique, scrambled for a chair lest he faint.

De Zurita requested a drink for his master of equal parts water and wine and Wisdom's man, Caffrey, slunk to the sideboard to prepare it.

Fortified by the drink, Navarro rasped in heavily accented English, "How can we speak of sums this large without seeing the merchandise?"

"As I clearly stated," Wisdom said, "you will be able to see them after a price has been agreed upon. If they are not as represented—one comely, young, live maiden, two live children, one boy, one girl, and one older and fatter live matron—then you may withdraw your bids. However, you know me to be an honest broker, so you may be assured of my representations. You will also know that I previously acquired and did trade in a live maiden. I believe the French count who obtained her was most pleased with his purchase. It is a great curiosity that live souls have come of late to these parts. I cannot explain it but I have had the pleasure to become the exclusive purveyor of this exceedingly rare and singular merchandise."

Navarro looked to Manrique, a small, dark man who turned away to check the weight of the purse under his cloak. He bent and said something to his lord. Navarro then asked, "And you say the maiden is fair?"

"Most fair," Wisdom said.

"Then I bid two thousand crowns," Navarro said.

The offered amount had now reached the sum-total for all of Wisdom's flesh trade for five years and he took more drink to steady his nerves. "Excellent. And it's back to you, Prince ..."

A heavy banging against his front door stopped him in mid-sentence. He sent Caffrey to see who it was while Prince Heirax muttered something that Wisdom was sure was a Macedonian curse.

Caffrey returned with a wax-sealed envelope and whispered something in Wisdom's ear. Wisdom broke the seal with a greasy finger, read the parchment and put it down, unable to hide a spreading and unctuous smile.

"Gentlemen, it seems the situation has changed. I have here a letter from Queen Matilda, herself. Yesterday, I informed the English crown of the new merchandise which had come into my possession and I have a response. She has submitted a bid of two thousand crowns."

"This is what I have bid," Navarro sniffed. "If I must, I will trump the lady by one additional crown."

"Ah, but she has made her offer for the children alone," Wisdom said grandly.

The Macedonians were furious and accused Wisdom of misrepresenting the nature of the auction but the broker held his ground. The two gentlemen took their leave in a huff, demanding to be returned at once to London.

Navarro was calmer and after speaking to his retainers put a different offer on the table.

"I must say, Solomon, that I did not have a clear vision for these children. I have little doubt I could find interested parties but I am certain there is a good demand in Iberia for a live maiden. I will give you seven hundred fifty crowns for her alone."

"What about the matron?"

"I will take her off your hands but not for another crown."

"I must have compensation for her."

"Then just the maiden," Navarro said. "Do we have a deal?"

"Very well," Wisdom said. "I will delight the Queen by letting her have the children and a nurse. You shall have the lady."

Navarro had Manrique count out the coins, subject to an inspection of the woman. He had one other condition. "Following our recent and unfortunate sea battle with Henry, we Iberians are persona non grata at court. We do not wish our presence here to be known to the emissaries of the queen so let us retire to a private chamber where we may inspect the maiden and complete our purchase."

"Caffrey," Wisdom said, "bring the gentlemen to my study and take the lady down to them. If they are pleased, send them off through the rear of the house. Count Navarro, your horses are in the stables, fed and watered. It has been a pleasure doing business with you."

When Caffrey unlocked the bedroom door, Delia was just finishing her alterations. Arabel stirred at the sound of the heavy latch raising.

"Get dressed," Caffrey said, pointing at Arabel. "You're to come downstairs with me."

Delia demanded to know why he wanted her alone but Caffrey just repeated himself. Arabel rubbed at her eyes and began to tear up over the realization that some of her turbulent dreams had been true. She was still in this awful place. She protested in a quiet voice so as not to disturb the children that she didn't want to leave them, but Caffrey was seething now and he withdrew a short knife from his belt and threatened to slit Delia's throat if she didn't hop to it.

"Just try, you filthy shit," Delia said, rising, dropping some of her sewing on the floor. She was bigger than he was. When she'd first joined MI5 she had taken self-defense training but when Caffrey approached her with a raised blade she blanched and sat back down on the bed.

"I'll go," Arabel said. "How long until I can return to the children?" she asked.

"You'll have to talk to my master 'bout that. I was told to fetch you, no more."

Delia gave Arabel her clothes. Her skirt and blouse now had ugly but serviceable buttons and her bra was sewn closed in the front.

"Will you please turn around so I can dress?" she said.

Caffrey's leathery face stretched into a gap-toothed, leering grin. "I will not."

"Then I'll dress under the covers," she said.

When she was done she carefully got out of bed to avoid waking Sam and Belle and lovingly gazed at them before turning to Delia.

"Will you look after them?"

Delia took her quivering lips as a sign she believed she might not be coming back.

"Of course I will, dear. But you'll return presently, I'm quite sure."

"But if I don't, will you tell them their mummy loves them?"

"I will, luv. Ten times a day. And I'll look after them as if they were my own. If something does happen and we find ourselves separated, remember. We will be rescued. We will be found."

11

John and Emily spent the night together trying their best to slow down time. By tacit, mutual consent, the evening was more domestic than romantic. They shared cooking chores and afterwards, she helped him tidy his flat. They cuddled on the sofa and watched TV, sticking to comedies. Before retiring to bed, she checked his wound and declared it clean as a whistle. They didn't make love, not because they didn't want to, but because she simply couldn't accept pleasure into her life, knowing the ordeal Arabel and the children must be facing. She didn't have to explain it to him. He understood.

Instead they lay there in the dark, talking about what they would do when this was over, how she would find a university job somewhere, anywhere, and how he would follow along and mold his life to fit hers. They didn't want to give in to fatigue because with sleep, time would begin to fly and morning would come too soon. But sleep was inevitable.

He was back in Afghanistan and that horrible scream was in his ears.

In the distance the Taliban-infested farmhouse was flashing orange in the black, moonless night, lit by 30mm cannon rounds spitting from the Black Hawk hovering a click away. Explosions punched holes in the mud-brick walls surrounding the compound, taking out the snipers who were using them for cover but sparing the main house and hopefully the raid's objective, Fazal Toofan, the high-value target John's Green Beret team had been tasked to take alive.

At that moment the mission objective was the farthest thing from his mind. John was focused on his medic, Ben Knebel, clutching his abdomen and screaming in agony next to the man he'd just been treating, SFO Stankiewicz.

John rushed over, cursing at the sniper who'd already been atomized by cannon fire. John had assumed a crouching position between the farmhouse and Knebel to protect him as he worked on Stankiewicz's leg. The bullet that got Knebel must have threaded a needle—a ridiculously fucked-up shot in a ridiculously fucked-up war.

By the time John made it to their side, Stankiewicz had transitioned from patient to medic, ignoring his own bullet hole to divert his pressure dressing to Knebel's belly, pushing down hard to staunch the flow.

John had to pull the earpiece from his canal because Knebel's screams in his headset mike were too loud. He ripped open another pressure dressing from Knebel's kit, tossed it to Stankiewicz and kept pressure on the medic's abdomen.

"Stank, tape yourself up. I've got doc. Doc, stay with me. I'm going to bind you up and give you candy, all right?"

Through gritted teeth, the medic yelled. "Pouch in my bag. Can't move my fucking legs. Fuck, fuck!"

John used a roll of surgical tape to bind the pressure dressing tight against his gut then unwrapped a fentanyl lollipop and shoved it between the medic's cheek and gum. Then he put his earpiece back and called in the helo.

"I need you to evac two casualties, one of them's my medic. Now!"

The Black Hawk pilot radioed back, "Are we extracting all of you?"

"No, just the casualties."

"That's going to leave you naked, Major."

"You get my men out now. On my beacon. We've still got work to do."

"Roger that. Our ETA is thirty seconds. We'll get another bird to pick you up. I'll get you their ETA when I've got it."

John told the wounded men to hold on for a few more seconds and radioed Mike Entwistle on the north side of the farmhouse. "Mike, we're going to be on our own for a while. Are you taking any more fire?"

"Negative. I think we've got 'em suppressed."

"All right. As soon as Stank and Doc are evac'd we're going to squeeze them from the north and the south, make entry, take our HVT, and get the fuck out of Dodge."

As the fentanyl kicked in, Knebel's screams faded away into something almost more disturbing, the high-pitched whimpering of a newly paralyzed man who seemed to understand that the life he knew was gone forever.

They awoke well before the alarm went off and took turns showering and dressing. They had carefully selected and modified their clothing to avoid the wardrobe malfunctions that had plagued them previously. All the fabrics and stitching were made of natural fibers, wooden buttons replaced plastic ones and metal zippers, and their boots had leather laces and soles.

They kept their conversation sparse and light; they didn't feel the need to remind themselves what would happen in a few hours. As he checked the contents of his canvas and leather backpack one last time, John remembered the dream he'd had and realized his current mindset was similar to his pre-mission thinking in Iraq and Afghanistan: concentrate on the preparation, not the execution. Once a mission started, it almost never went to plan. Training and attitude was what kept you alive.

When it was time to go, they collected their gear and turned out the lights. He saw her look wistfully at the dark flat and said, "Don't worry. We'll be back."

Rix and Murphy were up early to start a fire and begin cooking a breakfast porridge of wild oats sweetened with foraged honey. For a week they'd kept to the same daily routine—provide basic sustenance to their guests then set off into the woods to look for Molly and Christine.

The village of Ockendon was set in a clearing on poorly drained, boggy ground teeming with flies and gnats. When Rix and Murphy first led Martin and the others from the dangerous forest, the ramshackle village of crude thatched huts had seemed like a sanctuary, but after a week, it seemed more like a prison camp. Ever distrustful of their fellow villagers, Rix had all of them bed down in their one small cottage, using every square inch of floor for the purpose. For the last thirty years Rix and Murphy had lived there with Molly and Christine and it was plenty cramped with the four of them. Eight was more or less an absurdity. They had given their beds to Alice and Tracy and had taken to the floor with the men, Rix closest to the door and Murphy by the hearth. Martin had washed Tracy's punctured foot and after he had declared the wound minor, he had wrapped it in a reasonably clean piece of cloth. Murphy and Rix possessed a meager collection of men and women's clothes and shoes, and everyone had dealt with their wardrobe problems as best as they could.

Martin awoke at the first whiffs of smoke and tiptoed over sleeping bodies to squat by the fire.

"Morning," he whispered.

"How you doing, doc?" Rix asked.

"Hellaciously," he answered, his now-standard quip. "Going out again?"

"After some grub," Murphy said.

Rix stirred the heavy iron pot suspended over the fire and grunted but with each passing day he was losing hope.

"I'd like to go with you," Martin said. "I'm getting a serious case of cabin fever."

"It's too dangerous," Murphy said. "It's been a month since the sweepers last came through. They'll be coming again, they always do. Everyone in this fucking village knows you're in here. They may not know your secret but they know you're here. They'll grass you out in a heartbeat. You'll need every last one of you to defend the ladies."

Martin gestured at the makeshift weapons propped against the walls—wooden clubs, an iron bar, a bent sword.

"I've told you. I'm a doctor, not a fighter. None of us are. If they come we'll be taken."

Rix shook his head. "If they come you've got to fight," he whispered. "You lot will be scattered to the four winds. The women will be raped and sold off as sex slaves. They find out you and Tony are poufs, you'll be raped too. Just do as you're told, all right? We'll be back after a few hours to check on you."

Tony had been awake, listening with eyes closed. He propped himself up. "I know you don't want to hear it, but I don't think you're going to find Molly and Christine. And I object to your calling us poufs."

"You're right," Murphy fumed. "I bloody don't want to hear it so shut your fucking mouth before I shut it for you."

His outburst woke the others and they began to stir and sit up.

Martin jumped to Tony's defense. "It might not be a popular notion but if everything you've told us about this place is true then it stands to reason that whatever forces, physical or supernatural, that catapulted us here may have sent them back to our place and time."

"It's just a load of bollocks," Murphy said. "The lasses are in the forest somewhere. Either the rovers have them or they've already escaped and they're trying to get back to us."

Rix stirred the bubbling pot. "Maybe it's bollocks and maybe it isn't," he said. "You can say it's bollocks that a bunch of live people came to Hell but, here they are. I'll tell you one thing, Colin, I'd give anything to know that our lasses are right this minute strolling along some sunny High Street in the county of Kent in the country of England on the planet Earth in the year 2015, than in the clutches of some fucking rovers in this shithole of a land. But until we know it for a fact, we're going to keep looking for them."

Tracy began to do what she had done almost every waking hour—she began to cry. Alice had been her self-appointed caretaker when she wasn't sewing everyone's clothes. But this morning she seemed too lethargic to offer any more support. Charlie, sitting next to a yawning Eddie, picked up the slack by putting a large hand on Tracy's shoulder and telling her everything was going to be all right.

But none of them actually believed it.

During their first night in Hell, Murphy and Rix had returned to the cottage following a fruitless day-long search for Molly and Christine, and laid out the shocking realities of the situation to their six shell-shocked guests. Initially, none of them believed a word of it, even after the two hosts described in some detail the day they had both died in 1984.

"Do you have a better explanation for what you're seeing with your own eyes?" Murphy had asked contemptuously.

Martin, ever the rationalist, had replied, "No I don't. But that doesn't make your cock-and-bull story less so."

"When we first arrived here it was hard for us to accept it too," Rix said. "But it's the truth."

"If what you say is true, that one can't die here, then these lads' father and grandfather are not dead."

Rix had shaken his head. "Maybe yes, maybe no. I've never seen a live person in Hell before so I can't be sure."

Charlie had lifted his head from his chest at this turn of conversation. "You say they could be alive? We have to go back to the woods and get them."

"I said I didn't know," Rix had said.

"For fuck's sake, let's get a move on," Eddie had said springing to his feet.

"In the morning," Murphy had said. "The rovers who almost had you are likely to be out and about."

In the gloomy dawn Martin and Eddie had accompanied Rix and Murphy into the forest, retracing their route until they reached Charlie's father first. Martin had waved Eddie off as he inspected the headless, butchered body. He was very much dead and gone. At the river, they found his grandfather who had suffered the same gruesome fate. Much of his muscle mass had been cut away.

"I suppose you lot *can* die," Murphy had said, spitting into the stream. "You're lucky."

Walking back to the village behind the grieving son, Martin had said to

Murphy and Rix, "I'm afraid you've shown me nothing to support your contentions."

"Contentions," Murphy had laughed. "It's not contentions, it's fact. Tell you what. Tonight, I'll sneak you across the village to show you your proof."

When night fell, Murphy had been true to his word. Tony, fearful, had asked Martin not to leave but the doctor had been determined to get to the bottom of their predicament. The two men had crept past the shuttered cottages lining the muddy road and approached a low wooden building. Martin had recognized the sickly smell of decay well before they made it to the latched door and he had to place his hand over his mouth and nose to prevent gagging. Murphy had warned him to steel himself before unlatching the door and lifting his flaming torch over his head.

Martin had by necessity pressed his hand hard against his face, almost cutting off all the air but it wasn't enough. He had to hold his breath to prevent passing out. His sense of smell had been dulled, but the sights and sounds assaulted him and had left him reeling. The rotting room was filled with decomposing bodies that were very much alive. Pitiful cries and moans filled the morbid chamber. The liquefied mass of flesh covering the floor was in motion. Hundreds of arms and legs slowly churned the putrid sewer of humanity, distorted, melting faces contorted in agony.

"Enough?" Murphy had said.

Martin had nodded, fled, and vomited outside.

Murphy had latched the door and had managed to find enough compassion to pat the doctor's back.

"Now do you believe you're in Hell?"

Now on the morning of their seventh day in Hell, Rix ladled the porridge into shallow wooden bowls. He and Murphy wolfed down their breakfast while the others ate slowly in dull silence.

"Right, we're off then," Rix said, shouldering his musket. "Remember, if anyone comes to the door, stay quiet. If anyone tries to get in, fight them and fight them hard. We're growing fond of you lot."

"Speak for yourself," Murphy groused, pushing the door open and scowling at a scrawny man who was leading an emaciated horse down the road.

"Don't you look at me, mate," Murphy shouted at the man who picked up his pace at the threat. "I will fucking crush you if you so much as look at me again."

The forest was damp and humid. The rain had stopped but water dripped steadily from leaves and branches. Rix led the way. They looked for fresh footprints but found none. At times he called out for Molly. Murphy was in a foul mood and couldn't muster the lungpower to call for Cristine. Eventually they passed by the bodies. Even more of their flesh had been eaten, not by returning rovers but by foraging animals. Emerging from the woods into the large meadowland, Rix paused.

"I say we go south toward the river," he said.

"We went there two days ago," Murphy said.

"Any better idea?"

Murphy grunted.

"Well?" Rix asked.

"No. Fuck, Jason, I don't know. Maybe what that fruit said is true. Maybe they've gone back to Earth."

"Better than having them carried off by rovers."

"Yeah but …"

Murphy didn't have to say it. Rix finished the thought. "I know, I know, but how the fuck are we supposed to carry on without our girls?"

Rix set off across the vast meadow and Murphy followed along, his eyes drifting to a circling hawk that suddenly fell from the sky and sank its talons into a startled vole.

The recreation center was almost unrecognizable. The polished wooden floor was protectively covered in cheap carpet with cutouts for the cabling to connect the workstations and monitors to the server room in the main lab building. Technicians manned rows of long tables running pre-startup diagnostic protocols on the hardware and software systems. A false wall had been built in the middle of the hall to hold an array of large screens to track the operational status of the synchrotron and the twenty-five thousand magnets ringing greater London inside the MAAC underground tunnels.

A staging area for the traveling party had been established in one corner and there, Ben Wellington was waiting with Trevor when John and Emily arrived.

They exchanged grim smiles and got down to business with an absence of small talk.

"Missing one," John said.

"He's in reception," Trevor said. "They'll be bringing him over."

They had all settled on more or less similar uniforms—khaki or camo trousers, heavy-duty cotton shirts, cotton underwear, boots and leather jackets swapped-out with wooden buttons for zippers. They were checking each other's backpacks when Brian was escorted in.

He had adhered to the dress code and looked chipper and excited, sporting the enthusiasm of a boy itching to go on a camping trip.

"'Allo!" he said, reaching for and pumping everyone's hands. "All systems go?"

John stopped himself looking for a watch on his bare wrist. A digital countdown clock on the wall had to do. "We'll go down below in sixty mikes."

"Sixty mikes," Brian repeated, delighted. "I do love the military jargon. Now, I've heeded your brief and I've left all manner of gear in my car boot, including my favorite broadsword. You sure it won't pass muster?"

"As I've said, metal won't pass," Emily said.

Brian had only met her the day before and he'd been charmed out of his mind. He had told her, "I love beautiful women, I love the Scots, so I'm already madly in love with you." When it became clear she was spoken for he had pouted for the rest of their planning session.

"Have fun at the dentist?" Trevor asked.

Brian smiled to show off the new gaps in his mouth.

Now that everyone was here, Ben felt a need to deliver a small speech. "It goes without saying that this is a volunteer mission. It's clearly not too late to back out. There's no shame in it. So, I'm obliged to canvas your responses."

"I'm going," John said.

"Me too," Emily replied.

Trevor chimed in next. "I'm in."

And Brian said emphatically, "Wouldn't trade it for all the tea in China or all the Oscars in Hollywood."

"Right," Ben said, struggling to keep his composure. "God speed. I'll be off now for the final security checks for Dartford and South Ockendon. I'll be waiting for you right here in one month's time. Please don't be late."

"Good luck rounding up all the villains," Trevor said.

Ben shook his hand. "I'll do my best, my friend."

They resumed their equipment checks then passed around the books for everyone to inspect.

"Interesting selection," Brian said.

"The pen is mightier than the sword," John said.

"So I'm told, but I'm a damn sight better with one than the other," Brian said.

When all the bags were re-packed they sat on folding chairs, watching the technicians prepare. Emily wandered over to Matthew Coppens and David Laurent who were deeply into their countdown prep. Matthew looked up from his workstation.

"Hey," she said.

"Hey." He still looked plenty guilty over his role in the mess.

"How's it going?" she asked.

"Everything's online. No problems we can see. I was worried about having to move the control room but no glitches so far."

"It's strange to be on the outside looking in," she said.

"I was so happy when you came back. I wish you weren't going again."

"If it weren't for my family, I'd be sitting beside you, Matthew. I've got complete confidence in your ability to bring us home."

John turned to Brian, "So is Trev ready to slay dragons?"

"He's a very quick study, young Trevor is. More than ready, I'd say."

"I'd be happier with my old SA80 assault rifle than a bow and arrow," Trevor said.

"It's an ugly-ass weapon system," John said, "but I'd prefer it too. What did you tell your family?"

"I took my mum and dad for a curry last night and told them I'd been picked for some special assignment overseas. Slung some bullshit—covert this-and-that, need to know, etcetera. They couldn't understand it. Took them by surprise. They thought the days of worrying about me had long passed. Still, they're cool. I gave them Ben's number in case of …" His voice trailed off.

"That's funny," Brian said, jumping in. "I gave my ex-wives your number, Trev. Just in case."

With thirty minutes to go, the VIPs came in led by Anthony Trotter, overdressed for the occasion in a snug three-piece suit. Leroy Bitterman and Karen Smithwick followed, along with Campbell Bates from the FBI and George Lawrence from MI5. Bitterman made a beeline for the travellers.

"Well, it's almost time," Bitterman said.

"We're ready as we can be, sir," Emily said.

"I'm sure you are." He greeted everyone and said, "You must be the famous Brian Kilmeade. I'm Leroy Bitterman, the US energy secretary."

"I could use some of that," Brian said.

"Some of what?"

"Energy."

Bitterman laughed heartily. "Armed with a sense of humor, you can defeat almost any enemy. I believe your prime minister is watching from Number Ten. He tells me he's a fan of yours. Wave at the camera."

Brian obliged and blew a kiss. "If we were taking a camera crew with us I might finally get what I've always wanted—a US network reality show."

"Well, I know a few people in the business," Bitterman said, smiling. "I'll put in a good word for you."

"I'll hold you to that and if we get a deal I'll give you my good-for-nothing agent's ten percent."

Turning to Trevor, Bitterman said, "I hear you exceled in training, Mr.

Jones."

"I had a good teacher."

"Well, let's hope you don't need too much of it. And how are you doing, John? All healed up?"

"I'm good to go, sir."

"Glad to hear it. We'll be having sleepless nights until all of you return."

Trotter interrupted and told Bitterman he was wanted. The secure coms link with London, Washington, and the South Ockendon estate had been established. He acted as if the others weren't even there.

"Aren't you going to wish our colleagues good luck?" Bitterman clucked.

"Best of luck, chaps," Trotter said mechanically, walking away.

"Well, he's not what we'd call a warm and fuzzy type," Bitterman said, giving them a last wave.

From across the hall, Emily strained to listen to the department heads reporting out the status of the power-up. The super-cooled helium had been pumped into the array of twenty-five thousand magnets and the magnets' director had declared them to be at 1.7K, the temperature at which they became super-conducting and capable of bending beams of protons around the one-hundred-eighty kilometers of tunnels ringing London. The countdown toward full synchrotron power was progressing smoothly and at the fifteen-minute point, a security detail of MI5 men appeared to escort them down to the old control room. The control room and indeed the entire underground complex had been deemed too unstable for anyone but the departing souls for fear of sending anyone else through a widening dimensional portal.

After the familiar elevator ride down to the control-room level, they entered the strangely barren space that had been stripped of virtually all its electronics and now resembled a dismantled movie set. The only display was a red-numbered digital clock counting down to MAAC start-up. Multiple high-definition videocams studded the walls and speakers hung on the walls.

They walked down the tiered levels and eyed the large X taped onto the well of the theater floor, three meters directly over the muon spectrometer detector, a seven-story tall behemoth which was the collision point where opposing beams of proton particles would meet in an enormously high-energy state.

"So this is where the magic happens," Brian said.

The clock ran down to ten minutes.

The security team departed.

They heard the exit doors being locked and bolted.

Matthew Coppens' disembodied voice sounded from the speakers. "All right, we've got good visuals and audio on all of you. We'll ask you to take to the mark at the one-minute point. You're free to relax until that time."

"Can you believe he said relax?" John whispered to Emily.

Matthew came back apologetically. "Sorry, poor choice of words."

"The microphones seem to be working well, Matthew," Emily said, trying to smile at the cameras.

John leaned over and whispered directly into Emily's ear. "When we get back I'm going to keep you in bed for a solid month."

She grinned and said, "Matthew, I sincerely hope no one heard that."

"That's a negative, Emily."

"Thank God."

At T-minus-five minutes they heard a technician announce, "We have full power. Two hundred GeV acceleration."

At time zero, lead ion gas would be injected into the synchrotron where it would be accelerated and transferred into the MAAC. Two beams of proton particles, one traveling clockwise, the other counterclockwise, would be further accelerated to their collision speed of 30 TeV, circuiting greater London at near light speed, or eleven thousand times per second.

They heard David Laurence declare the muon detector online and fully operational.

At T-minus-one minute Matthew asked them to take to the mark and the four of them bunched together in a tight circle, their backpacks touching in the middle. Matthew initiated the injection and filling of the particle guns with the lead gas, and at thirty seconds he sought authorization from Leroy Bitterman to launch the beams.

Bitterman simply said, "Yes."

Matthew's tense voice boomed through the speakers, "…four-three-two-one. Initiate firing."

John reached for Emily's hand.

They heard Matthew calling out the rising energy read-outs.

"Four TeV, five, six, seven …"

"Nothing's happening," Brian said.

Emily said, "Too soon."

"Sixteen, eighteen, twenty, twenty-one, twenty-two, twenty-three, twenty-four …"

"Getting there," she whispered.

"Twenty-seven, twenty-eight, twenty-nine, thirty TeV. Full power!"

Emily squeezed down on John's hand so hard her knuckles ached.

12

The first one inside the makeshift control room to speak was Anthony Trotter. Although he had been briefed on what was likely to happen, the sight of it playing out on huge monitors seemed to unnerve him. He swore loudly then must have remembered that the remote audience included the prime minister and the president of the United States. A weak "Sorry," followed.

Ben Wellington urgently scanned the other camera feeds. The employee canteen from where Arabel Loughty, her children, and Delia May had disappeared was empty. Up and down the underground control room level, the halls and utility rooms were empty.

He returned to the control room displays.

John, Emily, Trevor, and Brian were gone and no one had taken their places.

"Automatic power-down has been initiated," Matthew called out, his voice now urgent and high-pitched. "They're gone."

Leroy Bitterman had quietly assumed Henry Quint's role as scientific head of MAAC and he calmly thanked Matthew and asked him to inform him when they were at zero TeV. Quint sat alone against the back wall, impotently clicking his ballpoint pen.

"All security teams," Ben radioed to the MI5 agents dispersed throughout the MAAC campus, "please report any unusual activity of any sort, any intruders."

Negative reports flooded in.

"Can we have all the feeds from South Ockendon on the main screens?" Ben asked.

The estate had been evacuated and cordoned off. Videocameras had been installed covering all streets and gardens. Motion-capture cameras had been placed inside all the empty houses.

There was no unusual activity.

"We're at zero power," Matthew announced. "Full shut-down achieved."

A disembodied American voice came through the control-room speakers. "This is President Jackson. Could someone please tell me what's happening?"

"Mr. President, this is Leroy Bitterman. As you can see, the traveling party has disappeared, presumably to the other dimensional space. That was expected. What seems unexpected is the absence of exchange activity. We had been anticipating a one-for-one swap as before. Four souls for four souls."

"And if that doesn't occur?" the president asked.

"I'm unsure of the implications at this time," Bitterman said.

Suddenly one of the motion-capture cameras at South Ockendon came to life and a sunlit lounge appeared on one of the screens.

"Which house is that?" Ben asked.

"It's number fourteen, the Hardcastle/Krause dwelling," one of Ben's agents reported.

"Put it on the main screen," Ben said. "Just there! Did you see that, by the china cabinet?"

"What the fuck, Jason? What the fucking fuck?"

Murphy was hyperventilating.

In one moment they were in the middle of an empty field of undulating grasses, in the next they were in a suburban lounge.

Rix shielded his eyes from the glare. He hadn't seen the sunshine in thirty years and it mesmerized him. As it flooded through the open curtains it cast his own shadow, something he'd forgotten existed. His elongated stilt legs almost made him laugh out loud.

He noticed that his hands were empty. His musket was gone and his shoulder pouch was too light. He squeezed at it. The musket balls were gone.

His eyes darted around the room. There was too much to absorb. Hundreds of objects, most of them familiar enough to trigger rushes of emotion, some wholly unfamiliar like the iPhone and digital car-key fob on the side table. He settled on a wall display of framed photographs.

"Colin, look at these," he said.

Murphy crept across the thick carpet as if it were a body-sucking swamp. He studied the photos and exclaimed, "It's the blokes. Martin and Tony."

"We're on Earth," Rix said, dropping to his knees, his eyes welling up. "We're back on bloody Earth."

Murphy stumbled around the lounge and wandered into the kitchen and when Rix joined him his head was already inside the refrigerator.

"Would you look at this?" Murphy said, holding up a can of beer. "Have you ever seen something so beautiful?"

He cracked open the can and started gulping it. Rix left him to his ecstasy and began searching the house.

"Molly?" he called out. "Molly, are you here? Christine?"

He ran up the stairs and looked into the bedrooms and the two baths. He came back downstairs and was about to announce that the house was deserted when the front door blew open and armed men in full riot dress stormed in, ordering him and Murphy on their bellies with their hands stretched out in front of them.

Rix complied but Murphy was defiant. "I'm not finished with my beer," he complained, remaining upright until two men took him roughly down, placed him in plastic cuffs, then hauled him back to his feet.

The lead MI5 officer in the tactical squad was in radio contact with Ben Wellington.

"Ask them who they are," Ben instructed.

"State your names," the officer said.

Back in the control room in Dartford, the cabinet room in Downing Street, and the situation room at the White House, the assembly saw and heard the responses from two men with London accents: Jason Rix and Colin Murphy.

"Do they have a peculiar odor?" Ben asked.

"They smell bloody awful," was the reply. "Putrid, really."

"Ask them when they died?"

"Say again? Did you say, ask them when they died?"

"Affirmative. Just ask them, please."

"When did you two die?" the officer asked hesitantly.

Rix seemed to understand that someone off-premises was watching and directing the questions. He looked around the room and spotted a lens affixed to the wall.

"Is that a camera?" he asked.

"Tell him he's correct," Ben instructed.

"Yes, it's a camera."

Rix looked into the lens and smiled. "The both of us, me and Murphy shuffled off the mortal coil in 1984."

Murphy got into the action, addressing the wall. "Be an angel and let me finish my beer."

"Where are we?" Rix asked.

The officer received permission to respond and told them they were in South Ockendon.

"Do you have our women?" Rix asked. "Christine and Molly."

They were asked for their full names.

"Christine Rix and Molly Murphy," Rix said. "They're our wives."

Chatter broke out in the control room.

Ben asked everyone to be quiet and directed the reply. Rix and Murphy were told the women were at large and that they would be brought in for questioning immediately.

"That's all right," Rix said to the camera. "We know the drill. We were coppers in our day."

The VIPs departed Dartford for London in government cars and Ben began to prepare for Rix and Murphy's interrogation. A room had already been prepped for the purpose. He had the recording devices checked, the medical team alerted to perform a preliminary assessment on the prisoners' arrival, and the canteen ready to feed them. He was about to ring his wife to let her know he was unlikely to be home for dinner when his mobile went off. It was an MI5 number at Thames House. One of the junior intelligence officers assigned to monitor radio traffic from the Metropolitan police and surrounding constabularies introduced herself and apologized in advance for the call.

"No need," Ben said. "I left clear instructions to be alerted if we picked up anything out of the ordinary."

"I believe this satisfies the criteria," she said stiffly, as if star struck by how many organizational rungs she had vaulted to be talking directly to Ben. "Police in Buckinghamshire have been called out to the Iver North Water Treatment Works to respond to an unauthorized entry into the facility."

As she talked, Ben put her on speaker to punch up a map on his phone.

"Go on," he said.

"The police are en route but emergency services have the caller on line and I'm continuing to monitor."

"What details have been provided?" Ben asked.

"Two intruders, both male, described as wandering about inside one of the facilities. The caller said they seemed to be, and I quote, 'in a daze.'"

"I see, anything else?"

"He approached to ask who they were and withdrew to call 999 when he became alarmed at their smell."

"Did you say, smell?"

"Yes, sir, their odor. He said it was repulsive."

Ben stared at the map. Iver, Buckinghamshire was west of London, about forty miles as the crow flies from Dartford. The water works was adjacent to the M25.

The MAAC tunnels ran directly underneath.

"Listen closely," Ben said, taking the phone off speaker, "and do exactly what I say. This is a matter of national security and I'm depending on you to get this absolutely right."

13

It was all too familiar.

The sad little village of Dartford was just as John and Emily had left it a week earlier—smelly, drab, and shabby. They stood in the middle of the road on the same spot they had straddled for their journey home. On taking their first steps they felt the mud tugging at their boots once again. The small cottages were shuttered, the road deserted.

Trevor and Brian turned in tight circles in silence.

"Are we in the right place, guv?" Trevor finally asked.

"As advertised," John said, slipping off his backpack. It was still heavy, a good sign. He checked its contents. Everything was there. The books had made it through.

Brian snapped out of his trance and dashed off, fighting the mud until he had his hands on the wooden club propped against one of the cottages. It was crudely fashioned from the bough of a tree. He rejoined the others, brandishing it with both hands.

"Good man," John said.

"That's why you're paying me the big money," Brian said. "It'll do until we find something with a sharp edge."

"I can't believe we're really back," Emily said.

"We knew what we were signing up for," John said. "In four weeks we'll be back on this spot heading home. With the others."

She gave a one-word reply. "Hopefully."

"Definitely."

She smiled at that. "Your American attitude comes in handy at times like this."

John motioned for everyone to follow him as he made his way across the road to Dirk's cottage. He didn't bother to knock. The structure was poorly built with gaps around the doorframe so he called out without shouting.

"Dirk, are you in there? Believe it or not, it's John Camp."

It was only a few strides from one end of the cottage to the next so John wasn't surprised that the door flung open immediately.

Dirk stared at him, his pupils constricting in the morning light. Duck peered over his shoulder.

It was Duck who spoke first. "I told you they'd come for 'em," he said. "I told you so!"

"How about letting us in?" John asked.

"'Course you can," Dirk said, standing aside to let them pass. "I reckon you missed us something awful."

"Yeah, like a bad hangover."

Emily had been hoping beyond hope that Arabel and the children would be there. When she saw they weren't, she deflated like a bad soufflé. Trevor was equally disappointed.

Dirk looked at Trevor and Brian with suspicion but carried on with John. "You're looking brighter than last we saw you."

"I'm doing much better, thanks. Miracle of modern medicine."

"Who are your mates, then?"

"This is Trevor and this is Brian. They've come to help us."

"You'll need plenty of that," Duck said urgently.

"Were they here?" Emily asked. "My sister, the children?"

"They wuz," Duck said. "And Delia as well. But they was taken. I swear, there weren't nothing me or my brother could do to stop it from 'appening."

"Do you know where they are?" she demanded.

"We do," Dirk said. "And we'll 'elp you good and proper. You're a man of your word, John Camp. You said you'd get my brother back and you did. Sit down, 'ave some of my ale and we'll tell you what we know."

The morning dragged on. All six of them were bearing the emotional scars of their seven days of captivity. Rix and Murphy hadn't been holding them captive but they had confined themselves to the cramped quarters because they feared showing themselves outdoors. Even the act of using the privy involved cracking the rear door to see if anyone was in the fields then dashing there and back. Tony had declared it worse than prison because at least there you'd know your sentence and understand your circumstances. But to Martin it was wholly analogous to prisoners being sent to Australia in the nineteenth century. When those poor wretches had arrived on the vast penal colony, they too had been strangers in a strange land and their hope of returning home was no more than a small, fading flame.

By late afternoon, they began to get nervous.

"Why haven't they returned?" Eddie asked.

"We're eating them out of house and home," Martin said. "They probably went hunting after looking for their wives."

"Maybe they were sucked back to Earth," Charlie said.

His brother snorted at him but Charlie asked him why he was being so dismissive.

"Yeah, sorry to doubt you," Eddie answered sarcastically. "I expect they found the magic wardrobe and pissed off to Narnia."

"I don't like it," Tony said. "This is the longest they've ever left us. What are we supposed to do if they don't return?"

Tracy began to blubber and Alice scolded Tony for setting her off but he was tired of walking on eggshells around the fragile woman.

"You're right," he fumed, "I should have said, what are we supposed to do even if they do return. We're buggered either way."

Amidst a backdrop of Tracy's sobs, the group argued amongst themselves for a time until Martin raised a hand and shushed them.

"Listen," he said.

At first it was more like an irregular vibration of the coarse floorboards but it morphed into a low rumble and then the unmistakable sound of galloping horses heading their way. Martin slightly opened the shutter on the road-facing window and saw men waving and pointing at their cottage.

He swore and glanced at the crude weapons Rix and Murphy had left behind.

"We're going to be taken," he muttered.

"Should we fight?" Eddie asked.

"We should not," Martin said. "I know what we were told but if we do we'll be hurt or worse."

"What will happen to us if we don't fight?" Alice said, going for the iron bar. "That's what I'm worried about."

Through her tears Tracy managed to say, "I don't want to go. Don't let them take me."

"Alice, put that bar down," Martin said. "You'll only get all of us killed."

"Where are they? Are they coming?" Tony asked desperately.

The raiding party came into Martin's view, ten or more riders, soldiers with slung rifles and belted swords which slapped against their horses' flanks.

The captain of the guard dismounted and began talking to the scrawny man with whom Murphy had exchanged words earlier.

Seconds later a voice loudly called out, "You lot in there. Come out with your hands held high or we shall come in and drag you out by your hair."

Martin and Tony looked at each other in sorrow and desperation but Eddie had another plan. He opened the rear door and bolted through it. Charlie needed no encouragement and followed along. The two of them sprinted past the outhouse into the surrounding field.

A soldier who had been sent to watch the rear of the house shouted that there were two men fleeing. He made off after them on horseback and was quickly joined by other riders.

At the same time, the captain of the guard ordered an assault on the house and men burst through front and rear doors with swords drawn.

Martin raised his hands into the air, shouted over Tracy's shrieks that they were surrendering, and begged them not to hurt anyone. Alice let the iron bar fall from her hands.

The captain, a young man with a mane of flowing hair, stepped into their midst and told Tracy to stop screaming as she was hurting his ears. He examined the four of them and smiled ear-to-ear. "It's true! They are decidedly different," he called through the door. "It's perfectly safe, Fletcher. You may enter without fear."

Fletcher, a greasy and waddling man with a pudgy, moon face and rubbery lips peered in. Once inside he inhaled the ambient air through his nostrils and declared his amazement.

"By Jupiter, it's true! They are far and away not the usual sorts. No they are not! Methinks the rumors swirling about have credence. These people are not dead, are they, captain?"

"I do not know what they are, Mr. Fletcher."

"Well, are you dead?" Fletcher asked.

Martin answered. "I'm a physician and I can assure you that we are very much alive."

"A physician!" Fletcher gushed. "And alive too. How extremely valuable. How did you come here if you are not dead?"

"I've no idea how it happened," Martin said. "One moment we were in our houses, the next moment we were here."

"It seems you are not the only ones," Fletcher said, moving amongst them, surveying his new property.

"There are others?" Tony asked.

"And what is your profession?" Fletcher asked him.

"I'm an architect."

"Really? A builder of edifices?"

"I design them. The men who escaped are builders."

There were shouts from the rear field. It sounded like the brothers might no longer be escapees.

"An architect. I see. Another valuable profession methinks. To your question, yes, we have heard tales that a colleague of mine, Solomon Wisdom, by way of Greenwich, recently brokered the sale of living arrivals and profited splendidly from the transaction. I did not believe these tales but now it seems they were so. And now, by Jupiter, I am to be richly rewarded myself."

"Also me," the captain said.

"Yes, captain," Fletcher said. "You will receive your usual percentage. We shall all prosper. A physician, an architect, a young, attractive wench and, well, another wench."

"Fuck you," Alice said.

"A wench with a mouth on her," Fletcher laughed. "Worth an extra few crowns for being feisty."

The captain had completed his inspection of the premises. "Where are the men who own this dwelling?"

"We don't know," Martin said. "They left us this morning and haven't returned."

"They will be severely punished for failing to report your arrival," the captain said. "Sweepers are not to be trifled with."

The rear door opened and the brothers were thrown in, their hands bound with rope. The soldiers manhandling them declared that something was different about the prisoners then realized there were four other different sorts already there. The captain told them to mind their own business and sent them outside to keep order among the villagers gathering in the road.

"Why did you run?" the captain asked the brothers.

"I don't know. Why do you smell like shit?" Eddie asked him back, his eyes blazing with hatred.

"How much are builders worth, Mr. Fletcher?" the captain said.

"A couple of crowns ordinarily. But I'd expect some sort of premium for their novelty."

"Take it out of my percentage then," the captain said, lifting the tip of his sword and running it through Eddie's chest.

"No!" Charlie screamed as Eddie collapsed to his knees.

Martin scrambled to help him but the blood gushed so violently from his pierced heart that he was gone in seconds.

Tracy howled in hysteria and the captain's men restrained a raging Charlie. The captain pushed Martin aside and inspected Eddie's lifeless body.

"It seems he was indeed, alive and that he is now, indeed dead," he said. "In the span of mere minutes I have seen two things I have not seen even once in all my time in Hell—men who are alive and a man who can be killed."

John and the others debated how best to travel to Greenwich but they all decided to defer to his judgment. It was John's opinion that an overland journey would require at least two horses with tack and enough weapons to fight their way through any situations they might encounter in the towns and villages along the route. Dirk agreed, his white-knuckle ride with John through Thamesmead still fresh in his mind. That left a river passage. It wouldn't be without its own challenges but, if successful, was bound to be quicker.

"What do you think?" John asked Dirk.

"I can tell you this," Dirk said. "There's been a steady procession of sailing ships coming up from the estuary this past fortnight, but they don't stop 'ere, do they? They sail right past."

"Heading where?"

"London, I expect, or the palace at 'ampton."

"Soldiers?"

"Definitely, I'd say. 'Enry's men."

John told everyone they were probably coming from Francia. He recounted the last time he saw King Henry, raging upon his black horse, exhorting his troops in the desperate midst of a battlefield rout at the hands of the Italians.

"Did he survive it?" Brian asked.

"I don't know," John said.

"I'd love to meet the man," Brian said. "Can you imagine?"

"It's quite the experience, but I don't think he'll be best pleased to see me again," John said.

"So how do we manage to capture a passing boat?" Trevor asked.

They discussed several tactical options, none of which sounded very practical until Emily, who'd been quiet, announced, "I know exactly how we can do it."

Before trekking to the river they stopped at Alfred Carpenter's empty house opposite the road from Dirk and Duck's place. Dirk and Duck stood guard outside while the rest of them made entry. Brian immediately spotted an object of desire, a rusty sword, short and heavy.

"This'll do nicely," he said, testing it in his hand. "It's a Roman design, a gladius, nicely balanced. I can get a good edge on this with a bit of elbow grease."

Before leaving, they added some knives and another club to their armamentarium and headed for the river, two miles away across marshlands. There were no boats in sight so Brian got to work, finding flat river stones and teaching Trevor how to hone the knives, wetting the stones with spittle. Then he began working on the sword under the shade of a small grove of trees.

Dirk and Duck squatted on the bank, tossing stones into the murky current like a couple of kids at play while Emily and John sat back, watching the hawks ply their trade in the lifeless, pale gray sky.

"Don't worry," he said, "we'll find them."

"God I hope so."

"We're less than a week behind them. It'll be okay."

"You'll like Arabel."

"How come I never met her?"

"It was only a matter of time," she said. "You haven't met my parents either."

"You think they'll approve?"

"Why wouldn't they?"

"Completely wrong pedigree. One, I'm not a Brit. Two, I'm not a scientist. Three, I'm a soldier. Four …"

"Four, I'm in love with you. That's all they'll need to know, plus all the mad heroic bits which we may or may not ever be permitted to speak about."

"Trevor's a soldier too. They'll have a double-whammy if he hooks up with Arabel."

"They'd do well to have both of you in the Loughty clan."

Dirk whistled for their attention. He pointed toward the east. A boat was approaching fast, its sails full of the afternoon breeze.

Brian came over and told them, "It's a river barge, about forty feet, flat-bottomed I'd be willing to bet to allow navigability in channels. Rigged with a mainmast and a mizzenmast. No cannon I can see. It was a typical late eighteenth century, nineteenth century design. Not a naval vessel but perfectly fine for ferrying provisions about."

"Is there anything you don't know about?" John asked.

Brian beamed. "Glad you brought me then?"

"I am."

"So am I," Emily said.

"I'd dearly love to have a spyglass," Brian said, "but I don't think I see many men on the deck."

Trevor drew closer. "There could be men below," he said.

"Doubt it," Brian said. "The hull's going to be too flat for that. Those what we see is those what we've got."

"Right, then," Emily said, standing. "It's show time. I do hope I don't go to Hell for this."

"Already there, luv," Brian said.

Dirk and Duck watched awestruck as she shed her denim jacket and undid the wooden buttons on her blouse. They whispered to each other when she stripped down to her cotton bra.

"Sorry boys," she said. "That's as far as I'm going."

John told the brothers to join them hiding behind trees as Emily, clad only in her bra and hip hugging khakis, went to the river's edge.

When the barge was a hundred yards away, she began waving at it and calling out. At first there was no reaction but suddenly, shouts emanated from the vessel and the tillerman jerked a change of course hard to port.

Emily held her ground and continued to wave as the barge steered directly for her.

"I make it seven men," John said.

"I agree," Brian said.

"What are those, pikes?" Trevor asked, pointing at a couple of long objects upright at the stern.

"More likely barge poles for maneuvering in the shallows," Brian said. "But at least a couple of blokes have swords on their belts. They're probably guards to protect the cargo. I doubt we'll have seven soldier-types to contend with."

"All right," John said, twisting his torso to test the pain and mobility around his flank wound. "Get ready to fight."

Dirk took a step back. "You do that. We'll just keep an eye on Miss Emily."

"You do all the looking you want but that's all you're going to do," John warned.

As the barge approached land, the men on board reached a fever pitch of excitement at the sight of a partially clad blonde siren waving them to the shore. She began backing up when a man jumped overboard and splashed toward her, anxious to beat his mates to the prize. A few sailors had the presence of mind to drop sail as the boat beached. Five men were soon in the water. That's when Emily began to move fast. She ran straight for the grove and kept going into the tall bulrushes.

John saw Brian cross himself and tighten his grip on the sword. Trevor and he would have to make do with clubs and if those failed, knives.

"Brian, I never asked you," John whispered, preparing to rise from his crouch, "have you ever killed anyone?"

Brian stood and said, "I've never even drawn blood, mate."

"First time for everything," Trevor said, straightening himself and taking a last deep breath before combat.

As the men approached the grove John stepped out from behind a tree, brandishing his club like a baseball bat. Brian joined him, a knife in one hand, the sword in the other, and Trevor circled around the grove to flank them.

One of the men cried it was a trap. He stopped in his tracks and he and two other soldiers drew swords. The other two appeared to be unarmed and began running back to the barge.

"Trev, you're going to have to stop them from sailing away," John shouted.

One of the soldiers, a ruddy-complexioned man, charged at John with an upraised sword but Brian stepped in front of him, shouting "action," as if the only way he could get ready to fight was with a director's cue ringing in his ear. The two other soldiers were holding back so John paused to see how Brian acquitted himself.

There was a single clang of metal upon metal and then unexpectedly the soldier stopped fighting. John saw why. Brian's knife hand was red and blood was oozing from the soldier's chest. The man gasped loudly a few times and collapsed in a heap.

Brian looked stunned.

John shouted at the two other swordsmen who looked no older than Dirk and Duck, "You want some of that, boys, just keep on coming. Otherwise throw down your swords and we'll let you walk away."

As the soldiers contemplated their next move, Trevor was making contact with the two unarmed men fleeing toward the boat, swinging at them with his club and shouting at them to halt. In a panic they complied and begged him not to hit them any more.

"Off you go then," Trevor instructed. "Run along the bank in the direction you came from and I'll stop thumping you, all right?"

They ran off, looking frantically over their shoulders to make sure he wasn't following.

Meanwhile, the swordsmen also thought better of fighting and tossed their weapons to the grass and fled, quickly catching up with their comrades.

The two sailors on the barge decided they too were not interested in hanging about. They jumped into the river and tried to free the boat from the bottom but Trevor yelled at them to stop pushing. When he got closer they panicked and furiously swam off downstream, sped by the current.

John knelt by the fallen soldier, checking his condition. On Earth he would have been dead, of course, but he wasn't dead; he continued to gasp and moan. Brian dropped both sword and knife and sat down on the grass in a daze.

"You all right?" John asked.

"Fuck me. I killed a man."

"He's not dead."

"I pierced his heart."

"Different rules here."

Brian came closer and shook his head at the sight of the man. "Apparently so."

"You're fast, you know, very fast," John said. "I'm impressed."

Brian shrugged and tried wiping his bloody hand in the grass. "What are we going to do with him?" he asked.

"We'll leave him as he lies. Nothing else to do."

Brian stood over the man and said, "Sorry, mate. Someone should've told you not to screw around with a man who's got his own show on the BBC."

Emily returned with Duck and Dirk, the two lads clearly disappointed she had chosen to put her shirt back on.

Trevor was calling at them from onboard the barge.

"Our ride's here," John said.

"Do you know how to sail?" Emily asked him.

"It's been a while, but I can probably get by."

Brian was busying himself gathering the dropped weapons and removing the fallen soldier's belt and scabbard. "I'm a fully qualified sailor," he offered.

"This man can do it all," John said, slapping him on the back.

"What do you want us to be doing?" Duck asked.

John told them to return to the village. "As soon as we find the others we'll come back and stay with you boys until the four weeks has passed."

"Tell Delia that Duck'll be waiting to see 'er again."

"I will," John said. "I'm sure that'll make her day."

"Safe journey then," Dirk said. "I'll busy myself making a fresh batch of beer. I know how you like your beer, John Camp."

"Christ, John," Emily said. "You've even got a reputation down here."

14

The dormitory wing at MAAC had been hastily converted into a prison by a small army of government contractors who installed bars on the doors, lavatory facilities, and interrogation rooms. As in real prisons, the jailers learned that televisions were effective pacifiers. The underworked and over trained guards from MI5 relieved their boredom by watching Alfred and the other three Hellers watch their TVs. None of these men had been alive past the eighteenth century and they exhibited a simian fascination with their screens, grabbing at images of food, pleasuring themselves at even modestly dressed women, cowering at cars, airplanes, and any action involving explosions and fire.

After only a few days of interrogations, Ben had decided that Alfred and his lot had little value. They were uneducated and crude and had spent their entire existence in Hell in and around Dartford. They had never even been to London and had no knowledge of affairs of state. They were, however, a notch above rovers, an assessment he noted in his report. Mitchum, a bona fide rover, was still recovering in his hospital bed but he would be coming to a cell in MAAC before long.

Ben paced the loading dock nervously, awaiting the newest arrivals from South Ockendon, Rix and Murphy, and the two intruders from the Iver North waterworks. The percussive thumping of an approaching helicopter drew him to the lawn and he shielded his eyes as the chopper touched down. The MI5 officers who offloaded the cuffed and shackled men were wearing surgical masks, gloves and paper over clothes that Ben found interesting since he hadn't issued a biohazard warning. It was likely a field decision in response to their odor.

He recognized the two men from the security cameras. He had decided to make the tactical gesture of welcoming them as law enforcement colleagues in the hopes of fostering a sense of camaraderie and using it to his benefit.

"Ben Wellington," he said. "Security Services. Sorry we can't shake hands. You'll be processed this way, officers."

Rix looked him over. "You in charge?"

"I'm in charge here. I have superiors."

"Old enough to shave?" Murphy asked.

"Just started. Come along."

"It beggars belief we're here," Rix said, letting the sunlight splash his face.

"I couldn't agree more," Ben said.

Inside, the men were allowed to luxuriate in hot showers and encouraged to use liberal amounts of body scent before being taken to individual cells for medical checks and a meal. While they were being processed the Iver intruders were choppered in and within seconds of greeting them Ben concluded they would be about as illuminating as Alfred Carpenter and his mates. They seemed dimwitted, almost feral, with short, powerful limbs and scared, darting eyes.

"What are your names?" Ben asked, as they were led up the loading dock stairs.

One of the men strained at his plastic restraints but didn't answer.

"Do you speak English?"

The man spit at him and said, "Sod off. What's 'appened to us?"

"Put spit masks on them and take them down the corridor to the intake personnel," Ben said to his men. "I'll deal with them later. Much later."

Once they were cleared by medical and fed, Ben had Rix and Murphy brought into an interview room. In an adjoining room his officers were set up to monitor the proceedings, do research on the fly, and communicate with Ben via an earpiece. The men wore freshly pressed jumpsuits and slippers.

"No need for restraints," Ben said to the agent who led them in.

The prisoners sat and rubbed their unbound wrists.

"First things first," Rix said. "Explain to us how this happened."

Ben smiled. "It's true then."

"What is?"

"That you were police officers. You're trying to control the interview."

"But you're not going to let us, are you?"

"I'll be happy to engage in some give and take, so let me try to answer your questions. Then I'd like you to answer mine."

He told them about the MAAC and provided his own simplified version of how a channel might have opened between their two worlds. Both men listened attentively and when he was done Ben asked if they were satisfied.

"When I was alive," Rix said, "I had no interest in Heaven or Hell or anything other than the here and now. I was mightily shocked when I wound up in Hell but I got used to it. I suppose I'll get used to being back on Earth."

"All right," Ben said. "May I please have your full names?"

Murphy raised his hand. "'Scuse me. My mate got to ask his one burning question. What about me?"

"Fair enough," Ben sighed. "Go ahead."

"Do we get to stay?"

"There's no easy answer to that. Our aim will be to send you back in one month's time but our ability to make that happen is uncertain. Now, your full names, dates of birth, and dates of death, if you please."

Rix went first: Jason Rix, born 8 January 1949, died 25 October 1984.

Then Murphy: Colin Murphy, born 16 June 1941, died 25 October 1984.

Ben's eyes narrowed. "You died on the same day?"

"Isn't that what best mates do?" Murphy said.

"Do?"

"Kick the bucket simultaneous like."

In his earpiece Ben heard, "That's confirmed. A Colin Murphy and a Jason Rix both died on that date in Romford. Accessing police databases."

"Were you both police officers at the time of your deaths?" Ben asked.

Rix replied, "We were. We were both with the Met. We were detectives."

"Ranks?"

"I was a DI," Rix said. "He was a Detective Sergeant."

"He had the rank but I had the looks," Murphy added.

"And what station were you working from? Romford?"

"Brick Lane," Rix said.

"Were you on the job at the time of your deaths?"

Murphy laughed. "We might have been on the clock but we were hardly on the job, if you know what I mean?"

"I'm afraid I don't."

Murphy leaned forward. "We were bent, weren't we?"

"I see," Ben said. "Illegal activities while on duty."

"You got it, sunshine," Murphy said.

Ben made a show of jotting notes while he received a blast of data in his ear.

A minute passed. He looked up at them then began reading from his pad. It was clear he was laboring to remain impassive. "On twenty-two October, 1984 you kidnapped one Jessica Stevenson, aged six, from her family home in Knightsbridge. You held her for ransom. You may have been unaware she had a medical condition. She died in your custody. On the night of 25 October both of you were found in a car in a lay-by in Romford, shot dead, along with your wives, Christine Rix and Molly Murphy. An accomplice of yours, one Lucas Hathaway, was later that same night killed in a shootout with armed police. It was established that his gun was the weapon used in your murders."

Rix had already noticed that Ben was wearing an earpiece. "In our day it would have taken someone a fair old while to come up with all that information. You've got someone in your ear who's done it in seconds. How's that possible?"

"Never mind about that. Is it correct?" Ben asked.

"Yeah. It's correct."

"Earlier, when you materialized inside the house in South Ockendon, you asked if we had your wives, Christine and Molly?"

"Well, do you?" Murphy asked.

"We do not. But we believe they are here."

Rix rose from his chair and Ben had to demand he sit back down.

"Where are they?"

"I asked you to please sit down." When he complied Ben continued, "We don't know where they are. We think five men who came here with them are holding them against their will. It's possible they are making their way to Nottingham."

"What men?" Rix asked, his fists clenching and unclenching.

"I believe you call them rovers."

Murphy and Rix exchanged glances. "How do you know about rovers?" Rix asked.

"This passage between our dimensions—it's happened before. Some of your lot have come here. Some of our people have gone back and forth. We've had debriefings."

"If you've got rovers here, you're in for a world of hurt," Murphy said.

"So I understand."

"Tell me why you think they've gone to Nottingham," Rix asked.

"We captured one of them, a man named Mitchum. Do you know him?"

"We don't know those scum by name," Murphy said.

"I believe you do know one of them by name. Lucas Hathaway."

Giles Farmer's bedsit in Lewisham was too small to swing a cat. From his bed he could touch his chair and from his chair he could touch the fridge. Sponsored ads on his *Bad Collisions* website and odd editing jobs for technical journals paid his rent and broadband service and kept him in Ramen noodles, but not much more. His career, if one could glamorize what he did with that label, had begun shortly after dropping out of Leeds University where he had been a restless student at the School of Physics and Astronomy.

Anthony Trotter's operatives at MI6, who had purposely strayed onto the domestic turf reserved for MI5, had been acquiring a dossier on Farmer. His tutors at Leeds had a somewhat different version about his leaving than his. On the biography section of his blog he wrote about his unconventional mind, his quest for "big answers to big questions." His tutors spoke of a highly irritating young man given to conspiracy theories who regularly disrupted lectures with absurd and off-the-mark comments. Though bright enough to complete his course, they strongly encouraged him to take time off to collect himself.

The year he found himself cut loose was the year the MAAC was scheduled for completion and commissioning. He threw himself into the blogosphere, taking up the cudgel of skeptics who saw a path fraught with waste and peril, and when the inaugural collider start-up was marred by an electrical fault causing a magnet quench and a helium explosion and fire, he had his platform. He spent two years railing against the huge cost of replacing the damaged superconducting magnets and warning of existential dangers to the planet should the project continue.

Farmer wasn't much of a drinker but the night before he had drunk four pints at a pub in Brixton where he had met his mate, Lenny Moore, who enjoyed his gadfly rants. And Lenny, gainfully employed, had been buying. This morning his head was thumping and while the kettle went on the boil he checked his email and Twitter. As soon as he was caffeinated enough he planned to finish the post he had been composing for a week.

It was the big one, the one he had been building toward for over a month when he began to notice telltale signs of weekly MAAC restarts registering on the power grid following the one publicly announced startup. To his mind he was nearing the critical mass of data accumulation that would force the government to come clean. He went searching for his bottle of aspirin to quiet his headache.

His laptop was on the small table by his chair and as he reached for it, he made his hand stop in midair. Farmer was particular in his habits. Although the bedsit was tiny and not scrupulously clean, it was meticulously tidy and organized. By habit, after using it, he always left the computer pinned to the far left corner of his tray-top table.

But now the laptop was a quarter-inch from the left side.

He stared at the machine for a few seconds then picked it up, shook off his sense of unease, and began to work. He scanned his work-in-progress, flitting from paragraph to paragraph. It went further than his previous posts, much further. After reminding his readers of the theoretical hazards of high-energy supercolliders that included the formation of microscopic black holes and strangelet production, he had laid out the sequence of recent unusual activities at the MAAC. The security breach for which a suspect allegedly had never been apprehended. The successive weekly power dips affecting the London grid, all compatible with MAAC firings that had never been acknowledged. The "bioterror" incident at South Ockendon that was subject to a severe information blackout. The lack of availability of Dr. Emily Loughty, a scientist who had been willing in the past to speak with him. The unwillingness of Dr. Loughty's father to be forthcoming. And now, the smoking gun, as he saw it. Amidst another London power grid dip, Farmer had turned on the police scanner app on his phone and heard a curious exchange between dispatchers and Buckinghamshire police units, directing them to respond to intruders at the Iver North waterworks, only to be waved off and informed that "other agencies" were responding.

Farmer began to type where he had left off the day before.

What, you may ask do an estate in South Ockendon, the Iver North Water Treatment Works, and the MAAC laboratory in Dartford have in common? I'll tell you: all three are located directly above supermagnet components of the MAAC and all three have now been the scene of "intruders." Would you know what I think, dear readers? I think that...

His screen froze.

He couldn't move the cursor with his track pad and none of the usual maneuvers could unfreeze it.

"Bugger, bugger, bugger," he muttered before re-booting.

The computer failed to properly reboot, landing him on a blank blue screen, not once or twice, but three times.

Alarmed he stood and began searching around the room for anything to corroborate his earlier observation about the out-of-position laptop.

"Are you fuckers watching me?" he said out loud. "Well are you?"

He whipped out his mobile phone and got a friend, Laurence, on the speaker.

"Laurence, Giles here. Listen I think I'm being hacked or watched or both. By whom? By them, of course. Listen, I need you to just stay on the line while I use my mobile as a signal detector. Yeah, just be quiet until I come back on the line."

He began systematically moving the phone around his tiny flat, listening for telltale clicks produced by the electromagnetic interference of a bugging device. Other than his friend's breathing, the phone was quiet until he passed it in front of the ventilation hood over the cooker.

Click, click.

He slowed down and repeated the maneuver and reproduced the clicking with each pass.

"Laurence, I've got to ring you back. Actually, I won't be ringing you back. They'll have your number now. If I go missing, go to *The Guardian* with the stuff we talked about. They'll be the most sympathetic."

Six miles away, an operative at MI6 working on an upper floor of the Albert Embankment, watched and listened on a monitor while Farmer unscrewed the vent cover and cursed the camera when he found it. When the bug went dead, the officer picked up a phone and rang upstairs.

"Sir, this is Evans in Special Surveillance. We've got a situation with Giles Farmer."

"What kind of situation?" Trotter asked.

"Farmer has found and neutralized our device in his flat."

"That's not very good, is it?"

"No sir. Fortunately, we wiped his blog before he could post an incriminating entry. I've just sent you a screen grab."

Trotter read it and grunted. "Well, keep following his telephone traffic and keep eyes on him."

"We don't have eyes on him, sir."

"Why the hell not?"

"The lawyers were concerned about using physical assets on a domestic target."

"Bugger the lawyers!" Trotter shouted. "This is a matter of high national threat and we're listening to the lawyers? You get eyes on him immediately and leave the bloody lawyers to me."

Farmer pocketed the tiny camera, took his wallet and keys and left his mobile phone behind. Ten minutes later he was catching his breath, his head buried in a newspaper, on a train from Lewisham to Charing Cross station. He looked up furtively every so often, wondering if any of his fellow passengers were onto him and if his life would ever return to normal.

Hathaway steered the Hyundai through the dark and largely deserted streets of Nottingham, trying to square his memory of the roads and architecture with what he was seeing.

"The streets are all mucked up," he mumbled.

"Easier for you, I reckon, than for me," Talley said, waking from another brief nap. "This whole land is mucked up. Makes my head spin."

"Would do," Hathaway said. "I'm foxed by thirty years of change. You've got three hundred years to square with."

"All these infernal machines and high buildings," Talley said, "I can't get on with it." He was about to perform a characteristic spit to mark his displeasure but remembered the car window.

"You saying you'd rather go back?"

Talley rubbed at his eyes. "No, I think I'll give this a go. Good grub, good molls. We almost arrived?"

"If I can find it."

"Who's the fellow?"

"My brother, Harold. If he's still about he'd be in his sixties."

"Likely to be any molls about?"

Hathaway didn't answer.

He eventually found his way to Sneinton, the neighborhood where he had grown up and where his parents were living at the time of his death. If he knew Harold, the shiftless, school-leaver he was, odds were he'd be right where the acorn fell, in the same house, on the same road, in the same neighborhood.

To Hathaway's pleasure, Holborn Avenue was in a time warp. The same long rows of two-story brick houses on either side of the dead-end road. The same fanciful Moorish arches leading to recessed front doors. The same rows of parked cars jammed half-on, half-off the sidewalks. The only difference he could see was that the brickwork on some of the houses had been painted white or tan and most of them had curious gray dishes with wires bolted onto the second stories.

"That's the one," Hathaway said to the others, slowing and pointing at the shabbiest house on the block. The bricks needed pointing and the paint trim was peeling.

"Are we getting out of this crate now?" Youngblood asked.

"Not yet," Hathaway said. "I'll scout it out first. Let's see if I remember how to parallel park."

There was a tight space past the house and he managed to cram the Hyundai into it. He told the men to stay put and keep out of sight. Chambers promptly relieved himself in the back seat.

Most of the houses were dark and this one was too. Hathaway tensed and rapped lightly on the door. He'd left his knife in the car but he didn't need it. He'd learned how to destroy people with his fists, feet, and teeth.

After a short while he knocked again, this time louder. There was a slight glow above his head and when he stepped back out of the archway, he saw a light had been switched on. Then the front window glowed and a muffled voice came through the door.

"Who's there?"

He made himself talk. "Is that Harold? Harold Hathaway?"

"Yeah. Who's this?"

His heart leapt. "If I told you, you wouldn't believe me."

"Piss off. Tell me who it is or I'm calling the police."

He took a very deep breath and said, "It's Lucas."

There was no response, none at all.

"I said it's Lucas. Your brother."

"Okay, you've got three seconds to leave or you're going to get nicked."

"Our cat was called Agatha. Our goldfish were Ronnie and Reggie. Mum's favorite food was chips and Daddies Sauce. Dad was drunk on barley wine nearly all the time."

After a long pause the door opened a crack, then a bit more. A fat, bald man appeared in his boxers, his gut ballooning a wife-beater undershirt. It wasn't until the door was open wide and the light from the hall fell upon Lucas that his brother's face fully registered what he was seeing. A second of an abjectly shocked expression was followed by collapse as the blood drained into his stout legs. He fell backwards into the hall.

From upstairs a woman called his name and asked if everything was all right.

Lest she ring the police, Hathaway called up. "It's all right. He's just fainted. It's a mate of his."

A woman, also in her sixties appeared at the top of the stairs. She looked like her round body had been stamped from the same mold as Harold's.

She came waddling down the stairs and got to her husband's side at the same time as he began to come around.

"Get him some water," Hathaway said.

"I don't know you," she said, cradling Harold's head. "Who are you?"

"A mate, like I said."

"He don't have no mates your age. What did you do to him? I'm going to ring the police."

Harold tried to get to his feet but only managed to sit. He stared at his brother. "It *is* you."

"Yeah."

"Who? Who is it, Harold? Should I ring emergency?"

"No! Just help me up."

Hathaway had phenomenal strength. He lifted his brother as if he were a child and carried him to the sitting room. Some of the furniture was familiar.

Harold came to completely. "How is it possible?" he asked, over and over.

"How is what possible?" his wife asked.

"It's Lucas, my brother."

"What do you mean, it's your brother. Your brother's been dead for thirty years."

"You look the same," Harold said. "Exactly the same as I remember you."

"You look different, mate," Hathaway said.

"Are you dead?" he asked in a rasping whisper.

"I don't know what I am, to be truthful. It's a ridiculously long story."

"You smell like you're dead."

"You smell like booze."

Harold told his wife to get him a large gin.

"Bring us a glass too," Hathaway said to the woman. "Listen, I've got some mates in the car. Mind if I bring them in?"

"Are they like you?" Harold asked.

"Similar, I'd say."

Molly and Christine made their way through dense woods until they came to farmland. They climbed a wire fence and in the near distance heard the lowing of cows in the dark.

"Better not be a bull about," Molly said.

Christine took her hand. "Better a bull than rovers."

They walked for at least a mile before they saw the roof of a farmhouse silhouetted against the starry sky.

"No lights," Christine said. "They're either asleep or away."

"You sure it's a good idea?" Molly asked.

"We're hungry, we're dirty, we're cut up. Yeah, let's try it on."

All the windows were pitch black and there were no cars in the driveway. They spent a few minutes in whispered debate before deciding to break a window with a rock. The sound of the glass shattering was louder than they hoped so they hid behind an outbuilding. When no lights came on, they returned to the house, unlatched the lounge window from the inside and climbed in.

Armed with brass lamps pulled from the mains as weapons, they made a slow and cautious tour of the dark house, floor by floor, searching for occupants. It was only when they finished creeping through the small bedrooms on the third floor that they were able to relax and begin to luxuriate in the idea of having the place for each other.

Unsure how near they were to the closest neighbors, they were reluctant to switch on lights. Instead, they found some candles and matches in the lounge and headed straight for the fridge. Inside, to their delight and amazement was a roast chicken, bowls of mashed potatoes, and vegetables, and in the freezer, several tubs of ice cream.

"This isn't Earth," Molly said. "It's Heaven."

When they couldn't eat another morsel they turned to the next object of their desire: the bathtubs. Each one filled their own hot tub, the water promptly turning brown and almost black from their grime. Christine decided to drain the tub and have a second fill with clean water. She spent a full hour in bliss, her skin wrinkling, her mind at peace for the first time in thirty years. But drying herself with a marvelous fluffy towel she saw herself in the mirror and began to cry. Gone were her saucy good looks and big hair. The woman in the mirror was skin and bones with gaps in her teeth and sagging breasts. It was a wonder that Jason still cherished her, though he hadn't exactly escaped the ravages of their harsh existence. Pulling herself together she found a bottle of cologne and applied it heavily to try and mask her odor. She couldn't bear to put her ragged, filthy clothes back on so she had a rummage through the bedroom dressers and wardrobes but the lady of the house was several sizes larger. Molly had been pursuing a similar course of ablutions but was having better luck in a daughter's room where she laid out several outfits on the bed. The two women spent a half an hour like teenagers, trying on clothes and laughing, but the reality of their situation intruded and they forced themselves to gather clothes, toiletries, and food in a sports backpack they found in one of the closets and reluctantly they left this bountiful, fantasy of a house.

Molly thought to check the outbuildings for vehicles and inside a barn they found a fairly new Cooper Mini in racing green. The keys weren't in the car so they re-entered the house and soon discovered a key ring on a peg in the kitchen.

The car interior was difficult to decipher and by the glow of the instrument panel they read the driver's manual and figured out how to start it.

"Do you need a map?" Molly asked as Christine drove off.

"Unless the roads have changed I know the way."

"Are you sure we should go there?"

"I don't know too many other places we can go."

Left behind in the kitchen was a note Christine wrote for the homeowners done in halting penmanship. It was the first time she had put pen to paper in three decades.

We're sorry for using your house and stealing some items. It was the best night we've had for a very long time. Please forgive us.

An emergency telecon was about to begin. Ben logged on at MAAC and before long the screen filled with participants joining from London and America. Ben opened with a preamble. He reminded everyone that the goalposts had shifted. One-for-one exchanges were still happening but now they were geographically dispersed around the huge MAAC oval. The appearance of the Iver Hellers was particularly disturbing.

Leroy Bitterman was at the US Embassy at Grovenor Square where he had been briefing the president on secure comms. He looked up from the map of Greater London spread before him and said, "It seems to me that the implications are profound. Each MAAC restart must be altering the dimensional fields in ways we don't understand. Previously the connection between them and us was only a pinhole. Now I would say it's a portal. We have no way of knowing what the restart in four weeks is going to do. I'm concerned that further collider activity will open the door wider. We don't want to see a floodgate. Fortunately we made the decision to have only one more restart."

Trotter, online from his perch at MI6, cleared his throat to announce he was about to speak. "For the record, I was against further collider activity. We should have slammed the door closed, locked it, and thrown away the key."

"And condemned twelve innocent bystanders to an awful fate," Bitterman said.

"I'm more concerned about the fate of sixty million Britons."

"That's hyperbole," Bitterman said.

"Is it? Can you give us an ironclad guarantee?"

"Of course not. We're all feeling around in the dark on this one."

Smithwick chimed in from her office in Whitehall. "I for one would not like to characterize our endeavors to the prime minister as feeling around in the dark.'"

"Is honesty discouraged at 10 Downing Street?" Bitterman countered.

Smithwick puckered her mouth and allowed Trotter to press on.

"In light of the Iver intruders," Trotter said, "which Dr. Bitterman just described as a profound development, and lacking scientific guarantees, I think we should make a recommendation to our respective governments to terminate all future activities at MAAC."

"We just sent a rescue party of four brave people over," Bitterman said, his voice rising. "The US government will not allow them to be abandoned and anyway, we're a month away from the next restart. We haven't even convened the first meeting of the scientific advisors who are being empaneled to help us mitigate the situation in which we find ourselves. My understanding is that this videocon was called to deal with practical and pressing matters. Mr. Wellington, I believe you had the first agenda item."

Ben minimized Trotter's feed but even in a thumbnail view, his smirking face was a distraction. He briefed the group about the status of all the prisoners now held at MAAC, the lack of new information about the

Hellers from South Ockendon, and then he expanded on the backgrounds and life histories of Jason Rix and Colin Murphy.

"Despite the new wrinkle of geographical separation," he said, "to date, the principle of parity seems to have been maintained," he said. "There have been sixteen people who have traversed from our side and sixteen Hellers we know of who have come to Earth. Therefore, it is incumbent on us, in order to have the best chance of recovering all sixteen of our people in one month's time, that we locate the missing Hellers. From our interviews with Rix and Murphy, it appears that two of these people are their wives, Christine Rix and Molly Murphy."

He put the photos of all four of them on the screen. They had been obtained from 1984 news stories about their murders.

"These women are likely traveling with a group of rovers which includes this man, Lucas Hathaway."

Another newspaper photo filled the screen.

"Hathaway was their murderer. To say there's bad blood amongst them is an understatement. The reason I bring this up to the group is that given the law enforcement backgrounds of Murphy and Rix, and given their zeal for finding their wives, I would like to take them up on their offer to help us in our investigations."

"And how would they do that?" Trotter asked, his face filling the screen again.

"They want to go into the field. We would accompany them at all times with armed guards and would give them zero freedom of independent movement."

"I vote no," Trotter said, "and I advise others to do the same. It's too risky. If they escape, you'll have two more runners to deal with. If they have any pertinent information on the potential whereabouts of the Hellers, then extract the information from their jail cells."

"They have rejected the idea of remotely assisting our inquiries," Ben said. "They were shoe-leather detectives and maintain they can only be effective if they are allowed to follow the trail in person and I am persuaded to agree with them."

"Are you quite sure you can keep them on leashes?" Smithwick asked.

"I am," Ben replied.

They voted; Trotter was the only one casting a no ballot. For the rest of the meeting he maintained a clench-jawed silence and failed to bring up the matter of Giles Farmer.

15

Brian skillfully maneuvered the flat-bottomed sailing barge upstream. When a fishing boat passed in the opposite direction, Emily hid amongst the cargo and passing fishermen seemed unaware that the crew of the barge was exotic.

From a distance, John recognized Solomon Wisdom's house perched on a high hill. Approaching Wisdom's dock, the men readied their weapons but there was no one about. Wisdom's boat was tied up. Brian maneuvered the craft to the opposite side of the dock and threw lines out to John and Trevor. They had plenty of swords to go around but Emily declined one.

"Guess you've got your own weapons," John joked, looking at her chest.

"Wait till you see me use my head," she said.

"What's the plan, guv?" Trevor asked.

"Last time I was here I didn't see armed guards," John said, glancing up at the big house. "But you never know. I think we should circle around and see if there are horses and wagons around the back, tents, signs of bivouacked troops."

"If there are?" Brian asked.

"We'll cross that bridge if we have to."

Despite the absence of sunshine it was warm and by the time they had looped around the steep hill to the rear of Wisdom's property they had worked up a sweat. They encountered no one along the way and by the look of things they weren't going to have a big fight on their hands.

"Now what?" Trevor asked.

"We knock on his door," John said.

They came around to the front of the house and John banged on the door with the butt of his sword. In time the large door opened and the manservant, Caffrey peered out. Seeing John he tried to shut it but John shouldered in, toppling the man.

Caffrey went for a belt knife but John pushed the tip of his sword to his breastbone and advised him to stand down. Trevor quickly relieved him of the blade and Brian, ever ready, tied his hands and feet with a length of hemp from the boat.

Wisdom called out from the study asking Caffrey who was at the door and when John and Emily barged in he leapt up from his desk and began searching for something to protect himself. When Trevor and Brian entered too, he seemed to accept his defeat.

"Sit down," John demanded.

Wisdom's knees buckled under him and his rump found the chair.

"So good to see the two of you again," Wisdom said unconvincingly.

"Well it's not so great seeing you again, you slimy bastard," John said.

"A man must do what he must do to survive in this harsh world," Wisdom said. "Everyone here has lost his moral compass, more or less. I am far from the worst."

"That may be," Emily said, "but you're well up on the league rankings. You sold me into slavery to the Duke of Guise, remember?"

"Not to mention lying to me about Emily and selling my ass to Henry," John said.

Wisdom attempted a toothy grin. "What can I say? Fortunately, both of you seem to be quite capable and resilient when adversity rears its head. Who are your colleagues and how is it that so many live persons are presently coming to our unfair land?"

"Never mind them," John said. "We're here to talk about two women and two children."

"Whomever do you mean?"

John asked Brian and Trevor to hold Wisdom's arms down and said,

"Okay, Solomon, we can do this the hard way or the easy way. It's your choice. I'm not messing around. Every minute, every day is precious. In twenty-seven days we've got to be back in Dartford with them to catch a ride home. We know they were here and my guess is you've already moved the merchandise. That's what they are to you. You're going to tell us where they went, one way or another. In ten seconds I'm going to cut off your left hand. Ten seconds later, your right hand. After that, well, use your imagination. Then I'm going to personally toss you into that rotting room you showed me down the hill. So here we go: ten, nine, eight …"

Wisdom strained against Brian and Trevor's iron grips then went limp. "Stop. I concede. They have gone to different places."

"You motherfucker!" Emily screamed, lunging at him.

Even John was surprised; he'd never heard her swear before but he completely agreed with her characterization of the skeletal man in black. He held her back and whispered something into her ear that had a calming effect.

"Where are they?" John asked coolly.

"The children and the woman called Delia went to Queen Matilda. The young woman, Arabel, went to King Pedro of Iberia."

Now it was Trevor's turn. "Do you mean to tell me you split up a mother from her children?"

When all Wisdom could do was nod weakly, Trevor released his grip and punched him full in the mouth, spraying the desk with blood and a yellow tooth.

He quickly apologized for losing it, but Emily thanked him instead.

John pulled a handkerchief from the pocket of Wisdom's frock coat and let him hold it to his mouth.

"If you want to stay out of the rotting room, you're going to tell us everything we need to know about how to find them. If I'm not convinced you've given us every single detail this won't end well for you. You may be an accomplished lying bastard but I've got a highly refined bullshit detector. Start talking."

Wisdom stared mournfully at his errant tooth and began to sing like a bird. When he was done he looked up at John the way a gladiator might look to an emperor to know his fate.

"All right, Solomon. I'm going to believe you. We're going to let you keep your fingers and your toes but there're consequences for what you did. Guys, take him and his goon outside and lash them together. We'll meet you in a few minutes."

Emily and he swept through the house. They found Wisdom's cook in the kitchen and told her to clear out if she knew what was good for her. She waddled out like a fat duck and when she saw her master being manhandled on the grass she kept going. John found a strongbox in the study and smashed it against the side of the fireplace a few times until it cracked open revealing a pile of gold and silver coins that he poured into his backpack. Then, lighting a candle from fireplace embers he began setting furniture and drapes alight.

Outside, smoke began billowing from open windows and Wisdom, bound, back-to-back with Caffrey, began hollering at the sight of his precious house put to torch.

"You'll need a new boat too," John said.

"You're sparing me?" Wisdom moaned, lying on his side, roped to Caffrey.

"Seems so."

"Why?"

"Because we're not the same as you," John said. "We're not evil scum."

All the way down the hill they heard Wisdom wailing over his losses. On the dock John said exactly what the others were expecting.

"I don't like it but we knew this might happen," he said. "We've got to split up. Emily and I will go to Hampton Palace for the kids and Delia. Brian and Trev, you'll need to find your way to Iberia for Arabel. It won't be easy."

"We're up for it," Trevor said. "We'll get her, Emily, don't you worry. Send you a text when we get there."

She hugged him and went moist in the eyes.

Then Trevor added, "So, Brian, you reckon you know how to get to

Spain?"

"Ordinarily I'd flag down a taxi to Heathrow."

"You, a taxi?" John said. "Chauffeured car, more likely."

Brian snorted. "Right you are. It's in my contract. In our present circumstance we'll need to make it to the estuary, tack south through the channel and sail to the Bay of Biscay. When we hit land we'll improvise. Mind if we take the more seaworthy vessel?"

"Your choice."

"The barge we came on then. You all right with the other one?"

"I'll figure it out," John said. "I don't need to tell you that we've got three weeks and six days. There weren't any clocks or watches inside so we'll have to keep track of each dawn then tack on four hours to get to 10 a.m. We'll meet back in Dartford when we can but there's no missing the deadline. You guys are great fighters—you've got your sticks. Let me give you some carrots to help you along."

He opened his backpack and gave them half the coins. Then he thought for a while and chose one of the books for them.

Brian inspected it and put it in his pack. "Hope they can read English."

They exchanged hugs and well wishes and split up. The wind was favorable for John and Emily's upstream journey; the currents favored Brian and Trevor's barge.

As the boats diverged they exchanged sad waves. "Will we see them again?" Emily asked.

John hoisted the mainsail and said, "The odds are long. But they're both outstanding men."

Their arrival at Hampton Court Palace did not go unnoticed. The palace docks were bustling with activity as men off-loaded provisions and military equipment from the French campaign. John was not as proficient a sailor as Brian and the best he could do was ram the dock with the prow of Wisdom's barge and toss a line to one of the astonished soldiers.

Stepping off John announced they were there to see the king or

Cromwell.

The nearest soldier, a limping one-eyed wretch, sniffed at them in alarm and declared them to be unusual beings.

"That's why they'll want to see us," John said.

"The king ain't here but he's coming."

"He survived Francia?" John asked.

"How do you know 'bout that?"

"I was there."

An officer pushed his way through the dockside throng who'd gathered to get a better look at Emily. He displayed a recent battle injury, his arm wrapped in a cloth, brown with dried blood.

"Stand aside, stand aside. You there, state your name."

"John Camp and Emily Loughty."

The young man had long blonde hair elegant, despite the dirty tangles. "Where are you from?" he demanded.

"Same place you're from, friend. But we're not dead," John said.

"How is that possible?"

"Please don't make us tell the story again," Emily said.

"The king knows all about us," John said. "Cromwell too."

"Then hand over your weapons and your pack."

"Weapons, yes, pack, no. You can look inside but that's as far as I'll go. Believe me, the king won't be happy if you take it from me."

The officer inspected John's pack. The silver and gold coins interested him more than the loose sheets of printed paper. He found no books. The officer surreptitiously took a silver piece for his troubles then returned the backpack and told them to follow. The dockworkers began to trundle along too but the officer barked at them to get back to their labors.

Inside the palace the officer found a court official and whispered in his ear. This man ushered them to the same room where John had cooled his heels the first time he visited the palace. John and Emily rested against a wall while the officer shifted his weight from side to side, fixing them with a contemptuous stare that irritated John no end.

"Did you pick up that wound in Francia?" John asked.

"I did. We were prepared for battle with the French to the west of Paris. The morning was heavy with fog. When the fighting began deadly bombs began flying through the air. We'd never seen anything like them. I was hit by shrapnel. Then the cavalry charged and all was lost."

"I'm sorry you were injured," John said.

"Why should you be?"

"Because I feel responsible. They were my grenades. I might have thrown the one that got you. In fact, I probably did."

The officer began to sputter in anger but the court retainer returned and told John and Emily to accompany him.

John looked back over his shoulder. "You ought to change that dressing. You don't want that wound to get infected."

They were taken to a small, well-appointed room where a smooth-shaven man with a bloodless complexion was waiting behind a large desk. Pinned against each corner were four soldiers armed with swords and pistols. The man behind the desk was narrow in the shoulders. His defining feature was a deep gully of a scar that ran all the way from his right ear down the cheek to the corner of his mouth. His clothes were a mixture of semi-modern and older garb.

He spoke with a strong Irish accent. "I am William Joyce, a member of the king's privy council. I was told two things: one, that you are not dead, and two, that you have previously been to this court."

John didn't much like his officious tone. "I don't recall seeing you here before," he said staring hard at his scar. "I never forget a face."

Perhaps as a reflex, Joyce fingered the scar before pulling his hand away, saying, "I'm quite sure I wouldn't forget yours either. Especially this lovely creature. You were here a month ago, I understand."

John stiffened at Joyce's interest in Emily. "I was, she wasn't," he said.

"I was in the hinterlands handling a matter of urgency for the crown," Joyce said. "When I returned, I learned the king was making preparations for a channel crossing, having routed the Iberians. I have remained here, holding down the fort, as you Americans say."

"How'd you know I was American?"

"Your accent, of course, and your brashness. I was born in Brooklyn in New York City, actually, and lived there as a child before my family moved back to Ireland."

"Oh yeah?" John said. "When was that?"

"In the early 1900s. And where are you from, my dear?" he asked Emily.

"I'm Scottish."

"I see." He addressed John. "Would you mind telling me how it is you were able to come to this land without first suffering a demise?"

"Don't look at me, pal. She's the scientist."

"How remarkable," Joyce said. "Well then, Miss …"

"Doctor. Loughty."

"Explain to me, doctor, if you would be so kind, how you got here."

He listened attentively, running a long digit over his scar and then pulling it away whenever he seemed to realize what he was doing. When Emily was done with her well-worn explanation he mumbled how extraordinary all this was then took a large breath and let the air out through pursed lips, making a sound like a horse.

He chided himself. "Mustn't do that," he said. "Reinforces stereotypes."

"What stereotypes are those?" John asked.

"You probably have no idea who I am. You're too young and I'm quite sure I'm a forgotten figure, but during the war, World War II, that is, the British called me Lord Haw-Haw, which always brought to mind a donkey. You know Hee-Haw."

"Why did they call you that?" Emily asked.

"It was supposed to be a term of derision, I suppose. I worked in propaganda and had a radio program that was broadcast into England from Hamburg. I was none too popular on this side of the channel."

"You worked for the Nazis," Emily said icily.

"I did indeed. And for speaking the truth about the Jews and the communists, I was executed at Wandsworth Prison in 1946."

"You were executed for being a traitor?" John asked.

"For that alone."

"Usually takes more than that to buy a ticket to Hell."

"Well, there was the small matter of taking revenge against the Jew bastard who took a razor to my face in 1924 following a political meeting. It wasn't even a meeting of fascists. It was a Conservative meeting! I joined Mosley's British Union of Fascists later on. Anyway, my friends and I found a couple of communist kikes and I took my revenge. Left more than a scar on their faces, I'll tell you that much."

"You're a real charmer, aren't you?" Emily said.

Suddenly turning darker he said, "What I am is no concern to you."

"Surprised you're not still with the Germans," she said. "Until recently Himmler was a big wheel over there."

"What do you mean until recently?"

"I snapped his neck a couple of weeks ago," John said.

"Did you now? That will weaken Barbarossa, won't it? In any event, I entered Hell in London. Solomon Wisdom spotted my talents and peddled me to the crown."

Joyce asked why John was smiling.

"Solomon's out of business for a while."

"Did you snap his neck too?"

"I restrained myself. But he's got some rebuilding to do."

"You're quite the rabble rouser, aren't you? If you try to do me harm, my guards will cut you down. To return to my story, though not a warrior, King Henry has appreciated my organizational skills and with Cromwell and other privy council members off to war, I am in command here. And now I have you and the others to deal with."

"What others?" Emily asked urgently.

"We've had a flood of you lot the past few days."

"Are the children here?" she demanded.

"Here's what I've observed with this bewildering influx of live souls," Joyce said, ignoring her question and leaning back in his chair. "You don't know your place. If you'd had the usual rite of passage, you would have just been through the rather unpleasant experience of dying. When that happens it doesn't take long to appreciate that this is your comeuppance for whatever moral turpitude you were guilty of. You quickly learn that there is no appeals process, no way of jawboning your way out of your eternal predicament. In short, you are beaten. You lot don't seem to know you're beaten and you don't know your place. Let me put it simply. I'm in charge. You're not. You have to answer my questions, I don't have to answer yours."

Emily was not going to be bullied. She gave him a withering look and said, "I'll ask you again: are the children here?"

Joyce stood in a fury and ordered the guards to seize them and take them to the jail.

"This isn't going to end well for you," John warned but the angry man was not going to back down.

At first John liked his chances—four to one with the weakling Joyce a non-factor, and he cracked his knuckles for action, but in seconds, another contingent of armed men swarmed the room and for the sake of Emily and their mission he allowed Joyce to take them prisoner.

High in the queen's wing of the palace, stiff afternoon breezes blew through the open windows of her chamber, billowing the curtains. A strong gust caught a bunch of flowers and toppled the vase off a table, sending it crashing onto the floor. Ordinarily, Queen Matilda would have had a fit over something like this but today nothing seemed to upset her. Her servants rushed to clean up the mess, casting sidelong glances, waiting for her to drop the hammer, but she remained unperturbed. Her full attention was elsewhere.

The children.

As she watched Belle and Sam play with a set of cups and saucers on the carpet, her face, which was usually hard and immobile, became soft as bread dough. While she watched the children, Delia watched her, protective as a hen but woefully lacking in any real ability to safeguard them.

"How old did you say they were?" Matilda asked.

"The boy is three, the girl is two," Delia said curtly.

"One forgets …" the queen said, her voice drifting off.

Delia pretended she didn't know what she meant. "Forgets what?"

"How they look. How they act. It has been, well, a very, very long time."

"They need to be with their mother."

"Do they?"

"Yes they do."

"And where did you say she was?"

"I don't know. Perhaps you could ask Solomon Wisdom."

"If my memory serves, I did not need a mother for any reason other than birth. I was raised by nannies and retainers."

"How long ago was that?"

"My head was not made for the mathematical sciences and I have no interest in the meaningless passage of time. I cannot tell you this. Suffice it to say, it was the twelfth century."

"Well, these children are from the twenty-first century. And in our time, children are cared for by their mothers."

The queen scowled at Delia and seeing Matilda's growing irritation, one of her ladies, Phoebe, a raven-haired beauty who hailed from the eighteenth century said, "You would do well, Miss Delia, to be more respectful to her majesty."

Delia, never one to be told how to behave, not in her own world or this one, was about to dig herself a deeper hole when Belle looked up and said, "Where's mummy? I want her."

The queen was quick to respond. "Never mind her. You may call me mummy if you wish, child."

"You're not our mummy," Sam said.

"Perhaps not, but I am your queen, young man, and you would do well to remember that."

"For God's sake," Delia cried. "It's daft to speak to a child that way."

Matilda raised her hand imperiously. "Enough! Lock her away," she ordered her guards. "I wish to see them play with my crockery in peace."

This was an area of the palace John hadn't seen during his last visit to Hampton Court. Surrounded by guards they passed through long, drab corridors until they stood before a small oak door, black with antiquity. One soldier lit a torch with a lamp and another unlocked the door with a large iron key. By torchlight the party descended a steep run of stone stairs into a cool, damp cellar.

"I don't like the look of this," Emily said.

"As soon as someone with a higher pay grade than that Nazi fuck finds out we're here, he's going to be walking around with his head under his arm," John said.

"I hope you're right. Every day down here will be a day utterly wasted."

They walked along a dark, narrow passageway until it opened into a larger torchlight space, a central guardroom surrounded by jail cells. Dirty, gaunt faces appeared at the barred windows and men called out at them pitifully in English, French, Spanish, Dutch. The soldier with the torch pointed at one of the cells and asked a gawking guard whether there was room for two more.

"I've got five in there already. It'll be a bit tight but when they get good and skinny after a month there'll be plenty of room."

The door was unlocked. It creaked open on ungreased hinges. John was expecting something like the rank odor of a rotting room but the smell wasn't bad at all. By the light of a feeble oil lamp he saw five shocked people, three men and two women, sitting on piles of straw. Though scared, they looked healthy and well nourished and John astonished them with his question.

"You guys wouldn't be from South Ockendon, would you?"

"How did you know that?" Martin asked.

"Educated guess," was his reply. "I'm John Camp, this is Emily Loughty."

"I'm so glad we found you," Emily said.

"Found us?" Alice asked. "You were looking for us?"

"We were," John said, getting down on his haunches. "There were eight of you, right?"

Charlie became unhinged. "I lost my dad, my granddad and my brother," he blubbered. "I'm the only one left. I'm all alone. I should have done more. It should have been me instead."

"I'm so sorry," Emily said. "How awful."

But Tony was in no mood for commiseration. "Look here. Who the hell are you? Where have you come from? How do you know about us? How did we get here? We want answers, goddamn it!"

"I just want to go home, can we go home now?" Tracy said numbly in an interruption that irritated Tony.

"Please be quiet," he snapped. "Let the man talk."

"Don't bully her," Alice said. "The poor woman's lost her children."

Emily dropped down beside Tracy. "Where were they?"

"At school. I was home and they were at school."

"Thank God they weren't caught up in this," Emily said, soothingly.

"Caught up in what?" Tony shouted. "Will you answer my fucking questions?"

"Okay, just relax, pal," John said.

Martin reached his hand out to steady Tony but the florid man pushed it away. "Tony, you're just going to make yourself ill," Martin implored.

"Before we answer your questions, please, can I ask you one?" Emily said. "Did you see any children here?"

"No," Alice said. "We were told there aren't any."

"My little niece and nephew are here. Did anyone speak of them?"

Alice shook her head.

"All right," John said. "Let's tell you what we know. This all started about six weeks ago."

John and Emily tag-teamed the narrative, beginning with the first MAAC startup that launched Emily into Hell and ending with the audience with William Joyce that landed them in the jail cell. Whenever Tony seemed inclined to ask a question, Martin prevented him from doing so with a gentle remark or a gesture. When John and Emily were finished Tony became angry and rose to make a statement directed at Emily.

"The arrogance," he said. "The sheer arrogance of you scientists.

Mucking about with nature. What do you expect? And we're the ones to suffer. I have nothing but contempt."

"That's not fair, Tony," Martin said. "They've come to rescue us and bring us home."

"Don't be blind," Martin said. "They came to rescue her family. They just happened to stumble upon us."

"Our mission is to bring everyone home," John said. "Finding you by accident is still finding you. I'll take a lucky break whenever I can get one."

"But you're prisoners just like us," Charlie said. "How are you going to get us out?"

John had a ready reply. "This fellow who threw us all in jail, this asshole William Joyce—my guess is that as soon as someone higher up finds out what he did, we'll be upstairs and he'll be in this cell."

"All right, fair enough," Martin said. "Now what?"

"I think we'll just have to wait," Emily said. "Now we've told you who we are. To see this through, we're going to need to cooperate and draw on all our skills. I'm keen to learn more about each one of you."

Martin volunteered to go first. "I'm a medical doctor," he said. "A consultant. Ordinarily I would have been at the hospital at ten in the morning but I had a canceled meeting and Tony and I had a bit of a spontaneous lie-in. It was a good morning. We were having coffee and reading the paper when, well ..."

"Yeah, it was a good morning until it became a shit morning," Tony said bitterly. "The thing is, Martin led me into indolence."

"Not for the first time," Martin said.

"Yes, not the first time for sure," Tony said. "I actually had a client meeting that morning. I called in sick at his urging. I'm an architect. My firm does a mixture of commercial and residential commissions. The client I postponed wants a truly garish trophy home in Hampshire to replace a country house he bought with lovely bones. I had been trying without success to get him to tastefully renovate but his intention is to level it and put up something very large and very nouveau. It actually wasn't a huge stretch to feign illness because the prospect of the meeting was making me nauseous."

"How long have the two of you been together?" Emily asked.

"Ten years," Martin said. "If we manage to get out of this alive we're going to get married."

"If I don't change my mind," Tony said.

"Everyone's invited," Martin said.

"I'm in," John said. "Shit, maybe we'll make it a double wedding."

"Are you asking?" Emily said.

John reached for her hand. "Maybe."

"Thank you, Martin and Tony, for setting a fine example," she said with a broad smile. "If the maybe turns into a yes, a double wedding it shall be."

"I'd like to come if we can get a babysitter," Tracy said softly.

"Bring the children," Martin said. "Tony's got what is it—six nieces and nephews? The more the merrier. I'm sorry, but I don't know the names of your children or even your husband's name. We've lived on the same street for years. It's our fault for not having you over."

"My husband is Dan. He's in IT for a city firm. You asked about skills. I don't have any beyond being a mum so I don't know how I can help."

"You've got lots of practical skills, luv," Alice said. "Don't sell yourself short."

"Thanks but beyond keeping a house, I'm useless really. Anyway, Martin, our son is Jeremy. He's eight. Our daughter is Eva. She's ten. I wonder where they are and what they're thinking. Do you think they've been told what happened to me? To us?"

"I'm not sure," Emily said, "but I doubt it. The authorities were …" She was going to say "hell-bent" but she caught herself. "They were determined to keep a lid on the situation. They were putting out a story about a bioterrorism threat on the estate so my guess is that your husband has been told you are in quarantine and can't communicate."

"That's good," Tracy said. "Dan's a trusting soul. He'll believe what he's told by the authorities. He'll be worried sick though."

"I'm sure he is," Emily said.

"Will I be able to tell him the truth when I get home?" Tracy asked.

"They'll probably try to keep all of you quiet," John said. "If you want my advice, make them pay through the nose for your silence."

"How much are my dad, my brother and my granddad worth?" Charlie asked. "How do you put a price on them?"

John nodded. "All I'm saying is that you guys are victims and victims are entitled to compensation. Mega-compensation. What's your story, son?"

"Me?" Charlie said. "I'm a builder. We were doing a renovation on the estate. It was just another working day. We were just cracking a thermos of tea when everything shifted. Forever."

"Okay," John said. "We've got a builder, a doctor, an architect, and most importantly with Tracy, a domestic goddess." He turned to Alice. "How about you?"

Alice sighed. "I'm a building inspector for the council. I was an electrician by trade but my company went bust. I don't think I've got any skills of use here. I haven't seen any lights or electrical fixtures. I'm divorced, no children any longer and I miss my cats. I hope my neighbor is looking after them."

"I think you're wrong about your skills, Alice," Emily said. "Some of them desperately want to build an electric grid but they've got large technology gaps to fill. They do have a limited battery capability which powers telegraph lines in Brittania and some of the continental areas."

"I'm not an engineer, dear, I'm only an electrician, but I'll do what I can to help everyone else."

As the day dragged on, John inspected every inch of the cell looking for escape possibilities but the walls were solid blocks of stone. The floors were hard-packed dirt that might have been amenable to tunneling. But even if they had digging implements it would be a multi-week project, ripe for discovery at any stage. The door to the cell was sturdy but wood was always vulnerable. The problem was the guards stationed on the other side.

The prisoners sat and chatted the hours away, sharing the remaining scraps of food from the morning rations and eyeing the dwindling lamp flame, the only thing keeping them from near-total darkness.

A face appeared in the barred window and the lock mechanism clunked open. In short order, several guards crammed into the cell and one of them pointed a flintlock pistol at John. It was clear they had identified him as the greatest potential threat. John and everyone else stood up.

"You! Move to the corner."

"Me?" John asked in a way that returned the menace in spades.

"Yes, you."

"Why?"

A guard with a fancy set of buttons on his tunic said, "Just do it or you'll get a lead ball in your head. And once we start shooting the rest of you will get it too."

John looked at Emily. Her pleading expression persuaded him to take a backward step toward the corner.

Fancy buttons then pointed at Emily and said, "You're to come with me."

At that John began to choreograph how he could take down the soldiers without getting his people hurt. He'd start by snatching the pistol in a lightning move, shooting fancy buttons then moving with speed to the others. But in tight quarters with so many civilians, it would be a miracle if innocents weren't shot or stabbed in the melee.

"Where are you taking me?" Emily demanded.

"William Joyce wishes your company," fancy buttons said with a leering tone.

That was all John needed to hear. He wasn't going to let Emily be taken.

It was time for violence.

"You men!" a voice boomed from the hall. "Stand aside!"

Fancy buttons recognized the speaker and ordered his guards to make room.

The robed man who swept into the cell with small, quick steps scanned the faces in the cell and settled on John's.

"John Camp," he exclaimed. "It *is* you."

"Mr. Cromwell," John said, feeling the fighting juices drain away. "I can't tell you how glad I am to see you again."

16

Thomas Cromwell was an ordinary-sized man but the strength of his presence made him seem larger.

"Why are these people in the dungeons?" he demanded.

Fancy buttons cowered at Cromwell's fiery countenance and said meekly, "Councilor Joyce so ordered it."

"Did he now? Well, I'll deal with him later. It seems that the door between our lands has opened wider, Mr. Camp. All of you, all of you live souls are guests of his majesty, King Henry. You will be given proper accommodation and ample food and drink. Now, Mr. Camp, please come with me. The royal party has just returned from our misadventure in Francia. The king, though indisposed, will want you to explain your actions."

"I'll come," John said, "but I'm not letting this woman out of my sight. Mr. Cromwell, I'd like to introduce Emily Loughty."

"Ah, the woman you so ardently sought. You have reunited. I see why you were so persistent. I am at your service, my lady."

"It's an honor to meet you, sir," she said.

"Hang on a second," Tony blurted out. "Is this *the* Thomas Cromwell?"

"In the flesh, or at least some infernal version of flesh," Cromwell replied.

"I just read a good book about you," Tony gushed. "This is absolutely amazing."

Cromwell squinted at Tony and said, "'Tis the season for amazement, my good man."

On entering King Henry's bedchamber, John and Emily were assaulted by more than the usual aroma of Hellers; there was a sickly sweet smell of infected flesh permeating the room. Henry was propped up on cushions, his face contorted in pain, his cheeks hollow.

Henry managed to raise a hand to point straight at John. "I knew I saw you on the battlefield. I told Cromwell it was you." He then pointed at the less than pleased Duke of Oxford, his mutton-chopped field commander and said, "You didn't believe me, Oxford, did you? You insisted that he was lost on the *Hellfire*. But you weren't lost at sea, were you, John Camp?"

"No Your Majesty, I wasn't," John said with smile. "The *Hellfire* lived on but was sunk by the Iberians on our return to England."

"What of my admiral? What of Norfolk?"

The particulars of the Duke of Norfolk's demise would not have been well received so John merely said, "He is below the waves, I'm afraid." Quickly changing the subject, he added, "This is Emily Loughty, the woman I sought."

John had never seen Emily at a loss for words but standing there in the presence of the most illustrious monarch in England's history left her struggling to maintain composure. She managed the first curtsy of her life and said, "I am pleased to meet you, Your Majesty."

"She is indeed a beauty," Henry said. "The loss of ships and admirals is a mere trifle in comparison. Yet I see you have not succeeded in returning to your own time and place."

"We were successful," John said, "but we've come back."

The king and Cromwell both registered their surprise and Henry asked why.

It was Emily who answered. "The passageway between our two worlds has widened, Your Majesty. My own sister and her two young children, among others, were transported here. John and I have returned to save them."

"How astonishing," Henry said, wincing in pain again. "If my soldiers only had your courage, well …"

John interrupted. "Solomon Wisdom sold the children to your wife."

"My wife? The queen?" Henry asked. "I would not know as I have just returned. I have not yet seen her. Cromwell, perhaps you can make inquiries."

"I will, Your Majesty."

"Now, I must visit with my physicians," Henry groaned. "I am most unwell. We will speak again soon. I am displeased by your actions against the crown, Mr. Camp. Very displeased. You must be held accountable."

John nodded but said, "One of the live men who's just been released from your jail is a physician. I think he ought to take a look at your wound."

"How do you know I have a wound?" Henry asked.

"I smelled it across the room."

The king looked upset then burst into laughter. "Your honesty sets you apart, Mr. Camp. Summon this live physician."

Martin peeled back the covers to reveal a grotesquely swollen leg. On his way to the king's bedchamber from the comfortable rooms the South Ockendon travellers had been given, Martin had told John and Emily about his apprehension about seeing, letting alone treating King Henry. Yet when the time came, John could see Martin slotting into a professional groove, gently but impassively lifting the king's nightdress to expose a purplish, bulging thigh and a deep wound oozing bloody pus.

Emily shuddered and looked away.

"Might I have a bowl of hot water?" Martin asked, searching the faces of the gaggle of retainers circling the bed. "And soap if you have it."

"What need have you for these?" Henry demanded.

"I would like to wash my hands before I examine you further."

"Why is that?"

"To cleanse my hands of germs. I don't wish to make matters worse."

"Why do you not cleanse your hands before touching my person?" the king demanded of his traditional physicians, archaic looking men with long robes and ample beards.

"If Your Majesty would like, we would be pleased to do so," one of them answered diplomatically.

In time a basin was produced and a woman brought in a dry cloth filled with irregularly shaped clods of soap. Martin sniffed at them then dug his thumbnail into a lump and declared it suitable. The soap didn't produce much lather. The king's physicians watched with a blend of fascination and mirth as he laboriously washed his hands. A clean square of linen was provided for him to dry off and after asking permission he began inspecting and palpating the royal legs. Both calves and thighs had bulging varicosities and pigmented scars from the chronic ulcerations that had plagued Henry in life. This Henry, though still a large man, was half the weight of the behemoth he had been at the time of his death at age fifty-five. In his final years on Earth he had been wheeled around his palaces and hoisted up stairs. The Henry of Hell was in many ways more robust and certainly more mobile. The left thigh had the fresh wound but the left calf had signs of a much older one. When a young man, Henry had suffered a fracture from a jousting accident that had almost claimed his life. For the remainder of his life he suffered an intermittently draining infection of his calf. When Martin inspected the gnarled limb he mumbled to himself that he suspected chronic osteomyelitis, a minor problem compared to the present, acute infection.

When the doctor moved on to a vigorous palpation of his wounded thigh Henry screamed in agony and Martin gave a perfunctory apology.

"What caused the puncture, do you know?" he asked. "Wood? Metal?"

"It was a fragment of iron," Henry said, using a cloth to wipe the beaded sweat from his forehead. "There were bombs exploding all around our person. I felt pain and saw a piece of the bomb had pierced my leggings and embedded in my flesh. I dug it out with my fingers and continued in battle. After we withdrew from the field the wound was bound and I was well enough. The swelling and pain occurred after some days and my agonies increased during the channel crossing."

Listening to this, John wondered if he might have thrown the offending hand grenade himself.

"Well, the wound is infected," Martin said, "and you have a deep abscess within your muscle. It must be drained rather urgently. If you would like me to do this I will need sterilized surgical instruments. Do you have these?"

One of the august physicians leaned in and said, "We have all manner of knives and lances. What is sterilized?"

"Bring me the instruments and I'll have a look at them. We'll need to boil them for a good ten minutes then lay them out on a boiled cloth to cool. That will kill the germs on them. Do you understand?"

"Do as he says," the king told the befuddled physician.

"Do you have anesthesia? Ether perhaps?" Martin asked.

After receiving blank stares Martin explained himself and was told that they could offer the king strong drink and a piece of leather to bite down on. Martin shook his head and asked what era these physicians hailed from. One was from the fifteenth century, the other from the seventeenth. Expecting little he asked about antibiotics. There were no such medicines, he was told so he inquired how they treated these kinds of suppurations.

One of the physicians, the more modern of the two, said, "We have several remedies for fetid and weeping wounds and indeed we have applied these to the king's person in the past. We use garlic applied to bandages. Honey is an effective agent. Ground flax seeds in milk on occasion."

The more ancient one added, "I find that a paste of chewed bread and salt when inserted into the wound is an excellent medicament and I would recommend this."

Martin sought out John and Emily's eyes to demonstrate what he thought about these folk remedies.

"All right," he said, "we've got a lot of work to do to save this leg and save this man."

Martin huddled in a corner with John and Emily and asked if they would assist him.

"Tony can't stand blood. Charlie's not in a good state of mind. Alice seems tough but I think she ought to stay with Tracy."

"Of course we'll help," Emily said. "What can we do?"

"I'm sure you've had your share of experience with battle trauma, John. I'd like you to assist with the surgery. Emily, I'm going to need you to make penicillin."

"You're joking, right?" she said.

"No, I'm dead serious. Even with draining the abscess, we've got to deal with extensive soft tissue infection which, if left untreated, will lead to a bloodstream infection and death."

"They don't die here, doc," John said.

"Well, something awfully close to death then. We're either going to need to find some moldy bread which would save us a couple of days, or absent that, we'll have to leave some bread in a hot, damp place to foster rapid mold formation. We need to replicate Alexander Flemming's classic work. I vaguely recall an article on survival medicine on how to make penicillin tea. I think we can assume that in a world without antibiotics, the bacteria in his wound will be exquisitely sensitive to penicillin. This will work in our favor. I'll tell you what I remember of the process then leave it in your hands, Emily. It's not particle physics but I'm sure you'll be capable."

"One batch of penicillin tea, coming up," she said, straining to smile. "We've got to save him. He's got to make his wife give us the children."

John refused to let Emily out of his sight so the two of them were taken to the kitchens located in a basement wing of the palace. The ovens were putting out intense heat. Sweating cooks and bakers sniffed and stared at them but were ordered to keep working. When they were shown the bread racks it was immediately clear that it would have been a greater challenge finding loaves free of mold. Emily chose one on a rear shelf which was covered in powdery, blue-green stuff and while she was admiring it, one of the retainers who'd accompanied them downstairs offered to scrape it clean for her.

"No, it's perfect the way it is," she said. "Please bring me a pot of warm water with a lid."

She broke the loaf into pieces and placed them in the pot and stirred the brew with a wooden ladle. Then she found a warm spot near an oven and announced to the wary kitchen staff that no one was allowed to touch it, by order of the king.

John escorted Emily to join Tony, Alice and the others and made his way back to the king's bedchamber. Henry was well on his way toward alcoholic oblivion, having downed an entire bottle of port.

"Is that you, John Camp?" he asked in a slurred bleariness.

"It is."

"Damn you, man. Damn you. You conspired against me. Do you know what I do with conspirators?"

"I can imagine."

"Have a drink with me and I'll tell you. Or maybe I'll sing you a song. Where's my lute? Someone fetch my lute!"

While John humored Henry and lifted a glass, Martin inspected the piping hot instruments cooling on a cloth. The only suture material was ordinary sewing thread that he doubted would hold up very well. He chose one of the small knives and a lance that looked more like a knitting needle and washed his hands again.

"I'm ready to proceed," he announced, checking to see if the knife was cool enough. "John, could you tie that cloth over my nose and mouth please."

The king mumbled, "Hiding from me, is he? No one hides from the king."

"Why are you doing this?" one of the physicians asked.

"Germs," Martin said.

"You keep insisting there are these creatures called germs which we cannot see," the physician exclaimed. "I wonder if you take us for fools."

"I'm quite sure you were the bee's knees in your day," Martin said, "but I assure you, germs do exist."

He lifted up Henry's nightshirt and announced he was going to clean the skin first with soap and water, and used a fresh cloth for the job.

"He looks good and drunk," Martin said quietly. "John, could you place that leather between his teeth to protect his tongue? It will hurt a great deal though I doubt he'll remember it."

"Bite down on this," John said.

"Bite or be bitten," Henry mumbled before clamping down.

"I'm ready to proceed, sir," Martin said. "I apologize in advance for causing you pain. I shall move as quickly as I can." He lowered his voice and told John that he wanted him to tie a cloth around his face too and be ready to pass the lance and squares of linen.

With the exception of an open, oozing fistula, the wound had largely closed on its own. Martin used the knife to open it wide, releasing a gush of green pus mixed with fresh blood. A deep groan emanated from Henry's locked jaw.

"Please hold his legs tighter," Martin told the strong men assigned the task. "John, could you mop some of that up so I can see what I'm doing?"

John soaked several pieces of linen with the putrid material. A young attendant tasked with holding a bucket to collect the soiled linens fainted dead away and had to be replaced.

"All right," Martin said, "now for the tricky bit. Hand me the lance. Without scans, we'll be flying blind. Assuming he doesn't have aberrant anatomy, I should be able to avoid major vessels."

The first thrust of the lance did nothing but convulse Henry with agony. The second time there was an audible pop and Martin's facial mask was sprayed with pus under pressure.

"Could you remove the cloth and replace it with another?" Martin said calmly. "And try to mop up as much of these secretions as you can while I apply some pressure to the surrounding tissues to fully evacuate the abscess."

Henry slipped into unconsciousness, making the rest of the procedure easier. Martin packed the deep wound with a long strip of linen and left a few inches protruding from the skin margins.

"Well, that's as much as we can do for now. Hopefully we'll have some penicillin to give him tomorrow. You did well, John, but there's one more thing you can do for me."

"Sure, anything."

"A glass of that port would go down very nicely."

That night, every few hours, Martin left the others to check on his patient who was febrile and delirious. The rest of them lounged on comfortable beds and enjoyed decent food and drink, except for Emily who was fuming and dissatisfied at Cromwell's pronouncement that Queen Matilda had refused to see him and claimed to have no information about the presence of children in the palace.

"What are we going to do?" she asked John.

"The hall's filled with soldiers. We could try and fight our way through them and find our way to the queen's quarters but I don't think we'll succeed. Let's hope Henry recovers and forces her to cooperate. That's the best we can do for now."

"How are you feeling?" she asked.

"Me? Why are you asking?"

"You had surgery yourself not so long ago. Remember?"

"Vaguely."

"At least we have Martin to take your stitches out," she said. "I didn't fancy the job. And if you need it we'll have some nice penicillin tea."

Emily eagerly lifted the lid on her pot of soggy bread. The broth was dark, brown and stinky, just as Martin had predicted. Following his instructions she strained it through a clean cloth into another pot, discarding the clumps of bread. Then, with John leading the way, she carefully carried the pot of brown liquid up to the king's chamber where Martin was waiting.

Henry was groggy and drenched with sweat. Martin and John propped him up on pillows as Emily ladled the smelly liquid into a glass.

"Is this enough?" she asked.

Martin shrugged. "I hope so. Not an exact science at this point. We'll aim to give him a glassful every four hours. You've got enough for a few days but to be safe you should start another batch."

They coaxed the liquid down Henry's throat little by little, encouraging him to stifle his gags, until the glass was empty.

"Now, we wait," Martin said.

Emily made her way to Cromwell who was speaking with the Duke of Suffolk in one corner.

"Well?" she demanded.

Cromwell looked at her wearily. "I have no news for you, m'lady."

"Were you able to see her?"

"I was not. She is not receiving visitors."

"Surely you must know what is going on inside your own palace."

"It is not my palace."

"I want to see her then," Emily insisted.

"I will pass along your request."

"You have to insist."

"M'lady, we are talking about the queen."

The transformation was remarkable. When Martin, John, and Emily came to see him the next morning the king was seated bolt upright in bed loudly slurping at a bowl of soup.

"You're not going to give me more of that foul tea, are you?" Henry demanded.

"You'll need to continue with it for a full week at least," Martin said, shifting the bedclothes to get at his leg. "It's looking much improved," he declared. "I'll just pull some of the packing out to allow the wound to close behind it. It shouldn't hurt much."

Henry hardly looked up from his soup bowl while Martin performed the maneuver. While Martin washed his hands at a sideboard, Henry beckoned Cromwell and whispered something to him.

Cromwell stood up straighter and announced ceremoniously, "As the king is feeling much improved, he believes it is high time to have John Camp explain to his person his actions with respect to the commandeering of his ship, *Hellfire*, and his aiding the king's enemies in Francia."

Emily was too impatient to succumb to Henry's agenda. "Excuse me," she said. "I want to see the children now. I insist that the queen allow us to see them."

"Where is Matilda?" Henry said, looking around the chamber as if he'd forgotten her existence. "Has she been to my bedside?"

"She has not, Your Majesty," Cromwell said.

"Why has she not? Did you not tell her that her good husband was ailing?"

"I endeavored to speak with her but I was told she is not seeing visitors or receiving messages."

"Is she not well? Perhaps this modern physician should be sent to her."

"I will attempt to speak with her presently," Cromwell said. "I will relay to her your request for her company."

"It is not a request, it is a demand. Do not keep me waiting any longer," Henry shouted, his mood turning black. "Now Mr. Camp, I demand an explanation for your transgressions. You would know that neither my illness, nor my expeditious recovery, would allow you to escape my wrath. Men who cross me do so only once. Explain yourself so I may determine your punishment."

John let Emily know with a thin-lipped shake of his head that they'd pushed Henry as far as they could for the moment. It was time to use Malcolm Gough's brain droppings. He hoped the professor's stellar reputation as a Henry scholar was justified; he was about to find out.

"What would *I* do if I were face-to-face with a living, breathing Henry and had to convince him I had a just reason for betraying him?" the professor had asked with a bemused expression. "Well, I would probably have gotten my affairs in order prior to the audience, because Henry was not one to forgive and forget when he believed he had been deceived or crossed. He had tens of thousands put to death as a testament to his iron will. He wasn't only a fan of execution, but of what he called, dreadful execution—slow, painful methods intended to serve as a warning against any future interference with his religious and secular agendas. But, if I were going to try to save my skin, I suppose I would appeal to his vanity. I would remind him of the greatness of his accomplishments as a king and, for the purpose of this fanciful exercise, I would describe to this reincarnated Henry, the durability of his legacy. When it was clear that this tact was going to fail—and fail it probably would—I would endeavor to use whatever leverage I might possess to make some kind of a deal. Henry was, after all, a pragmatist. He was a megalomaniac but a pragmatic one."

John assumed a posture suggesting penitence, fingers interlaced at his waist, head ever so slightly bowed. "First of all, Your Majesty, I think that I failed to properly express my awe in meeting you a month ago. I was very much a stranger in a strange land and it was difficult for me to fully appreciate the enormity of meeting the greatest king that England has ever known."

Henry nodded and called for some watered-down wine.

"I hope you've been told by new arrivals to your realm over the years," John continued, "that your legacy is unrivaled by other monarchs. You singlehandedly reshaped the religious landscape of your empire and established a uniquely English church, neither a slave to Rome or to Luther. You singlehandedly bestowed on English kingship a profound new dignity and unified your country as never before, giving your people pride. Your singular vision established England as a force to be reckoned with throughout Europe. Your campaigns in France are still admired by military men. You, with the able assistance of Thomas Cromwell, established a central legal and administrative structure for governing your diverse realm, which brought peace and stability to what had previously been large areas of lawlessness and violence."

He paused to read the room. Henry was hanging on every word and Cromwell looked extremely pleased at his mention. He kept piling it on, recalling the professor's advice. "You established the English navy as the greatest force on the high seas and that naval supremacy shaped the history of England for centuries to come. You were the ablest builder of all the kings and queens of England and your palaces and fortifications still stand today. And incredibly you were also a scholar, a writer, and an artist. Your books are still read five hundred years on, your music is still sung. You were a king, who by exercise of your mastery of all of the affairs of the state and the soul, was not only feared for your might but also loved by your subjects for your spirit and pride."

He stopped long enough to let the king fill the vacuum.

Henry waved at a retainer to fill his cup and had another few gulps. "These are fine words, Mr. Camp, chosen, I presume to defang the beast. I have heard these songs of praise over the full span of my interminable residence in this foul land, and by and large, I cannot and will not argue with the inherent truthfulness you now impart. Yet, I have also heard loathsome judgments of my person. Tyrant. Betrayer. Usurper. I have even been told I am best known, not for the fine things of which you have spoken, but for having six wives and beheading two. But I say this in my defense of the harsh judgments under which my reputation labors. Was I cruel? Yes! Did this cruelty condemn me to Hell? Yes again, though the fact of this wholly unfair and irrational condemnation has led me to forsake the faith for which I fought my entire earthly life. My cruelty had a purpose, sir. A fine and noble purpose. Moving a country is nearly as difficult a task as moving a mountain. Love can move a country but a little. Fear can move it much further and much faster. I could not have achieved what I had to achieve without an iron will and an iron fist."

"I imagine that philosophy serves you here as well," John said.

"It does, sir, though in Hell, there is no need to bother with love which is a meaningless thing. Fear is the king of emotions in this realm."

Cromwell asked the king if he might speak and he was given permission.

"Mr. Camp has voiced his admiration for the character and deeds of his majesty, yet he has nonetheless engaged in exploits which have harmed the crown. How does he reconcile thought and deed?"

John was ready to use the next arrow in his quiver. "In order to survive and achieve my goals I had to quickly learn the lay of the land of your world. I only had a month to find this good woman and bring her home. The doorway between our worlds was going to be open for only a short time and I knew I had to quickly get to Francia. I needed a ship."

"I believe I promised you passage if you fashioned me these singing cannon," Henry said, his voice rising.

"We both know the Duke of Norfolk wasn't going to let that happen. As soon as the battle with the Iberians was over, he was going to take me prisoner or kill me."

"If he had, this would not have been my undertaking," the king said.

"Perhaps not, but it would have happened," John insisted.

"Yet once you reached Francia, you made allegiances with the French and the Italians to do war against King Henry," Cromwell said. "You cannot deny this. You were seen on the battlefield opposing us at Argenteuil. As a result, Brittania has been weakened and our enemies grow stronger. We have heard that the Great Bear of Russia, Czar Joseph, senses our weakness in defeat and is making plans to sail for our shores with his armies. You have wounded Brittania as if you had, by your very own hand, pierced the thigh of King Henry. How will you explain your treachery?"

The analogy was ironic but it wouldn't have helped matters to smile at it. "Like I said," John protested, "I had to learn how to survive here. I needed help to rescue Emily. The Italians and their new king provided that help."

"This new monarch," Henry growled, "this man called Garibaldi. He is not of noble birth. He is a commoner and yet he would be a king. You betrayed me to a common criminal and now you must pay. I have a certain fondness for you, John Camp, but I cannot let that interfere with what I must do and the example I must send to all who are answerable to the crown. I was fond of Thomas More. I was fond of Anne Boleyn. I was even fond of our good friend, Cromwell, but I did to them what I must do to you."

Emily looked panicky and was about to say something but John raised a hand to quiet her. He wasn't altogether surprised at the failure of his first two arrows. He confidently reached for the third.

"All right. I understand you're angry at what I did and I appreciate that you've got to keep up appearances. You don't stay king for five hundred years by being a soft touch."

"What does this mean: soft touch?"

"Forgiving. Nice. Easy. Weak. All those things. But here's something else I know about you, Your Majesty. You're also very intelligent, very shrewd. You know a good bargain when you see it and I'd like to offer you a very good bargain."

Henry handed his wine to a servant then propped himself higher on his pillows and demanded that the cushion under his wounded thigh be repositioned.

"What bargain do you propose?"

"I want you to give us the children and the woman your queen purchased from Solomon Wisdom. I want free and safe passage back to Dartford for them, myself, Emily, and the five other living persons who are now guests in your palace. And in exchange, I will give you something that no other ruler in Hell has, something that will give you unimaginable power and superiority."

Henry betrayed himself with a fleeting, greedy smile. "And what, pray tell, is this, Mr. Camp?"

"I will give you books. I will give you some very important books."

John and Emily sailed the great river alone. Henry had given his assurances that they would not be followed and they felt certain no one was as they navigated the swift downstream currents to the spot, about four miles away, where they had hidden the books.

The landmark John had chosen to mark the spot was a rotting pier with just enough substance to tie up their barge and support their weight. The crumbling foundation of a stone house, a few yards from the riverbank, was the spot they'd chosen as they made their way from Greenwich. John had transferred all the books to Emily's pack after ripping out the first few pages from one set. At the king's bedside, John had produced the pages as proof of the goods and an astonished Henry had read them, passing page by page to Cromwell to inspect, and had declared that a deal would be done.

"Bring me these books," he had said, "and I will have the queen relinquish these children, if indeed she has them, and I will give you all free and unfettered passage and my guarantee of safety until such time as you may be able to return to your own realm."

"We'll need to see the children first," John had said.

Henry had laughed. "I am well versed in the art of the trade," he had said. "You will receive what you require and I will receive what I desire. You have the word of this king and that is a sure currency even in Hell."

The books, wrapped in cloth, were concealed in a shallow hole he had dug, covered by rubble. John unwrapped the cloth revealing two copies of six books, a total of twelve. He removed the five he'd ripped pages from.

"I'm glad you decided against giving him a copy of the sixth," Emily said. "As it is, it bothers me that three of the five can be used for cruelty."

"Technology's always been a double-edged sword," he said, hiding the books again. "Even with supercolliders."

He wished he hadn't made the remark but she let him off the hook by saying, "At least we can be certain that only good can come from the other two."

A whippy westerly wind picked up in intensity and it began to rain. A flock of jays following the river eastward seemed to be almost stationary against the dull sky. A large sailing barge came into view from the west, sped by three masts of full black sails and a contingent of men putting their backs into twenty pairs of oars.

"They're really hauling ass," John said, as the barge disappeared around a river bend. "Too bad we're going the opposite direction."

The strong, unfavorable wind and the heavy current conspired to make their return journey to Hampton Court arduous. John shouted into the wind more than once that it would have been faster to walk, and after several painful hours they arrived back at the palace soaked to the skin.

Cromwell met them in the great hall and asked if they had been successful.

"We're wet but the books are dry," John said.

"May I lay my eyes upon them?" the chancellor asked anxiously.

"Let's not waste time," John said. "Let's see the king and let's see the children."

"Have you seen them?" Emily asked.

"I have not but the queen has received a message from the king and I am assured they are well," Cromwell said, turning his back to them and taking off through the hall. "Follow me. The king is most impatient."

Henry was eating again. He raised a greasy hand and used the joint of meat to beckon them into his bedchamber. "You have taken an intolerably long while to return. Do you have them?" he called out as they approached.

Emily answered. "We do. May we please see the children now?"

Henry shouted to the column of retainers lined up against the wall. "You heard the woman. Fetch the queen and the children." He called for a cloth to wipe his hands and said, "They will arrive forthwith. Now the books, if you please."

John and Emily were still dripping wet but Henry took no notice of their plight.

"What order would you like to see them?" John asked.

Henry had the look of a young lad about to receive presents. "Surprise me," he said. "Delight me."

John looked into his pack, pulled out the first volume, and held it up to Henry's eyes.

"Excellent!" the king exclaimed. "I was just reading its frontispiece again." He fished through his bedclothes for the torn sheets and read out loud, "The blast furnace is the key which unlocks Nature's stores of iron for our use. It is unique in having been unchanged in principle for several centuries, and in having no substitute. If the blast furnace were taken from us civilization would be halted.' Did you hear that, Cromwell? Civilization would be halted. Well, methinks that our civilization has indeed been halted. We must have improved furnaces. Now show me this book."

The book John handed him was *Blast Furnace Construction in America* by Joseph Esrey Johnson, written in 1917. Henry avidly thumbed through it murmuring and cooing like a happy songbird.

"Look at these behemoths! These furnaces dwarf my largest forges. This tome is filled with fine illustrations and construction plans. Cromwell, summon my master forger, William, and have him come to the palace this very day. I wish him to study this text and study it well. I would have him build me my own behemoth. Think of the cannon we can forge with iron from the Norselands and behemoth furnaces!"

"It's not only cannon you can build," Emily said. "You can make rails for railway tracks and locomotive engines to ride on them. You can make bridges and stronger buildings. You can make a better life for your people."

"My subjects will have worse lives if they are conquered by Russians, that I can tell you. We need finer weapons first and foremost. If the ranks of those who are condemned to Hell weren't swollen with imbeciles and ruffians then we would have learned how to make these furnaces already. The only thing a murderer or a rapist is good for is murdering and raping. Give me the next book."

John reached into the bag and produced, *Steam Boilers, Engines and Turbines*, a 1908 book by Sydney Walker.

"Blast furnaces are one leg of the stool," John said, holding it up. "The second is being able to make the large steam engines and turbines to power them and make them hot enough. Water wheels can only go so far. We saw small steam engines in Europa used to power automobiles but larger ones don't exist here as far as we know. This book teaches how to build them."

Henry leafed through the book and marveled at the illustrations. Then he said, "Show me the third leg of the stool."

That was *Bessemer Steel, Ores and Methods*, a book published in 1882 by Thomas Fitch. John explained, "You want to be able to produce more than just large amounts of steel. You want to produce high quality steel that's consistently strong and won't rupture. Remember the singing cannon that exploded the day the Iberians attacked?"

"I do indeed. You led us to believe that this defect could be assuaged by utilizing the iron from the Norse mines."

"Yes, that iron has the lowest phosphorous content and phosphorous is the enemy of good steel. In the nineteenth century an Englishman named Bessemer invented a process for turning any iron ore into the highest quality steel and he made iron very inexpensive to produce. This book teaches how to make Bessemer steel. It's the third leg of your stool."

Like a greedy boy, Henry wanted more.

John asked Emily to present the fourth book.

"This book was written by another Englishman," she said. "It does not teach how to make weapons or engines or indeed anything you can hold in your hand. It teaches you how to hold things in your heart. It is meant to inspire, to make you laugh, to make you cry. It is food for the human spirit, something you need dearly here, in my humble opinion. I give you the *Complete Works of William Shakespeare*, the greatest poet in the history of mankind."

Henry received the heavy book with two hands and opened it to one page then another before his eye was caught by a familiar name. "Behold! He writes of my ancestor, King Henry the Fifth!" He paused to read a passage to himself then said, "Listen all to these fine words, as fine as I have ever seen: 'And Crispin Crispian shall ne'er go by, From this day to the ending of the world, But we in it shall be remember'd; We few, we happy few, we band of brothers; For he to-day that sheds his blood with me, Shall be my brother; be he ne'er so vile, This day shall gentle his condition: And gentlemen in England now a-bed, Shall think themselves accursed they were not here, And hold their manhoods cheap whiles any speaks, That fought with us upon Saint Crispin's day.'"

A tear ran down his cheek.

"And now for the last book," John said.

"I am glad you saved it for the last," Henry said, reaching for the torn pages he'd received. "For it is the greatest of them all. Though I have forsaken God, as there is no salvation to be had any longer, I have often tried to remember the sweet passages I learned in my youth. But memories fade, though flesh fadeth not."

The fifth book was the Bible, and not just any edition but the English bible, prepared by Myles Coverdale, under commission by King Henry, to be used throughout his realm by his new Church of England.

Henry said, holding out his hands, "It is the Great Bible, my bible." The cover page had an illustration of Henry, seated on his throne, watched over by God, disseminating copies of his new Bible to his Protestant clergy. "It looks like my very copy. See this Cromwell? Do you see this?"

"I do, Your Majesty. I remember the Great Bible well. It was I who devised the edict that every church in your land possess one copy."

"This is the book which I will presently read and study to the exclusion of the others," Henry declared. "I will refresh my memory of the word of God and see what use there is of His divine words in such a place as …"

A retainer rushed into the bedchamber in a dead run and slid to a halt on the stone floor.

"What is the reason for your haste?" the king said with obvious irritation at the interruption.

"It is the queen," the man almost shouted. "She is gone!"

John and Emily looked at each other in alarm.

"Gone?" Henry asked. "What mean you, gone?"

"She and her retinue have departed the palace."

"When was this and why was I not told?" the king shouted. "Cromwell, did you know of this?"

"I knew not, Your Majesty."

"They left some four hours past," the servant said. "They sailed off on the queen's barge."

"The children!" Emily cried out. "Did she take the children?"

"None are left behind in her royal apartment," the retainer said. "All are gone."

"Does her barge have black sails?" John asked.

"It does," Cromwell said. "How did you know this?"

"We passed it on the river. With the wind and the current they've got a huge head start. The deal was, the books for the children. You've got the books, we don't have the children."

"It is not the fault of his majesty," Cromwell countered. "The queen has undertaken this action of her own accord."

"Did she know she had to hand over the children?" Emily said.

"She was so advised," Cromwell said.

"Where did she take them?" Emily asked, choking back tears.

"Perhaps to London," Henry said. "My palace in Whitehall pleases her."

"I beg of you, sire," the servant said. "I had occasion to question a palace guard stationed in the corridor outside the queen's chambers. He heard one of the queen's ladies complaining of having to go to Francia."

"Where in Francia?" John demanded.

"I do not know," the servant said, cringing.

"She might be making for Normandy," Cromwell said. "She has an affinity for the region and knows the Duke of Normandy well. She died in Rouen, you know, and in Hell she made her return to Britannia."

"There is also Strasbourg," Henry said. "Do not eliminate Strasbourg from consideration."

"Yes," Cromwell said, "she may elect to go to Strasbourg," Cromwell said. "She also has ancient kinship to this region and in years past, when we had alliances with Francia, she was entertained by the duke of Alsace who has a fine castle there."

"We've got to leave immediately," John said. "We're getting our people and we're leaving. Your majesty, I'm counting on you to keep your word and let us go."

"I will do so," Henry said, "though I would have you leave your physician behind to minister to my person until I am healed."

"We all go together. I'll have him see you before we go and leave instructions with your own physicians."

"Very well," the king said. "You may leave."

"One more thing," John said. "If we don't catch up with her, can her barge make a channel crossing or will she need to transfer to another ship?"

"It is well capable of making full passage," Cromwell said.

"Well our barge isn't. We need a ship."

"The Duke of Suffolk will accompany you downriver," Henry said, "and he will sail with you to Francia if need be. Now take your leave so I may read my Bible."

Cromwell had to churn his legs to keep up with John and Emily and by the time they arrived at the guest wing, he was dangerously out of breath.

Bursting through the door, John immediately saw that something was wrong. Charlie was nursing a split lip, Alice was crying, and Martin and Tony were fitfully staring out the windows.

John didn't see Tracy. "Where is she?" he asked.

"Some men came for her," Charlie said. "I tried to stop them. I did try but they popped me one."

"Where did they take her?"

"To William Joyce."

"Cromwell!" John shouted. "Take me there."

Cromwell nodded, too breathless to speak.

"When I get back, we're leaving," John said.

"Did you get your niece and nephew?" Alice asked.

"The queen ran off with them," Emily said. "We're going after her. John, I'm coming with you."

They hurried off, with Cromwell panting and leading the way through the labyrinthine palace.

There were guards outside Joyce's private rooms but at the sight of the chancellor, they melted away.

John tried the door but it was locked and Cromwell had to muster enough breath to announce his presence.

The door unlatched and a shirtless Joyce opened it, but at the sight of John he tried to slam it shut. John put his weight against it and set the door slamming into Joyce's chest, bowling him over.

John put his boot on Joyce's neck and shouted for Tracy.

Hesitantly, Tracy emerged from another room, clutching a torn shirt to her nakedness. Emily ran to her and Tracy began wailing pitifully.

"Here, take my robe," Cromwell said, shedding his outergarment. John saw he had a dagger on an inner belt.

Emily took the robe, put her arm around Tracy, and shut the door behind them.

"Can I have that?" John asked Cromwell.

Cromwell nodded and gave him the knife. "You may put it to good purpose, Mr. Camp. To be truthful, I never liked or trusted this man. The king favors recent arrivals, thinking it gives him certain advantages, but I could not see the merit in giving this man high office. It is now out of my hands and into yours."

John removed his boot and Joyce stood up, rubbing his throat.

"What are you going to do?" Joyce asked.

"What do you think?"

"I bedded her. So what? That's what men do here. Whenever and wherever they want. I'm a member of the privy council. You can't touch me."

John closed the distance between the two of them with one long stride and plunged Cromwell's dagger between his third and fourth ribs just to the left of his breastbone. Heart blood welled from the chest wound. Joyce went down gasping, and lying on his back he searched John's face, then Cromwell's.

"Is there a rotting room around for this piece of trash?" John asked.

"As it happens, we have a particularly large one close by," Cromwell said with a smile.

17

Hathaway's brother, Harold, got very drunk on gin and kept blubbering about how he couldn't get his head around what was happening.

"You was dead. I was at your funeral. I can take you to see your grave. It's just down the road. I tackle the weeds from time to time. You was dead and now you're in my lounge."

"Don't want to see my bloody grave," Hathaway hissed.

The three other rovers, Talley, Youngblood, and Chambers sniggered and kept tucking into the meat sandwiches rustled up by Harold's wife, Maisey, and passing around his last bottle of gin.

"I like the grub here," Chambers said, mayonnaise dripping onto his shirt.

"Where's she gone?" Youngblood asked.

"She's upstairs," Hathaway said. "She's not too keen on us, that's for damn sure. I cut the phone line so we're all right."

"What's a phone line?" Chambers asked.

"Don't worry about it."

Talley got up and wobbled on his feet. "I'm going out back for a shit," he announced.

"I'm going to teach you about indoor plumbing," Hathaway said. "Prepare to be amazed."

When he returned from his tutorial, Hathaway asked Chambers where Youngblood had gone.

"Dunno," was the boozy reply.

Hathaway ducked into the kitchen and came back empty-handed, mumbling, "Bloody hell."

Just then Maisey screamed.

Hathaway bounded up the stairs to find Youngblood, trousers around ankles, on top of Maisey on her bed. Youngblood was a powerful brute, nearly half-again the size of Hathaway, so Hathaway shied away from anything resembling a fair fight. He grabbed a crystal ashtray and slammed it into Youngblood's head. The blow didn't knock him out but it stunned him and allowed Maisey to roll off the bed onto the floor.

Crying hysterically, she began to crawl to the door but Hathaway warned her not to leave the house.

"Leave me be!" she shouted. "He tried to, well you know what."

"I just saved you, you old cow but I won't save you again if you try to leave. Now put some clothes on and keep your mouth shut, all right?"

Talley called up the stairs and asked what was happening and Hathaway told him to make sure that the woman didn't try to escape. She collected some clothes from the wardrobe and stumbled across the hall to the bathroom.

Youngblood lay on his back, holding his head and spouting invectives. When he tried to sit up Hathaway clobbered him again, this time splitting the ashtray in two and opening a gash in his forehead.

Talley and Chambers climbed the stairs to have a look.

"What've you done to him, then?" Talley asked.

"He was raping," Hathaway said.

"What's the matter with that?" Chambers asked.

"Nothing if it weren't my brother's wife."

"Where is she?" Talley asked.

"In the loo."

"With the indoor shitter?"

"Yeah."

"I don't see the worth of it," Talley said. "Plot of ground serves the same purpose."

Downstairs, Talley and Chambers finished off the gin and the few cans of beer on the sideboard and began trashing the place looking for more. Harold told them to stop but then, in his drunkenness, decided to join in, rummaging through the pantry for a bottle of good whiskey that may or may not have already been consumed on his last birthday.

Hathaway shook his head and tried to figure out how to switch on the strange, flat television but he got ready for a scuffle when Youngblood came stumbling down the stairs. The big man was too woozy for a fight and seemed to forget how it was that his head got split open. The blood ran down his face and onto his clothes and Talley tossed him a sofa cushion to hold against his gash.

"Where's Maisey?" Harold asked, returning to the lounge empty-handed.

"She's gone to bed," Hathaway said.

Harold grumbled, "Always the death of a party, get it? I'm unable to find one more drop of drink. What to do, what to do?"

"Is there a tavern about?" Talley asked.

"There are some excellent establishments," Harold said, wagging a finger to make the point.

"I don't think that's a good idea," Hathaway said.

"Well I do," Talley disagreed.

"We'll be courting trouble," Hathaway said.

Talley laughed. "When have we ever turned from trouble? I say we go to the tavern."

"When's closing time?" Hathaway asked his brother.

Harold squinted at the mantel clock. "Half eleven on a good night. It's past last orders but the landlord's a good bloke. He'll serve me."

"You're staying here with your wife," Hathaway said. "Got any rope?"

"In the cupboard," Harold said helpfully. "Why?"

With Hathaway shaking his head at the insanity of showing themselves and with Youngblood still pressing a cushion to his bloody head, the four rovers shut the door, leaving Harold and Maisey behind trussed up but very much alive.

The Carpenter's Arms was only around the corner on Sneinton Dale, a deserted commercial street. Hathaway remembered it from the old days, and while the block was studded with unfamiliar shops with unfamiliar names, at least from the outside, the pub looked much the same as he remembered.

Before crossing the threshold he asked Talley if he was sure he wanted to do this but Talley only swore and pushed on through the door.

It was a weekday and nearly closing time and the patronage was light. Three young men stood at the bar, chatting with the publican. Another two older gents sat at a table nursing the last of their pints. Another young man was dropping pound coins into a fruit machine that was banging out an inane, synthesized tune.

Everyone turned and stared at their entrance.

One of the men at the bar, a cocky lad with two full sleeves of tattoos, said to his mates, "Would you get a look at these geezers?"

"Bring us ale," Talley barked to the landlord, finding a seat at one of the many empty tables.

The landlord had thick arms bulging from rolled-up sleeves. He looked at the four men quizzically and said, "First of all, we don't do table service. Second, it's customary to specify which ale you want."

Hathaway intervened, pointing at one of the taps. "Four pints of Fullers."

The landlord nodded and began pulling pints while the young men whispered and giggled among themselves.

"That'll be thirteen pound, twenty," the publican said.

"Say what?" Hathaway answered, staring at the pints incredulously. "Thirteen pounds! Have you gone mad?"

"Me? Have *you* gone mad, mate?" the landlord flung back. "What do you think beer costs?"

Hathaway drifted back to his day; in 1985 beer was about seventy pence a pint. "I don't know, about three quid?"

All the locals were hanging on every word and the youth closest to Hathaway, emboldened by the whispered proddings of his mates, said,

"Who are you, Rip Fucking Winkle come back to winge over the price of beer?"

"Was I talking to you?" Hathaway said.

"I dunno, was you?" the kid said, puffing his t-shirted chest.

Hathaway decided to ignore the provocation. He pulled the twenties out of his pocket and reluctantly peeled one off.

"Oooo, twenty quid," the youth said. "Surprised you've not got a pocket of pennies."

One kid chimed in, "Why don't you take the change and buy yourself some clothes to replace the rags you're wearing?"

Followed by another's comment, "And a proper bandage for that bloke so he don't have to use a cushion on his face."

"Knock it off," the landlord said, seeming to sense a nasty situation brewing. "Let 'em drink their pints in peace." But then he apparently couldn't resist piling on himself and said with a smirk, "Especially pints which weigh in at three pound thirty a time!"

To the sound of laughter Hathaway carried two pints back to the table and returned for the other two.

"Mister, did you know you smelled like shit?" the first kid said, finishing his own beer and putting the mug down hard on the mat.

The kid on the fruit machine came over and sniffed hard. "He does smell like shit don't he? It's customary to wash the pong off before coming into a public house."

"Maybe they're pig farmers and the smell's permanent," the other kid said.

Hathaway had enough. He delivered the remaining beer to the table and watched Talley and the other rovers drink them down in powerful gulps.

Hathaway turned back to the loudmouths and said, "Any of you ever killed a man? Raped a woman? Raped a child?"

"Here!" the landlord shouted. "I'll have no talk like that in my pub."

Hathaway turned a deaf ear to him and said, "If you have, I'll see you in Hell."

The carnage that ensued was swift and furious.

At the sight of Hathaway pounding a knife into a chest, Talley and the others were on their feet and swarming on the youths, stabbing bellies, slashing throats in a bloodletting befitting an abattoir. The landlord tried to flee to the lounge bar but Chambers was over the bar counter with a rather elegant vault catching the man with one knife-blow to the back and another through the thin part of the skull.

That left the two older men who remained frozen at their table, watching the events unfold as if they were on a movie screen.

When Talley approached them it became clear they were both very drunk.

"We won't say nothing, will we?" one of them slurred.

"I know you won't," Talley said.

"We'll be off now," the other said, his voice shaking as much as his hands.

"Here's the good thing," Talley said, his kitchen knife dripping blood on the floor. "We've had proper grub and our bellies are full. So we won't be eating you after."

"After what?" the first man asked in terror.

Talley raised the knife. "After this."

Ben's mobile woke him out of a dreamless sleep. Ordinarily he muted his phone at night so as not to disturb his wife, but he wasn't taking the chance of missing a vibration. Brahms's Third Symphony set him reaching for the unit and his wife moaning in irritation.

It was 2 a.m.

He listened, asked only a few questions in a low voice and got up.

"What is it?" his wife asked.

"Sorry, I've got to go."

"Where?"

"Nottingham."

"Bloody hell. Don't wake the children."

He lived in a mews in Kensington, a swanky pile he would not have been able to afford on a civil servant's salary. But he was from money, lots of money, and his parents had bought the place for them when the second child arrived. The house had become an asset in his rise through the ranks at MI5 as he strategically invited superiors over for couples' suppers, reinforcing the impression that he was one of them—which he was. Now, as he tiptoed through the dark house, scooping up car keys and swigging orange juice directly from the carton, a no-no in front of his wife, he became grimly resolute. He would not allow the horrors of what had apparently just happened in Nottingham to invade the world of his innocent, sleeping girls.

At half past four in the morning an MI5 helicopter deposited Ben, a small forensics team, and his two guests in Green's Mill Park in Sneinton, a short distance from the Carpenter's Arms.

During the flight, Murphy had raised his voice over the din, "Are you sure there weren't any female victims?"

"That's what I was told," Ben had replied, opening a laptop computer and logging on to a cellular network.

He had called up a map of Nottingham and soon was looking at a street view of the Carpenter's Arms.

Rix had been looking over his shoulder. "Is that a live camera feed?"

"No, it's archived from a previous drive-by."

"Just of Nottingham?"

"No, much of the country, in fact much of the western world."

"Bloody hell."

"Is this only for spooks like you lot?"

"No, it's for anyone with a computer. Costs nothing to use. We spooks have access to live closed circuit TV feeds, mostly from urban areas, but not from this part of Nottingham."

"And you can look things up, fast."

"We can. Anyone can."

"Show me."

"You move the cursor up to this box by sliding your finger then typing in what you want to find out."

"Now show me how your people were able to find out about Murphy and me."

Ben had obliged and Googled their names. A host of archived newspaper articles had filled the screen detailing the tragic events of 1985.

"Fuck me," Rix had said. "Being a copper's got to be dead easy now."

"Some things are easier, some are harder."

"And you can use this to find people you're looking for?"

"That's right. You just type in their name and follow your nose."

"Anyone can do it."

"Anyone."

"Who's got these computers?"

"Most everyone these days in one form or another."

"And what if you don't have one, then what do you do?"

"There are public places in cities and towns called Internet cafes where you can rent them for a small fee. Anything else you'd like to know?"

When they landed, a police van drove them the rest of the way. Knots of neighbors woken by police and ambulance sirens lingered outside the taped-off pub and a few print reporters tried to ask questions as Ben and his team breezed by on their way to a crime-scene tent erected by the rear entrance. They donned disposable coveralls and booties. The Chief Constable of the Nottinghamshire Police was waiting for them inside. He came forward and introduced himself, holding up his gloved hands to excuse the lack of hand shaking.

"Chris Plume, Chief Constable. We all look the same in these monkey suits."

"Ben Wellington, security services. May we have a look?"

"These men with you?" Plume said, wrinkling his nose and staring at Murphy and Rix.

"They are."

"I see. How's your stomach?" Plume asked.

"That bad, eh?"

"Worst I've ever seen. It's a challenge walking about and finding bits of floor not covered in blood."

"How many casualties?"

"Six patrons and the publican. It was his missus who sounded the alarm when he failed to come home after closing time. She sent their eldest son down here to check on him and, well, you'll see what he found. While we were responding to this incident, we received a 999 call to an address on Holborn Avenue, a few streets away. The nature of the call was curious to say the least. Not three minutes later, you lot called from London. I didn't know MI5 had the capability of listening in on the 999 network nationwide."

"Should be no comment," Ben said, "but we do. In special situations."

"That's what you've got here, Mr. Wellington. A right special situation. Would you mind telling me what we're dealing with here? Pub killings aren't the usual purview of MI5."

"We don't believe it's an ordinary pub killing."

"Do you have reason to suspect a terroristic connection?"

"We do which is why we'll be invoking primary jurisdiction."

"Might this be related to the South Ockendon terrorism investigation?"

"I couldn't comment on that. I'm sure you understand."

As they donned their forensics gear Murphy asked Ben why it was necessary to gown up.

"So we don't contaminate the crime scene with our own footprints, fingerprints, clothes fibers, DNA."

Rix chuckled. "Waste of time. We know who did this, and anyway it'll never go to trial, will it?"

Ben couldn't disagree but he simply said, "Well, let's keep up appearances. For the local police."

Ben was the first inside and he stopped in his tracks just beyond the threshold of the public bar. He hoped that his hesitation would be taken as a sign of wanting to absorb the big picture, but in reality he had to steady his nerves. He had seen death from violence before but not often and not on this scale. Work at MI5, particularly at his level, was a largely bloodless affair but this was not. It was a massacre of unfathomable proportion.

He gingerly stepped forward, minding the chief constable's admonition.

Finding non-bloody patches of floor to tread on was like playing hopscotch.

The six victims immediately visible were not simply murdered, and somehow the word butchered didn't seem appropriate either, since butchers are methodical and purposeful in their work. These men were slashed, stabbed, and even dismembered in the kind of apparently wanton frenzy that implied, what was it, he thought?—almost an orgiastic sadism.

Rix and Murphy looked at each other and nodded.

"Rover work," Rix said.

"No doubt about it," Murphy added.

"Please keep your voices down," Ben told them. "How can you be so sure?"

"They don't just take a man down," Rix said. "They destroy him. It's their way. They enjoy maiming, they enjoy eating, they enjoy striking fear into the hearts of ordinary Hellers like us."

"I see. Well have a look about if you will," Ben said, trying to keep a professional tone. "See if anything catches your eye which might give us an indication on where they might have gone from here."

The chief constable sidled over to Ben's side. "Those two seem a bit rough around the edges for MI5, I would have thought."

"We've expanded our recruitment efforts of late."

"Have you now?"

Ben watched as Rix called Murphy over behind the bar to have a look at the landlord. "I want to go to Holborn Avenue as soon as we're done here," Ben told the chief constable.

"Of course. We've got the house secured. Were you able to listen to the entirety of the 999 call?"

"I was."

"What did you make of it?"

"Which part?"

"The part where the bloke says that his brother's come back from the dead and tied him and his missus up."

"Ah yes, that part."

"Well?"

"The man sounded intoxicated," Ben said, peeling himself away.

They elected to walk the few blocks to Holborn Avenue to trace the path the rovers would have taken and to look for CCTV cameras positioned along the way. The chief constable promised to canvas shop owners along Sneinton Dale in the morning and confiscate all recordings.

Ben caught up with Murphy and Rix who were several paces ahead. "Anything catch your eye?" he asked.

"Yeah, they're well fed," Murphy said.

"How do you know that?"

"Because none of them were gnawed on," Murphy said, as if it was the most obvious of all forensic conclusions.

There was a police cordon in front of Harold and Maisey's house. Ben informed Plume that he wasn't needed for the interviews and the chief constable grumbled that he might as well go home to bed. Ben didn't disabuse him of the notion.

Harold was sitting on his threadbare sofa in the lounge nursing a cup of tea. Maisey sat beside him holding a cushion to her chest, lightly rocking back and forth. They looked up when Ben entered with the two Hellers.

Maisey clutched the cushion tighter and began to cry and Harold sniffed the air and said excitedly, "What? More of them? Get them away from us!"

Ben identified himself and ordered the two Nottinghamshire officers to leave the house and when they were gone he told Harold and Maisey that they were perfectly safe.

"The Security Service is quite concerned for your safety and welfare, Mr. and Mrs. Hathaway. These gentlemen are assisting us in our inquiries. They are not like the men you had in your house earlier."

"Do you believe us?" Harold asked excitedly. "The police told us I was drunk, which maybe I was, but it was still the truth."

"Yes, I believe you," Ben said. "May we sit?"

"Are you dead too?" Maisey asked Rix and Murphy.

"Do we look dead, luv?" Murphy said.

"No, but they didn't neither."

Ben wasn't interested in the conversation progressing along these lines. "We understand you believe that one of the men was your brother," he said.

"I don't believe it," Harold said. "It was him. It was Lucas. I don't know how it was him but it *was* him."

"What do you think, Mrs. Hathaway?"

"I wouldn't know, would I? He was dead before I ever met my Harold."

"I see. So I take it that the men didn't return here after visiting the Carpenter's Arms tonight."

"They did not," Harold said. "I undid my ropes and called the police. Lucas and the others didn't come back."

Rix couldn't seem to stand listening to Ben conducting the interview on his own. "How many men were with Lucas?"

"There was three others," Harold said.

"Did you catch their names?"

"Only one of them. They called him Talley."

Ben saw the impact the name had on the men. He let Rix carry on. "Did Lucas or these men talk about any women?"

Maisey had wanted to speak and she interrupted. "Was that the one who tried to have his way with me? Was that the one called Talley?"

"That was another one," Harold said.

"How come you didn't do nothing to stop him?" she yelled.

"I didn't know nothing about it, did I?" Harold said. "It was Lucas who busted it up to his credit."

"Were two women mentioned?" Murphy asked.

"No, no women," Harold said.

"How did they arrive here tonight?" Rix asked.

Harold shrugged. "By car I presume."

"You didn't see it?"

"That's what I presume means."

"Did they say where they'd been before they got here?"

"They didn't say and I didn't ask. Somehow the question of how my brother had returned from the dead was more on my mind than their bloody itinerary."

"And what did they offer by way of explanation?" Ben asked.

"They didn't offer nothing by way of explanation. Just that it was so."

"Did any of them say where they might go next?" Ben asked.

Harold and Maisey both shook their heads.

Ben thought for a moment and followed up with, "Would Lucas have any other relations or ex-wives or girlfriends he might want to contact after all these years?"

"Relations, no. He was never married. As to girlfriends, I wouldn't have a clue. I was still a lad in Nottingham when he was off to London."

Suddenly Maisey said something puzzling to Ben. "You know, we don't have much money."

Ben asked why she was mentioning this.

"Well, Harold and I was talking quietly amongst ourselves a short while ago that we could probably make a lot of money selling our stories to *The Sun* about how his dead brother come and visited us."

"I see. Well, it's a matter of national security that you not do so. I'm sure you're both very patriotic individuals."

"Sure we are," Maisey said. "Queen and country and all that. But we really don't have much money."

Ben stood up and the Hellers followed suit. "I think I can give you the assurances of Her Majesty's Government," Ben said, "that your cooperation and your silence on this sensitive matter would entitle you to a cash award."

Harold started to protest. "We don't need no government ..."

"Shut up, Harold. You wasn't nearly violated tonight by a dead man. We'd be most grateful to get the cash."

On the street, just beyond the incident tape, Ben motioned Rix over and noticed with a tinge of alarm that Murphy had wandered off. A policeman was doing a roll-up and Murphy was bumming some tobacco and papers off the curious man. Before the officer could ask where Murphy was from, Ben collared him and led him off, and as they walked, Murphy happily rolled a cigarette one-handed, as if he'd never stopped.

"Still got it," Murphy said proudly. "They wouldn't give me any in Dartford. No smoking policy or some such bollocks." He called over to the policeman for a light and a box of matches flew through the air. When he inhaled the first drag pure pleasure overcame him and he closed his eyes. "So much better than sex," he said.

"Awfully glad to hear it," Ben said. "More importantly, we have no idea where your rovers have gone. I would think it would take the better part of eight hours to assemble all the CCTV data and see if we can identify them leaving the pub and the number plate of a car they may be driving. By then they will be far afield and possibly in another vehicle. So our best bet is you. Where do you think they might be heading next?"

Murphy was too preoccupied with nicotine to answer. Rix said, "From what I hear, Talley's an ancient cunt, hundreds of years removed from this world. I couldn't say about the other two. Don't know who they are. Then there's Hathaway. Come to think of it, he had a girlfriend who came from Suffolk, didn't he, Murph?"

Murphy shrugged and blew a perfect smoke ring, then launched another smaller ring through it, followed by a "did you see that?"

"She was always saying that she was going to go back and live in her parents' pretty little cottage one day and leave London in the rear view mirror."

"Which village?" Ben asked.

"I think it was called Hoxne," Rix said.

Murphy smiled and blew another ring. "Yeah, that's my recollection too," he said.

"What was her name?" Ben asked pulling out a small pad from his jacket pocket.

"Janice," Rix said. "I can't recall her last name. How about you, Murph?"

"Your memory's better than mine. I thought it was Jane."

"No, it was Janice."

"Do you remember her address?" Ben asked.

Rix said, "No, but she used to keep a picture of that cottage on a corkboard in her kitchen and I used to see it every time I went in there for a beer. I'd remember it if I saw it."

"Then I suppose we're going to Suffolk," Ben said.

Murphy stubbed out the spent roll-up. "We're with you, Benjamin, as long as we stop at a tobacconist along the way."

The morning haze hadn't burned off yet but the promise of sunshine thrilled them. Before leaving the car they liberally splashed on stolen cologne. On the sidewalk they furtively glanced at passersby for any reaction.

"I think we're good," Christine said after a while.

"You sure you remember where he lived?" Molly asked.

"Not the address but the place. It doesn't look so different. It was near where Peter Sellers was born. Wonder if Gareth's still alive?"

They were in Southsea, only half a mile from the seaside. The morning air held seagulls and the promise of walks on the beach. Christine thought back on her days here, pushing a pram down to Clarence Pier and watching her toddler play with a bucket and spade while she sat on a towel curling her toes in the sand.

Passing the Sellers Coffee House Molly said she'd die for a coffee, setting the two of them into a refreshing spasm of giggles. They carried on, pounding the pavement until Christine satisfied herself that Nightingale Road was the right street.

Surveying the rows of tall, cream-colored terraced houses with bay windows, Molly said that it seemed awfully posh.

"It wasn't his money," Christine said. "It was his dad's. He moved in with the old bastard after we split."

"He might not be here any more."

"If he's still alive he'll still be here provided he was left with enough inheritance to pay the rates." She stopped and looked up and down at one of the row houses. "This is it."

There were a few letters stuffed into the mail slot. She pulled them out.

"Told you. This is Gareth's house."

"Come on then," Molly urged. "I need to use the loo. Only advantage that Down has. You can go anywhere."

Christine steeled herself. Gareth would be well into his seventies. Would she even recognize him? Would he recognize her? What would she say to him? How could she not have rehearsed what she'd say?

She forced her finger against the bell and waited. She rang again and heard a muffled "I'm coming," and after a long pause the door opened and an elderly man, smaller than the man she remembered but with the same watery blue eyes and beakish nose stared at her for an exceedingly long time without speaking.

She felt compelled to break the silence. "Gareth. It *is* me."

His dry lips moved. Nothing came out. Molly stepped out from behind Christine. She'd been friendly with Christine when Gareth was still her husband. She'd been the one who introduced her to Murph's best mate, Colin Rix, and Gareth had hated her for it.

"Yeah, it's me as well," Molly said. "Couple of bad pennies, eh?"

The words finally came out. "I'm sorry, I don't understand."

"'Course you don't," Christine said. "Can we come in?"

"No!" he said, getting agitated. "I mean, I don't understand. What's happening to me? Have I died? Did I just die?"

"You're not dead, Gareth. Calm yourself or you will be ill. Please let us in and we'll explain everything. Nothing bad's going to happen to you."

He backed away from the door and let them in. The ordinariness of showing Molly where the bathroom was located seemed to settle his nerves. He and Christine waited in the hall without saying anything. When Molly emerged he led them to the lounge but Christine asked if they could go to the kitchen instead.

"I'll make some tea," she said. She almost laughed out loud at the simple statement. In Hell, making a cup of tea was like trying to fly by flapping your arms: impossible.

She remembered her father-in-law's kitchen and when she went to the cupboard where the tea bags used to be kept, there they were, down to the same brand. Gareth steadied himself with a liver-spotted hand on a chair, watching her fill an electric kettle.

"Sit down, Gareth. It's okay."

"You've got biscuits, I hope," Molly said.

He sat on a cane-backed chair and pointed to one of the cupboards. Molly came back to the table beaming and holding a pack of biscuits.

"Squashed fly. My favorite. This is going to be marvelous."

Gareth could only stare while Christine served the tea. The two women gulped them down as if they were mugs of cold water on a hot day and Molly ate one biscuit after another, oohing and ahhing at the taste of each raisin.

Christine was pouring more hot water onto new tea bags when Gareth lost it.

He pounded the table with a clenched fist and shouted, "Who the hell are you?"

"You know who we are, Gareth," Christine said.

"You died," he croaked.

"We did," she said gently. "We were murdered."

"You got what you deserved," he muttered before realizing the absurdity of the conversation and getting angry again. "Stop it! You're imposters trying to pull a fast one on an old man. If you don't leave I'm calling the police."

"Gareth, you can ask me anything. Ask me something that no one else could ever know, no one but me."

His pale blue eyes became watery. "Tell me what the last thing Christine ever said to me."

The moment flooded into her mind and overwhelmed her with its vividness. She was certain she hadn't thought about it for thirty years. The two of them were in their bedroom in London. She was throwing her clothes into a bag and he was sitting on the bed, crying. She had zippered the bag and lugged it off the bed, holding it the crooked way a small woman manages a heavy suitcase.

She spoke the exact words, "Tell Gavin his mummy will always love him," then began to sob.

Gareth blinked at his own tears and in an instant, Molly joined in, until the three of them had wet faces.

"Christine," he whispered. "How?"

"There's more than just this world of ours, Gareth. The Bible was right. I don't know if there's a Heaven but I'm here to tell you, there is a Hell."

Gareth was asleep in his chair. Molly had dozed off on the sofa. Christine was sleepy but she fought the urge, preferring to experience the evening as long as she could, for who knew when this world might disappear? She opened a cabinet and ran her fingers over Gareth's mother's tarnished silver and his father's collection of Toby jugs. One of the faces reminded her ever so slightly of Jason's and she pictured him sitting in their awful hut in Ockendon grieving over her disappearance. He'd be thinking the rovers got her. He'd remember her for a hundred years, maybe longer but would he remember her forever? She shook him from her mind, not because she didn't miss him but because he had always told her since they arrived in Hell that if anything happened to him, she had to do whatever she needed to do to keep herself intact. You will not wind up in a rotting room, he'd say. You will stay whole. Far better to be a lord's concubine than spend eternity in a rotting room. Now she found herself somewhere far different and far better than any scenario Jason might have imagined but the danger was no less acute. She still had to survive.

Towards the end of her long conversation with Gareth, he had asked her with a weariness which had reduced his voice to a sigh, what she intended to do.

"Do?" she had asked. "I want to feel safe. I want to sleep in a real bed. I want to eat a steak. I want a million cups of tea. I don't want to go back there."

"But where will you go? You can't stay here."

She had wished he hadn't said that. She had wished he'd been able to forgive her for leaving him for another man, for abandoning her ten-year-old son to start another life with lusty and virile Jason Rix. But why should he? He was an old bitter man with curdled memories. It probably gave him some satisfaction that she had received the ultimate punishment for the life she chose.

She turned to the sideboard. She had seen there was a collection of framed photos. She hadn't been ready to face them but now she set her jaw and drew closer. Her eyes darted from one photo of her son to another, taking in an entire disjointed childhood and manhood in mere seconds. Then all of a sudden, her handsome young man had a pretty woman by his side and then a baby boy and then, in the last photo she saw before turning away in joy and despair, a baby girl.

Gareth woke at the sound of her blowing her nose into a bathroom tissue.

"Where does Gavin live?" she asked.

"Portsmouth," he said.

"I want to see him."

Gareth had reluctantly, very reluctantly agreed. The wait was agonizing. Christine did her best to make herself presentable while Molly gobbled up everything sweet in the kitchen. When the doorbell finally rang Christine hurriedly applied a fresh coat of cologne and spritzed Molly as an afterthought.

From the sitting room she heard a man ask, "What was so important I had to drop everything, Dad? You're not sick, are you?"

Gareth's voice was stilted. "I'm not sick. There's someone who wants to see you."

"Who?"

"She's in the lounge."

A man with a close-cropped beard came in. The ten-year-old boy she remembered was there in the forty-year-old face looking back at her. He was a larger, more robust man than his dad, more like Christine's own father.

He glanced at Molly on the sofa, her fingers frosted with powdered sugar, and said hello to Christine.

"I'm Gavin. You wanted to see me?"

She struggled with her composure. "Yes. I'm a friend of your dad's. I wanted to meet his son."

"Oh yeah? What's your name?"

She hesitated too long to come up with, "Jane."

Gavin sniffed the air, sending her heart racing. "Hello Jane. You ladies do like your perfume."

Molly found that funny, cackled a few times, then shut up.

"How do you know dad then?"

"I used to live in the area."

He seemed to study her face. "Did we ever meet?"

"When you were very young, Gavin. I'm sure you don't remember."

"I've got to say, you look familiar."

Gareth sat on his chair and said emphatically, "You were too young."

"If I was too young, how old was she? We look about the same age. How old are you, Jane, if you don't mind me asking?"

"Older than I look." She was desperate to change the subject. "Gareth, why don't I put the kettle on?"

When she came back into the lounge with a tray, Gavin wasn't there.

"Where'd he go?" she asked.

"He's upstairs. I don't know why," Gareth said, working into a state. "I knew this was a terrible idea. You should leave. I'll tell him you had to leave. I wish you hadn't come. I'm confused by all of this. It's not right. You shouldn't have come."

"It's okay, Gareth," she said. "I saw him. It was good. He looks a fine man. I'll say goodbye and we'll go."

"I don't want to go," Molly said, slurping her tea.

There were heavy footsteps coming down the stairs and Gavin came back in. He was holding an old scrapbook open to a page of photographs.

He put the book in front of Christine's face and said, "Tell me how it is that you look exactly like the mother who walked out on me when I was ten? Tell me that, Jane."

18

Over a fortnight had passed since the decisive battles in the outskirts of Paris that had laid the table for the victory of the combined Italian and French forces over the armies of Brittania, Germania, and Russia. Skirmishes had continued on a daily basis but the great war had passed into history and no one in the know doubted that John Camp's weapons were pivotal to the outcome. His percussion grenades had wreaked havoc among King Henry's forces to the west of Paris and his La Hitte Cannon had pulverized the German and Russian armies to the east.

In the aftermath, Henry had limped back to Brittania in a controlled retreat, Barbarossa had decamped for his castle lair in Marksburg, and Stalin had followed him there for consultations. Francia was peaceful again.

The Italians remained in Paris, ostensibly guests of King Maximilien, though in truth he had not proffered a formal invitation. He complained daily to the Duke of Orleans and his principal minister, Guy Forneau that he would have preferred for King Giuseppe to depart for Rome.

"I don't trust him, Forneau," the king had said. "And he is only a soldier, a commoner who has no appreciation for what is required to be a monarch."

Forneau had ground his teeth at the remark. Had Robespierre forgotten his own common blood? Who was he to disparage a man such as Giuseppe Garibaldi whose blood may have been common but whose heart was noble?

"Your Majesty will surely acknowledge that without the help of the

Italians, Barbarossa would now be sitting on your throne. Besides, Garibaldi is recovering from his battle wound and cannot easily travel such great distances."

"When he has sufficiently recovered, we will cordially see him off," the king had said. "There is room in Francia for but one king."

Robespierre's palace was grand enough that the Italian party had their own wing far removed from Maximilien's private chambers and halls. Forneau had rather short legs and an asthmatic constitution so the long walks shuttling between the two wings were taxing. On this night he arrived in Garibaldi's room to find Maximilien's physician attending to the Italian's thigh wound. He was a twentieth-century doctor who had murdered a hospital administrator for having him struck off for attending to patients while drunk. In Hell, his love affair with the grape continued. Forneau smelled wine on his breath and hovered nearby to make sure that Garibaldi was receiving competent care.

"The wound is clean, quite clean," the doctor told Garibaldi in their mutual tongue of English. "The time of danger has passed."

He clumsily tried to re-wrap the bandage but Caravaggio elbowed him aside and re-did the job perfectly, completing it with an elegant bow.

"Good night, doctor," the artist said with a derisive wave. "Don't get lost on your way home."

Forneau waited for the doctor to stumble off before saying anything. Antonio and Simon who were playing cards at a small table across the room, threw their hands down and joined the men at Garibaldi's bedside.

"I believe you are healing despite this doctor's efforts," Forneau said.

Garibaldi smiled and swung his legs off the bed. "In my day, the nurses would say that God is watching over you. With neither God nor the physician to credit, I would say that I'm simply fortunate. How is Robespierre? I haven't seen him in a good while."

"He grows restless over your presence," Forneau said.

"He's not the only one who's restless," Simon grumbled. "What are we still doing here? If you ask me we should have followed the Ruskies and the Huns and finished them off."

"I agree with him," Antonio said, pleasing Simon no end. "We removed the hook and set the fish free. We should have eaten it."

Garibaldi reached for the cane Caravaggio had carved for him and used it to hobble to a chair. "To extend Antonio's analogy further," he said, "I would say that if we had attempted to eat the fish, the bones would have lodged in our throats. We were fortunate to prevail but if we had extended our lines to make chase to Germania then we might have lost all we gained. This game of ours will be won by consolidation. Who would have imagined, only a month ago that we would have succeeded in toppling that monster, Cesare Borgia, and taking up peaceful residence in King Maximilien's palace?"

"Yes, I agree," Forneau nodded. "Francia is the next pearl in your necklace."

"*Our* necklace, Guy," Garibaldi said. "Well, we mocked the doctor well enough for drinking wine but now I would like some too."

Simon poured and they pulled chairs into a circle.

"Now that you are out of danger," Forneau said, "I believe we may proceed with the next step in our plan."

"Do you think Orleans has the backbone?" Garibaldi asked.

"On his own, no. But with the assurance of my support, I believe so. Recall that he is the one who made the proposal to me. He wishes to wear the crown so badly I imagine he dreams of it and is disappointed in the morning when he finds his head unadorned."

"Can we control the events which will follow?" Antonio asked.

"Nothing is certain, but I believe so," Forneau answered. "It would be far too dangerous for me to poll the nobles at court but I believe that they are no better disposed to Orleans than they are to the king. They chafe under cruel and capricious rule."

"Orleans would be a tyrant too if he had the chance," Caravaggio snapped.

"You are not wrong, my friend," Forneau said. "Any of the nobles would, in time, become as bad a tyrant as Robespierre."

"How do you know I won't too?" Garibaldi said under his breath.

"Sorry, what?" Simon asked.

He repeated himself loudly.

"Because we know you," Antonio responded, seemingly annoyed that their leader would doubt his own virtues.

"Don't be so sure," Garibaldi said. "You must be ever vigilant, even with me. If I become a tyrant I expect you good men to act, swiftly and surely."

Simon got up to refill his glass and said lightly, "Well, I'm optimistic. You've been king for a month now, Giuseppe, and you haven't fucked up yet."

Forneau had a cryptic note sent to the Duke of Orleans and waited for a response. It came quickly with a single word written on a card delivered on a silver tray: Come. Forneau wondered why the ink was smudged.

When he arrived at the duke's rooms, one of his retainers escorted Forneau inside. Orleans was soaking in a tub which explained the smudge. He squinted and called for his thick spectacles then stood, exposing his unimpressive manhood, before servants produced a towel and a robe. Orleans flopped onto a divan and dismissed all of his attendants.

"What is it you want?" Orleans asked, his long, wet hair dripping on the floorboards. "Your message was opaque."

"It is not so much what I want, my good duke. It is what you desire."

Orleans seemed to understand. "I see," he said, his mood brightening. "Have you been reflecting on my proposal?"

"I have."

"And what have you concluded?"

"I believe the time to strike is upon us."

"Really? With the Italians here? Would it not be better to wait until they have departed?"

"Their presence could work to our advantage."

"How so? Is it not a complication? They have a successful alliance with Robespierre. I would be a new actor upon the stage."

Forneau nodded earnestly. "You forget that Garibaldi is also, as you so aptly put it, a new actor upon the stage. He is open to new circumstances. And I know from speaking with his intimates that he thinks poorly of our king. In fact, I am told in private he calls him a foolish peacock of a man."

"He is a foolish peacock, is he not?" Orleans laughed.

"There is more," Forneau said.

"Yes?"

"Garibaldi has also told his people that he has immense respect for you as a military commander and thinks you would make a far more substantial and reliable ally for his country."

Orleans was now too excited to contain himself. He got up from his chair and strutted around the room, his robe flapping open.

"When?" he asked. "When should we do the deed?"

"The king will announce a grand banquet to be held tomorrow night for his nobles and the Italians. At that banquet he will congratulate King Giuseppe on his recovery and wish him well on his return to Italia."

"In other words, bugger off, Giuseppe. Back to Rome and thank you very much."

"That is the idea. I believe you would be making a bold statement to our nobles and our Italian allies to strike a blow at this very banquet. Think of it, by tomorrow night, you would be sleeping in the king's bed, no, your new bed."

"And what would you require of me for your fealty?" Orleans asked.

"Nothing more than my service as loyal councilor to your person."

"Nothing else? Not even a heavy purse of gold and a bevy of fetching slaves?"

Forneau let his mouth crack into a smile. "Well, perhaps a small purse and one or two pleasant wenches."

The royal banquet was a tense affair with a palpable sense of portent in the air. The Italians knew what was coming, Forneau knew, and so did Orleans. Perhaps Orleans had even told a few confidants. The one man who was assuredly oblivious was Robespierre who was in a positively giddy mood, basking in the defeat of indomitable enemies and buoyed by the imminent departure of the Italians. He ate and drank with abandon and laughed riotously at his own jokes and those of sycophantic nobles at his table.

Seated to his right was Garibaldi and to his left Orleans. Garibaldi had no appetite. He always ate sparingly before a battle and tonight was no exception. There would be a battle—whether it would be a terrible and bloody one was an open question. The French nobility, these men surrounding them throughout the great hall, all of them arrogant, preening, drinking, whoring—they would have to be placated or destroyed. If they were to be placated, his words would be the instrument. He drank his wine in tiny sips to keep his head clear.

Servants flooded the hall with groaning platters of some sort of charred meats. Robespierre suddenly rose, choosing this moment to address the gathering. He looked prissy with his tight, powder blue garments and oiled, highly coiffed white hair. His voice was high-pitched, more like a woman's.

As the king was about to begin his remarks, Garibaldi saw Orleans trying to make eye contact, as if seeking a dose of courage for what he was about to do. The old Italian avoided his eyes and instead sought out Antonio and Simon at a nearby table. He nodded at them. They rudely and loudly declared that they had to take a piss, and off they went, leaving the hall together.

If Robespierre was offended by the slight, he failed to let it register on his jovial, sweating face. "My friends, my allies, over the past fortnight we have not failed to celebrate our great victory over not one, not two, but three formidable enemies, the English dogs, the German wolves, and the Russian bears. But on this night, the celebration reaches a crescendo and my kitchens have prepared a special festive course, platters of roasted dogs, wolves, and bears!"

The French nobles erupted in applause while the Italians had a more muted response.

"You must tell me which you enjoy the most," the king continued. "Of course, a great victory oft requires a great ally and we now have such an ally in the Kingdom of Italia, our friends to the south. We are joyful that their courageous new monarch, King Giuseppe, has fully recovered from his battle wound but saddened that he must now return to his own lands. We will miss him greatly. To remember his time in Francia, we will be loading his wagons with barrels of our finest wines and perhaps we may expect in return barrels of the king's finest olive oil."

"Of course," Garibaldi replied loudly. "You may count on it."

As applause rang out Garibaldi saw Orleans slide his chair back.

Robespierre had a sip of wine and continued, "As much as you love your king, I am sure you will want me to keep my speech short so you may …"

Orleans stood and caught the king's startled gaze.

"Yes, you will keep it short!" Orleans shouted, plunging a dagger into the king's throat with a sharp, upward move.

All in the hall rose and gasped as the king's plate filled with blood.

Robespierre's eyes were wild. He tried to speak but was unable. Instinctively he clasped his hands to his throat to stop the bleeding but it was a futile gesture. But as his legs were about to give out his countenance changed and he sought out Orleans' face. His rage seemed to soften and become a sadness of sorts and his lips formed two syllables: *pour quoi?*

"Why?" Orleans bellowed to the bleeding king who had slumped back to his chair. "Why? Because you are weak and I am strong. Because I have waited for this moment for years, decades, centuries. Because I am the better man to be king and my reign will be …"

"A very short one," Simon shouted as he and Antonio appeared from behind the royal table.

Antonio had a sword he had stashed in a serving room and he swung it hard and high, grunting with effort as the blade sliced through skin, muscle, ligaments, and finally the duke's vertebrae and spinal cord. With a geyser of blood Orleans's head fell from his shoulders and thudded onto the floor.

Robespierre's eyes followed the head as it rolled away and then he pitched forward onto his dinner plate.

The French nobility called out in rage and began ranting at the Italians. Many drew their weapons and the Italian contingent reached for theirs too but was ordered to stand down by Garibaldi. Even Antonio threw down his bloody sword and stood beside Simon, arms folded, chin out. It was then that Forneau, who had been quietly seated halfway down the royal table, rose up and lifted his arms.

"My fellow countrymen! Please be calm! Please be serene! You must listen to me. You all know me and I know you. Sit and let me speak to you. I beg of you."

The astonished crowd numbly obeyed but none put away their blades and pistols.

"I am sure that King Maximilien and the Duke of Orleans can still hear me and that is good. We have all long suffered under the cruel and capricious yoke of Robespierre and Orleans would have been no better, perhaps worse. It is high time we had a ruler who was a better man, a man who could help us rise higher, a man who could bring a modicum of goodness to this evil existence to which we have been condemned."

The Duke of Burgundy, seated near to Forneau called out, "And you? You, Forneau? A bureaucrat? You believe you are that man?"

Forneau quickly extinguished the catcalls by raising his arms again and saying, "To this I say, no! No, I am not this man."

Someone cried, "Then who?"

Forneau walked behind Garibaldi and said, "This. This is the man."

More than one yelled that he was an Italian. Had Forneau forgotten this was Francia?

Garibaldi rose, concealing his aches and pains with a placid expression. "My friends, you are French. I am Italian. The differences we possess in language, culture, and heritage might have been worthy of discussion, even war during our earthly days but they seem so terribly small in our current situation. We are no longer divided by petty differences over religious practices, over marriages and succession, over family dominance. All these things have been washed away by the consequences of our wickedness. We can continue to act with wickedness and selfishness, as most of us have acted for decades and centuries, or we can explore a different path."

"What path?" Burgundy demanded.

Garibaldi's voice gave out, perhaps from exertion, perhaps from emotion. People in the hall had to lean forward and strain to hear his words. "For all my days in Hell," he said, "I have lamented not the deed that condemned me here, for there is nothing to be done about the past. I have lamented the life we live here and I have always asked, is there a better way? Is there a way to make this place more humane, not only for the likes of us who are privileged to live in palaces and fine houses and to have enough food to eat and wine to drink, but to all the wretches of Hell? Is there a way to make our existence less brutish? Is there a way to bring a ray of hope into our gray skies? Is there a way for men and women to live in less fear?"

A woman, one of the many courtesans in the palace, began to weep openly, and soon others joined her, and their sobs became the orchestra for the rest of his speech.

"And how do you intend to accomplish this lofty goal of yours, my dear Giuseppe?" Burgundy said, his tongue dripping acid. "My apologies. King Giuseppe. I almost forgot you have been king for an entire month."

Garibaldi paused for a long while, an uncomfortably long while, and the hall grew quieter. Even the sobbing became softer. "I don't know," he said.

"You don't know?" Burgundy said with a mocking tone.

"I'd be a fool to say I knew with any certainty how to achieve this," the Italian replied. "But here are my ideas: to start, we have to eliminate each and every tyrant who calls himself a king, men like Borgia and Robespierre who grew intoxicated with their own power. We need fresh voices."

"Like yours?" a noble asked.

"Yes, like mine, as imperfect as I am. We need to take down all the kings and tyrants who stand in our way. I am a soldier. I understand that force is often required to change a world, especially this world. But when this is done, and it will not happen in one year, ten years, maybe even a hundred years, then we can end our ceaseless wars and conquests and turn inwards to building a future with less fear, wiping out all rovers from the face of Hell, adding a touch of humanity to rotting rooms, treating women as equal beings, not as property, building workshops and factories, and teaching skills to men and women for the betterment of all people. We will never have children here but that doesn't mean we don't have to think about the future and plan for better days to come."

His throat was dry. He reached for his wine glass and by the time it left his lips something happened. It started as two clapping hands. Then there were four, then a dozen and soon, the entire hall erupted in applause and shouts until even the Duke of Burgundy joined in, reluctantly at first, then enthusiastically.

Forneau seized the moment to shout at the top of his lungs, "I proclaim this man, this extraordinary man, Giuseppe Garibaldi, king of a united and proud Francia-Italia empire!"

Garibaldi felt a tear running down his face. He brushed it away and gestured for Forneau's ear.

"What do you think old Maximilien is thinking about all this?" he whispered through the din.

Forneau smiled. "We shall never hear his opinion of your fine words but I will find him a most humane rotting room. I will even have it decorated with some of his favorite ornaments."

The festivities lasted but a single day. Garibaldi had convened a war council with his Italian generals and French nobles to consider a strategy for dealing with the threat of the Russians and Germans regrouping for a counter-attack. Burgundy, a pomposity of a man, had begun maneuvering the previous night and Garibaldi had decided it would be necessary to extend additional rank and consideration to keep his allegiance. So he became Grand Duke Godfrey of Burgundy and received one of Robespierre's ornate palaces near Paris as compensation. Other nobles would have to be satisfied as well in one way or another but Garibaldi asked Forneau, as his Lord Regent, to sort out all the tiresome details.

Word came to the council room that a rider had arrived from Italia with a need to see King Giuseppe immediately. Garibaldi left the chamber and a few minutes later Antonio, Simon, and Caravaggio were called to join him.

Garibaldi paced while the exhausted messenger, too weak to stand, sat and lifted a vessel of ale to his parched lips.

Antonio saw his master's bleak look and asked what was happening.

"This good man has ridden day and night for nearly three weeks to deliver an urgent and troubling message. We have a problem, gentlemen, a very large problem."

"What problem?" Caravaggio asked.

"The Macedonian has invaded Italia."

"The bastard," Antonio uttered. "Where is he? How many men?"

"Tell them what you told me," Garibaldi urged the messenger.

The man lifted his heavy head. His eyes were deeply sunken, his voice little more than a whisper. "Their ships landed near Lecce. There were many, many soldiers, thousands I was told and hundreds of horses. They were marching toward Napoli when I was sent by the Duke of Amalfi to warn you. Surely their intention was Roma but I cannot say whether they have succeeded."

"Caterina," Antonio gasped. Since toppling Cesare Borgia, Antonio had not ceased talking about Borgia's beautiful queen, Caterina Sforza.

"Lovesick fool," Simon mumbled to himself.

"What did you say?" Antonio challenged.

"I said you're a lovesick fool."

"Lovesick? Perhaps. A fool? No. I do not know if she will ever be mine but I know with certainty that she is in danger. Master, let me return to Italia to help mount a defense against these invaders."

Garibaldi nodded but held up a finger to signify he needed to think. He walked the perimeter of the reception room three times before speaking. "Nothing important is ever easy but our task is difficult indeed. We were fortunate to defeat the Germans and the Russians. Without the help of John Camp, we may not have succeeded. He is gone now. We are still here. But the Germans and the Russians have not gone to sleep. They will surely fight another day and next time, well, we may not be so lucky. We were fortunate to swiftly dispatch Maximilien and make this pact with Francia. But pacts may form and pacts may dissolve. This one will take care and feeding. Now we have another challenge, perhaps the greatest. Italia's old adversary has pounced while we are far from home. We must fight a war on many fronts. I wish I were a younger man. So much to do, so much ..."

Antonio pressed him for an answer to his request.

"Yes, Antonio. You may leave us and return to Roma. Take one thousand men. Mobilize an army as you sweep south across Italia. Defeat the Macedonian."

"This will surely leave us in a weakened position here," Caravaggio said.

"Yes," Garibaldi said. "This is why we must seek another ally."

"Who?" Simon asked.

"One who is no friend of the Germans and the Russians. One who despises the English and will surely be glad we sent Henry back across the channel with his tail between his legs. We must make a pact with Pedro. We need an alliance with the Iberians."

Brian's mantra was never lose sight of land. The only way we'll get lost and therefore buggered, he said, is if we lose sight of land. Beyond that, there was the small matter of provisions. They had set sail with only enough food and water for several days and they needed to beach the boat periodically to forage on the shore.

For a week, they kept to plan, sailing south through the channel, hugging the coast of Francia. They made their first landfall along the beaches of Normandy one evening and had the great luck to happen upon a small settlement of lightly armed and non-bellicose fishermen, an ancient tribe, who sniffed and stared but gave them no trouble when they offered a sword in exchange for a barrel of rainwater and a basket of dried fish. The barter was accomplished with some artful pointing without a shred of common language.

The plan went awry past Jersey when a storm hit at night, blowing their barge out to sea. The flat-bottomed vessel was ill equipped for the deep swells and had it not been for Brian's excellent seamanship they would not have survived the ordeal.

It was still dark when the seas calmed. Seasick but happy to be alive, they slept for a while in the comfort of a quiet ocean, and then awoke at first light to face their predicament.

Trevor chewed on a piece of fish and looked around. The sky and water were identical shades of grayish blue. "Remember the thing about losing sight of land?" Trevor asked.

"I remember it because I said it, mate," Brian said. "We are well and truly buggered, but fear not, we're not permanently buggered. Mind you, it would be grand if we had a compass, which we don't, or could see the position of the sun, which we can't."

"I once saw something about magnetizing a needle and floating it on a leaf," Trevor said, helpfully, spitting out a fishbone.

"Trouble is," Brian said, "we'd need a needle or a piece of wire, which we don't have. Now, if we did, you could rub the heck out of said needle or wire with a piece of silk or wool and said needle or wire would be magnetized. But we still wouldn't know which way was north and which way was south, absent a handy glimpse of the sun. All we'd have is a north-south line. Not entirely useless but not hugely useful. No, my young friend, we need to use our eyes and our ears to get our arses out of this sling. Look for birds, young Trevor, and listen for the roar of the surf."

For the next few hours they watched the skies for gulls. Finally, Trevor spotted one.

"Which way's the damned thing heading?" he asked, spinning around the deck until he was dizzy.

"Seems to be going in circles, much like yourself," Brian said. "He's not a particularly helpful creature. We need less confused ones."

In time they saw three birds heading in a reasonably straight line.

"You think we should follow that lot?" Brian asked, raising the sail.

"Absolutely."

"No. We. Should. Not," Brian said poking Trevor in the chest each time for emphasis. "At dawn seabirds fly away from land looking for food.

At dusk they fly toward land to roost for the night. Lesson over. Let's sail in the opposite direction and keep your ears pricked for the surf. Let's get ourselves un-lost."

Queen Matilda's ship made landfall in the low provinces of Francia. Sam and Belle had found the notion of river and channel crossings a great adventure and they had strained at Delia's grasping hands as they disembarked on the gangplank. Delia had never been a fan of any boat smaller than the Queen Mary and her stomach still churned with nausea for hours after landfall. The covered wagons the Earl of Southampton had procured for the queen's party at Ostend were not to her usual royal standards but time was of the essence and he did the best he could under the extraordinary circumstances. Southampton was the queen's man; he had been so for well over a hundred years. But no one in Brittania served only the queen. His neck belonged to Henry and by being pressed into this last-minute flight by Matilda, Southampton feared that his long run of good fortune might be coming to an end. For all he knew, the king had dispatched men to find his errant queen and bring her to yoke. He doubted Henry would ever allow him to return to court and he had whiled away the sea passage wondering if he had the facility to learn French.

The lowlands of Europa had changed hands countless times between Francia and Germania. For the last two centuries Francia had managed to hold onto them at the cost of an expensive garrison of troops in the key border towns of Liège and Bastogne and by keeping the bribes flowing to the Duke of Luxembourg. Luxembourg hated the Germans and the French equally but feared King Frederick and the Germans more, so he had remained in King Maximilien's camp.

Matilda rode in her own carriage with some of her ladies and her strongbox which was laden with gold, silver, and gemstones. Southampton had kitted out her carriage with cushions and fabrics from her barge but it was still a plebeian affair and she complained bitterly whenever the duke rode alongside. Delia and the children followed in their own small carriage that bounced and rolled worse than the ship, causing Delia prolonged misery. A wagon train of servants and cooks snaked along the open countryside accompanied by over two dozen men at arms, riding newly-purchased horses.

The children spent their time looking out the window at the horses, nominating this one, then that one, their favorite.

"I like the brown one," Belle said, prodding Sam to look.

"I see three brown ones," Sam said.

"*That* one!" she insisted, pointing.

"I don't like that one at all," Sam replied, becoming restive.

"What about that yellow one?" Belle asked, poking his arm.

"I don't want to play anymore," he moaned.

"But I do!" she screamed in a piercing high pitch, hurting Sam's ears and triggering a punch to her leg.

"Children, stop it, please," Delia begged.

Belle dissolved into tears and started calling for her mother. Before long, Sam was joining the refrain.

"We'll be seeing your mummy soon, children. Please, please, please don't cry." But in saying this, Delia lost control of her own emotions and turned away from them to stare at the bleak countryside. Off to one side, a forest loomed, so dark and dense it looked like a black curtain. She wondered what horrors lurked in those woods.

Then she too began to cry.

Inside that forest a column of men rode their horses in single file along a narrow path crisscrossed with thick roots. At their lead was the one-eyed, bowlegged brute, the ancient Frankish king who no longer had a kingdom, but who roamed and plundered the countryside, wielding his thick-handled axe.

Clovis watched Matilda's wagon train from afar as it winked in and out through the gaps in the trees.

He didn't know who rode inside the wagons but judging from the heavy guard, they were bound to be important and they were bound to have treasure he wanted and treasure he would most certainly come to possess.

19

The morning sun was bright and cheerful but the ruddy-faced farmer was not happy. He cursed at the two police constables from Eye who had the gall to drive onto his farmland, flag his tractor down, and halt his planting. After they told him what they wanted he became livid, stamping his feet and threatening to call his local MP.

"You do not have my permission to have a helicopter put down on my farm!" he yelled. "Where are we, the Soviet Union? This is private property, for God's sake."

The younger officer knew the man's family. "Sorry, Gerald," he said. "It's a rotten thing to ask, but the way the call came to us, it's not a request. Some blokes from London, MI5 is what we hear, have urgent business in the village and this is the closest place to land, so they've determined."

"Think of it as your patriotic duty," the older officer added.

"Patriotic duty?" the farmer fumed. "I'll tell you what's patriotic duty. It's reminding yahoos like you and our pathetic government that it's planting season and that driving around my land and landing helicopters will trample and scatter my seeds. How stupid are you fellows, anyways?"

But it was settled and the farmer could only pull out his mobile phone and call his wife because she, at least, would be sympathetic to his plight.

The helicopter came into sight flying from the west. The pilot circled once then put his skids down on the rich soil a short distance from the police car. The farmer retreated to the cab of his tractor to protect his eyes from the rotor wash and emerged to challenge the men who were exiting.

Ben and two of his agents got out first followed my Murphy and Rix.

"Ben Wellington, Security Service," Ben said to the older policeman. "Thank you for your assistance."

"You're most welcome. I'm Constable Kent."

The farmer was yelling at them but the younger officer ordered him back.

"He seems angry," Ben said.

"Planting season," Kent said.

"I see. Well, hopefully we won't inconvenience him for long. I wonder if you could keep my pilot company until we return."

The policeman gave the Hellers a sidelong glance and said to Ben, "Where are you off to, if I might ask?"

"Not far. Low Street."

"Might we be of assistance with an address or a name?"

"Thank you, no. We'll be fine."

"We've never had the Security Service on this patch before," the constable said.

"Haven't you?" Ben said, brushing past. "First time for everything."

They emerged from the field and walked down a small lane that ended on Low Street across from The Swan, the only pub in the village of Hoxne. Rix turned to the right and with hands on hips looked up the street while Murphy lit a roll-up. The village had only eight hundred residents and early in the morning there was not a soul about.

Ben came up behind Rix. "Where to, Jason?" he asked.

"It's up this way, I expect. I'll know it when I see it."

They walked up the street past the post office and general store and they were about to pass the village's red telephone booth when Murphy stopped and looked inside.

"Someone's nicked the telephone," he said, amused.

"They're for show now," Ben said. "Everyone's got mobile phones."

"Bloody ridiculous," Murphy replied as they carried on past a covered bench set on a patch of green.

Ben watched Rix as he studied each cottage lining the street. Some were thatched, others not, some brick, some stucco, all of them postcard-pretty. Then Rix stopped at a white one with a tile roof and a trellis of ivy around the front door.

"Is it this one?" Ben asked.

"Yeah, this is it."

"Are you sure?"

"I said this was it, didn't I?"

"All right then. Stand aside please."

Ben knocked on the door. A curtain covering the window to the right of the door parted and the door opened. A sturdy middle-aged woman answered and said hello as if it were a question. She looked Ben up and down then bent her neck from side to side to see men behind him.

"Hello, madam," Ben said. "My name is Ben Wellington from the Security Service." He produced his identity card which she read and handed back. "We're investigating a matter of national security. We have reason to believe that you may have recently been contacted by a man who is the subject of our inquiries."

"I should stop you," she said. "I don't live here. I'm a home caregiver. I look after the owner, Mrs. Hardcastle."

"Is she here?"

"She is, but she's asleep."

"Do you think we might wake her to answer a few questions?"

"I don't think that would be a good idea," the woman said. "She's poorly today with a cold. She's ninety. Did you know that?"

"I did not."

"I put her down for a nap after breakfast. She's foggy from the tablets her doctor prescribed. So you see, it wouldn't do any good to wake her."

"Are you here every day?" Ben asked.

"Five days a week. Another woman calls in on weekends."

"Does she have a daughter?" Ben asked.

"I wouldn't know. If she does I've never met her."

"Could I ask if a man has come calling for her recently?"

"Not while I was here."

"Does the name Lucas Hathaway mean anything to you?"

"I'm afraid not."

"Could you give me a few seconds, please?" Ben said. He stepped away from the door and spoke to Rix. "Are you certain this is the right house?"

"It's the one in the photo. I'm positive."

"Well, it may be the house but there's no telling if the woman here is the mother of Hathaway's girlfriend. That woman might have moved or passed away years ago."

"Why don't you ask how long she's lived here?" Rix suggested.

Ben called over to the caregiver and asked the question.

"Far as I know, she's always been in the village. There's a picture inside of her as a young woman in this very house."

"We've come all this way," Rix said. "We should search the house."

"What's the point?" Ben asked.

"Ma'am," Rix called out. "Do you stay the nights here?"

"Oh no, I come in the morning and leave after I give her some lunch. She can get by but we do help her with meals. A woman from the village helps with cleaning and laundry."

Rix said to Ben, "Hathaway could've come and hidden himself. This lady wouldn't necessarily know."

Ben looked skeptical but asked whether they could have a look around inside and the garden.

"You look like a nice man and your identification card looks genuine but I've learned the hard way not to be too trusting. And as it's not my house, I don't feel comfortable."

"If the police accompanied us, would that be more satisfactory?" Ben asked.

The woman nodded and politely shut the door.

In five minutes, one of Ben's agents returned with Constable Kent.

"I did offer my assistance," Kent said.

"Yes, and now I am taking you up on your offer," Ben said, rapping on the door. "Let's try again."

The caregiver knew the officer and made way for a search as long as everyone promised to be quiet. The house was small and Ben's men waited outside. The caregiver wrinkled her nose at Rix and Murphy and retreated to the kitchen with the policeman for a cup of tea, saying loudly enough for them to hear that some men ought to use deodorant.

There were only three rooms downstairs and two upstairs and with a postage-stamp of a garden with no shed the search was over quickly. They peeked into the old lady's bedroom where they heard snoring and saw a white-haired head poking from the bedclothes. Downstairs in the sitting room, Rix examined the framed photos on a table. He picked one up for a closer look.

"What is it?" Ben asked.

"Nothing," Rix said, quickly putting it down. He saw a photo album in a bookshelf and leafed through it while Murphy went out for another smoke.

Rix's lower lip protruded.

"What is it?" Ben asked.

"This is her."

Ben slid the photo from the plastic. An attractive brunette with a shag cut and bell-bottomed jeans stood beside a tree in the back garden of the cottage. The date was inked on the back: 1979.

"This is Hathaway's girlfriend?"

Rix nodded and returned the photo to the album. He paged forward, looked at a few more photos and shut the book with a slap.

"Well, there's no indication he's been here," Ben said.

"He still could come," Rix said.

"I suppose so," Ben said. "We'll have the local constables keep an eye on the place. They seem keen to help Her Majesty's government."

They were on the M1 motorway again, this time heading south. Talley, wide awake, sat beside Hathaway while Youngblood and Chambers slept in the back. All of them were so crimson-stained it was as if they had bathed in a vat of blood.

"I don't know where we're going," Hathaway said in a dull tone.

"You're asking *me*, where we ought to go? Fuck if I know," Talley said.

"Just saying."

"There's but one thing running through my mind," Talley said.

"What's that?"

"Finding the molls."

"Why do you care?"

"Because I do, that's why. They're the ones that got us into the troubles we're in."

Hathaway screwed up his face in thought for a while then said in exasperation, "You're blaming them for us getting sent here? If you recall we were chasing them to do rape and worse when it happened."

"I do blame them."

"Your logic's all bolloxed up."

Talley erupted, waking the men in the back. "If I didn't need you for turning the wheel of this machine and getting us from here to there I'd cut out your liver and I'd eat it in front of your stupid face. Don't you ever backtalk me again. You hear, Hathaway? You hear?"

Hathaway climbed down. "Yeah, sure, Talley, sure. Whatever you say."

"I want to find them and crash 'em good and proper."

From the back seat Youngblood said, "I want to find 'em too. I've got unfinished business between their legs."

Chambers sniggered at that.

Hathaway said, "Look, I've been after them as long as I've been in Hell but Rix and Murphy were always protecting them. I'd like nothing better than crashing them but I don't know where they are, do I?" Hathaway said.

"You're from their time," Talley said. "You tell me. Where would they go?"

Hathaway said he didn't have a clue and drove in silence for a few miles. Then he added, "I called in at Jason and Christine's flat one night to pick up something. She was waving a letter about she'd had from her ex's lawyer. Something about support for their son."

"What's an ex?" Talley asked.

"Ex-husband. She was divorced, split up from him."

"So she'd want to see her son, wouldn't she?" Talley said. "Where's he likely to be?"

"No way of telling. I don't even remember what his name was. But I do recall her ex-husband's name. She was like, fucking Gareth this and fucking Gareth that."

"Steer the machine to Gareth, then."

"It's not that easy. I need to remember his last name. Then I need to remember where he lived. Then we need to see if he's still alive."

"Well, think on it."

Hathaway began to do just that, spurred on by the nubbin of a memory that there was something peculiar about the man's name. He'd seen the lawyer's letter; they'd had a laugh.

What was the geezer's name?

Was it South or Southern?

No, it was something like that, wasn't it? A direction. North? East? West?

West, that was it, he thought. But why would he remember that?

Then he had it: because his name was West and he was from Southsea. A silly juxtaposition had somehow stayed in his brain for thirty years, to Hell and back.

"I need to find a telephone book," Hathaway said. "If he's still alive and still where he used to be then maybe we can find him and maybe we can find his son and maybe we can find the molls."

"Good," Talley said. "'Cause I want to crash 'em good and proper."

It was no small task finding an address for Gareth West.

First Hathaway pulled into a rest stop on the motorway near Leicester and slowly cruised it, looking for a phone box. He dared not go inside the restaurant or petrol station in his bloodstained state. Next he exited the M1 again for the B roads, looking for a phone box in small towns and villages.

Finally he spotted one in a village and with a handful of change from the center console, he hurried inside to find, to his astonishment, no phone, no wires, no anything, just an empty kiosk.

He drove on. Youngblood and Chambers clamored for grub and on seeing an elderly man carrying a pint of milk and a newspaper from his car to his front door, he decided to be opportunistic. The house was far from neighbors and the man was easy pickings.

They drove off some hours after Hathaway forced the man to show him how to call directory enquiries, after Talley slit the old fellow's throat, after they cleaned out the pantry and fridge, after they slept for a while, after they helped themselves to changes of clothes, and after Hathaway had taken the maps and siphoned off the petrol from the old man's car.

Feeling refreshed, they returned to the motorway heading for Southsea.

The four Hellers arrived at Nightingale Road in the evening. Hathaway parked the car and got out leaving the others behind. The terraced house had G. West stenciled above the mail slot. He rang and Gareth's muffled voice came through asking who it was.

"I've got a package for Mr. West," Hathaway said, using a reliable gambit from his life of crime.

Gareth unlocked the door and Hathaway easily pushed his way in.

Several minutes later, Hathaway went to fetch his three companions. Inside they found Gareth tied to a chair with a tea towel crammed into his mouth. Blood trickled down a nostril.

"They were here," Hathaway told Talley.

"The molls was here?"

"Yeah. They've cleared off."

"You certain 'bout that?"

"It's what he said. But we need to have a look around."

"Do it. Any drink about?"

Talley sat on a chair in the kitchen drinking brandy from the bottle while Gareth stared at him, his blue eyes watery but unblinking.

"You want to say something to me?" Talley asked.

Gareth nodded and Talley pulled out his gag.

"Say it, but don't shout or I'll crash you."

"You're from there, aren't you?" Gareth asked.

"From there? Yeah, I'm from there. What about it?"

"Why are you here?"

"I'm looking for the molls."

Gareth said he didn't understand.

"Molls. You know, the women we was with."

"Christine and Molly were here. I told the other man that."

"You sure they've lit off?"

"They're gone."

"Where'd they go?"

"I have no idea."

"We'll see 'bout that, won't we?"

He stuffed the tea towel back in Gareth's mouth and swigged brandy until Hathaway and the others returned to the kitchen.

"They're nowhere to be found," Chambers said.

"He says he doesn't know where they went to," Talley said.

Hathaway pulled out the tea towel again. "Did they have a car?" he asked.

Gareth asked for water. Hathaway filled a glass from the sink and put it to his lips. He drank thirstily and said, "I think so."

"You've got a son, right?"

Gareth wouldn't answer.

"Look," Hathaway said. "We'll find him and then he'll be tied to a chair too. We don't care about him, just Christine and Molly, all right?"

"Leave my son alone," Gareth said, trembling with anger. "He came over and saw Christine. He wasn't believing her. He wanted nothing to do with her. He left before they did. You won't find them with him."

"There you go, that wasn't so hard, was it?" Hathaway said. "Don't you feel good you spared your son all the bother?"

"Will you leave now?" Gareth asked.

"Soon, soon," Hathaway said. "Now think on this. Who else would the ladies wish to see after all these years? Any friends or relations still alive and kicking?"

"I wouldn't know anything about Molly."

"Christine?"

"Her sister's in London. I told her that. Her mother, Gavin's gran, is still alive too."

"All right then, Gareth. Why don't you tell me about sis and gran."

Hathaway found a pen and an old envelope and joked that he'd probably forgotten how to write. Gareth gave him the addresses. Talley wandered off and came back after a rummage in the hall closet.

"Finished with him?" he asked Hathaway.

Hathaway said he was.

"I'll crash him then," Talley said, swinging the heavy hammer he'd found in Gareth's toolbox.

If Giles Farmer had ever doubted the wealth of his friend, Ian Strindberg, his two-day stay at his flat in Belgravia had put an end to it. His guest bedroom on Eaton Mews overlooked a leafy garden and its en-suite bathroom alone was nearly as large as his entire bedsit. He'd pretty much had the town house to himself because shortly after he arrived Ian had to pop off to Brussels for business. Giles had always been at a loss to understand what it was that Ian did. It was something to do with insurance or re-insurance, but he glazed over on the details. Chums from university, Ian had always lent an ear and an occasional few pounds to his eccentric pal as he tilted at windmills.

Giles had spent his time in this lap of luxury feeling cut-off and adrift. He dared not log onto his own email or blog site from Ian's desktop for fear of being tracked. Likewise, he was scared to contact any of his network of conspiracy theorists. Unsure of the robustness of government web-crawlers, he wasn't even comfortable searching for power-grid perturbations or information about the South Ockendon and Iver North incidents. That left occupying himself with television, radio, and a Trollope novel.

Stir-crazy as he was, he welcomed Ian's keys fiddling in the door and his voice calling to see if Giles was still about.

He met him in the lounge.

"How're you getting on then?" Ian asked.

"Going out of my flipping gourd."

"That bad? Come on. Let's get some wine in you. Red or white?"

"Both."

"That's my lad. Sorry I couldn't give you the time of day before. I'm all ears now. Tell me your tale of woe. Who did you say was spying on you?"

Ian kicked off his loafers and stretched his long legs onto an ottoman. He sipped wine and furrowed his brow at Giles's story and examined the small camera Giles had plucked from his cooker's ventilation hood.

"Christ, Giles, how do you know it's still not transmitting?"

"Because it's not connected to a power source?"

"Don't be snide," Ian said. "I was only an economics major, remember?"

"Sorry."

"I mean seriously, I can't even change a light bulb. Look, mate, planting a camera in a man's house is hard-core. I'm no expert but I think they'd need an order of the High Court. My cousin Harry's a lawyer. I could ask him."

Giles waved his hands like he was playing tambourines. "Don't talk to anyone. If it's a lawful operation, they'd need a court order. If it's a black-ops job then they can do anything they want."

"Who are they?"

"MI5. MI6. Army intelligence. Some other group of assholes we don't even know exists."

"And you think all this is because you've been rattling their cages?"

"I think I'm onto something really scary, Ian. Something's gone very wrong with their precious supercollider. I think they want to shut me down and they'll do anything to keep me quiet. I don't know where else to go. Can I stay a few days longer until I figure it out?"

Ian wet his lips with his tongue and pulled his fingers through his pompadour. "Sure you can, mate. No worries."

20

King Henry's lord admiral, the Duke of Suffolk, seemed poorly suited to his job. Norfolk, his previous naval commander whom John had committed to the sea floor, had been arrogantly comfortable in his command of a naval vessel. Suffolk was ill at ease on the high seas and had spent all his time in his cabin, never appearing once at the captain's table during their passage to Francia.

John had asked the captain of the *Whirlwind* about the man.

"Norfolk was a bastard but a capable bastard. Suffolk's a horse's arse but the king seems to like him. What else matters?"

When they arrived at Dover, Suffolk had cost them a precious few days, insisting that the *Whirlwind* be kitted out with excessive provisions for the brief channel crossing. John had asked repeatedly why they needed so many barrels of wine, ale, and food for a journey to the French coast but Suffolk had shut down his enquiries and had sent out foraging parties to strip the surrounding towns of food and drink.

It was dawn and all the Earthers were on deck watching the hazy coast of Francia. John drew a short line on the piece of paper he kept in his pocket. Seven lines, their seventh day in Hell. The days were passing too quickly and they had made little progress. Arabel, Delia, and the children eluded them. They had no way of knowing how Brian and Trevor were getting on in their passage to Iberia. But when he looked into the apprehensive but appreciative faces of Martin, Tony, Charlie, Alice, and

Tracy, he took some solace. They had rescued these people, hadn't they, given them hope, saved them at least for a time?

Suffolk came onto the deck and weaved toward them on his bandy legs. John didn't know if he was drunk or seasick or both but when he came closer there was no alcohol on his breath.

"Ah, good, captain," Suffolk said to the ship's master. "You are flying the white flag."

"We wouldn't want to be holed by those cannon, would we, sir," the captain said.

"Where?" Suffolk asked in alarm.

John pointed at two dark pillboxes on the cliffs. They were at Calais. He had landed there weeks earlier in his quest for Emily. His landing party had taken fire from these cliffs and he wasn't keen on history repeating itself.

"Do you think they will honor the flag of truce?" Suffolk asked.

"There's only one way to find out," John said.

The *Whirlwind* dropped anchor a few hundred yards from the coast. By the captain's reckoning they could have drawn in closer but Suffolk was too wary of the French artillery. A rowing crew took the landing party into shore, one of the sailors holding aloft an oar with a white flag flying.

By the time they made landfall, a French troop had assembled on the beach, their muskets ready.

John and Emily helped Alice and Charlie helped Tracy through calf-deep waters. Once they were onshore the longboat was hastily turned and the English sailors rowed off.

The leader of the greeting party asked in a haughty French who they were and why they thought they could land at will on the sovereign territory of Francia. All the while he stared at the women.

John started to ask if anyone among the soldiers spoke English when Tony interrupted to translate.

"Why didn't you say you spoke French?" John asked.

"Never thought about it. Anyway, I'm glad to be of some use," Tony said.

John said, "Tell him we've come from far away, from the land of the living. Tell him King Maximilien knows us and that we are friends with Minister Forneau. Tell him we helped Francia defeat the English, German, and Russian armies. Tell him we're on our way to Paris and need their assistance."

The soldiers seemed astonished at what Tony was saying. They approached slowly and sniffed. One toothless man got too close to Tracy and reached out to touch her, making her cringe and whimper. After her assault by William Joyce, Tracy had been even more brittle than before and Emily stepped in protectively with an expert martial-arts kick, sweeping the man's leg and toppling him.

Rather than provoking them, the French soldiers found the maneuver hilarious. When the laughter died down and the man picked himself up, their leader told them to follow along. But first he required John to hand over his sword and pistol and searched their packs. John's pack was heavy with the rest of the books they'd stopped to recover along the way from Hampton Court to Dover, but the soldiers were wholly disinterested in them.

"That move of yours was amazing," Alice told Emily as they trudged through the soft beach sand toward a trail leading up the cliffs.

"John taught me everything I know," she said. "It's called Krav Maga."

"My best student," John said.

"I'd like to learn," Alice said. "Seems an essential skill in this bloody place."

"I should learn too," Charlie said sadly. "My brothers could fight but I was always rubbish."

"Tell you what," John said. "We'll teach you a few moves when we have the chance."

"Count me out," Tony said. "I abhor violence."

"I'll sit it out too," Martin said. "We're birds of a feather, Tony and I."

When they reached the cliff top the lead soldier pointed to a tower in the distance and said it belonged to the Earl of Calais. It proved to be a two-mile trek through marshland and when they arrived the soldiers guarded them outside the small castle while their captain entered through the portcullis.

Emily noticed something in the distance and pointed it out to John.

"Do you see that?" she asked.

"Telegraph poles," he said. "I heard the French had the technology. They probably use it to send word to Paris about invasions."

A one-armed man emerged from the castle, awkwardly buttoning his ruffled coat and fussing with his long hair to make himself presentable.

"Is it true?" he muttered on seeing the Earthers. "Can it be true?"

Tony stepped forward to translate but the earl shifted to broken English to address them. "I am the Earl of Calais. My eyes they are amazed to what I am seeing. How is possible?"

"We'll explain later," John said, "but first I need your help to get to Paris. We need horses and wagons. We have urgent business with King Maximilien and Minister Forneau."

"But the king, he is no more," the earl said, gesturing a throat slash. "The telegraph brings the news. Maximilien is destroyed."

"Is this bad?" Martin asked John.

"Depends." John asked the earl who the new king was.

"It is too incredible," the earl said. "He is not even French."

John grinned. "It wouldn't be Giuseppe Garibaldi, would it?"

"But how could this be known to you?" the earl asked.

"Just a lucky guess."

"You know this man?"

John said, "I'd say we're very good friends with Garibaldi."

The earl saw an opening for himself. "Would you tell King Giuseppe the news that the Earl of Calais is good man who helped his strange friends to achieve Paris?"

John nodded eagerly. "We will tell him that you are a terrific guy and if you give us an armed escort to Paris we'll tell him you are the single greatest earl in all of Francia."

He had died when he was young, a strapping man of thirty-five, murdered by his own bastard brother. Pedro of Castile, whom history would call

Pedro the Cruel for his panoply of monstrous acts, departed the world in 1369 as King of Castile and León to become a far more powerful and ruthless king in Hell. To be sure, many pitiless Iberians would follow him Down, and many would try to seize the reins of power from his iron fist, but Pedro was strong and cunning. In all of Europa, only King Frederick of Germania had a longer grip on power.

He had chosen as his seat of power the Iberian region he had known best in life and he built his great castle in Burgos, the arid city where he had been born. From there he waged constant campaigns over the centuries against his perpetual European enemies, attacking, defending, attacking, defending. His latest adventure, striking at the English with his great armada, had ended in an ignominious defeat that had set him into a rage from which he had not yet recovered.

Following the debacle at sea, he had summoned the Duke of Medina Sidonia, his naval commander, to Burgos to give an account of himself. The king had listened long and patiently to tales of whistling cannon balls hurled incredible distances from English batteries then put a long finger to his full lips.

"I can no longer bear to hear your voice," Pedro had said. On his command, his palace guard then seized the duke and held him down while Pedro pulled on his tongue with tongs and cut it away, instructing his cook to fry it in oil for his supper.

The castle was at the highest geographical point above the River Arlanzón with a commanding view over the central Iberian plateau. It was widely considered the most impenetrable fortress in all of Europa. From the squalid town an intruding army would first have to penetrate the outermost curtain wall patrolled by archers and soldiers wielding stones and oil to rain down on enemy heads. Then a drawbridge would have to be lowered to bypass a deep ditch. The bridge itself would funnel advancing foes into a narrow passageway where crossbow and pike men would meet them in the outer bailey. Another drawbridge led to the middle bailey and then a third drawbridge pierced the inner curtain wall to the heart of the castle, the inner bailey, where the king and his court resided in the royal apartments.

This was the route Arabel Loughty took to reach the castle keep.

On her arduous sea and land journey, Count Navarro, the Iberian ambassador to the English court, and his loyal officials, De Zurita and Manrique, had personally accompanied her. Navarro's dysentery worsened during the journey and by the time they arrived in Burgos he was panting and unresponsive. King Pedro had no interest in his condition. Ambassadors could easily be replaced. When informed about the arrival of this precious cargo Pedro at first scoffed at the notion that a living woman had been procured, but de Zurita and Manrique, though unable to offer any explanation for her presence, nevertheless swore on pain of eternal torture that Arabel was no Heller and moreover, that she was a fetching beauty. With that, centuries of ennui dropped away and in a frenzy of excitement, Pedro ordered his seamstresses to fashion new outfits for himself and this special woman, his cooks to lay on a feast, his cellar master to decant his best wines and ports. He would entertain Arabel that very evening.

Arabel had spent her journey in perpetual tears, distraught over being torn from her children and fearful she would never see them or home again. The only reason she had survived the passage was because of the kind attention and encouragement of Garsea Manrique, an imp of a man who used his small stature and puckish face to amuse her as best he could.

"Miss Arabel, I beg of you not to cry," he had said repeatedly in his excellent English whenever he came to bring her food and drink. "If only I could see you smile, my miserable existence would be very much improved."

Eventually to humor him she had managed a fleeting smile.

Then he had said, "If only I could hear you laugh, my sad troubles would seem but small things."

Eventually she had blessed him with a small laugh.

Finally, he had said, "If only you would tell me tales of your happy life on Earth, I would be your faithful servant forever and ever."

By the time they arrived in Burgos, they had become fast friends and the only thing that would dry her tears was the wicked smile and lilting voice of the small man. Señor de Zurita, a more educated and substantial man than the frivolous Manrique was wholly without humor, but he recognized the calming effect the imp had on the woman. So when they arrived at the castle, he insisted that Manrique have a room beside hers to keep her in the best possible spirits for the king.

High in the castle keep, Arabel awoke from a nap on the evening of her first day in Burgos, to see Manrique dangling his short legs off the edge of her comfortable bed.

"How did you sleep, Lady Arabel?" he asked.

Her lower lip quivered. "I dreamt I was home with my babies. But I'm not."

"But I am also your baby, am I not?" he said sticking his thumb in his mouth and eliciting half a grin. "While you were in sweet, sweet slumber, ladies of the household were laboring with needle and thread and they have made you a beautiful new dress to wear to meet the king."

"I don't want to meet the king."

"But you must. He is the king and he commands it. I was told by servants of the household that he has been as excited as a puppy dog."

She sighed loudly. "Tell me about him."

"I was trying to do just that during the whole of our journey but you would not listen."

"I suppose I'd better listen now."

"Well, he is a fine figure of a man, young and robust. I have seen him with mine own eyes for, oh my goodness, two hundred years or more since I did myself arrive, and I have rarely seen him afflicted by illness. He is strong in body and mind, an able hunter, able soldier, formidable ruler."

"What was he in life?"

"He was a king. An ancient one, ruling well before my own time."

"How ancient?"

"Oh my goodness. Hundreds and hundreds and hundreds of years gone past. I do not even know."

"Does he have a wife, a woman? Garsea, I don't even know the questions to ask."

"He has a queen, Queen Mécia. In life she was a Portuguese woman of noble birth, not as ancient as the king, but more ancient than your Garsea. In truth I do not know her well because she chooses to live in a palace in Bilbao. She has a very strong temper and I do not think the king likes to be in her presence. As to other women, well, of course, he is a man and a king and kings have many women. Any woman he desires, he can have."

"Will he?" She seemed unable to finish.

"Will he what?"

She shook her head. "Will he force himself on me?"

"Oh my goodness, Lady Arabel. I could not possibly speak on such a subject. Come now. Rise and perform your ablutions. You will meet the ladies who will attend to your needs. They will bathe you, powder you, bring you cakes and sweet wine, and at the appointed hour, they will dress you and bring you to the king who is laying on a feast in your honor. Did I tell you he is as excited as a young puppy?"

She did not resist the onslaught of servants who descended on her, plain women with dull eyes who were skin-and-bones thin and spoke no English. She could tell they knew she was different from them, but because they feared her or feared the king, they assiduously avoided eye contact. She submerged in a wooden tub but when she allowed her eyes to close succumbing to the pleasure of soaking in the soapy warm water, in her mind she saw Sam and Belle asleep in Solomon Wisdom's house. Recoiling, she bit her lip hard to subject herself to pain.

The servants backed away when she began to cry but suddenly something came to her that brought her tears to an abrupt halt.

What would Emily do, she thought?

What would Emily do?

Ever since she was a young girl, she had looked up to her older sister. Emily had always been the smarter of the two, more ambitious, and infinitely more accomplished. While Emily was getting advanced degrees in physics, she was temping in London and going to wine bars. While Emily was building MAAC she was in Australia working as a waitress on Bondi Beach. While Emily was elevated to research director of the Hercules project she was having babies, and while Emily was running half-marathons and learning martial arts she was a TV-watching single mom, reeling from the untimely death of her husband.

But now she was being tested in a way that Emily herself had been tested.

Emily had survived.

Emily had survived and had made it home. She would have to rally and do the same. For her children. For herself. She had to be strong.

She had to survive.

Maybe she wasn't as clever as Emily. Maybe she wasn't as fit as Emily. Maybe she didn't know how to defend herself. But she was a Loughty and Loughtys were tough old Scots.

She would survive.

The female servants seemed to sense a change had come over her and whispered among themselves in their native tongue.

Arabel climbed from the tub and when a woman came forward to dry her she snatched the towel away and dried herself.

She pointed at the red silk dress laid out on the bed so they would understand her.

"I'm ready to see the king."

When she entered the grand and vaulted banqueting hall, her red gown dusting the floorboards, Arabel felt hundreds of eyes upon her. Men and women stood, not by protocol, but to catch a better glimpse of her. She tried to control her breathing and with each deep inhalation her bosom swelled and threatened to burst from the revealing dress.

All of a sudden she was aware of Manrique by her side. He was dressed in a fancy waistcoat and long jacket, which made him look much like a lawn jockey. He must have interpreted her smile as signifying delight and he told her he was happy to see her too.

He offered his small hand and said, "I will accompany Lady Arabel to the king's table. He is anxious …"

"I know, like a puppy."

"Precisely."

The highest nobles of the court were positioned at the front of the hall at the elevated table that had to be reached by a short run of stairs. An imperious man dressed like a peacock in a colorful, ruffled doublet stepped away from his chair and approached.

"Is that him?" Arabel asked.

"Oh no," Manrique said. "That is the Duke of Aragon."

When they were face to face the duke sniffed at her with such abandonment that she wondered where it might end but Manrique broke the spell by introducing her in Spanish.

Aragon replied sonorously and Manrique translated.

"He said you are like a precious flower, my lady. He believes the king will be delighted. You will sit between his majesty and the duke."

"And you?" she said. "You know I can only say hola, adiós, and buenas noches."

"Fear not. I will be hovering over your shoulder like a hummingbird."

At the center of the table was an empty chair Manrique said was hers. Next to it was an ornately carved, high-backed chair with a silk cushion that so precisely matched her dress, Arabel wondered if it had been cut from the same cloth.

The hall was so quiet that the scrape of wood on wood from the simple act of the duke pulling out her chair seemed jarring and loud. She sat and looked over the hall of bearded men and a smattering of women and felt like an actor on a stage, an actor who had not only forgotten her lines but the very subject of the play.

All eyes suddenly turned from her to the rear corner of the room. There she saw a fairly young, swarthy man enter through a curtain. He had an oval face, a full beard, short and black, and long curly hair spilling out from under a wide-brimmed, floppy hat. He was not a large man, perhaps her height. Like the Duke of Aragon, Pedro had adopted a style of dress more of the seventeenth century than his own era and he was resplendent in a green and silver doublet and velvet sash, wide lacy collar, shiny green breeches, and black boots.

Pedro saw her from across the room and seemed to pay attention to no one else as he made his way forward. In response she neither smiled nor frowned. When he stood before her, looking first at her face, then her bosom, she heard Manrique speaking her name in some kind of formal presentation.

Pedro said nothing in return but Manrique confused her by saying, "The king extends his welcome to you and wishes to learn about your person."

As Pedro took his ornate chair, Arabel whispered, "But he didn't say anything at all."

"He did not have to speak," the little man said enigmatically. "You may sit now."

Pedro nodded to no one in particular and servers appeared from all corners of the hall bearing trays of meats and game pies. A servant filled his goblet, then Arabel's and the duke's.

The king began conversing earnestly with Aragon as if she were not seated between them. She drank some wine and tasted some roasted meat that was tough but delicious. Both men leaned in front of her to speak. Aragon smelled as unpleasant as all the Hellers but the king's aroma was masked by aromatic perfume.

Finally, in exasperation turned to Manrique. "What are they talking about?"

"They speak of the Moors. They are raiding the south. Always when we are weak, they invade."

On their journey, Manrique and de Zurita had spoken of the recent defeat of the Iberian navy at the hands of the English.

"Weak because of the British?" she asked.

"Yes, I am sure."

"Does the king know I'm British?"

"He does not mind, I think."

In time the men stopped their conversation. Pedro then smiled broadly and said something to her, several sentences worth.

Manrique leaned over her shoulder and said, "The king says he is most interested to know how a live woman has come to Hell. He says the price paid for you was not too great for you are very beautiful. He says that you have very beautiful breasts too."

"Did he now?" she said.

"Yes, this is what he says."

"First tell him that I am flattered. Then tell him I will not sleep with him. Finally tell him that if he tries to force himself on me I will kill myself."

Manrique's face fell. "You wish me to say these things?"

"Just as I have said."

"I hope I will survive this night," Manrique said.

After Pedro heard the translation he fell silent for several moments before laughing uproariously.

All conversation stopped at the other tables.

Pedro replied to Manrique who appeared visibly relieved. "The king says he is a patient man who has been in Hell for a very long time. He says it is his fate to remain here forever. He will not force himself on the lady. He says he will wait for as long as it takes until the lady decided she will force herself upon him."

Standing five-feet four-inches in stockinged feet, Joseph Stalin had always relied on the strength of his personality to make him seem a much larger man and now, raging and florid, he seemed enormous.

He and his senior staff were being housed in a fine house off the inner bailey of King Frederick's Marksburg Castle high over the Rhine but he complained of feeling like a bear in a cage.

"Bears must be free," he bellowed in Georgian. "I must be free."

Only some of his generals and advisors spoke his native language. Pasha, an Englishman, leaned over to General Kutuzov and asked, in his shaky Russian, what the tsar had said.

Kutuzov, a big-bellied, fat-lipped man with downy white hair whispered back, "Something about bears, I think."

Stalin switched to Russian to continue his rant. "This German, this medieval barbarian whose face looks like a prune pit, this fucker Barbarossa likes nothing better than plumping up his position by keeping me waiting in this ugly castle."

"I am assured we will have the promised war council tonight," Kutuzov said.

"Who gave you this assurance?" Stalin asked.

"The Duke of Thuringia."

"Him?" Stalin said. "Thuringia? He is as ancient and ridiculous as his master."

"He believes he is a contender to be named chancellor to replace …"

"Do not even dare to say that toad's name."

"Well, to be named the new chancellor."

Heinrich Himmler had been left behind in the mud after John Camp broke his neck the day the Germans and Russians were routed. It was the only piece of good news Stalin had received after his ignominious defeat. He hoped Himmler's body had been torn apart by wolves. Anything less would have been too good for him.

"Doesn't the king have anyone more able than that old fool, Thuringia?"

Kutuzov said, "Himmler made fast work of all his rivals. I apologize. I was not supposed to mention his name."

Stalin rolled his eyes at his bumptious field marshal whose most illustrious campaign in life had been to repel Napoleon's invasion of Russia in 1812.

"Rainald van Dassel was the last effective advisor the king possessed," Kutuzov continued. "Himmler, sorry, effectively purged many at his own level of command, and when he took Rainald's head last month, there was no one else but him who might be considered a credible chancellor. Now there is a dearth of able men for King Frederick to choose from."

"Perhaps we can exploit this situation," Stalin said.

"How so?" Kutuzov asked.

"I'll say no more," Stalin replied with a tug on his moustache and a wink. "Now Pasha, tell me what you have discovered about this new

English cannon."

The Russians had claimed a single victory in the midst of an overall defeat at the hands of the Italians and French. One of the carriages carrying Garibaldi's singing cannon had broken an axle and had to be left behind. A squad of Russian soldiers had come upon it and had managed by sheer brawn to transfer it into a heavy wagon. On the army's retreat from Francia, they had moved the captured piece into Germania where Pasha had led a group of military men and forgers in its evaluation. Pasha had just recently arrived in Marksburg to make his report.

Pasha disliked speaking in Russian. Before he died he had acquired rudimentary proficiency as a Russian reader, mainly of scientific articles, but in his seven-year residence in Hell, almost all of it spent in Russia, he had been force-fed the language like a goose being prepared for foie gras.

"I will start by saying what I always say," he began. "I am not a weapon's specialist and I am not a metallurgist."

Stalin dismissed this with a wave. "And I will reply the way I always reply. You have a brilliant technical mind. A twenty-first century mind. Eventually our Russian empire will catch up with you. For now, you must work with the seventeenth, eighteenth, and nineteenth-century technologies available. The cannon, if you please."

Pasha sighed, heaving his painfully thin chest and pushing the gray curls from his eyes. He had been bony and pigeon-chested in life and in Hell he had lost more weight. Stalin, his ardent protector and benefactor, had made sure he had ample rations and favorable accommodations but his chronic depression had pulled him down like an anchor. The only thing that induced him to eat at all was his fear of winding up in a rotting room.

"The cannon has a simple but clever design. I know little of the history of cannon-making but the military men tell me it is probably a late nineteenth-century innovation that was brief-lived and eclipsed by the more technologically advanced designs made possible by large, efficient blast furnaces."

Stalin nodded his large block-like head. "We need to find engineers who can build us large furnaces. We need to be first to achieve this in this stinking world of ours. But until we do, we must make smaller innovations."

"I agree, of course," Pasha said. "The innovations of the Italian weapon are ones we can easily reverse engineer. The cannon itself is conventional but the barrel has been rifled with deep spiral channels. The artillery shells have lugs welded onto them and fit perfectly into these grooves. Upon firing, vigorous spin is imparted onto the shells and a spinning shell will travel straighter and farther. It is this spin that produces the whistling sound we all heard that day."

"They positioned these cannon on high ground overlooking our encampment," Kutuzov said, "and exacted a terrible toll from a great distance."

"Why didn't we have this design?" Stalin demanded.

Pasha shrugged. "As I've told you many times, these kinds of technologies are short-lived. It is rather hit or miss whether someone comes to Hell who knows of the technology, stays intact long enough to pass the knowledge along, and is at the right place and the right time to have the technology implemented."

"But the Italians had this confluence," Stalin said angrily.

"Apparently so," Pasha said. "The good news is we should be able to produce an unlimited number once we deliver the captured weapon to the forges in our territory."

"We must make this happen immediately," Stalin said. "These weapons were the margin of the enemy's victory. Who could have imagined the combined might of Russia and Germania being thwarted by Francia and Italia. We must not wait to return to the motherland. The Germans have excellent forges, no?"

Kutuzov shook his head making his jowls flap. "We cannot let them have the knowledge. Today they are allies, tomorrow they are foes."

"I am aware of this," Stalin said. "Please hold onto the thought. Now, let us turn to the agenda for this war council tonight."

"May I leave now?" Pasha said.

"No, stay. I like having you around. Your sour face always cheers me up.

Now, *we* must drive the agenda tonight, not the Germans. What do *we* want to happen?"

"We should send for fresh troops and re-engage Francia first and then Italia," Kutuzov said firmly. "Maximilien must be punished. Then Borgia."

Stalin looked around the chamber and pointed. "Come out from your little hiding place, Yagoda, and tell them what you've told me."

Colonel Yagoda, Stalin's head of his secret police, stepped from the shadows. Yagoda had led Russia's secret police in life, only to be purged by Stalin in a show trial, then stripped naked, beaten and shot by his deputy, who then suffered the same fate under Beria. In Hell, Yagoda had eked out his survival as a lowly soldier in Tsar Ivan's army. When Stalin made his own entry to Hell, he quickly got his bearings, evaded the tsar's sweepers, and began finding and courting all the former cronies and acolytes he could find in and around Moscow. There was no shortage of them including scores he had himself purged. His message to these men was simple: join with me, forget the past, and together we will topple the mentally unstable Ivan. Under Tsar Joseph your lot in Hell will be much improved. Yagoda had signed on.

Yagoda often engendered sniggers because he looked remarkably like a very large rat. "Although we require confirmation," Yagoda said, "we have heard about significant developments within the French and Italian camps. Maximilien is destroyed. Borgia is destroyed and he was not in Francia at all. The two empires have joined together under a single new king."

"Who?" an astonished Kutuzov exclaimed. "Who is this man?"

"Giuseppe Garibaldi," Yagoda said.

"Garibaldi?" the general said. "He was a rather minor figure on the world stage, was he not?"

Stalin tapped impatiently on his armrest. "What a man was or was not on Earth is of no matter here. If Garibaldi has accomplished this, he is a master manipulator. Yagoda, I want a confirmation. If it is so I am inclined to throw our weight against Henry in Britannia. He is wounded, we hear, and it would be useful to add his territory to ours."

"Henry has annexed the Norselands," Yagoda said. "We would get two territories for the price of one."

Stalin nodded and stood, a sign they all recognized. He was finished. "Come sober to the war council tonight," Stalin demanded. "You will see a good show and will want to remember it."

At nightfall the large Russian delegation made its way across the main bailey to King Frederick's great banqueting hall. The hall was candlelit but still nearly black as night. The multiple thick support columns rising from the floor made it seem like the gathering was being held in a forest. The banqueting table had been moved aside to make room for a large circle of high-backed chairs.

The German delegation rose politely when Stalin and his company entered. Absent the king who was not yet in attendance, the Duke of Thuringia was the most senior man on the German side and he took it upon himself to mingle with his allies. He shuffled over on his arthritic hips and shook Stalin's hand. It was a weak handshake and Stalin almost crushed Thuringia's fingers in a show of vigor.

Thuringia spoke in English, a language Stalin could understand. "We will commence when Barbarossa arrives," he said, reclaiming his hand.

"We can start now," Stalin said loudly in Russian. He instructed a man on his staff, a German speaker, to translate.

The Germans took offense but they were soon distracted by the entry of their king's twin bodyguards, the hulking and muscular young men who never left their master's side even in bed. Hans and Johann carried a large wooden chest by its handles into the room and placed it in the center of the circle.

"What is the meaning of this?" Thuringia asked in astonishment.

"I have two things to show all of you," Stalin said, seeming to savor the moments while his words were being translated. "Gentlemen, please remove the first object from the box."

The musclebound men opened the lid, reached down, and pulled out the naked and headless body of an old man. When they threw it upon the floor, the arms and legs moved, as if searching around for their head.

The circle of men came closer and some asked in German and Russian who this was.

"Now, for the second," Stalin announced.

A head was produced, a head with a wispy white beard and a pink, scaly scalp. Hans held it up. The dull eyes seemed to search the room and the dry lips opened and closed.

Duke Thuringia cried out, "Hans and Johann, what have you done?"

Johann spat at Barbarossa's head and addressed him as if he were still whole. "You treated us worse than dogs for hundreds of years, you old shit. Tsar Joseph, he treats us like men, and he has given us more gold in one day than you have ever given us. You have gotten what you have long deserved."

The German nobles were in shock. Their king had survived in Hell for a thousand years. But before anyone even thought to draw a weapon Stalin had climbed onto a chair and pleaded for their attention.

"Please, gentlemen, sit and listen to me," Stalin began, allowing his translator to jump in at each dramatic pause. "Even though Hell is perpetual and neverending, it is changing in front of our eyes. King Maximilien is gone. King Borgia is gone. Francia and Italia have united. The old guard is falling, new ones rise. Tonight, I will present to you, my German friends, a new vision for our shared future, a future where a united Russia and Germania, led by Stalin, will conquer not only all of Europa, but all of the dominions of Hell. Listen to my words. Listen in peace and think about the riches and pleasures that await all of you who have the vision to join with me."

It had been a very long time since Queen Matilda had seen the Earl of Strasbourg's residence. He called it a castle but to her eye, it was paltry, hardly more than one of her husband's many hunting lodges. It rose high over the city on a bank of the Ill River and looked somewhat cheerful compared to the rest of the bleak city structures because it was made of rose-colored stone.

The Earl of Southampton had ridden ahead to inform Strasbourg of the queen's imminent arrival. When her wagon train reached the castle drawbridge, Southampton was waiting for her.

He came to her wagon and she instantly saw there was a problem.

"What is the matter, Southampton?" she asked. "You look far too gloomy for my liking."

"It seems that the earl is not in Strasbourg."

"Is he not?" she snapped. "When will he return?"

"He is in Paris, my lady, with a party of Alsatian men-at-arms, having been summoned some time ago to aid in the defense of Francia."

"Do you mean to say that he took up arms against King Henry?" she asked in amazement.

"That is so, my lady."

"And his return?"

"The household has no news. They do say that you are most welcome and they will do their utmost to afford you all the comforts they can muster."

"Well, what choice do we have, Southampton? We can't wander the countryside, can we?"

"No, my lady. My only concern is fortification. I saw few armed men about and our own party is too small to mount a stout defense of so large a castle."

"Large?" she asked with raised brows. "It seems rather small to mine eyes."

When nightfall came, Sam and Belle slept together in their new bed high in the castle keep and Delia sat beside them in quiet despair. She had never in her life felt so far away from home and so terribly lonely. Her friends and colleagues had always said she had a sunny disposition and she had always bristled at the label, as if it reduced her credibility within the ranks of the jaded so-and-so's of the Security Service. But even she would admit she was hardly a depressive. Her disposition had been put to the ultimate test in the aftermath of her husband's fatal heart attack; she had kept herself remarkably positive throughout the ordeal and in the lonely years that followed.

She had nothing remotely resembling a sunny thought that night. The flagon of red wine left by a moronic and leering servant was her only solace.

Now on hearing those noises in the distance she regretted her three cups of wine. At first they sounded like distant voices engaged in animated discussion. Growing louder they sounded more like shouts and then, alarmingly, screams. She tried the door but it wouldn't budge. She held off banging on it lest she wake the children but when the commotion was too loud and close to ignore she pounded on the door and used her limited French to call for help.

"What's the matter, Auntie Delia?" Sam said, rubbing his eyes.

"Oh, nothing, dear, go back to sleep."

"But you were shouting."

"I know. I'm sorry for waking you."

The latch moved and the door flew open. Southampton was standing there, sword in hand, a hand red with blood.

"Quickly," he said. "Take the children and follow me."

Delia couldn't take her eyes off the blood dripping off the sword. "What's happening?"

"We've been attacked. The queen has been mortally wounded. Hurry, or all is lost."

Delia rushed to the bedside and picked up Belle who remained asleep in her arms. Sam sat on the edge of the bed staring in fascination at the earl's sword.

A second sword came into view, this one emerging from the earl's chest.

Southampton cried out and blood began to trickle from his mouth. A heavy boot pushed him aside and a short, thick man peered into the room brandishing a sword in one hand and an axe in the other.

Delia stared at the brute's one good eye while Clovis examined her and the children with the satisfied expression of a man who was about to become extremely wealthy.

21

Rix and Murphy drank coffee and stared out the helicopter windows glad to be out of their Dartford holding cells. Ben sat apart from them, fitfully re-hashing a fight he'd had with his wife over breakfast. She was a tolerant woman, a trooper, who well understood the pressures of being an MI5 wife but no previous assignment had ever taxed their family life as strenuously. She was used to his inability to talk about his work but she was not accustomed to his foul moods and flashes of anger toward her and their daughters. Their argument had occurred while he hurriedly dressed following a dawn call from the office. Ben had to wave off the girls' school pageant that evening.

"That's the second time in a row, Ben," she had complained.

"The bad guys don't seem to adhere to the school calendar, you know."

"Look, I'm sure you're keeping the nation safe from the bad guys, darling," she'd said with a biting tone, "but your daughters are growing up without you."

"You've no idea," he had said, slipping on his shoes. "No bloody idea."

"You're right. I have no ideas, none at all. I'm just an empty-headed, stay-at-home mum. And don't bother calling later. I know you'll be home after we've already gone to bed. You always are."

They put down in front of a general aviation hanger at the Southampton Airport where a car whisked them the fifteen miles to Southsea. The Hampshire Constabulary had set up an interview room at the Southsea Police Station. Weary of dealing with curious coppers, Ben had arranged for direct access to the interview room from a loading-dock door, no police participation in the interviews, and no video recording. The lawyers at MI5 had attended to the formalities.

Murphy and Rix sat alone behind a two-way mirror; given the circumstances, Ben had decided to conduct the interview alone.

"Hello, Gavin," Ben said on entering the room. "My name is Wellington."

Gavin West picked his head off his arms. He looked exhausted.

"Are you the one I had to wait for?"

"I believe so."

"I don't know why they wouldn't let me go home. I'm being treated like I'm the criminal."

"I understand."

"Do you know how long I've been kept here?"

"Since before midnight, I believe."

"That's right. All bloody night and half the bloody morning."

"When I'm done you'll be allowed to leave."

"I'd better or there'll be hell to pay."

Ben's mouth curled faintly. "Why don't you start from the beginning?"

"Beginning of what?"

"Finding your father."

Gavin shook his head in disgust. "It's like I told every single officer who's spoken to me at the house and here, I started ringing my dad after supper last night and he didn't pick up. I thought maybe he went to the pub."

"Did he do that often? Go to the pub?"

"No, not often. That's why I was uneasy. I couldn't go to bed without knowing where he was so I drove over from Portsmouth. That's when I …" He choked on his words.

"I'm sorry. This must be difficult."

Sorrow turned to anger. "Difficult? The fuck you say. Difficult? Seeing your father tied to a chair, his head bashed in, blood everywhere? It was horrible."

"Yes, I'm sure it was. Listen, Gavin, I don't need to inconvenience you regarding routine police matters so I won't be asking you about the state of the house, missing items, et cetera. I want to probe a statement you made to the officers last night about calling around to your father's house a few days ago and seeing a woman who purported to be your mother, Christine. Could you tell me what you told them?"

On the other side of the mirror Rix and Murphy leaned forward.

"He called me up. Said he wanted me to come by but wouldn't say why. When I arrived there were two women with him, one who wanted to see me. She said her name was Jane. That she was a friend of dad's."

"Did the other woman give her name?"

"No."

"I see, go on."

"This Jane woman, she said she used to live in the area and that she'd met me when I was young. But that didn't make any sense, did it?"

"Why not?"

"Because she was no older than me. I'm thirty-six. She looked about the same. On the beat-up side, like you get from sleeping rough, you know, but not much older than me."

"And did you ask her about that?"

"I did. She said she was older than she looked."

"And did you believe her?"

"No, it was rubbish."

"Did you call her on it?"

"I did more than that. Something in the back of my mind set me off. There was something about her I thought I recognized. When I was young something happened that everyone hid from me. But kids find out stuff, don't they?"

"What happened?"

"My mother was killed. Along with the scumbag she ran off with, some copper. She left my dad and me and fell in with this geezer who was a bad apple. They kidnapped a girl and killed her and they got killed for it. Got what they deserved. Anyway, my dad had a photo album of when I was a tyke, when we were still a family. I used to sneak looks at those photos when I was a teenager. This woman, this Jane. I remembered her face and sure enough when I got the photo album out, it was just like her."

"Your mother."

"That's right."

Ben had a copy of the photo sent to MI5 by the police. "Is this the photo?"

"Yeah, that's it."

"And the woman, Jane, looked just like this?"

"Near enough."

"And you confronted Jane with the photo?"

"Yeah, I did."

"What did she say?"

"She said she was my mother. She started to cry and so did my dad."

"And what did you do?"

"Well, I didn't cry if that's what you're asking. I got angry. Look, Mr. Wellington, I'm not Albert Einstein but I'm not Forest Gump, either. It was bullshit. Some kind of a scam on an old man."

"Did you tell her that you thought she was perpetrating a scam?"

"I did tell her that."

"And her response?"

"She told me there were things in this world that we couldn't understand. I told her she was a fucking bitch who was either wearing some kind of Hollywood mask or had plastic surgery to try to fool us."

"Did she deny that?"

"'Course she did."

"And then what happened?"

"I told her we weren't buying whatever it was she was selling and told her to sod off and leave my dad alone."

"And did she and the other woman leave?"

"They had to didn't they?"

"Did they say where they were going?"

"No. And I didn't ask."

"Did they call a taxi? Did they have a car?"

"The other woman took car keys from her bag."

"Could you see the make of car from the keys? Did you see them getting into the car?"

"No to both."

"All right. Did your father believe that Jane was your mother?"

"He did, but I think he wanted to believe it. An old man's mind playing tricks on him."

"Do you think these women came back and murdered your father?"

"'Course I do. Who else? You've got to catch them, Mr. Wellington and bring them to justice for murdering a kind old man."

"You've been very helpful, Gavin. Is there anything else you haven't mentioned I wonder?"

"No, that's it."

"Anything about the way these women might have smelled? Their aroma?"

"Yeah, there was. Both of them were reeking of perfume. It was almost too much being in the same room as them. What was that all about?"

Ben went into the observation room and sat with Murphy and Rix.

The room was thick with Murphy's roll-up smoke.

"I don't think smoking is allowed," he said.

Murphy lit another.

"Do you think Christine and Molly killed him?" Ben asked.

"What do you think, Benjamin?" Rix said in a mocking tone.

"No, I don't. In addition to the victim's fingerprints, Gavin's, and your wives, there were at least four sets of unidentifiable prints inside the flat. How did the rovers know where to find Gareth West?"

"Had to be Hathaway," Murphy said. "Christine must've mentioned her ex to him. All he'd need was his name and the city."

"Of course it was Hathaway," Rix said. "We used to have that piece of garbage at our flat, shuttling dope in and out."

"Why do you think they're looking for the women?" Ben asked. "Why don't they just forget about them?"

"They're twisted bastards, aren't they?" Murphy said. "They'll be blaming them for winding up here. They'll be wanting their revenge. It's the way they are."

"Blaming the victims," Ben said, "Marvelous. Well, the good news is that they didn't find your wives. The bad news is we're no closer to finding any of them and the body count is rising."

Christine and Molly drove around London lacking any sense of purpose. Their route and pace were as aimless and listless as their emotions. Gareth had given them what cash he had in his flat and had shouted at them to go. They had left him behind in a state of confusion and agitation.

Ahead, Molly saw the dome and spires of St. Paul's.

"Fancy going to church?" she said.

"Fuck off," Christine replied. "Not funny."

"We've got to go somewhere, luv. How 'bout the cinema then? Sit in the dark, have ice lollies and popcorn?"

"We need a plan." Christine said.

"I know what we can do. We can sell our story to the *News of the World* then go on the tele and make millions. What do you reckon they'd call us? Hell birds?"

That almost made Christine laugh. Almost.

"Did you see how much Gavin hated me?" she said.

"He didn't hate you. I don't think hate entered into it."

"If he believed it was me he would have hated me. I abandoned him. What kind of a mother leaves her boy?"

"A mother who was head-over-heels with Jason. Don't forget that Gareth West was a domineering, soul sucking bastard. You were at wit's end, darling. You needed a fresh start and you took it. More power to you. And Jason wasn't going to be any kind of father figure to the boy. It wasn't in him. Gavin was better off growing up with one father. And with what happened to us, well, he was spared all that."

Christine took it in. A young couple on the sidewalk caught her eye. They were mucking about and having fun. "You're not wrong," she said wistfully.

"'Course I'm not. Maybe I could get my own show on the tele. Advice on life and love from Dr. Hell Bird. So, what did you decide?"

"On what?"

"On seeing your sister. We're not far from Stoke Newington."

"I didn't like her when she was young. She was a cow. Now she'll be an old cow."

"Well I've got no one in this world or the next besides Murph," Molly said.

"All right, then," Christine said. "I didn't want to but we'll go visit my mum."

The address was a small Victorian cottage on a leafy street in Stoke Newington. Hathaway drove past it a few times then found a parking space on a small dead-end road near a mechanic's garage. Talley held up his hand to protect his sensitive eyes from the bright sun. They had two bottles of Gareth West's liquor to occupy their time and they would wait until night.

Waking in the darkness, the booze long gone, they piled out of the car and pissed on the deserted road. When they got to the cottage it was pitch dark. Hathaway rang the bell and when there was no answer he went around to the back, broke a window with a rock, and let the others in.

"We'd best keep the lights off."

"Suits me," said Talley. "This land's too bright for my liking."

Hathaway fumbled for a pair of candlesticks on the mantle and lit the wicks on the kitchen cooker. Inside the fridge there was a box curiously labeled as wine. Hathaway figured out how to use the plastic spout and tasted it.

"What a world," he said. "Wine in a fucking box."

He passed the wine box to the others to keep them quiet while he had a proper look around.

The wardrobes in the bedrooms were filled with old-lady clothes. There was a TV in the lounge that was flat and alien but there was an old boxy set in one of the bedrooms that he thought he might be able to figure out. There was an accumulation of mail on the floor under the slot. All of it was addressed to a Helen Mandeville.

The kitchen and pantry shelves were stocked with an abundance of canned and dry goods and an overage of loo paper. It seemed Christine's sister was a food hoarder. In the lounge a breakfront cabinet was filled with cheap, floral china. He pulled open the lower doors and whistled. It seemed she was a booze hoarder too.

"I reckon we could stay here a while," he announced to the others, tossing liquor bottles around to eager hands.

22

While pondering his next military move, Stalin took possession of Barbarossa's palace, directing it to be cleaned and scrubbed, removing every filthy remnant of the ancient king.

"Burn his clothes, burn his mattress, burn everything that burns," he had said.

When the bonfire in the main bailey had finally died out, a small army of servants moved all of Stalin's possessions and those of his generals and advisors into the rejuvenated palace.

"How long must we stay in this damned place?" Field Marshal Kutuzov had asked after inspecting his own chilly quarters.

"What's your hurry?" Stalin had asked.

"I prefer Moscow," the general had replied.

"We all prefer Moscow," the tsar had said. "But we are soldiers, Mikhail, and soldiers fight. Marksburg is a better place to launch our conquest of Europa than Moscow. Do I need to draw you a map?"

"Then let's get on with it," Kutuzov had sniffed. "Let's march on the Norselands which will fall like a house of sticks then sail to Britannia and take London from the north. You have seen my war plan."

"Soon, soon, Mikhail, but we must consolidate our position in Germania first. Any German officer and noble who is not completely loyal and trustworthy must be purged and replaced with men we own, men whom we can trust. Otherwise, as soon as we leave Marksburg, some devil will try to install himself as the new king and all our gains will be wiped out."

It was nighttime and Stalin sat alone in the king's damp great hall staring at burning logs. He pulled a blanket over his lap and felt himself beginning to drift off.

His personal manservant tiptoed in. Nikita, a freckled young man, had been at his side since Stalin first seized the reins of power from mad old Tsar Ivan. Ivan had ruled over Russia for over four hundred years, more than living up to his earthly moniker, Ivan the Terrible.

Nikita inched into view and waited to be acknowledged.

"What is it?" Stalin asked. "Are you going to scold me for sleeping in my chair?"

"Apologies for disturbing you. A party of men has arrived at the castle. Their leader, a barbarian, I am told, demanded to see Barbarossa and when informed of his demise, demanded to see you instead."

"I'm sure it can wait until the morning. But if he does not have the grace to wait until then, have the guards destroy him. I have no patience for barbarians. There are too many of them about. Has my bed been warmed?"

Nikita bowed his head, something he always did when he was about to contradict the tsar. "Apologies, Tsar Joseph, but this barbarian has a great treasure he wants to sell to you."

"Treasure?" Stalin bellowed. "This palace is filled with treasure. If I see one more golden plate or jeweled ring I'll vomit. Now, Nikita ..."

"Children," the young man blurted out.

"What did you say?"

"Children. He has children."

"That's absurd," Stalin said, growing angrier. "Have the barbarian shot."

"I refused to disturb you unless I saw for myself. He produced a small boy. Very young, certainly no more than five or six if my memory of children suffices. The boy was scared. His face was wet with tears. The barbarian claims he also has a girl at his camp, even younger. And a woman who tends them."

"You saw this boy? And you haven't been drinking?"

"Only a little wine. Not enough to imagine a child."

"This makes no sense," Stalin said, throwing off his blanket and pointing toward his boots. "The laws of Hell are inviolate. Children do not come here."

"But, Tsar Joseph," Nikita said, "these children are not dead."

Stalin had another drink to steady his nerves. He had been waiting for over an hour for the barbarian to return to the castle with all his "treasure."

From across the great hall he watched a contingent of his imperial guards march in and suddenly part ranks, revealing a squat, one-eyed chieftain dressed in skins and furs, and behind him, a plump, middle-aged woman holding hands with a small boy and a smaller girl.

"They speak English," Nikita whispered to Stalin.

Stalin ignored Clovis and brushed past him without a word, leaving the brute to mutter something in his guttural tongue.

Delia eyed the tsar suspiciously with an expression to suggest she recognized, but couldn't quite place him.

"Please don't come any closer," Delia said. "You'll scare the children."

Stalin dropped to a knee. "I do not want to make them scared," he said in English. He had a look of utter wonder in his eyes. "What is your name, madam?"

"Delia. Delia May."

"Welcome, Mrs. May. I am pleased to welcome you and your little ones. I am Stalin. Joseph Stalin."

She blanched and blurted out, "Jesus Christ."

The tsar's moustache curled upwards. "He is not here, only Stalin."

"I thought I recognized you," she mumbled.

Stalin sniffed the air. "It is true," he said. "You do not have the smell of death upon you."

"Fortunately, no."

"How is this?"

"Do you have time for a rather long story?"

"Yes, yes, I'm sorry. There will be time. What are their names?"

"The boy is Sam, the girl is Belle."

"Look how beautiful they are. Look how sweet. They are yours?"

"Heavens, no. I'm just looking after them. They were separated from their mother."

"Who is also a living woman?" Stalin asked.

"She is."

"Can I speak to children, please?"

"If you don't scare them."

Just then, Clovis began to talk loudly, making the children cry out in fear.

Stalin rose and asked what the barbarian was saying. The Duke of Thuringia and a gaggle of German noblemen had crept into the hall and the old duke came forward, volunteering his assistance.

"He speaks an ancient dialect, my tsar," the duke said. "He asks how much you will pay for these trophies?"

"Give him a bag of coins and send him away," Stalin shouted to Thuringia. "The bastard is making the little ones cry."

The duke went over to Clovis and spoke to him, eliciting a toothless smile and a vigorous head nod and the imperial soldiers led him away.

Word of the visitors had spread through the castle and Russians and Germans alike began to filter in. Kutuzov came in, tucking in his tunic and Pasha arrived with his shoes untied, the laces flapping on the stone floor.

Stalin dropped to his knees again and splayed his arms out wide. "Children, come. Sam and Belle come. Come and greet your Uncle Joe."

Delia told the children it was safe to come out from behind her. Sam emerged first and took a tentative step forward.

"How old is Sam?" Stalin asked.

"I'm three."

"Oh, such a big boy. How old is little girl?"

From behind Delia a small voice said, "I'm two."

Stalin wiped tears from his cheeks and blew his nose into a handkerchief. "Such precious children. I am in shock. Never would I have imagined such a thing."

"We're in a state of shock as well," Delia said.

Stalin stood again. "You are English, Mrs. May, are you not?"

"I am indeed."

"And where in England are you from?" he asked.

"London but our jumping off point to come here was Dartford, in Kent."

From across the hall a voice rang out in English. Pasha pushed forward through the gathering crowd. "I'm sorry," he asked. "Did you say you were from Dartford?"

The journey from Calais to Paris had not been without incident but the Earl of Calais's armed men had dealt with rovers and brigands with ruthless efficiency. John had guarded his own group with weapons at the ready but the earl's men did the dirty work, shedding blood and rolling heads at the smallest provocation.

Weary and exhausted, they arrived in a monochrome Paris shrouded in a heavy canopy of cooking fires. John pointed it out to the Earthers, the great palace on the Île de la Cité.

"That's it," he said.

"Our Paris is magical," Tony told Martin, choking on the smoke. "This Paris is crap."

"If they've got beds and baths, I'll not complain too loudly," Alice said.

Emily put her hand on John's shoulder. "Giuseppe's the only man in Hell I look forward to seeing again," she said.

"Not Caravaggio?" John asked.

"Well, him too," she grinned. "He's gorgeous. And did I say talented?"

The Earl of Calais led the way to the guard stations flanking the great castle drawbridge. After an animated discussion with the captain of the guard he returned, waving his one arm.

"I explained to these men who you are and who I am," the earl said. "They are summoning high officials."

"Garibaldi?" John asked.

"I am hopeful. I would like to meet this new king. Do not forget to tell him that I have been helping you and your strange friends."

"Believe me. You're going to get a medal."

After a long wait, the captain of the guard summoned the earl who in turn summoned John. The huge drawbridge slowly lowered and the group walked across the river and through the outermost defensive wall of the castle.

From a distance a man hurried toward them and judging by the awkwardness of his locomotion, it was clear he was unaccustomed to running.

When he got close enough, John saw who it was and called out, "Guy! How are you?"

"John Camp!" Forneau yelled. "I cannot believe it is you."

Puffing and wheezing from the exertion he clasped John's shoulders and John pumped his hand.

"Were you not able to return to your own world?" Forneau asked.

"No, we made it but we've come back. I'll explain everything but first I'd like to introduce you to Emily Loughty."

Forneau bowed deeply, his chest continuing to heave. "Giuseppe told me she was beautiful and now I see it with my own eyes. I am honored to know you, my good lady."

She did her best version of a curtsy and said she'd heard many good things about him.

"Come, come, inside," Forneau told them. "There is much to talk about."

The Earl of Calais stepped forward and introduced himself and began explaining how he had volunteered to help them across the wilderness to Paris.

"Yes, yes," Forneau said, with a dismissive wave. "You will be rewarded for your service, monsieur. You are surely a friend to the crown. Tomorrow we shall conduct our business."

"Does Giuseppe know we're here?" John asked, politely edging the earl aside.

"But he isn't here, John. He and most of our Italian friends have departed."

The news left John and Emily despairing.

"Where is he?" John said.

"He has gone to Iberia to seek an alliance with King Pedro. Much has happened in a short time. Please come inside. We will talk."

"We don't have a lot of time," John said. "We need your help. The Queen of Brittania is in Francia …"

"Yes, yes, I know," Forneau said. "My spies have reported the news to me. She was in Strasbourg but she has been destroyed by the warlord, Clovis."

Emily let out a visceral cry. She knew the one-eyed beast all too well. "Oh my God, John. The children!"

"Children?" Forneau said. "You know of these children?"

"My niece and nephew," she said. "That's why we're here."

"Tell me what you know, Guy," John demanded.

"I did not believe what I was told but now, perhaps, I do. In Strasbourg children were said to be seized by Clovis. He delivered them to Marksburg in exchange for gold. That is where they are. Marksburg."

"Barbarossa has them?" Emily said, her voice quavering.

"No, not him. He is no more. The Russian tsar has taken control of Germania. Tsar Joseph has them."

"I saw him," Emily told John. "I saw Joseph Stalin when I was a prisoner in the German camp."

"I remember," John said gently, trying to assuage her panic. "You told me."

"We've got to go to Marksburg," she said urgently. "We've got to go there now."

"Please, you must rest first," Forneau said. "And you cannot just present yourself and expect to succeed in your quest. The tsar and his German allies have a formidable army. You will need much in the way of aid."

It was then that Forneau noticed Martin, Tony and the others huddled together a short distance away. He walked slowly toward them, sampling the air and shaking his head in awe.

"So many live souls," he said. "The passage between our two worlds has become larger, has it not? I am Guy Forneau, lord regent to the new king. I welcome you to Francia."

"Is this Spain?" Trevor asked.

"Hang on," Brian said, surveying the vast, rocky beach. "Let me check what the sign says. Or better yet, I'll just power up the sat-nav."

"Stupid question."

They tugged and pushed and got the barge as far onto the beach as they could, then tied a line around a boulder to secure it, though Brian was dubious it would hold once the tide came in.

"Actually it wasn't a completely stupid question," Brian finally said. "I sailed around the Bay of Biscay years ago. This inlet looks like one I remember. If I'm right, this is Santander. 'Course the Santander I remember was a major port filled with cruise ships and this beach was stacked with high-rise flats and that hillside was covered in houses with lovely salmon-colored roofs. Other than that it looks exactly the same. Fancy a sangria?"

"Did anyone ever tell you that you get really irritating sometimes?"

"Only all of my ex-wives. And my girlfriends. And my agent, Ronnie. And the crew on my shows."

They gathered their possessions, their swords, packs, and remaining food and water and began walking the beach, relying on Brian's belief that Bilbao was to the east. They had no idea about the location of Burgos. Trevor was sick of hearing Brian say that they'd just have to ring up the Automobile Association for directions.

In the distance they saw some fishermen casting nets and they headed inland to avoid contact. The beach turned to scrubland then meadowland. There was smoke rising to the east. It started as a few wisps then became a solid column of dark gray against the pale sky. Trevor reckoned it was about two miles away.

A mile closer, the smoke had not abated and they saw the reason why. Flames were visible, rising from a broad base.

"We should give that a miss," Trevor said.

Brian agreed. "We can flank it to the south but we'd best not get too far off course."

Closer still they saw that the conflagration was coming from burning houses. A village was up in flames. Within a few hundred yards they heard the first screams, male voices bellowing in pain and fear. Then lone, high-pitched screams which grew louder and louder.

A woman came into view, running toward them from the burning village.

Then four men running after her, shouting and waving swords.

Brian and Trevor looked at each other with the same puckered expression that needed no words. Chivalry was going to get the better of them.

"At least let's make quick work of it," Trevor said. "This isn't why we're here."

"We're on the same page," Brian said, drawing his sword.

The woman saw them and froze, likely believing she was trapped.

"Aqui, aqui! Amigos!" Brian yelled, using most of the Spanish he knew.

The woman glanced over her shoulder at the approaching men. She was young and barefooted, with black hair and a long peasant skirt. She made her decision and ran toward Brian.

Trevor and Brian held their ground and the woman ran past them, her eyes flashing with fear. She kept going and stopped fifty yards beyond.

The approaching men seemed to realize a fight was coming and they slowed their pace to shout instructions to one another.

"Sword in right hand, knife in left," Brian said, giving his student a quick refresher course. "And take off your backpack."

"Wish I had my nine millimeter," Trevor said, breathing hard in anticipation.

"You and me both. Ancient weapons are rubbish, aren't they?"

The swordsmen split into two groups and began a flanking maneuver, first at a trot, then a full run.

"Steady, steady," Brian said, his back to Trevor. "Put one down fast and it'll be one-on-one."

At first contact, the attackers seemed to recognize that something was different about their adversaries but there was no time for more than combat.

Brian surprised his two foes by charging them, his sword high, before dropping low and slashing one of them in the hamstring with his knife. Before Brian could capitalize on the advantage, the other one was on him, necessitating a series of parries.

Trevor stayed planted, leaning slightly forward on the balls of his feet, as Brian had instructed. His two foes did a coordinated attack and he had to deal with two blades coming at him in concert. He blocked one but the other got through, slicing his jacket. He braced for pain but felt none. Angered at the close call he launched a furious counterattack, surprising himself by yelling like a maniac.

His vocalization proved helpful. One of the men hesitated just long enough for Trevor's downward chop to strike home before his adversary could muster an effective defense. His sword hit the man's shoulder and his tan shirt turned red. The second man, the one who had sliced his jacket, reacted swiftly and swung his weapon with so much force into Trevor's parry that Trevor's sword flew out of his hand. The man smiled and seemed to dare him to bend down to pick it up. Trevor shifted the knife into his right hand and prepared to be slaughtered.

From the corner of his eye, Trevor saw a blade come into view. Brian lit into Trevor's would-be executioner and the man reacted just in time to clash swords. That gave Trevor enough time to glance at the two bodies lying on the ground, handily dispatched by the man from the BBC.

The other soldier whom Trevor had wounded tried to bring his sword back into play but his shoulder was too damaged. He chose to run back toward the burning village.

"Need any help?" Trevor called out.

"No, stay away," Brian shouted. "I don't want to hit you by mistake."

Brian and his opponent clashed and traded blows for a long minute and then they stopped as abruptly as they had started. The soldier looked down at something sticking into his flank and dropped his sword, choosing to use both hands for another purpose. He removed Brian's knife, held it quizzically then fell forward, his blood fouling the grass.

Trevor turned to look at the woman. She let out a yelp and began running again.

"Hey," he called out. "It's all right. They can't hurt you now."

He heard Brian say, "But *they* can."

Then he saw what Brian saw. A large group of men on horseback were galloping toward them from the village, coming fast.

"What do we do?" Trevor asked.

Brian threw down his weapons and held up his hands. "We surrender or we die. And I'm not too keen on dying in a minute."

Trevor did the same and the two men awaited whatever was coming.

Most of the horses pulled up just short of them but a few charged past aiming for the fleeing woman.

The riders eyed Trevor and Brian suspiciously. Brian looked over his shoulder and saw the woman being scooped from the ground by one of the horsemen and thrown onto his saddle.

One of the riders was dressed far better than the rest. A middle-aged man with a pock-marked swarthy face, he wore a black doublet, black leggings and a floppy black hat secured with a chin strap. He dismounted and in Spanish, instructed one of his men to secure the weapons before he approached. Others dragged away the still-moving bodies of their comrades.

Then he stepped forward, staring and sniffing, screwing up his face in puzzlement.

"Who are you?" he asked in Spanish.

Brian understood the question and answered in English. "My name is Brian and my friend is Trevor. Do you speak English?"

The man answered, "English, yes, a little. Where are you from? You are not from here."

Brian slowly lowered his arms, prompting the man to say, "no, no." Brian obeyed and the man had them searched before he allowed them to put their arms down.

"We're from England," Brian said.

"Brittania?"

"No, England. We're not from Hell. We're from Earth," Trevor said.

"We are all from Earth, señor. We died first. Have you died first?"

Trevor said, "We're alive."

"Impossible."

"We're alive, all right," Brian said. "Some scientists sent us here."

"For why?"

"To find our friends," Trevor said.

"Who are these friends?"

"Other live people. Two women and two children who've been sent to Hell by mistake."

"I do not understand what you say. Tell me, why you destroy my men?"

"They were chasing that woman," Brian said.

"She belong to me," the man said. "The village of Astillero belong to me. If I say burn the village, the village is burned. If I say take the woman, the woman is taked."

"And you are?" Trevor asked.

"I am Prince Diego de Anera, the crown prince of Bilbao. You will come with me."

"Will you help us?" Trevor asked. "One of our friends, a woman, is in Iberia, in Burgos we think. We need to find her."

"Yes, I help you. You can pay? You have gold?"

"Better than gold," Brian said. "There's something very valuable in that bag."

The prince picked up the backpack and opened it.

"This?" he asked, holding up the book.

"Yes."

The prince opened it then quickly shut it. "I cannot read your language."

"That's okay. We can translate it," Trevor said.

"Why is valuable?"

"Because it teaches how to make bombs," Trevor said. "Very big bombs."

The prince raised his eyebrows and ordered four of his riders to double-up and offered horses.

"Come. We go to my house in Bilbao."

"That suits us fine," Brian said. "Feeling good about riding that horse, Trev?"

Trevor let out a string of curses.

"Don't let the animal know you're scared of it. You'll do fine."

"Better than her."

The fleeing woman was being paraded past them. She raised her head from the saddle and gave them a woeful look as her captor took her back to the village and an uncertain fate.

"We can't save them all," Brian said.

23

He had arrived in Hell weak as a kitten. But he had been rescued from the Babylonian slave traders who swept him up. Loyal Macedonian soldiers who had preceded him to Hell had nurtured him. Having regained his legendary strength he had returned to his Aegean homeland.

For twenty-three centuries in Hell the young man had fought enemies far and wide, conquering territory, losing territory, and conquering it again. But most of all he had fought the terrible sameness and boredom of neverending time.

"Better to be a king than a slave," he had told his comrades countless times, "but better still to be freed from this prison with no bars which is stronger than any jail."

But there was no release and he had little choice but to live out this existence of attacking and defending in limitless cycles of violence.

King Alexander of Macedonia had been told by more modern arrivals of the name which history had given him. Alexander the Great. The name was a source of pride. He *had* been great, had he not? He had created the largest empire of the ancient world, stretching from Greece to Egypt and into the Indian subcontinent. He had never been defeated in battle.

But in Hell, his military success had been far more limited. His soldiers were not as brave and disciplined as those he commanded in life. They did not fight for the glory of the gods because they no longer believed the gods existed. Many of his best men never made it to Hell at all, proving to him that battlefield killings were not universal acts of condemnation. It was only those soldiers who had committed atrocities on civilians, on prisoners, on innocents who found their way into Alexander's afterlife ranks. These men were an undisciplined and fractious lot. And the more modern Macedonians and Greeks who arrived in his Aegean kingdom were not as superb fighters as his ancient warriors. Those men had been real men, he chronically lamented.

He had long ceased pondering the reason he had been sent Down. Had it been the Thracian general he slayed because the man had dared to look him in the eye rather than cast his gaze downward like an obedient prisoner? Or the Indian boy he had strangled in his bed? Or his own soldiers he had executed for relieving themselves inside the tomb of Cyrus the Great? He no longer thought about such things.

Astride his white horse, his shoulder muscles rippled under his bronzed skin when he pulled the reins hard and brought the beast to a halt. He was at the tip of the spear, the front of a long column of Macedonian and Slavic fighters. He had been with a few of these men for two millennia, though most of his early comrades were rotting in ditches or on lakebeds. The luckier ones who had fallen in battle or from disease were deposited in rotting rooms. At least that conferred some honor. He had prepared his own royal rotting room to house his remains if and when the day of need came to pass.

Below him stretched the Bay of Naples and the crowded grimy city that sprawled from the high cliffs all the way to the edge of the sea.

"Do you see that, Cleitus?" he said to the young general by his side, a very old friend he had killed in life after a drunken quarrel. "They must know we are here. They must know of our march from the south. And yet, where is their army? Where are their preparations?"

Cleitus laughed. "This new king of theirs must be a donkey. Off he goes through the front door of his house chasing enemies to the north and he leaves the back door open and unguarded."

"Let us get on with it," Alexander sighed. "This city is poor and ugly. The faster we vanquish it, the faster we take Rome."

Two French steam cars noisily chugged along the rutted road sending wildlife fleeing. John drove the lead car with Emily at his side and Alice, Tracy, and Tony crammed in the rear seat. Charlie, whose claim that he could drive any vehicle ever invented proved to be true, drove the second car with Martin beside him and three armed French soldiers handpicked by Forneau in the back.

Forneau had a firm idea which southern route Garibaldi and the Italian army was taking.

"They will march due south to Toulouse," Forneau had advised, "then due west to the coast to avoid the mountain crossing. From there, they will enter Iberia near Irun and then to Burgos."

John's rough calculations, factoring the Italians' head start and their relative speeds, led him to believe the automobiles could catch up to the army before it crossed into Iberian territory.

The first day and first night passed without incident. They sped through the countryside and John was able to give the towns a wide berth. When they did have to pass through villages, the residents reacted as those had done the last time he'd driven these machines through Europa: they cowered behind closed shutters, scared of the noise and the imperial might the machines represented. When night fell, the French soldiers, fearful of rovers, wanted to stop but the road was good enough and well enough illuminated by the headlamps that John wanted to carry on. Only when it was clear his passengers needed rest and the boilers needed recharging with water, did he agree to pull up. Luckily, as soon as the cars were shut down, they heard the pleasant sound of running water and found a good stream by the side of the road.

They slept on top of blankets and furs in the warm night air, apprehensive, though comfortable despite the buzzing insects. John and the soldiers kept a rotating watch and at first light he and Charlie primed the boilers for the day ahead.

"I'm just going to take the ladies into the woods a bit," Emily said, loading the blankets into the car.

"Want me to keep guard?" John asked.

"We'll be fine."

He pulled out his flintlock pistol from his belt and put powder into the pan. "Here."

She took it and said, "Back in a jiffy."

John was so close to the heating, rattling, and chugging boilers that he almost didn't hear the gunshot.

When the French soldiers saw him running they followed, drawing their swords.

"Should we stay here?" Tony yelled after them, but they had disappeared into the thicket.

John saw the body lying beside a fallen, dead tree.

It was a scrawny man in ragged clothes clutching a curved rover's knife in his hand, a perfectly round, black hole in his forehead.

Emily was standing protectively in front of Alice and Tracy, the pistol still smoking in her hand. Tracy was hysterical and Alice was trying to comfort her.

"Was he the only one?" John called out.

"There were more," Emily said, surprisingly calmly. "They were sneaking up on us. The others ran off."

Seeing John, Alice stepped forward. "Is he dead?"

"Not dead, remember?" John said, kicking his knife away, "But his rover days are over."

Emily dropped the pistol and started shaking like a cold, wet dog. He wrapped her up in his arms and nuzzled her until she was ready to get going.

"Pretty good shot," he whispered.

"I think I closed my eyes."

"I doubt it. You're fierce, know that?"

She talked into his shoulder. "I just want to find Arabel and the children and go home."

"Then let's hit the road."

On the third morning of their journey, with the smoke of thousands of cooking fires drifting upwards from the nearby city of Toulouse, they spotted the horses and wagons at the rear of the Italian column.

"Do you think that's them?" Emily asked John.

"If we've hit the wrong army we're in trouble."

Tony half-rose in his seat and caught Martin's attention in the trailing car. There was no point in shouting over the racket but he pointed down the road and Martin seemed to understand, waving back and giving a thumbs-up.

The first Italian soldiers to hear the cars coming turned and readied their weapons. Word spread down the line. John slowed his car and approached in as non-threatening a way as possible, waving his free hand in a greeting.

When he got within fifty yards he braked hard forcing Charlie to do the same.

A sharpshooter was training his rifle.

"Get down!" John shouted, pushing Emily below the windscreen.

But before the rifleman could pull the trigger another Italian soldier began shouting at him to lower his weapon. That man came running toward the car, waving his arms, shouting John's name: "Signore Camp! Signore Camp," and John recognized him as a member of his squad who'd charged the English, hurling hand grenades in the attack that had turned the tide for Garibaldi's forces.

John stood at the wheel and shouted, "Ciao Mario!" and then to his companions, "It's okay. I know this guy."

Mario came to the driver's side of the car and said in broken English, "Is you! You no go home?"

"I went home, si. Now I'm back. This is my friend, Emily."

She reached out her arm but Mario rushed over to her side and kissed her on both cheeks.

"Stay, stay," Mario said. "I get Re Giuseppe."

The Italian line stretched down the road and it took quite a while for

Garibaldi to appear on horseback, flanked by Caravaggio and Simon Wright and accompanied by a protective guard of his most loyal soldiers.

John and the others got out of the cars, the French soldiers electing to stretch on the grassy verge.

Garibaldi dismounted dressed in the same soldier's uniform and red shirt John had last seen him wearing. No finery, no royal regalia, just a tired old soldier with a heavily lined face and a neat white beard. He approached them limping noticeably.

"John and Emily," Garibaldi said, seizing John's shoulders with his arthritic hands and smiling warmly at Emily. "My emotions are mixed. It is wonderful to see friends again, especially friends to whom we owe so much. Yet, I am heartsick that you have failed to return to your homes."

"We didn't fail," John said. "We came back."

"But why?"

"To bring these people back," John said, gesturing at the other Earthers. "And to find others."

"My sister," Emily said. "And her children got caught up in this mess. We're looking for them."

Garibaldi shook his head and was about to say more when Caravaggio came forward, giving Emily his full attention.

"Once more I am able to gaze upon this face," he said. "May I kiss it?"

"You may," she said, laughing.

"John, you will not shoot me?" Caravaggio said.

"One kiss, you're fine, two, you're in trouble," John said.

Simon shook John's hand hard. "Good to see you, my friend. How's this French bucket of rust holding up?"

"It's running a little rough. Maybe you can take a look at it."

"My pleasure." Simon's eye turned to Alice. "Don't be a rude bugger. Introduce your friends, then."

John motioned Charlie and Martin over and each one said a hello when John called their names.

"Everyone," John said. "This is Giuseppe Garibaldi, king of Italia and now king of Francia too. He's a great man and I'm proud to call him a friend. And these gentlemen are also great men. This is Simon Wright, soldier, patriot, and master boilermaker, and this is Michelangelo Caravaggio, one of the greatest painters of all time."

John had told Martin and Tony about possibly meeting Caravaggio but the art lovers were star struck and stammering in his presence, which pleased the artist but also was embarrassing as they fawned more over him than the king.

Simon wandered over to Charlie, Tracy, and Alice and began chatting with them, asking where they were from and how they managed to get into this pickle barrel.

"I don't understand it," Alice said. "You'll have to ask Emily about that."

"A boilermaker, are you?" Charlie said. "I'm a builder myself. Alice is an electrician, a good one."

"Are you now?" Simon said, nodding and smiling. "A lady who knows electrics. Here's Emily, a scientist and here's you, an electrician. The ladies in your time are doing the work of men. And you, my dear?"

Tracy lifted her head. "Me? I'm just a mother."

"No small job, that!" Simon said cheerfully. "May I inquire after your children?"

"They're with their father, I hope. They were at school when ..." With that, she began to cry and Alice rubbed her back in a motherly way.

"There, there," Simon said. "Mr. John Camp will get you back to them, I'm quite sure. He's a good man to have by your side."

There was much to discuss but Garibaldi was anxious that they not lose a day's march. After dismissing the French soldiers to return to Paris with fresh horses, they headed west toward the coast, John driving one car and Simon volunteering to drive the other. Charlie was relegated to the back seat with Tracy. Alice, at Simon's insistence rode up front.

That night Garibaldi ordered his cooks to prepare a feast of celebration which proved to be a feast in name only since provisions were tight. They ate the same hard bread, dry meat, and vegetable stew the rest of the army ate but Caravaggio assured one and all that at least the wine, with barrels liberated from Robespierre's cellars, was special.

Garibaldi sat on a bench between John and Emily and listened as they told him about their encounter with King Henry, their journey to Paris, and their impressions of a post-Robespierre Francia.

"You've done well to add France to your kingdom," John said.

Garibaldi responded with a thin smile. "As a soldier you know that taking territory is one thing, holding it is something very different, and sometimes more difficult."

"Forneau's a good man to mind the store," John said and Emily agreed.

"He is," Garibaldi said, "but there are ambitious French nobles in the wings and the possibility of a German and Russian counterattack is very real. Moreover, there are problems back home with reports of an invasion force from Macedonia. Antonio has taken a thousand men back to Italia to deal with the threat. It was not an ideal time to leave Paris. The new order I seek must take its strength from the support of the common man, exploiting any morsels of good that remain in their souls. I haven't had any time to let the people know my goals. Not the Italians, not the French. For those that even know they have a new king, they do not know that I see a new way for us to live in Hell. They do not know that I seek a better path, where every man and woman in this sorry place might rise up from despair and hopelessness. I would have liked to travel my new kingdom and lift up the spirits of my subjects but I could not do so. First I have to strengthen our hand with an Iberian alliance and that is why we go to Burgos, to seek an audience with King Pedro."

"What do you think he'll say?" John asked.

"I really don't know which is why it was necessary to bring a sizable force, in case he would prefer to fight. He is known for his arrogance and intransigence. But, my friends, these are my problems. Now tell me yours," he said, patting Emily's hand.

"My sister and her children, a boy and a girl were waiting at my laboratory for my return. When John and I came back, they were transported here along with another woman."

"Here? You mean children have come to this place?" Garibaldi said in distress. "How awful. How cruel. Where are they now?"

"Guy told us they're in Marksburg," John said.

"Barbarossa has them?" Garibaldi asked.

"You haven't heard?" John said.

"Heard what?"

"Stalin put him down and put himself in charge."

Garibaldi's head drooped. "A combined Germania and Russia. This quest for a new order has become even more difficult."

"We didn't dare ride into Marksburg and demand that Stalin just hand them over," Emily said. "We needed your help."

Garibaldi nodded. "And help you I shall, which is why an alliance with the Iberians is a matter of even greater urgency. I am sure you would prefer if we immediately turned north toward Germania but we are so close to Burgos."

John and Emily exchanged a glance. They both began to speak but John deferred to her.

"I think what both of us are going to say," she said, "is that since we're close we should go to Burgos first. My sister was split up from the children. They're with a living woman named Delia. Arabel was sold to Pedro."

John added, "We have two friends who came over with us who were trying to get to Burgos to rescue her. So here's our plan: let's try to find all three of them, travel together to Marksburg then return as one group to England."

"We're up against the clock again, I'm afraid," Emily said. "We only have twenty days to get everyone back to England to catch our ride home."

Garibaldi said, "Then we shall break camp at first light and proceed to Burgos with all haste."

Garibaldi started to stand but winced and clutched his thigh.

"How's that wound doing, Giuseppe?" John asked.

"It was fine, but now the reddening and the aching have returned."

That man over there, Martin, is a doctor. King Henry had an infection. He made some medicine that helped him. Can I have him take a look at you?"

"Send him to my tent," Garibaldi said. "An old man looks forward to his bed the way a young man looks forward to a woman."

The campfire flared and sputtered when Simon tossed more dried wood upon it. Caravaggio had made it his personal mission to try to cheer up Tracy, declaring that nothing in Hell was worse than seeing a woman weep.

Earlier Tracy had insisted she didn't have a clue who Caravaggio was. "I didn't take art in school," she had said.

"All right," Tony had said, rolling his eyes, "but we're talking about Caravaggio, for Christ's sake!"

"Leave her alone," Martin had scolded. "You're such a snob. Not everyone knows who he is."

"Well I've never met someone who doesn't know him and adore him. This has made the whole Hell thing so much more tolerable. Can you imagine the bragging we'll be able to do when we get back?"

"*If* we get back," Martin had whispered directly into his ear.

"Tell me about these children of yours," Caravaggio said to Tracy, pulling his trusty sketchpad from his shoulder bag.

"Well, Louis is such a smart little boy. He can ..."

"No, not what they do, how they look. Give me every small detail and I will draw them for you so you can look upon their faces."

"You can do that?" she asked, brightening.

"I can do."

She described the two children in every detail. The shape of their faces, their noses, lips and cheeks, their eyes, ears and hair. Illuminated by the campfire, Caravaggio sketched a facial feature on a sheet of paper in charcoal, and when she approved, he reproduced it on a master sheet. Slowly but surely, the faces of her two children emerged, a boy and a girl nearly cheek-to-cheek. The whole time, Tony stood over his shoulder and watched the master at work. The architect had his arms tightly wrapped around his chest as if trying to prevent it from heaving. When Caravaggio was done he presented the sheet to Tracy who responded with tears of sorrow and joy. Her release of emotions was contagious and Tony joined in.

"It's amazing," Tony said.

"You like?" the artist asked.

"I can't believe I've been able to watch Caravaggio, sorry, you, drawing. I feel like I've died and …"

"Sorry," Caravaggio said. "Not heaven."

Tony smiled. "Yeah, still. I do some sketching myself."

"You are artist?"

"Not really. I'm an architect."

"You make buildings."

"Yes."

Caravaggio passed him his pad and a piece of sharpened charcoal. "Show me a building you made."

Tony blushed and took the materials. He sat on the ground with his back to the fire and began sketching one of the London skyscrapers he'd designed. It was a soaring tower with a bold curving façade and when he showed it to the great artist he praised it to the sky.

"Can I hug you?" Tony asked.

"Hug? You mean with arms?" Caravaggio said. "Yes."

Martin emerged from Garibaldi's tent just in time to see the men embracing.

"Excuse me?" Martin said.

Tony looked sheepish and released his hold. Martin beckoned Tony with a finger.

"What are you doing?" he asked.

"He liked my sketch," Tony said.

"Did you happen to notice that he's seriously good-looking?" Martin said.

Tony feigned an expression of surprise. "Is he?" That defused Martin's anger and Tony finished with, "Anyway, you smell better than him. How's your patient?"

"He's got a wound infection. We'll make another batch of penicillin tea. I'm going to leave bread out to start it molding. What's with them?" He pointed at Alice and Simon who were sitting close to one another by the fire.

"Romance is in the air," Tony said.

Simon tossed another handful of dry wood into the fire and said, "So you've got a trade, then."

Alice nodded. "As I said, I'm a qualified electrician."

"Many women in your guild?"

"No, not too many. I wasn't going to let that get in my way, was I? Much use for boilermakers here?"

"Not much. Only boilers I've seen are these small ones for the cars and I doubt there's more than twenty of them in all of Europa."

"Any need for electricians?" she asked.

"Well, not really. I mean we've got crude batteries for powering the telegraph but nothing else that I know of. I wish we had electric lights. It does get powerful dark in the night." He paused for a while before saying, "Can I ask you something, Alice?"

"Go on then."

"Back home, do you have, well, a man in your life? A husband? A gentleman friend?"

She shook her head. "I had a husband but divorced him, what, ten years back when I was thirty. I never remarried and I've been single ever since."

"No gentlemen?"

She laughed. "No. The reason I'm laughing is some of my girlfriends were recently trying to get me to do something called Internet dating."

Simon repeated the words as if they were from a foreign language.

"Don't ask me to explain," she said. "But it's a way people get together nowadays."

"Did you do this—what was it—infernal dating?"

"I did not. What do I need a man for anyway?"

"We've got some uses, I reckon."

"A few, maybe. Do you like cats?"

"Like them well enough. Only the rich have them for mousing and ratting. Regular folks eat them."

"Heavens! If I saw anyone trying to kill a cat I'd thump them good," she said.

"You don't see them about much but if I spot someone trying to do one harm I'll join you in the enterprise."

"Were you married?" she asked.

"I was not. I had a mind to at one point in my life but it never happened. Maybe if I hadn't done what I did."

"What did you do?"

"I'll tell you, Alice, though I'm not proud of it. It was in 1901. I was thirty-six and full of piss and vinegar. When I drank I got boisterous as do many a man. I was in a tavern and another fellow, a man with whom I had some acquaintance, well, we got into it and one thing led to another. Fists were flying, then chairs, and I beaned him good with one that was unusually sturdy as chairs go and it did him in. I was arrested, tried, convicted, and the crown duly carried out the sentence. Death by hanging. And here am I, poor Simon Wright, boiler maker and Heller."

"I never pictured Hell would have nice men like you," she said.

He beamed. "You think I'm nice?"

"Yes. Yes I do."

"And I don't smell too bad. I'm told our lot has a peculiar odor. I did scrub myself the best I could before coming out to sit beside you and rubbed some wildflowers from the meadow over my person."

She smiled back. "You know, I hardly notice it."

Garibaldi limped out of the tent and found John and Emily sitting on a log by the fire.

"Your physician tells me my situation is not grave. He intends to brew me some medicinal tea. Thank you for making him available."

"I'm glad it's not serious," John said. "Have a seat."

Garibaldi lowered himself to the log.

John got his pack and told him they had something to give him.

"Do you?" the old man asked, intrigued.

"We figured out a way to bring you some useful items from the Earth."

"You're going to like them," Emily said.

"I can scarcely contain myself," Garibaldi said.

John pulled them all out and said, "Books, Giuseppe. We brought you books."

Garibaldi gasped and eagerly held out his arms to take the heavy stack to his chest where he held them like a baby.

"I have a very small library in Rome," he said. "Each book is a treasure, written by hand from someone's imperfect memory of a work known to them during life. I can scarcely believe I am about to see real books. Which ones did you choose, I wonder?"

"Have a look," John said.

He carefully put the six books down on the dry ground and began examining them one by one.

He began with *Steam Boilers, Engines and Turbines,* moved to *Blast Furnace Construction in America, Bessemer Steel, Ores and Methods* then the one book which King Henry had not received, *The Chemistry of Powder and Explosives* by Tenney L. Davis.

Garibaldi looked up and said, "Do you have any idea how these books, when placed into the right hands, can change the face of our world? Change it for good. Or evil?"

"I think we do," John said. "I need to tell you that we had to use five of them to get King Henry to free us and to give us a ship to get here."

"Which one did he not receive?"

"The book on explosives."

"Ah, good," the old man said. "This one can do immediate harm in the wrong hands."

Emily interjected, "But we gave the second copy to our friends to use for barter in Spain."

"That is worrisome," Garibaldi said. "Let us hope for the best. Let me look at the rest."

He looked up from the copy of the Bible and gave them a wink. "You know, I was not a religious man but most men here are, or at least were so. It will have an intoxicating effect that I will be pleased to exploit to our greater purpose. And last?"

"The best for last," John said.

Garibaldi's eyes moistened when he saw *The Complete Works of William Shakespeare* in his hands. "Now you have truly made an old man happy. Come here, both of you, so that I may plant a kiss on your cheeks. I will retire to my tent but I will not sleep. I will be spending the night caressing this blessed book with my eyes."

On the outskirts of Bilbao Prince Diego de Anera pointed out Queen Mécia's palace in the center of the city, a yellow stone fortress with impressive fortifications. The queen, he explained, would be interested in their book and would pay handsomely to have an advantage over her husband, King Pedro.

"They are not with war but they are not with peace," the prince said.

"Will she help us get to Burgos?" Trevor asked.

"I think yes," the prince replied.

The prince's own house, located about a mile away, was far more modest, a squat brick structure with a protective outer wall, though it was huge by the standards of virtually every other building in the city. But no sooner had they arrived inside the courtyard than the prince showed his true colors by ordering them seized and placed into heavy wrist irons.

"What about our deal?" Trevor yelled.

The prince merely shrugged and disappeared through a doorway carrying their book.

They were led by their manacled hands to a side entrance where, with quick words, they were passed to another set of guards who sniffed at them like hungry dogs and took them down a set of steps into a cool, dark cellar. The five guards jabbered in Spanish as they marched Brian and Trevor to a rank cell block, filled with moaning and clamoring prisoners.

As one of the men was unlocking the cell door Trevor said to Brian, "If this door closes on us, we're fucked."

"Couldn't agree more."

"How are you in hand-to-hand fighting?" Trevor asked.

"Only man I ever punched for real was my second wife's divorce lawyer.

Hurt my hand. I'd prefer a weapon."

"Then let's get you one."

"Right, follow my lead," Brian said.

They were pushed inside against one of the stones. The empty cell was putrid with an overflowing bucket of slop and filthy piles of hay. The guards laughed and began to leave but Brian did something extraordinary to make them turn and stare.

He began singing a Victorian music hall song and doing a soft-shoe dance.

I'm a flirt as you'll discover,
All my sweethearts I can tease,
When I stroll out with my lover,
Don't I like a gentle squeeze.
When an arm around your waist is stealing,
Oh, it thrills you through and through,
Who can describe the scrumptious feeling,
This is what you'd better say and do,
Get away, Johnnie, I'm sure there's someone by,
Get away, Johnnie, to kiss me don't you try.
Get away you naughty man, or I shall kick and strike,
Well get away a little closer if you like.

It wasn't only the guards who watched in amazement. Trevor was reasonably gobsmacked too and it was only at the end of the routine that he understood what Brian was up to.

Brian held out his manacled hands and said, "Por favor, señores, por favor."

The guards laughed and nodded and two men began to fiddle with the keyholes of both prisoners' handcuffs.

The second that one of Trevor's manacles fell free he swung it, still attached to his other wrist and crashed the heavy iron piece into his guard's temple, sending him reeling backwards onto the ground. Brian's guard dropped his keys before finishing the job and began to pull his sword but Trevor was on him, delivering a punch to his face that collapsed his cheekbone, incapacitating him with pain and setting him stumbling out of the cell into the corridor. The three other guards charged and Trevor engaged them with fists, elbows, and head-butts before they could get their swords out.

Brian dropped to his knees to retrieve the set of keys and fumbled for the right one while Trevor fought on. The moment he succeeded in unlocking his left wrist, he received a kick to the chin from one of the soldiers and when the stars cleared he heard Trevor say, "Take this and get the man outside the cell."

Brian nodded and took the sword, scrambling out in time to see a guard weaving around the corner.

Trevor fought on against the three guards, taking blows but relentlessly giving them back, tying up their arms so that no more swords could be drawn. Finally one of the soldiers was able to step back and unsheathe his weapon. He raised it high and swung it toward Trevor's neck.

All Trevor saw was the sword and an attached arm fall onto the floor. Brian was behind the man, his own sword bloody.

"Take a rest, mate," Brian said, laying into the two intact men and within seconds, all of the guards were in a spreading pool of their own blood.

"All right?" Brian said.

Trevor's lip was split and his cheek was swollen. "I'll live. Did you get the other one?"

"Yeah. He's finished. Let's get out of this shithole."

In the corridor, the other prisoners had heard the commotion and from their cells they were shouting up a storm.

Trevor retrieved a ring of keys from one of the fallen guards. "What do you say we keep the prince busy?"

Soon the cell doors were opening and skeletal men began to stream out into the corridor, some so hungry they fell upon the fallen guards ripping their flesh with their teeth, others making a move toward freedom.

Brian and Trevor were well ahead of them, running up the stairs and into the first floor of the fine house.

"This way," Brian said, pointing toward a way out.

"We've got to get the book back," Trevor said.

Brian sighed but didn't argue. They began sneaking down a hall.

"What was that back there?" Trevor whispered.

"You mean the song and dance?"

"Is that what it was?"

"Bit of old-timey nonsense. It's called *Get Away, Johnnie*. Impressed?"

"Not really."

They smelled food cooking. The kitchen was to their left so they took a turn to the right. They crept toward an open door and peeked into an ornate room where the prince was seated by his hearth, his feet on an ottoman. The book was on a nearby table next to the backpack.

Servants ran in from another entrance and in a panic, informed the prince that there had been a prisoner escape. The prince sprang up, grabbed his sword and ran out.

Trevor slipped in and took the book and soon they were in an alleyway behind the house, the ramparts of the queen's palace just visible over the walls.

"That's where we're going," Trevor said.

"It's a shame not to give Prince Arsewipe what he deserves," Brian groused.

"Back at the village you said it best," Trevor said. "We can't save all the innocents. We also can't crush all the bastards."

24

Hunger made them pull off the motorway and stop at a small village shop.

Christine spritzed herself with cologne before going inside where she filled a basket with snack food. She hastily paid the bored teenage countergirl and sat in the car with Molly at the side of the road, stuffing themselves with gooey treats.

They drove off through the quiet village. It was late afternoon and passing a village primary school Molly slowed down and pointed at a small boy sitting alone on a bench by the gate.

"Is he crying?" she asked.

"I think he is," Christine said. "Pull over."

"What?"

"Pull over. I'll just nip out and see if he's all right."

"We shouldn't."

But Christine insisted and out she went. As she knelt beside him a police car pulled up a few car lengths behind their Mini and the lone officer began typing into his dashboard computer.

Molly spotted him in the rearview mirror and frantically tried to decide what to do. But before she could signal Christine the young officer got out of his vehicle, sauntered over and tapped on her window.

"Could you roll down your window, please?" he said.

She complied and asked as calmly as she could, "What's the trouble, officer?"

"Is this your car, madam?"

"It's my friend's. She lent it to me."

"I'm afraid it's showing as reported stolen. Would you mind getting out so we can sort this out?"

She closed her eyes in despair and when she opened them the policeman was no longer at her window.

Christine was.

Molly tried to open her door but the policeman's body was blocking it. She slid over to the passenger side and went around to see Christine holding a stray flint nodule in her hand.

"Did you kill him?" Molly asked.

"No! I didn't hit him nearly that hard. Come on, help me get him into his car."

Molly looked around. The only one who'd witnessed the attack was the small boy who had stopped crying. He watched in fascination as the two women dragged the officer and stuffed him into his driver's seat.

"Jesus, Mary, and Joseph, let's get away from here," Molly said, just as another car lurched to the curb, braking too hard.

A young blonde got out and began weaving toward the boy.

"Where the fuck have you been?" she shouted at him.

"I've been here, mummy, waiting for you," he said in a plaintive voice.

"Get in the bloody car."

Christine's face contorted into a rage.

"Don't," Molly said, but it was too late.

Christine approached the woman. She had her son's arm in a rough grasp, the first throes of giving him a shake.

"Take your hand off of him," Christine demanded.

The blonde turned and said, "Who the hell are you to tell me what to do with my son?"

"I'm the one who's going to thrash you, you drunken cow."

"You and what army?" She yanked the boy's arm and made him yelp.

Christine gave the woman a sharp shove, sending her to the ground rump first.

"Know what?" the woman said. "I'm going to speak to that copper. I'll have you nicked."

She managed to get onto her wobbly legs whereupon Christine landed a fist to her jaw putting her down and out.

"Is mummy all right?" the boy asked.

"She's just having a kip," Christine said. "Come on, Molly, help me drag another one."

They laid the blonde out on the back seat of her car. The boy answered Christine's question: no one else lived at their house. Christine drove the woman's car and Molly followed in the Mini. The boy, seven-year-old Roger, was able to give turn-by-turn directions to a detached cottage with an overgrown garden at the edge of the village. Molly pulled into the drive and tucked the Mini behind a hedge, well hidden from the road, and helped drag the woman inside.

"She's more drunk than punched-out," Christine said.

The boy was already watching the tele when they finished tieing her with lamp cord onto a love seat in the small conservatory overlooking the back garden.

Roger looked up and said, "Can I have some tea?"

"'Course you can," Christine said. "What do you usually have?"

"Cereal," he replied.

"What? For your tea? Auntie Christine can do better than that."

She spent the next half hour re-learning how to make tea while Molly sat with Roger, both of them happily watching cartoons. The tray Christine eventually produced had several rounds of a serviceable Welsh rarebit and a glass of chocolate milk.

"What about me?" Molly asked.

"Make your own bloody tea. You okay, luv?"

The boy nodded and tucked in. "Will you be staying?" he asked.

"I don't think your mom will like that," Christine answered.

"She won't mind."

"What would we do with ourselves while you're in school?"

"It's term break for a whole week."

In the kitchen Molly told Christine the boy had told her that his dad didn't live with them anymore and that his mum was often mad at him.

"There's more booze in the cupboards than food," Christine said. "He's a sweet little boy who deserves better than a drunk for a mum."

Molly shrugged and helped herself to some of that booze. "Well, leave her ropes loose enough so she can wiggle free and let's get back on the road."

"I don't want to leave."

"What's that supposed to mean?"

"What it sounds like. I'm tired of running. I want to settle in for a while. This is a nice house. Roger's a treat. Don't you miss being around children?"

"Excuse me, missy?" Molly said. "Isn't there one tiny problem you're forgetting?"

"Monster mum? No I haven't forgotten her," Christine said. "I think mummy dearest needs to sober up for a week. Do her a world of good."

Murphy finished his supper and pushed his tray away. He got up and began pacing back and forth to the side of the bunk beds.

"Stir crazy?" Rix called down from the top bunk.

"Might say."

"It's a gilded cage, mate."

Murphy leaned his back against the locked door of their Dartford detention cell. "Do you know how many times I dreamed of having good food, a soft bed, flush toilets, tele?" he asked.

Rix didn't have to answer.

"But I'll tell you this: I'd trade it all for knowing our girls are safe."

The TV in the next cell switched on very loud.

Murphy pounded on the door. It had taken a while but Alfred, the sixteenth-century oaf in the adjacent cell had learned how to operate the TV, but he was woefully hard of hearing. He'd been given headphones but he kept forgetting how to use them.

"Come on guards!" Murphy shouted. "Make him put on the bloody headphones."

The guards in the hallway responded and soon quiet was restored.

Rix dangled his feet off the bunk. "I reckon they're doing fine. They'll be on the run, breaking into empty houses, eating up a storm, sleeping in comfort, hopefully finding some good wine along the way."

"It's Hathaway I'm worried about." Murphy said his name like a curse word.

For thirty years, every single day in Hell had been dominated by their hatred of the man. Hathaway had murdered them, but that wasn't the worst of it. He and the band of rovers he'd joined had made it their mission to terrorize them and their pitiful village of Ockendon, returning time and time again to wreak havoc and pick off their fellow villagers one by one.

Rix hopped down and helped himself to a soda from the mini-fridge. "I will take his head one day and when I do, I'll keep it in a box and take it out from time to time and play footies with it."

"So you've said."

Rix grabbed Murphy by his collar and shoved him against the wall, dropping the soda can on the floor. "Tell me about all your triumphs then, Murph. What's your record in draining the fucking swamp?"

Murphy didn't fight back. In fact he dolefully agreed and Rix let him go, waving at the security camera to let the guards know they needn't intervene.

"Hathaway won't find them," Murphy said.

Rix turned on the TV and cranked the volume so they could talk without being picked up on the cell's mics. "He tried. He found her ex."

"Yeah, but it was a dead-end."

Rix retrieved the soda from under the bed and popped the tab, spraying cola everywhere. "For old Gareth it was a very dead-end."

"You think Christine will try to find her mum?" Murphy asked, his mouth close to Rix's ear.

"Maybe yes, maybe no."

"Well, maybe we should be straight with Ben."

"Let's be honest, Murph. We want our girls back. They're running and I'm sure they're scared. We miss them so much it hurts. But if they're found, they'll send all of us back to Hell. That's their intention, isn't it? We love them too bloody much to have them return."

"Damned if we find them, damned if we don't," Murphy said.

Rix nodded. "We're fucking damned all right."

Trotter set his fiery eyes upon his desk blotter. He habitually looked downwards while he was hearing something he didn't like. He waited until his aides had stopped talking before raising his head and fixing them with a withering gaze.

"Off the grid," he said.

"Yes, sir," one of the analysts said. "Very much so. No digital fingerprints of any sort."

"And what about actual fingerprints?"

"Sorry?"

"Giles Farmer has real fingers, has he not? And real toes, and real legs, and a real face. If you'd done as I asked and had real operatives with real eyes on him he wouldn't have been able to slip the noose."

"The lawyers ..." The analyst looked like he regretted saying the word and Trotter punished him by jumping down his throat.

When the tongue lashing was over they all sat in silence until Trotter composed himself and said, "Let me see the list of everyone Farmer called, texted, Facebooked, Tweeted, emailed, anythinged in the past month."

He took the dossier and paged through it.

"It's a bloody lot of people," Trotter said.

"He's rather well-connected," one of the analysts said. "Having said that we've applied certain filters to prioritize and probability-weight his contacts based on the closeness of his relationships, length of friendships, prior support for his conspiracy theories. We've narrowed them down to just over a dozen people who we believe are the most likely to be harboring him. It's the last page of the dossier."

Trotter glanced at the alphabetical list. The first name was Melissa Abelard, the last one, Chris Tabor. All but three had London addresses. Ian Strindberg was not on the list.

"I assume that aware, as you now are, of my views on surveillance that you have eyes on all these locations?"

The analysts nodded.

"And what about electronic surveillance?"

"Telephones, Internet, yes," an analyst said. "Getting listening devices into all these houses and flats would, I'm sure you'd agree, be challenging, and would have to be ex-judicial and therefore subject to a level of detection risk. But if you ..."

"No, that will do for now," Trotter said, checking his clock. "Keep me posted. I'm late for another meeting."

He logged into the videocon of the conference already in progress from a secure facility in Whitehall. Trotter had never intended to sit still for all of it since he was quite sure the level of scientific mumbo jumbo would have been a waste of his time. He had watched Leroy Bitterman's opening remarks earlier in the day; now he wanted to hear the conclusions and judging from Bitterman's comments, the meeting was down to the short strokes.

Trotter used his trackpad to train the cameras successively on each quadrant of the conference table. Previously, he had reviewed the security clearances of the participating physicists and had voiced the concern, notwithstanding their confidentiality agreements, whether they could be trusted with the enormity of the disclosures. Now, studying the strain evident on their faces, he continued to worry about them keeping their mouths shut. Bitterman had insisted that these were all top-level people who had solid track records as government consultants and besides, what choice did they have? Outside experts were required.

"I don't know how to shut down the portal we've created, Mr. Trotter," Bitterman had said. "Do you?"

The CIA, FBI, and MI5 had all signed off on the meeting and finally Trotter and MI6 had reluctantly agreed.

Anton Meissner, professor of high-energy physics from MIT, politely raised his hand and Bitterman acknowledged him.

"Most of us here today have participated in the Hercules experiment in one way or another over the years," Meissner said, "and I don't think there were any dissenters to the final protocols which contemplated raising the collider energies in a stepwise fashion. We all thought it was right to explore lower energies before proceeding to 30 TeV, not because we had outsized concerns about strangelet production, but because it just seemed prudent." He angrily pointed at Henry Quint who was present at the back of the room having not been afforded a seat of honor at the table. Singled out, Quint bowed his head. "Henry, I don't know what possessed you to leapfrog to thirty but now we've got a heck of a mess to clean up. The problem is, none of us knows how to fix this. We've got self-propagating waves of poorly understood and highly exotic graviton-strangelet quantum fields, that's clear enough, but I don't think we've got any experimental apparati for testing ways to shut these fields down. It's going to be down to theoretical models."

Marcel DuBois, from CERN in Geneva, agreed and said, "I think we have to throw a lot of supercomputing power at the problem. It would be helpful to broaden the base well beyond those physicists here today, Leroy. Each of us could suggest additional people."

Bitterman shook his head. "Our goverments are mightily worried about leaks. The UK, in particular, is determined not to have panic and unrest among the civilian population. I'm afraid we're going to have to restrict information flows to this group only."

"I think that's a bad idea," Evan Kirkman from Oxford said.

"We'll agree to revisit the decision," Bitterman said. "But for now it has to stand."

Greta Velling from the Freie Universität of Berlin said, "Look, someone's got to say it, so let it be me. You're planning on firing up the collider again in nineteen days. That can't be a good thing. I'm not saying we know it will make things worse but I don't see how it can improve the situation. The aberrant quantum fields are bound to propagate further even if we were to shut down the collider as soon as our people return."

"So you would advocate what?" Bitterman asked.

"I would say, don't run the collider again," Velling said. "Find the extra-dimensionals who haven't been rounded up, bundle them with the ones you've caught, and figure out what to do with them. Hopefully we won't have additional transfers."

"And strand our people on the other side?" Bitterman asked.

Velling said "Yes," at the same time that Trotter shouted it out loud to himself.

"Well, I say, no," Marcel DuBois said emphatically, slapping the table hard. "Emily Loughty worked for me. I know her very well. We all know her and like her. She's braver by far than all of us put together and we owe her, the equally brave men who undertook a rescue mission, and the poor people who got swept up in this disaster, the full measure of our support. I suggest we all go home, sharpen our pencils, and use our brains to solve this problem."

Trotter scanned the faces of the scientists and when he saw that Velling had few if any supporters he clicked off the screen and threw a pen across the room.

25

Antonio had finally arrived.

Seated in his saddle he drank in the vast palace soaring over the muddy streets of the sprawling city. To him it was still Rome's Borgia Palace, and though King Cesare was headless in a rotting room, he suspected that Romans would continue to call it by that name for a long time.

He munched on a rind of crust waiting for his emissary to return. All his men were dog-tired. They had journeyed from Paris to Rome at break-neck speed, some falling from their saddles in exhaustion.

"For Garibaldi!" he had cried to rally them. "For Italia!" But only to himself he had said, "For Caterina."

Caterina Sforza, Borgia's beautiful and tragic queen, trapped in her ornate cage for centuries by her monstrous husband, now freed from her yoke by Garibaldi's uprising to live as a free woman.

When last he saw her, the smell of gunpowder permeating the inner sanctum of the palace, he had wiped the blood of the destroyed Borgia king from her cheek. She had asked his name and he had proudly introduced himself. She had said the words which he had repeated to himself many times a day: "I do not know my fate, but if your master does indeed spare me, I would know you better, Antonio."

Now with the Macedonians advancing from the Aegean, Caterina had to be saved again. And when he did, he would be bolder this time. He would master his shyness and ask to know her better. Much better.

His emissary returned and gave Antonio the news he was hoping to receive. Caterina was well and would receive him that very evening. As they spoke, provisions were being delivered from the palace to Garibaldi's nearby palazzo, where Antonio and his soldiers would be bivouacked.

Antonio rode to the palazzo giddy with anticipation. He would wash away his grime and try to find some suitable clothes. He would lubricate himself with wine—just enough to loosen his tongue, but not enough to turn it foolish. He would not lay with her that night, even if she wished it. First he had to attend to the defense of Rome. Later, when the Macedonians had been sent fleeing back to their ships, then he would claim his prize and all his miserable years in Hell would, at least for a night, fade from memory.

It was dark when Antonio and his lieutenants rode to the palace. The streets were calm, the taverns they passed filled with knots of merchants, the only men with money to spend on another man's beer. The approach to the palace was lit with torches. Passing through the outer portcullis, which was manned by rigid guards, Antonio wondered who these men were. Caterina's private soldiers? Remnants of Borgia's guard? Garibaldi loyalists? He would have to know this if he was to mount a defense of the city. If there were any question as to their mettle, he would replace them with members of his own brigade.

In the inner courtyard he dismounted and led his contingent of soldiers inside through galleries festooned with the magnificent oils that Caravaggio had painted under Borgia's patronage.

He caught sight of himself in a large mirror, one of the palace's treasures, and while he was pleased at the way his long black hair flowed from under his new cap, one of Garibaldi's lent by a servant at the palazzo, he self-consciously realized he had forgotten to have his dusty boots cleaned. That weighed on his mind while he waited in the throne room, hands clasped behind his frock coat.

When she appeared, preceded by her ladies and bodyguards, she looked as fetching as he had remembered. She had died in her forties, a striking beauty of her day, and while most beautiful women saw their good looks ground down by the ravages of Hell, Caterina had been unusually pampered. She remained quite lovely, with delicate, fine features and reddish hair that framed her face in curlicues. She was wearing the same green velvet dress Antonio had seen the day Borgia was overthrown. He wondered if she was, perhaps, sending him a message.

He bowed deeply.

"Antonio Di Constanzo," she said, after settling upon her old throne. "Come."

She held out her hand and he kissed it, allowing his lips to linger on her skin for an improper second too long.

"My lady, I bring you greetings from King Giuseppe."

She smiled. "I am still not used to calling Signore Garibaldi, king. How is he?"

"He is well, my lady. He has won a great battle against the combined forces of the Germans and Russians."

"Has he? With the assistance of that living man who throws bombs?"

"Yes, this man, John Camp, was of great help, as was the alliance King Giuseppe was able to forge with the French. In fact, he has made a coup against King Maximilien and now he is the monarch of a combined Italian and French kingdom."

"That is indeed remarkable. He has come such a long way in such a short time. I wonder where it will all lead?"

"To a better Europa, my lady. To a better Hell."

She smiled. "A better Hell. Fine words. Tell me, Antonio, why have you returned to Rome?"

"We have received word of an invasion force of Macedonians and Slavs landing upon our shores. Surely you are aware."

"I am indeed."

"King Giuseppe asked me to lead a force of the finest Italian soldiers to defend our kingdom and that is what I have done. I would meet tonight with those commanders who have remained in Italia while we fought in foreign lands. I would march south to intercept the Macedonians before they are able to lay siege to Rome."

"But why would you march south, Antonio?" she asked.

"Because, my lady, I presume that is where the attackers find themselves. They would take Naples, then march on Rome itself."

"I really do not think you have to go to such trouble," Caterina said, removing her yellow scarf and letting it fall to the ground.

Antonio stooped to retrieve the garment but as he did, Caterina's guards launched their spears at Antonio's men, impaling them with ruthless efficiency.

Antonio abruptly straightened and went for his sword but a dozen guards rushed him and despite his struggles his arms were pinned to his side.

A young, bronzed and muscular man in a leather battle skirt and the purple regalia of the Macedonian army entered the hall and stood beside Caterina.

"What is this treachery?" Antonio shouted over the moans of his wounded men.

The Macedonian answered in rudimentary Italian. "I save you from a march, signore. I am not in the south. I am before you."

"Who are you?" Antonio demanded.

The young man flashed a smile, not at him but at Caterina who responded by sliding her tongue seductively between pouting lips. Antonio saw he had a dagger in his hand. He tried to break free but was subdued with a knee to a kidney.

"I am King Alexander," he said, closing the distance between them with a few long strides and burying the knife to the hilt between Antonio's ribs. "But you may call me Alexander the Great."

After hours of watching the comings and goings around Queen Mécia's palace, Trevor and Brian came to the conclusion there was no easy way to get inside. They thought there might be an opportunity of stowing away in a delivery wagon but at the main gate they saw soldiers pushing swords through bushels of produce strapped to a cart.

Standing in a nearby alleyway, turning away from the wretches who passed them by, Brian said, "I reckon we should just go up to the gate and surrender and hope we don't get summarily executed."

"I don't love the idea," Trevor said, but just then, soldiers with muskets began marching down the alley from both directions, shouting at them to lay down their weapons.

"Like it better now?" Brian asked, tossing down his sword.

An officer poked a pistol against Trevor's chest and began screaming at him.

"What's he saying?" Trevor asked.

"Best I can tell he's asking whether you're a Moorish spy," Brian said.

"For fuck's sake, tell him I'm not."

"You think?"

They were roughly bundled into the palace where the manhandling continued. Stripped of their belongings and their book, they found themselves roped together, back-to-back, inside a windowless room decorated with a few good pieces of furniture.

A well-dressed man entered and in an apparent state of alarm he began addressing them in rapid-fire Portuguese. When that produced blank stares, he switched to Spanish.

"English," Brian said, speaking slowly. "Do you speak English?"

The man looked surprised. "English? Yes, I can speak English. Who are you? Why you here? Are you spies? Why you seem so different?"

"We're not spies," Trevor said. "And I'm not Moorish. I don't even know what that is."

"We're here to see the queen," Brian said. "We're friends. We brought her a very special book. Did you see it?"

The Portuguese man said he did and it puzzled him greatly.

"Untie us and we'll give you all the answers," Brian said. "Prepare to be amazed."

The man was Felipe Guomez, principal advisor to Queen Mécia, a courtly, nervous man who became increasingly agitated when they told him who they were and what they wanted. To each of his "is impossibles," they countered with "no, it's true," until Guomez threw his hands in the air and admitted that perhaps they were telling the truth after all.

"I have heard that King Pedro, he consorts with a woman who is like you, by which I mean live in the flesh. I did not believe this but now maybe I believe. Perhaps this is the woman you seek."

"That's definitely her," Trevor said, jumping out of his skin.

"Wait here," Guomez said. "I speak with the queen."

Queen Mécia must have been gorgeous in her youth, and she had probably still been handsome when she died of the plague in her forties. Centuries in Hell had left her with the listless eyes and flat countenance common to long-term Hellers, but owing to her high status and good nutrition, she retained a voluptuousness that she accentuated with a low-cut gown.

When Trevor and Brian were summoned to see her in an intimate audience chamber she looked them up and down but aimed her attention squarely at Brian.

She spoke no English, relying on Guomez to translate. He had clearly briefed her; she did not demand any further explanation of their situation. Rather she began with two interesting questions: was Hell anything like they had expected and how did they intend to return to the land of the living?

Trevor began to answer when she stopped him in midsentence and said, "No him."

"I think she fancies you," Trevor whispered.

"Fuck me," Brian whispered back, then answered that he wasn't really a religious man so he hadn't believed Hell existed at all.

The queen laughed at that and bade him to continue.

"Having said that," he said, "I suppose I would have expected more of the fire and brimstone that you read about, Satan and his minions, that sort of thing. Nothing like this, if you must know."

"I too was surprised by what I found here," she said. "For some it is terrifying. For me it is dull and boring. I crave excitement."

"Spice of life," he said.

She nodded vigorously and repeated the second question.

He told her he didn't understand how all this worked but that there were clever scientists in the modern times who had a machine to send them to Hell and bring them back. "We've got to get ourselves and the woman we're looking for, the one your husband the king's got, back to England in about two and a half weeks. They're going to push a button and, poof, we'll be back home."

She seemed delighted by the word poof and after she understood its meaning she said it over and over.

"Tell me about this woman you seek?" she asked. "Is she yours?"

"Mine?" Brian said. "Heavens no. I've never even met her." He angled a thumb at Trevor. "She's a friend of his."

"Boa, boa," she said and Guomez affected her pleased tone, "Good, good."

"You're toast," Trevor whispered.

The queen added, "So, about this woman: my confidants in Burgos told me there was a strange new woman who has commanded the attention of the king. He often acquires new concubines. Perhaps this is your woman."

Brian said, "We think it's her. That's why we need to get to Burgos."

The queen said something to Guomez who held up their book, *The Chemistry of Powder and Explosives,* and she asked, "What is this book? Why is it of value?"

Brian affected the confidence of the BBC presenter he was to sell its importance. "What Señor Guomez has in his hand can change everything for Your Majesty. This book holds the secret recipes developed over many years that will allow you to make powerful weapons to defeat your enemies. Do you have many scientists lying about?"

"Not so many," Guomez replied for her. "They do not usually come."

Undeterred, Brian said, "Well, no mind. Anyone who can follow a recipe can use this book to make big bombs and such."

"Can these bombs defeat the Moors?" she asked.

"Absolutely. Moors, anyone."

"Is he a scientist?" she asked, waving toward Trevor with the back of her hand.

"No, but he's a military man," Brian said.

"Can he make these bombs?"

"I expect he can."

"Why'd you say that?" Trevor whispered.

"Play along, will you?" Brian whispered back before quickly turning to her and saying, "He says he definitely can. So what I would respectfully request from Your Majesty, is your help in getting us to Burgos to secure the release of his woman friend."

"I may consider doing as you ask," she said. "However, I would need to know more. You will dine with me tonight."

"Both of us?" Brian asked hopefully.

Guomez didn't have to translate her response but he did, "No, just you."

26

The arrival of the steam cars provided an opportunity that Garibaldi seized upon. He had worried that Pedro would misinterpret his arrival on Iberian soil with a fighting force as an act of aggression. The cars allowed him to rapidly send an emissary ahead. He tapped Caravaggio to be his agent to smooth relations. Simon volunteered to drive one of the cars and a twentieth-century Italian named Alfonso received a lesson in its operation and drove the other. The rest of the delegation was comprised of trusted soldiers for protection against bandits, rovers, and hostile Iberians.

With Burgos in sight, Caravaggio tied white flags to muskets in each car. They chugged into the city where they received a decidedly unfriendly welcome from Iberian troops who surrounded and disarmed them and seized the vehicles. Caravaggio maintained a cooperative and friendly demeanor during the ordeal and persuaded Simon to do the same.

A captain was summoned from a nearby barracks. Caravaggio's Spanish and the captain's Italian weren't adequate for communication but they discovered both spoke enough French to get by.

"I don't understand," the captain said. "Do you represent the king of Francia or the king of Italia?"

"Both," Caravaggio replied with a charming grin. "Because they are one in the same, King Giuseppe."

The captain eagerly listened to all the gory details of Garibaldi's and Forneau's coup d'état then slapped the artist on the back, declared that he liked his new Italian friend and that he would see if he could arrange an audience at the palace.

Garibaldi heard the steam cars approaching from the Iberian side of the border before he saw them. By the time Simon pulled into the Italian campsite, everyone had assembled to greet the returning delegation. John, Emily, and all of the Earthers crowded around to listen.

Caravaggio jumped out and embraced Garibaldi, telling him their mission had been successful. King Pedro had been convinced of the merits of a discussion on an alliance and had sent word to his military commanders to give the Italian mission safe passage to proceed to Burgos.

Caravaggio said, "He seemed quite interested in learning the details of your rise to power in Italia and Francia. He was impressed but also a bit concerned, I would say."

"He has every reason to be concerned," Garibaldi said. "Pedro is a tyrant. I have no love for tyrants."

Emily was chomping at the bit. "Did you ask about my sister?"

"I tried to raise the matter," Caravaggio said. "However, my audience with the king was brief and he deflected my question. So I really don't know."

John wanted to know if he'd seen or heard about Trevor and Brian.

"Again, no," Caravaggio said. "I had occasion to speak with the Duke of Aragon, a man who dresses like a colorful bird, and I inquired if there were any living people at his court. He asked me if I had gone mad."

John comforted Emily and said, "We'll get in there and we'll get the truth. If she's in Burgos we'll find her."

Simon sought out Alice and snuck around to tap her on the shoulder. She jumped.

"I got you a present," he said.

She seemed pleased. "You did?"

From behind his back he produced a small bouquet of wilted purple and yellow flowers.

"Spanish flowers. Picked them myself."

"They're lovely. I was worried about you. Everyone was saying how brave you were to volunteer."

"Someone had to drive the bloody car. Caravaggio can paint and draw and charm the ladies but he can't fire up a boiler."

"The world needs all sorts. Without tradesmen like us, where would the artists be?"

"My thoughts precisely," he said.

"I saved you some supper."

"I'm starving," he said, patting his belly. "The Italian grub's better than the Spanish. Yet another reason for supporting the aspirations of our Giuseppe."

Pedro was in a fury.

No sooner had Caravaggio and the Italian delegation withdrawn from his court than the Duke of Aragon informed him that Queen Mécia had arrived from Bilbao with a large retinue.

"She just comes here?" Pedro shouted. "Without being summoned? How dare she. She knows this is a violation of our protocols."

Their protocols, hammered out almost a century earlier after interminable negotiations with royal intermediaries, detailed the separation of royal households and the means by which the king and queen communicated with one another. That communication had always been sparse and mainly limited to matters of military cooperation. The queen commanded her own militia and from time to time, Pedro requested her assistance in mounting a war or defending against invaders, always with payments and *quid pro quos* involved. In his recent defeat at sea at the hands of the English, Pedro had negotiated for the use of twenty of her galleons and hundreds of soldiers and mariners. However, he truly hated the sight of her, and her spontaneous appearance without prior notice and agreement was an affront. Besides, he had other matters on his mind. The invading Moors were making alarming progress in the south and although the Duke of Madrid had assured him his army would vanquish them on the field, the deed had not yet been fulfilled. Furthermore, a power-hungry Italian was coming to negotiate and undoubtedly try to take advantage of him, and his mind was possessed by a captivating live woman who was forcing him by dint of sheer personality and charm to become an ordinary, weak-kneed suitor, rather than a king who took what he wanted.

"The queen's people are saying she comes on a matter of great importance," Aragon said. "The message is enigmatic but it is this: she has something for you and will ask for something in return. She awaits your summons in her caravan."

Out of petulance and spite, Pedro kept her waiting for several hours. Then he finally received her in his throne room with the full complement of his nobledom assembled in the chamber for maximal, intimidating effect. Though it was a warm day he wore his fur-lined robe and the heavy and uncomfortable gold crown he rarely used.

When she entered, he hardly looked at her, his animosity too great. It was two of her companions who caught his eye, a dark-skinned and a light-skinned man who both exuded a certain defiance and lack of submissiveness he had only seen once before in Hell.

The queen bowed ever so slightly and gestured to the empty throne beside him that protocol dictated she be allowed to sit there in his presence. He nodded and she took her place.

He addressed her looking out at the assembly and she replied in a similar, stilted manner.

"Why have you come to my court, absent official notice?"

"I take no pleasure in the visit," she answered in Spanish. "I come on a matter of great mutual interest."

"Does it involve these strangers I see before me?"

"It does."

"Come forward," Pedro commanded and when Trevor and Brian didn't respond the queen informed him that they spoke only English. She offered Felipe Guomez as a translator but Pedro called for Garsea Manrique to come forward instead. The small man scampered through the assembly and obediently began his assignment.

"The king bids you to approach his person," he told Brian and Trevor.

"Sure thing," Trevor said. They came within several feet of the throne before Aragon held up his hand, told them to halt and asked whether they possessed any weapons.

"None," Brian answered.

Pedro tilted his head from side to side and asked, "Are you living?"

"We are," Trevor said.

"How many more of your ilk are there?" the king asked.

"I'm not sure of the exact number," Trevor said. "Four of us came over together. There's another group of four and possibly another group of eight. But I think you know about one of them already. Her name is Arabel Loughty and we think she's here."

Pedro listened to the translation, visibly bristling at the last two sentences.

The king told Manrique, "Tell him I know nothing about this woman."

When Trevor replied that he didn't believe him, Pedro became incandescent and ranted for a full minute, his neck veins bulging, until Manrique inquired whether he wished him to attempt to translate the tirade.

The queen interjected that translation was not necessary and said, "Now Pedro. I have heard about the arrival of this woman in your court. There is no need to pretend otherwise. These two men cannot force you to show her to them. They wish to bargain with you."

Pedro looked at her for the first time. "What kind of bargain?"

"They have brought from Earth a wondrous book which contains all the recipes for making giant bombs with which to vanquish your enemies. Iberia is vulnerable. You made it so with the defeat of your armada. The Moors are rampaging. For the sake of your kingdom and mine, you need to possess this book. They will trade it for the woman."

"Where is this book?" he asked.

"It is safe with me."

"Why don't you just give it to me and I will slit their throats?"

"What's he saying?" Trevor whispered to Brian.

"Doubt it's friendly."

The queen replied that she had given them her word they would be safe.

The king smirked. "Break your word."

"I will not do so."

"Maybe I should slit your throat," he said, smiling brightly at the thought.

"You won't do that for the reason you have not already done so. You need my army. If you destroy me, you'll have an internal war on your hands and if that happens, Iberia falls to its enemies. Let them see the woman. You may have one of your people examine the book. If both sides agree, we will strike a deal."

Brian and Trevor were taken to the wing of the palace allocated to the queen and her extensive entourage. Their room wasn't locked but Pedro's soldiers were stationed in the corridor. They ate some fruit and sampled a flagon of wine left by their beds.

"What do you think he's going to do?" Trevor asked.

"He's going to let us see Arabel," Brian said. "After that it's going to depend on how much he likes the book. I reckon there's a deal to be done."

"There'd better be. I don't see a Plan B taking shape."

"Me neither. Don't fancy the odds of using force. Two of us versus thousands of Spaniards."

"Why's the queen going to the mat for us?" Trevor asked.

Brian grinned. "Like I said, we had a productive dinner the other night."

"You haven't come clean with me," Trevor said. "Tell me you didn't sleep with her."

"A gentleman never tells."

"Jesus, Brian! She's dead. You slept with a dead woman?"

He offered up an insouciant shrug. "She looks a lot like my first wife, Gloria. I fancied Gloria before I stopped fancying her and that's all I'm going to say about it. Toss me another bunch of grapes, will you?"

Jugurtha, King of Numidia, proudly sat on his huge horse surveying the grassy plain. In the distance, to the north, the city of Madrid showed itself by the smoke of its wood fires. Between him and the city, a force of Iberians spread out in defensive formations, with cavalry at the front, archers behind, infantry to the rear, and light artillery at the flanks. The Duke of Madrid rode back and forth in front of his lines but all Jugurtha could see from his vantage point was a plumed helmet bouncing up and down.

Jugurtha's principal commanders, all high-born men from Berber and North African tribes, caught up with him and sought his instructions.

"The hour is upon us," the king said. "Today Madrid, tomorrow Burgos. When we have sucked Iberia dry and gotten fat from its riches, we will feast on the rest of Europa. Are the men ready?"

Tariq, his Libyan commander, replied that the men were excited to do battle. Jugurtha turned to admire the endless sea of polished shields.

"They will try to punch holes in our lines with cannon fire," Jugurtha said.

Tariq laughed. "I was not so sure our maneuver would work but it has. The enemy marched from Madrid to face us without any awareness of our forces flanking them to the east and west."

"It is time to grind their bones to dust," the king said. He called for a man to hand him his bow then lit an arrow wrapped in an oil-soaked cloth and launched it high into the air toward the Iberian line.

Before the flaming arrow touched the ground, his Moorish cannon, concealed in the high grasses outflanking the Iberian forces, fired their opening salvos and the air turned black with a lethal hail of Moorish arrows.

The Duke of Madrid's plume soon disappeared from sight.

27

When they were ten miles from Burgos, the Duke of Aragon and a hundred members of Pedro's royal guard personally met the Italian expedition. It was an escort arranged during Caravaggio's visit to the palace so there was a sense of caution among the Italians but no feeling of menace.

Garibaldi met the duke and invited him to ride with him in a steam car but Aragon politely refused, eyeing the machine with enormous suspicion.

"Is there an animal inside it?" he asked in his excellent Italian.

"You don't have these?" Garibaldi asked.

"We do not, nor would we wish to possess something that assaults the ears and disturbs the senses."

"Well, they are useful machines," Garibaldi said. "If we conclude an alliance, I'll give King Pedro one of them as a gift."

"I am quite sure he will accept it though I do not believe he will wish to travel inside. He has many fine horses and carriages."

"You have left your siege weapons at the border?" the duke asked the king.

"We have brought a single cannon, another gift for Pedro. I assure you, we come in peace."

"We have many cannon, Your Majesty," Aragon said.

"None like this," Garibaldi said. "This one sings."

Before they entered the walled city of Burgos through its northern gate, Caravaggio reminded Garibaldi that it was time to take his dose of penicillin tea. The king gulped it and made a face.

"Our welcoming party," Garibaldi said, pointing to the top of the thick, stone walls.

On its battlements, Iberian archers and artillerymen peered down on them, weapons at the ready. The Italian train of steam cars, horses, and wagons snaked through the narrow streets. Curious residents hung out their windows and stood on roofs to watch the spectacle. The Italian soldiers nervously watched for any sign of an ambush but they rode unimpeded to the plaza of the royal palace where Aragon instructed a camp be erected for the ordinary soldiers.

"You and your ranking officers will stay inside the palace, of course," the duke told Garibaldi when Simon had quieted the boiler. "There will be a welcome dinner tonight, hosted by his majesty."

"I have something to tell you," Garibaldi said to the curious Aragon. "I have some interesting members of my party. They are not soldiers. They are not Italians. In fact, they are not from Hell."

Aragon followed Garibaldi to one of the covered wagons and when the old king pulled the flap back, John and the Earthers began to climb down.

Garibaldi studied Aragon's face and seemed perplexed at his impassivity.

"Alive," Aragon said, bouncing his finger in the air, counting heads. "Seven living souls."

"You don't seem surprised," Garibaldi said.

"Why should I be? It is becoming an everyday occurrence. We already have such persons staying at his majesty's court."

"Two men and a woman?"

The duke nodded. "I could not tell this to your envoy, Signore Caravaggio, but now I am able."

Garibaldi turned to the Earthers. "John and Emily," he said in English. "I have good news for you."

The reunion took place in a formal room at the palace. John and Emily stood at the ready; Martin, Tony, Alice, Tracy, and Charlie sat on cushioned settees. As each minute passed the tension mounted until the doors finally opened.

Brian came out first, sporting a bright smile. Trevor and Arabel entered together, holding hands and when Arabel saw her sister she ran for her. The two women embraced and wept on each other's shoulders.

"You made it," John told the men.

"'Course we did," Brian said, pumping his hand. "Never a doubt."

"We made a pretty good team," Trevor said, giving John a bear hug.

"I expect you've got a few stories to tell," John said.

Trevor nodded. "I expect you do too. Why are you here? You were supposed to get the kids."

"Complicated story but we needed help. Garibaldi had to strengthen his hand with the Iberians before taking on the Germans and Russians. I expect Arabel was happy to see you."

"Happy's not the word. She's had a rough time but she's a survivor."

"Runs in the family," John said.

"She's gutted over her kids."

"I'm sure she is."

Trevor gestured at the others. "Tell me those aren't the South Ockendon lot."

"What's left of them. They've had a tough time too. Let me introduce you."

Emily and Arabel retreated to a sofa to be alone with one another.

"You came for me," Arabel said, reaching for Emily's hands. "You actually returned to this horrid place."

"I had to find you. It was never a question."

"Sam and Belle." She choked on their names. "Do you know where they are?"

"They're in Germany. We know where."

"Then why did you come for me?" she cried. "They're the ones you need to save."

"We're going to get them," Emily said. "We'll all go together. Then we're going home."

"How?"

"We'll need to get back to Dartford. The collider will be fired up to bring us back. I'll explain later."

"I'm sorry but I hate your collider," Arabel said, pulling her hands back.

"No, I'm sorry. I feel it's all my fault."

John overheard and came over. "It wasn't Emily's fault. Her boss was responsible."

"Arabel, I'd like you to meet John Camp."

She started to get up but he dropped to his haunches to greet her. "I've heard a lot about you," he said.

"So, this is John," Arabel said. "I don't know why we didn't meet before."

"I think Emily was keeping me under wraps until she'd cured me of bad habits."

"Well, it's a pleasure to finally say hello. Even under these circumstances."

"How're you holding up?" John asked.

Her eyes welled up. "I've had to dig deep. I kept asking myself, what would Emily do?"

Emily hugged her tight.

"How are mom and dad?" Arabel asked.

"As well as can be expected. I'm sure they haven't lost hope."

"Do you want to meet the others?" John asked.

"Were they at the MAAC too?" Arabel asked.

Emily shook her head. "Innocent bystanders, a distance away, I'm afraid. You'll like them. They're good people."

Hewing to King Pedro's wishes, a panel of negotiators met that afternoon prior to the state dinner. Pedro felt it beneath his position to involve himself in details and he left it to Aragon and other nobles to meet with the Italian delegation to discuss the particulars of an alliance. Garibaldi felt it was nonsense not to participate directly but his people persuaded him that offense might be taken by the asymmetry. So Garibaldi's closest advisors including Caravaggio and Simon sat across the table to try to hammer out a deal. Aragon was baffled by the absence of nobility on the Italian side and Caravaggio explained that theirs was more or less a people's monarchy.

"Garibaldi is a soldier at heart," he said. "I am a painter. Simon is a boilermaker. We all came to follow him because we believe he offers another way to live in Hell, a better way. We don't hate nobility. Some of my best friends are dukes."

"I am so pleased to hear that," Aragon said with a dollop of sarcasm. "I trust the French nobility is likewise heartened."

"We shall see about that," Caravaggio said.

"Well, your strange Italian ideas are of no concern to us. Let us explore the matter at hand. Why should we make an alliance with you?"

"It's simple," Simon said. "Germania and Russia have formed a pact. Each was strong. Together they are stronger. I'll wager that united under the tsar they're plotting their next moves. Maybe Brittania's next. Maybe it's us. Maybe it's you. They'll be wanting all of Europa, that's for sure."

"Perhaps," Aragon said. "I do not know their intentions."

"Forgive me for saying this," Caravaggio said. "I am but an artist, not a man of politics and war, but Iberia is weak at the moment. You lost a war with the English. We hear you have a problem with the Moors." For effect, he drained his wine and tipped over his goblet. "This could be your fate. Join with us in a grand Iberian-Italian-French alliance and let us together, disturb the plans of Tsar Joseph before he is able to send us all to our eternal rot."

The royal dinner, though hastily arranged, was carefully choreographed but to Pedro no detail was more important than the seating arrangements.

While Aragon negotiated, Pedro had fussed over the seating charts until he was satisfied he had achieved the desired effect. When he thought he was finished, Queen Mécia came along and demanded changes.

To reach accommodation, a single long royal table was scrapped in favor of multiple round tables, and a small army of servants scrambled to set up the banqueting hall in time for the commencement of festivities.

Garibaldi complained about the pomp and protocol but he agreed to remain in the wings and enter the hall at the exact moment Pedro entered, that moment heralded by the thumping beat of a dozen drums. Wearing his best uniform he nevertheless looked like a peasant compared to the ornately robed and carefully coiffed Pedro. The two men entered from opposite ends of the hall and were to meet in the front of the hall to the applause of hundreds of diners.

Garibaldi wondered how they would converse but suddenly a tiny man appeared at his side, introduced himself as Garsea Manrique, humble servant and translator. Pedro slowed his pace so that Garibaldi arrived first at the greeting point and had to wait for him. Pedro approached and welcomed him with a slight bow and an outstretched hand.

"Welcome to Iberia, King Giuseppe," Pedro said.

"It is an honor to meet you, King Pedro."

"Come, you will sit beside me, of course," Pedro said.

The seating at the king's table was an awkward blend of protocol and desire. To Pedro's left was Garibaldi and to his right was Queen Mécia. Aragon sat to her right. Brian was given a seat directly across from the queen and as a counterbalance; Arabel had been forced to split up from Emily and was placed across from Pedro. To complete the circle, Caravaggio sat beside Garibaldi and delighted the queen by producing a small, flattering sketch of her. Manrique stood behind the seated monarchs, his diminutive height perfect for the occasion.

At a nearby table, commanding the curiosity of the Iberian court, the Earthers were grouped together.

"If Pedro so much as puts a hand on her, I'll break it off," Emily said, staring over at the royal table.

"I'll help you do it," Trevor said.

"God, I hope the food's decent," Charlie said. "I'm starved."

"You and me both," Alice said, catching Simon's eye at a nearby table.

Martin and Tony participated in the round of formal toasts that followed.

"Here's to you," Martin said. "I can't believe how brave you've been."

"Ditto," Tony replied. "Absolutely, positively ditto."

At the royal table Pedro speared a capon and said to Garibaldi, "So, I have been informed that we have the basis for a pact."

"That's what I understand as well."

Pedro was speaking through a mouth full of greasy poultry. Brian whispered, "Messy eater," to Arabel, producing a delighted snort.

"I haven't laughed much lately," she admitted.

Manrique began to translate his king's speech. "With this pact, Italia and Francia will assist us in our adventures against the English and we will help you in your campaign against the Germans and Russians."

"That is so," Garibaldi said. "However, there may be a need to broaden this military cooperation to deal with our Macedonian and your Moorish problems."

"I know not of your so-called Macedonian problem, Giuseppe, but I can assure you that we have no Moorish problem. I am expecting a messenger at any time to bring me news that the Duke of Madrid has met and crushed the Moors."

"Well, let's drink to that," Garibaldi said, raising his glass. "Left unsaid is the matter of timing. Henry has retreated to Britannia so there is no urgency to action. Stalin has set up shop in Marksburg where he's a threat to us. I propose we proceed there jointly with all due haste. When he's been destroyed or chased back to Russia with his tail between his legs, then we can discuss how best to deal with the English."

"Our people can hammer out the details when they produce the final protocols," Pedro said dismissively. "But tell me," he said, leaning in and crowding out Manrique. "How do I know you will not endeavor to take my head the way you took those of Borgia and Robespierre? I have been in this realm for a very long time and I have never seen a man acquire power so expeditiously. It is a feat that is impressive and fearsome. You must be a ruthless man. A very ruthless man. But let me tell you this, Giuseppe. I do not wish to lose my head. I have grown fond of it."

"You have nothing to fear, Pedro. Cesare Borgia and Maximilien Robespierre were not as loved by their people as I'm sure you are. There was a hunger for change and I provided it."

"Hunger?" Pedro said in astonishment. "Why would I care if the people are hungry for food or shelter or change or anything at all? They are pond scum. That is why they are here."

"Well, I suppose that makes us royal pond scum," Garibaldi said.

When Manrique translated this, Aragon raised his head from his plate in astonishment, Queen Mécia cackled in delight, and Caravaggio snorted his approval and began sketching something on his ever-ready pad. Pedro, however, frowned dyspeptically and attacked another capon.

There was a commotion at the rear of the hall that turned heads. Pedro dispatched Aragon to see what the matter was. He returned with a wounded soldier, his arm bloody and hanging limply, his head bandaged.

"What is the meaning of this?" Pedro asked Aragon, looking at the wounded man with scorn.

"This man has come here from Madrid," Aragon said, hesitating as if afraid to continue.

"Yes? Yes?" the king said.

"I am sorry to report that the Duke of Madrid and his army have been destroyed."

"Destroyed? What do you mean destroyed?"

Garibaldi pressed Manrique to translate and he exchanged troubled glances with Caravaggio.

"What do you think is happening?" Emily asked John.

"I don't know but it doesn't look good."

Aragon elaborated. The Moors had overwhelmed the duke's positions and had wiped out thousands. Their numbers were superior. Their tactics were superior.

Pedro tossed his knife down weakly. "Madrid?" he asked. "The Moors have taken Madrid?"

The messenger bowed his head and replied, "No, sire, they spent but a brief time plundering for food, then departed the city."

"Why would they do that?" Pedro asked. "Where have they gone?"

"Here, Your Majesty," the messenger said. "They are here in Burgos. They have already taken up positions to the south, the north, the east, and the west."

Garibaldi told Caravaggio, "So much for not having a Moorish problem."

The artist closed his pad on his drawing of two frogs sitting on lily pads amidst pond scum, wearing crowns rakishly tilted upon their heads.

That night the Earthers urgently huddled with the Italians.

"We've got no choice," John said. "We've got to fight our way out of this."

"I'm afraid that is so," Garibaldi said. "Aragon tells me they have but two thousand soldiers within the city. Many of their men were dispatched to Madrid."

"Plus our five hundred," Simon said.

Caravaggio said, "I spoke with the Iberians who fled with the messenger to Burgos. Thousands upon thousands of Moors closed in on Madrid's army like a crab closes its pincers upon its victim."

"How were they armed?" Simon asked.

"Bowmen and swordsmen and lancers on horseback. Light and heavy cannon. Some muskets and pistols but not in abundance," Caravaggio said.

"Superior numbers and superior tactics," Brian said. "I'll bet they're a disciplined lot."

"Here's the problem," John said. "We're sitting in a walled city. By the looks of them the walls are well-built and should be able to withstand bombardment for a good while."

Tony came over. "I agree. If they're the same all around the perimeter as the section we passed through entering the city, they're twenty feet thick. And did you notice their exterior concave profile? That's ideal for deflecting artillery fire."

"So why's that a problem?" Charlie asked.

"Because the attackers will approach this like a siege," John said. "They'll huff and they'll puff for a while, but as long as the walls hold they'll change tactics and just starve us out. They'll supply themselves by looting surrounding towns and villages, maybe even sending supply lines back to Madrid. We've got seventeen days to get back to Dartford. A siege could last seventeen weeks."

"A vexing problem, indeed," Garibaldi said. "Perhaps we can try to break through the Moorish lines and send for relief troops from Francia. Outrun them with the steam automobiles."

"Fool's errand," Simon grumbled. "I'll do it if you order it but I won't like it."

A voice called out from the far side of the room. Brian had been pacing. He wheeled and said, "We need to turn the tables."

"What do you mean?" Trevor asked.

"He means we don't do defense," John said. "We play offense."

"Right you are," Brian said.

"Surely you don't advocate attacking them outside the city walls," Garibaldi said.

"I don't," John said. "When I was lying around in the hospital recovering from surgery I did some thinking and a bit of research. If there's a good forge inside the city we might be able to give these Moors a few things they've never seen before."

Caravaggio volunteered to ask Aragon about forges.

"It's too bad we can't get our singing cannon up onto these walls," Simon said.

"Who says we can't?" Tony said, asking Caravaggio for some charcoal and paper. "I might be able to design something."

"Here's the thing," Emily said. "I don't trust Pedro as far as I can throw the slimy bastard. If we save his bacon, how do we know he'll honor his commitment to release us, release Arabel, who he was positively leering at over supper, and give us the soldiers we'll need to secure Sam and Belle's rescue?"

Garibaldi answered, "We will be vigilant, we will be cautious, and at the first sign of betrayal we will crush him without mercy."

28

The royal forge at Burgos was a low brick complex with a beehive-shaped furnace and a tall, round chimneystack which rose to the height of the city walls. The master forger's name was Eduardo, a thin, wiry man who didn't look strong enough to wield the heavy implements of his trade, but what he lacked in brawn, he made up for in speed, running from one station to another, exhorting his men to work faster.

For the first time since arriving in Hell, John let Emily well out of sight to visit the forge while she stayed with Arabel at the palace. The urgency of their situation demanded they split up. Tony, Charlie, and Caravaggio went to the city walls and began working with a small army of carpenters. Trevor, Garibaldi, and Simon ascended the ramparts with Aragon and his officers and surveyed the plain. As the messenger had reported, a large body of men dotted the fields surrounding the city, and through his spyglass, Garibaldi saw hundreds of tents and cooking fires and cannon pieces being wheeled into position. Martin worked at the palace with Alice and Tracy and the royal physicians, assembling and refining surgical tools and making bandages. Emily and Arabel began making what was to be a huge batch of penicillin tea for the inevitable wound infections that would follow.

At the forge John paired with Brian to bring the plans in his head to reality. Working with an interpreter they asked the eighteenth-century Eduardo to show them his best rifles and the man produced a finely carved flintlock bearing Pedro's royal arms.

John and Brian peered down the barrel and dismissed it as smooth-bored.

"You've got rifled barrels, no?" John asked.

"Of course we have rifled barrels," Eduardo sniffed. "You asked for the best quality, not the most accurate."

John and Brian both agreed that Eduardo's rifling technique was good but the musket shot he made was a smooth, lead ball.

"Here's the problem," John said. "It's the same problem I saw in a forge in Brittania. With your rifles and these bullets, your effective range is only going to be about fifty yards."

"No more than that," Brian agreed.

"Haven't more recent arrivals told you about modern bullet designs?" John asked.

"The modern men are idiots," Eduardo complained. "They know nothing about how a forge works. They ask me why I do not have this and why I do not have that but they have no idea how to make these wild inventions. So I kick their asses out the door."

John had used Caravaggio's supplies to make some drawings the previous night and he and Brian showed Eduardo what they wanted to accomplish. The forger listened and questioned and grunted and finally nodded enthusiastically.

"These things, I can make," the man said.

"Then let's get cracking," Brian said. "We'll need thousands of these, a few dozen of these, and a few hundred of these."

"How long do I have?" the forger asked.

"If we're not sending these up to the city walls by tomorrow, you'll need to learn how to speak Moorish," Brian said.

"It is Berber," the translator said helpfully. "These Moors speak the Berber language."

"Then we had better start making the molds," Eduardo said, scurrying off with John's drawings.

Throughout the day Burgos was host to a frenzy of activity. All the city gates were sealed and panicked residents hid behind closed shutters. Pedro's soldiers went door-to-door, commandeering bread and beer and pressing reluctant, able-bodied men into service as musket re-loaders and, should the walls be breached, cannon fodder.

Later in the day Pedro emerged from the palace surrounded by his royal protectors to be transported by carriage to the walls. He climbed to the top with Manrique running at his heels like a small dog and was irritated to see Garibaldi there, roaming the ramparts, very much the man in charge.

"Good day, Giuseppe," Pedro said. "What do we have here?"

"We have a big battle coming. Let me show you where they'll be launching their cannon fusillades. They've got our necks in a fairly tight noose."

Pedro treated Garibaldi more like the commander of his army than a fellow monarch, but if the behavior rankled Garibaldi, he didn't show it, although Simon was livid. Later, Garibaldi would tell him that he had been a soldier for far longer than he had been a king and he was quite comfortable to be in the role of the latter.

Completing the tour, Pedro peered down within the city, curious at the noise of hammering.

"What is that?" he asked.

Garibaldi replied, "One of the living men is an architect. He has designed a tower with a series of winches to raise our very heavy and very special cannon to the top of the wall where it will be invaluable to our efforts."

"Very well," Pedro said. "I will leave you to your preparations, Giuseppe. I must return to the palace for my mid-day meal."

Garibaldi smiled. "I'll be sure to send word if the situation changes."

Queen Mécia summoned her man Guomez and asked to be informed of the military preparations. When Guomez seemed excessively vague on the details she asked to see Brian. Guomez returned to tell her that Brian had left the palace and had gone to work in the royal forge and she astonished her attendants by demanding to be taken there.

The furnace had been roaring for many hours and the air inside was beyond stifling. All the men, including Brian and John were shirtless, laboring side-by-side with the Hellers pouring molten lead and iron into newly minted molds.

The presence of royalty in their midst was a great rarity, and the presence of the queen was unprecedented. Forge workers were even more incredulous at the sight of Queen Mécia than they had been when John and Brian entered that morning. Most fell to the ground to take a knee. She gasped at the toxic atmosphere and called for a fan but her attendants had not thought to bring one. Guomez hastened to Brian and informed him that her majesty had come to see him. He rolled his eyes, grabbed his shirt and accompanied her into the fresh air.

"I cannot get reliable news about our preparations," she told him, while one of her ladies mopped her brow and her décolletage. "You are a military man, Senhor Brian. Please inform me."

"Well let me tell you this, Your Majesty," he said with an unfocused grin. "First we're going to razzle them, then we're going to dazzle them, and finally we're going to kick their Moorish asses out of your fine country."

Guomez looked perplexed and asked for help with his translation. Brian apologized and admitted he was a little woozy from the heat and in a minute he emerged from the forge with a tray of manufactured items.

When he completed his show-and-tell, the queen called for one of her servants to approach and bring her a small wooden box. She opened it and removed a chunky gold ring set with a carnelian gemstone. "You are indeed a remarkable gentleman, Senhor Brian. Please accept this ring as a token of my great affection."

Perhaps it was because he was still loopy from dehydration but after he admired the ring and slipped it onto one of his fingers he stepped forward and brazenly planted a kiss on her lips. Her entourage gasped in horror and Guomez looked like he was going to be ill, but the queen seemed delighted and she departed with a youthful spring to her step.

At the first light of the next day Jugurtha ordered the bombardment of Burgos to commence. Tariq the Libyan, under the cover of darkness, had personally ridden to the city walls and inspected them for areas of weakness and had reported back that they were of solid construction and would be unlikely to yield to cannon fire. Still, Jugurtha knew that there was much to be gained by subjecting the Iberians to a campaign of terror and if he could manage to get some pieces close enough he might be able to lob the odd ball over the wall and inflict some real damage.

John and Brian heard the shots at the forge where they had been working through the night. Garibaldi, his Italian commanders, and Trevor had slept at the palace but arrived on the ramparts with Aragon and his senior officers before dawn. They ducked at the sight of artillery flashes but the first rounds landed well short of the walls.

"Their nearest cannon are five hundred yards and yet they miss," Aragon told Garibaldi. "They will begin to creep closer but I do not wish to return cannon fire yet. They will know we are not in range ourselves."

"I concur," Garibaldi said.

"When will your living men deliver the new weapons?" Aragon asked.

"I had a report last night that they were making excellent progress. Hopefully we'll see the initial batches soon. I think we'll have to wait longer for the singing cannon. The lifting tower is only half-erected."

The two men walked a ways and looked down at the construction below and Garibaldi shouted a greeting.

"Good morning, gentlemen!"

Tony, Charlie, and Caravaggio craned their necks. The large singing cannon was on its carriage, hoisting ropes attached and at the ready. They assured Garibaldi that by the afternoon they would be in a position to begin the lift.

At the palace the women awoke to the sound of cannon fire. Emily and Arabel were squeezed together on the same bed out of choice. Alice and Tracy slept in separate beds in the same chamber.

"It's starting," Emily said.

Alice was already on her feet. "We'd better get to it then. I hope the men are safe."

"You mean you hope that Simon's safe," Tracy said.

Alice splashed some water on her face from the communal basin. "Oh stop it!" she laughed.

"We've all seen the way the two of you look at each other," Emily said, putting her boots on.

"For Christ's sake," Alice said. "Have you noticed he's dead?"

"Good men are hard to come by, alive or dead," Tracy said. "I hope my man is holding up."

Arabel was out of bed now too. "Then let's get cracking. We need to get to Germany then get home."

There was another volley of cannon fire.

"Let's see how our penicillin tea is getting on," Emily said. "I think we're going to need it."

Trevor arrived at the forge to check on the progress. He found Brian and John, dirty, sweaty and exhausted, breaking apart molds and inspecting their handiwork.

"How's it going?" Trevor asked.

"We've got quite the production line going," Brian said.

"I think it's going fine," John said, "but we're going to need another full day at least to make the quantity we need. We heard the cannon fire. How close are they?"

"About five hundred yards and falling short. They're already repositioning."

"They'll be wanting to draw fire from the Iberian cannon on the walls to test their effective range," Brian said. "Bit of cat and mouse. We shouldn't respond yet."

"We're not," Trevor said. "We're standing pat."

"Good," John said. He held up a heavy iron cylinder, still warm from the mold. "Want to help us test this?"

"How do you mean test it?"

Brian said, "He means, want to help us blow something up?"

"Always up for a good explosion."

"We'll need a target inside the city," John said. "Something solid and expendable to see if the percussion system works."

"I'll go check with the duke," Trevor said.

"No, he'll just have us blow up some poor sucker's house." John said. "I know how these guys think. See if you can find something yourself."

Trevor left and returned an hour later. There was an abandoned and partially wrecked stone building located at the end of a long alleyway, not far from the forge. The nearest houses were far enough away that shrapnel wouldn't be a problem. That's where they went with Eduardo and a gaggle of other forge workers.

As Brian was setting up the test John showed Trevor how the system was supposed to work.

"It's called a Hale rocket," he said. "It was designed by William Hale in 1844 as an improvement over the Congreve rocket which was a primitive contraption with a long wooden guide stick, kind of like a fireworks rocket. This iron cylinder is a foot long and weighs about twelve pounds. There's about a pound of gunpowder in the business end, here in the head, and about half a pound in the butt end for propulsion. A fuse sets it off, which is this bit of rope stuffed through the fuse hole. The thing that gives it accuracy and distance are these three exhaust ports that should give the rocket spin. If we've built it right, it should have a range of two thousand yards or more."

"This was used?" Trevor asked.

"Absolutely, in the Civil War, the Mexican War, in Crimea, Africa, you name it. It was good for softening up enemy positions. It got obsoleted pretty fast by modern artillery design which is probably why we haven't seen it here but if it works, they've got it now."

"We're teaching these tossers how to blow themselves up," Trevor said.

John gave him a quick shrug. "I guess we'll be out of the running for a Nobel peace prize."

Brian said he was ready. The other component of the Hale rocket was the launcher, a long, hollow iron tube, closed on one side, resting on a bipod with a fuse hole for ignition. Rather than using a typical forty-five degree firing angle, for the test, Brian removed the tripod and set up the tube horizontally, lashed to a wooden box.

John took the rocket, gently pushed it down the launching tube and ran the fuse out the firing port of the launcher. The target was about a hundred yards down the alleyway. After adjusting the aim and making sure no hapless Iberians wandered into harm's way, John got Eduardo to touch his torch to the fuse.

The rope burned for several seconds and the rocket ignited, sparking and flaming through the air with a high-pitched scream and an instant later it impacted the stone structure with a huge explosion.

Rocks, mortar, and iron shrapnel scattered everywhere.

"Fuck, yeah!" Brian shouted.

John pumped Trevor's hand and said, "Now we've got to make a whole lot more. Come back to the forge and I'll show you how the bullets came out."

Iberians from the surrounding neighborhood came running to the scene.

"Is it the Moors?" they cried.

"No, no," Eduardo said. "It is our industry. We have a wonderful new weapon to defeat them."

At the forge John took Trevor to a barrel filled with conical forms of lead.

"Ever see something like this before?" John asked, plucking one out and tossing it to Trevor.

"Nope."

"It's called a Minié ball. A Frenchman, Minié, invented it mid-nineteenth century but the Americans in the Civil War called them Minnies as in Minnie Mouse. The idea was to improve accuracy and range of the old lead musket balls, the kind these guys here mostly use. They know how to rifle a gun barrel that helps but the lead ball doesn't get a good purchase on the grooves. These hollow bullets expand from the gunpowder gasses and these grooves grip the rifling. We made them just a bit smaller than the bore of their muskets."

"You tested them?"

"Last night. They're good. I didn't do any long distance firing but they'll do the trick."

"What's the range?"

"Effective range, three hundred yards, maximal range, about a half a mile. About a five-fold improvement over lead balls."

"How many have you made?"

"Not enough. Tell Giuseppe we'll be ready tomorrow morning."

By nightfall Jugurtha had finally inched his cannon close enough to strike the city walls but the Iberians held their return fire to encourage the Moors to come even closer. But the walls held up. Over an evening glass of tea, Jugurtha and Tariq decided to use the cover of darkness to move within three hundred yards. At dawn they would unleash a furious barrage to see if the walls could be holed from that distance. If they did enough damage they would pour their infantry into the city. If not, they would employ siege tactics. They were in no hurry. The prize was too large for haste.

That night, Trevor escorted Emily and Arabel to the forge to bring food to Brian and John. They sat outside in the cooler air and ate bread, hard-boiled eggs, and cheese. Emily reported on palace activities. The penicillin tea was coming along nicely, bandages had been cut and rolled, surgical instruments boiled. Trevor told them about Tony and Charlie's progress on the cannon lift. The tower was now just over wall height and the horse-powered winching would begin soon. After they ate, John showed them the barrels of Minié balls, the stacks of rocket launchers, and the crates of Hale rockets. By morning, they'd be ready.

When it was time to return to the palace Emily begged John to get a little rest. Through the forge entrance the furnace cast a wide, orange glow but they found a shadow where they could hold each other.

"Stay inside the palace tomorrow," John said. "Don't leave under any circumstances unless I come and get you. Let the wounded come to you."

"Where will you be?"

"On the wall with the others."

"Oh God, John, I'm so scared."

"We'll be fine. Superior technology always prevails."

"Not always," she said. "My superior technology got us into this mess."

"Stop beating yourself up. Keep Arabel's spirits up. She's got to believe we'll get Sam and Belle back."

Trevor and Arabel were visible in the arc of orange light. They were holding hands.

"Can you believe it?" Emily asked.

"Of course I do. We're not the only ones bitten by the love bug. Now go. I'll see you when I see you."

She kissed him and said, "Take a nap, all right?"

When they left John took her advice, telling Brian to wake him in an hour. He found a dark, grassy spot on the side of the forge, sat with his back to the warm brick wall and closed his eyes.

The Black Hawk lifted up taking Stankiewicz and Knebel out of harm's way.

John breathed a sigh of relief when it didn't pick up any RPG or small arms fire from inside the farmhouse. With the wounded sorted out he turned his attention to the primary mission. He scanned the compound through night-vision goggles. The mud perimeter walls had been largely obliterated by cannon fire and there were no thermal images. The Taliban firing from the wall were either dead or back inside the house. The goats were incinerated.

"All right, listen up," he said into his helmet mike, "Stank and Doc'll be fine. Mike's squad's going to approach from the north, my squad from the south. Masks on. When we're close enough, on my order, we hit the house with flash-bangs and gas and make entry. If they're hostile they get smoked. They put their hands where we can see them, they get cuffed, hands and ankles, and stripped for haji vests. T-baum identifies the HVT. We take him and evac. The others we leave. Alive. We'll let the rats have them. Understood?"

He got a bunch of affirmatives.

"T-baum, did I hear you?"

"Yeah, yeah, I'm good."

"Okay, take the left flank. I'll take the right. Everyone else on my squad, straight down the pike. Okay, guys, stay low and move."

They crawled on their bellies pushing off the rocky soil with their kneepads. When John was about fifty feet from the front door of the farmhouse, Entwistle radioed that he was within range of deploying the flash-bang grenades through the rear windows.

"T-baum, you good to put gas through the window to the left of the door?" John radioed.

"Yeah, got it," he radioed back.

"All right," John radioed. "On my mark, Mike, do the flash-bangs and T-Baum, do the gas. Everyone else, on detonation, see you inside."

John prepared to give his command. On his flank he saw Tannenbaum, green and glowing, rise to one knee and take aim, a gas canister loaded in his grenade launcher.

There was a flash from the front window. For a fraction of a second, John thought that someone had jumped the gun on the flash-bangs but then he saw a green mist erupting from Tannenbaum's head.

"203s! 203s!" John yelled, calling for 40mm grenade fire. "Smoke them all to Hell!"

Well before dawn, the ramparts of Burgos were fully manned with Iberians and their Italian allies. Jugurtha's main force was concentrated at the south side of the city where he had also concentrated his cannon batteries, having made an assessment that the city walls were most vulnerable there.

John and Garibaldi passed the spyglass between them trying to see what troop movements had occurred during the night, and as the inky blackness of the night sky faded they had their answer.

"What do you suppose is the distance of their cannon?" Garibaldi asked him.

"No more than three hundred yards," John said.

"And their infantry?"

"Another hundred yards further."

They made a circuit of the ramparts checking on the encircling forces. There were a few cannon at all compass points and a thin band of troops ringing the city.

"They want to respond to an exodus from the other gates but they've put most of their fire power to the south," John said.

Back at the south ramparts they found Aragon who informed them his troops were assembled and ready in the south-gate square and the streets that led to it.

"Where is Pedro?" Garibaldi asked.

"He is at the palace. He is not fond of the early morning."

Garibaldi smirked, "Well I hope he'll be able to stay asleep. It's going to get noisy."

John found Brian, Trevor, and Charlie beside the singing cannon. Brian was inspecting the rope work on the carriage.

"What do you think?" John asked.

"The aiming point looks good but I'm a little concerned about the recoil," Brian said.

"You should be. Unchecked it'll snap back twenty feet. It was an issue on the gun decks."

"We need to cinch the stays tighter," Charlie said. "I think it could punch out the back wall and it's a long way down."

"Go for it," John said.

Just then Jugurtha's cannon opened up and the wall rumbled with each impact. Showers of stones were thrown into the air.

"Did I say hurry?" John added.

The Moors' cannon were trained mostly on the south gates, heavy oak doors fashioned with multiple layers of wood, their grains running at ninety degrees to one another for strength. The panels were held together with huge iron studs and the doors were mounted deeply within a protective stone barbican connected to the ramparts with necked walkways. The target was relatively small and the initial volleys were wide of the mark.

"Are we ready?" Garibaldi asked John.

"Give us a few more minutes to tie the cannon down better."

Soon Charlie ran over, ducking his head below the crenellations.

"We've sorted it," he said.

John shook his hand. "I want to tell you something."

Charlie looked like he was going to get a scolding but he was surprised.

"I know you've been beating yourself up," John said. "I know you've been saying that maybe you could have done this and maybe you could have done that to save your family. That's all horseshit. You're here because you were the strongest, fastest, and bravest of the bunch. You're a good man, Charlie, and I'm proud to have you by my side in a fight."

"You mean that?" Charlie said, choking on his words.

"I wouldn't have said it if I didn't mean it. Good luck today and keep your head down."

Garibaldi approached Aragon. "We are ready," he said. "I would be most grateful if you could give the order to your men to fire. I will do the same in Italian and we shall have a battle."

Aragon smiled and said, "I have been anxious to see how your new weapons perform."

"So am I," Garibaldi said. "Much depends on it."

Aragon raised his arm and shouted, "Open fire!" Garibaldi did the same.

From the plain below, just behind his line of cannon, Jugurtha saw the dark ramparts erupt in hundreds of points of orange fire. One of the flashes was huge and his horse reared in fear when a shell from the singing cannon shrieked overhead and landed to his rear. The round tore through a dense concentration of Moorish infantrymen and archers leaving a bloody gash in the earth.

At the same time Hale rockets whistled into the ranks of the artillerymen, felling dozens. Minié balls fired by Iberian and Italian sharpshooters pocked the lines.

Jugurtha shouted for his commander, Tariq, to order the cannon pulled back but Tariq was already down on the ground clutching at a melon-sized hole in his chest from a direct rocket hit.

The rocket and bullet fire kept coming and hundreds of frontline troops fell victim. On the ramparts, reloaders and shooters were finding their rhythm and kept the hail of steel and lead coming. Simon and Brian, wadding stuffed in their ears, worked the singing cannon and soon another shell ripped apart the main body of Moors.

Despite Jugurtha's shouts and threats, the Moors broke ranks and began fleeing, leaving their cannon behind. The infantry, archers and cavalrymen in the rear also panicked in anticipation of a third singing shell exploding in their midst. Then a Minié ball slammed into Jugurtha's raging, open mouth, shattering teeth and tumbling through the base of his skull. Only a stirrup prevented him from falling all the way to the grass. His horse bolted and raced through the lines ahead of the retreating Moors, his head bouncing on the hard ground.

Through the smoke, Garibaldi saw the disarray. He put down his spyglass and told Aragon the ground attack should commence.

Aragon dropped a red cloth onto the city-side of the wall and they began streaming out the south gates, riding and running toward the fleeing Moors, whooping triumphantly.

With that Aragon announced he was going to the palace to inform the king the battle had turned. "He will wish to attend the dénouement."

"I will await his arrival with bated breath," Garibaldi said with a smile.

In the palace everyone milled around Martin's casualty ward awaiting the first victims. Martin and Tony sat in one corner talking quietly. Alice and Tracy sat on a cot, jumping at each volley of fire, and Arabel and Emily paced the floor in lockstep.

When the doors opened they expected to see stretcher-bearers but instead an armed guard of Iberians barged in. They marched directly to the sisters and grabbed them by their wrists, pulling them toward the door.

"Leave us alone!" Emily shouted. "What are you doing?"

Emily bit down on a soldier's hand and when he loosened his grip she pulled free and began putting her Krav Maga training into gear. With a kick to the groin and the heel of her hand to his nose, the man stumbled backwards.

"Get away from them!" Tony shouted but when he came forward, a soldier drew his sword, prompting Martin to pull him back.

Tracy and Alice screamed and Emily was about to attack the man holding Arabel when a powerful arm clamped her neck in a chokehold. In seconds she went limp. The soldiers dragged the women away, leaving the others in shock. The door latch was dropped into its slot from the outside and the four of them were trapped.

There was no inside latch. Tony grabbed one of Martin's surgical knives and began trying to slide it between the door and the frame.

"Please hurry," Alice cried. "We've got to help them."

On the ramparts the firing had been halted to avoid friendly-fire casualties during the ground assault. Some elite elements of Jugurtha's brigades stayed to fight but most were already in full flight to the south. As word of the rout spread, Moorish troops encircling the city abandoned their positions and fled too.

John congratulated Caravaggio and Simon and hugged Brian and Trevor.

"Superior technology will win every bloody time," Brian said.

"Amen to that," Trevor said.

"Let's head back to the palace and get the others," John said. "I'll talk to Giuseppe to see when he's going to be ready to head out to Marksburg."

Then they heard Tony shouting and saw him running along the ramparts toward them.

He reached them panting and breathless. "You've got to come!" he gasped. "They've been taken!"

"Who?" John said in a panic.

"Emily and Arabel."

"I don't know where but they're gone. Martin's with Alice and Tracy."

Simon ran over. "What did you say about Alice?"

"She's okay, it's Emily and Arabel," Tony said.

Trevor was already running for the stairs and John lit off after him, followed by Simon.

Brian shouted that he was coming too but John wheeled around and told him to stay put in case the battle flared.

There were a couple of rifles propped against the wall next to a barrel of Minié balls. John stopped to grab a couple of powder horns, stuffed his pockets with ammunition then picked up the rifles.

John tossed Trevor a rifle and they sprinted through the congested streets of Burgos and into the main palace entrance that was wide open and unattended. Simon and Tony went straight to the room where Alice was holed up and John and Trevor ran through the halls looking for answers.

Near the banqueting hall they saw Queen Mécia sweeping past with Guomez and her attendants.

She raised a hand to stop the procession and hurried over and spoke to them.

Guomez translated, "Her Majesty wants to know how is Senhor Brian."

"He's fine," John said. "Does she know what happened to our women, Emily and Arabel?"

"Oh yes, she most certainly does," Guomez answered.

The queen began furiously answering the translated question.

"She says that Pedro, may he putrefy in a commoner's rotting room, seized the women and departed the city with his royal guards. It seems he has reneged on the assurances he gave in conjunction with King Giuseppe's alliance."

"Where'd they go?" Trevor shouted.

"She believes it is León. He has a fortified palace there where he enjoys whoring and hunting."

"Which direction?" John asked.

"West."

As they sped off, Guomez called after them, "She says she hopes you destroy the filthy bastard."

In the main bailey they saw some saddled horses at the ready.

"How's your riding?" John asked.

"It'll have to do, won't it?"

Before mounting they quickly loaded both rifles, shouldered them on their straps, then rode from the palace heading for the west gate.

Outside the city they kicked their horses to a gallop and John led the way through the abandoned Moorish line. The grass was trampled and tracks were indecipherable until they had ridden a mile or so. At that point the Moors had turned south and the grass was less disturbed, revealing the clear impressions of wagon wheels and horse's hooves.

Ahead, sandwiched between the green grass and the light gray sky was a brown speck.

"I think that's them," John shouted. "Try to keep up."

He kicked his horse and it responded. Trevor squeezed the reins so hard his hands shook and dug his heels into the horse's flanks. The two men raced ahead.

The royal carriage was not roomy. Emily was crammed beside Arabel on a bench, their knees pressing up against King Pedro and the Duke of Aragon. Aragon had a fancy pistol in his hand. Both women stared icily at their captors.

"Don't worry," Emily told Arabel. "They'll come."

"I'm not worried," Arabel said. "I'm angry. I'm very, very angry."

In twenty minutes John and Trevor were half a mile behind.

"I'm going to shoot from the saddle, you're going to have to pass and re-load. Can you do that?"

"Ride with no hands?" Trevor shouted back. "What's the worse that could happen?"

They kept getting closer.

John saw there were eight outriders, four horsemen on each side of the carriage. When he thought he was in range he tucked the reins under his crotch, unshouldered the rifle and took aim.

Emily heard the shot and from the carriage window saw a man fall.

Aragon shouted to the carriageman to go faster.

"John's a very good shot," Emily said.

"I hope Trevor's not on a horse," Arabel said. "He told me he hates riding."

Emily glowered at the king and said, "You look scared, you bastard."

"What is she saying?" Pedro asked Aragon.

"I do not know, Your Majesty" the duke replied. "I am sure it is of no consequence."

Riding side-by-side, John tossed his spent rifle to Trevor and once Trevor had secured it, he passed the loaded one back. While John took aim Trevor began the close-to-impossible task of staying in the saddle while muzzle-loading powder and bullet. He almost fell but through sheer will he poured the powder from a horn as John dropped another rider.

"Did it!" Trevor shouted.

"Good man!" John replied as they exchanged rifles again.

When a third man fell, the other riders apparently decided they did not like their backs turned to this sharpshooter. Despite a lack of royal orders, five remaining soldiers pulled up, turned their horses, and with swords drawn they charged.

There wasn't time to reload. John flipped the rifle around and gripped the warm barrel like a baseball bat and Trevor did the same but in doing this he finally lost his balance and slid out of the saddle, hitting the ground hard.

When he picked himself up, in pain but with no broken bones, John was way ahead, swinging his butt stock into an Iberian's face.

Trevor ignored the sharp pain in his hip and took off running, closing the gap until he was close to the action. John was flailing his rifle keeping the slashing swords at bay but Trevor saw one of the soldiers pull a pistol from his belt and cock the trigger.

He wasn't going to get there in time so he threw his rifle as hard as he could. It spun through the air and missed the gunman.

But it struck his horse.

The animal bucked hard and the soldier came off. Trevor was on him, punching away, crushing his face more and more with each blow.

When the man went limp Trevor found his pistol underneath him and pivoted just as a swordsman was about to strike him. The lead ball tore into his throat.

Emily leaned out the carriage window and saw John and Trevor receding in the distance.

Aragon shouted at her to sit back down and pointed his pistol for emphasis then angrily cocked it. She shouted back that she didn't speak Spanish and when he continued on she sat down hard then with all her might thrust her right foot into Aragon's nose.

The gun fell and she began grappling for it. The king began to fumble for a dagger but Arabel copied her sister and started to pummel him with her feet.

Aragon, bleeding from his nose, suddenly stopped fighting and told the king they had to surrender. Emily was pointing the pistol at them.

"Tell the driver to stop," Emily commanded.

The king and duke looked at each other not comprehending.

She tried French. "Arrêt, arrêt!"

Aragon called out to the driver to halt and the carriage slowed and stopped.

Emily opened the door and motioned with the pistol. Aragon climbed down first, followed by Pedro.

"I hope John and Trevor are all right," Arabel said and she began to exit the carriage, blocking Emily's line of sight.

"Wait!" Emily said. "He's still got a knife," but it was too late.

Pedro pulled her down and when Emily regained her line of sight, Arabel had a dagger at her throat.

"Easy, easy," Emily said to Arabel, to the king, to herself. She carefully stepped down, keeping the pistol trained on the king.

"God, don't shoot," Arabel said.

"I won't but let's not tell them that."

Aragon began shouting and pointing.

They heard John's voice behind her. "It's okay. We're here."

"Arabel, don't move a muscle," Trevor said.

"Can I breathe?"

"Yeah, you can do that."

Pedro shouted at them to stay back. To strike home his meaning he pricked the skin of her throat with the tip of the knife.

"Okay, okay, we're not coming closer," Trevor said.

"Emily, I want you to take three steps back and hand me the pistol," John said.

"You don't have a gun?" she asked. She sounded very afraid.

"Not a loaded one. Is yours loaded?"

"It's the duke's. He's been acting like it's loaded."

Trevor spoke up. "I want the shot. Give it to me, Emily."

"You want it?" John asked.

"Yeah, I want it."

"All right, Emily, give it to Trev."

Trevor quickly took the pistol from her. Aragon and Pedro began shouting. The king pulled Arabel's hair back to fully expose her neck to the dagger.

Trevor gripped the pistol with both hands and assumed a firing stance. He was eight feet away and Arabel blocked all but a few square inches of Pedro's head. "Arabel," he said. "I don't even want you to breathe now, all right?"

She took a deep breath and held it.

Trevor pulled the trigger.

Arabel dropped to the grass and Emily screamed.

Pedro's right eye was gone.

He fell beside her and began convulsing.

Emily went to her. "Are you okay?" she shouted.

Arabel opened her eyes and replied with a glassy stare. "I'm fine. What happened?"

"The good guy took out the bad guy," John said, rubbing Trevor's shoulders.

Aragon seized the opportunity to flee and was twenty feet away when John picked up the dagger, tested its weight, and threw it hard. It rotated several times and stuck deep in the duke's back.

The carriageman was still in his seat, rigid as a board. John pulled him down, frisked him, and let him run away.

"Climb in, ladies, and gentleman," John said. "This ride's on me."

When they arrived back into the palace they found their friends in the main bailey overjoyed to see them. They were crowded around Simon who had been busily charging the boiler of one of the steam cars to go after them. He let out the steam and the long sigh the boiler made seemed to speak for all of them. Alice came over to him and Simon draped his thick arm around her shoulder.

"So very good to see you safe," Garibaldi said.

"Is the fight over?" John asked.

"The Moors are no longer a threat," he replied. "And Pedro?"

"Trevor shot him. He's history. Aragon's not doing too well either."

Guomez called out the news to Queen Mécia who was coming into the courtyard.

Her exuberant smile said it all.

"The queen is pleased," Guomez said. "Greatly pleased."

"Our pact was with Iberia," Garibaldi told Guomez, "not with Pedro. I wish to know whether the queen intends to honor this pact?"

"I will honor our alliance with one condition," she replied.

Garibaldi looked at Caravaggio and Simon and frowned. "Ask her what is her condition."

"It is this," she said. "I do not wish to rule Iberia. I have neither the head nor the stomach for it. You, King Giuseppe, you seem to be a good man and an able monarch. You will be the new king of Iberia. I wish only to return to Bilbao and enjoy the status of queen mother."

As Guomez translated, Garibaldi's face lit up. "Tell her I accept her most generous condition. We will need to depart at first light tomorrow with a large contingent of your—I mean our army. We must make haste to Germania to rescue this woman's poor children."

Arabel wept at the news.

"I have one more condition," the queen said, pointing straight at Brian. "Before you leave, I will dine tonight with Senhor Brian."

29

Stalin had been expecting his visitors.

A day earlier he had been informed that a steam car of French manufacture had arrived at Marksburg under a flag of truce. Nevertheless, German and Russian soldiers patrolling the winding access road to the hillside castle on the Rhine had disarmed the driver and passenger before allowing them any farther.

It was rat-faced Colonel Yagoda who had interviewed the one who claimed to be the spokesman.

"What is your name?" Yagoda had asked in English, their common language.

"I am Michelangelo Merisi da Caravaggio."

"I'm sorry, did you say Caravaggio?"

"In the flesh."

"Caravaggio, the painter?"

"I am a painter, yes."

Yagoda was unaccustomed to amazement but that is what had flashed on his face. "What are you doing here?" he had asked.

"In Germania or in Hell?"

"In Hell!"

"I murdered a man. Well, accidentally murdered him. I only wanted to cut off his balls but I was a poor surgeon."

"I know the work of Caravaggio. I revere his paintings. You say you wish to see the tsar. However, I cannot represent your identity to Tsar Joseph without proof."

"Then give me a piece of paper or parchment."

Yagoda had a small stack of precious paper in his traveling desk. He had handed over a sheet with a leaded pencil.

Caravaggio had hunched over the paper. In under a minute he was done.

Yagoda had trembled. It was a haunting image of a young, winged angel, her breast pierced by an arrow.

"You *are* Caravaggio," he had muttered.

"At your service."

Nikita knocked on Stalin's door. The tsar was seated at his writing desk, reviewing Field Marshal Kutuzov's refined invasion plans of Britannia.

"The two visitors and Colonel Yagoda are here to see you," the young freckle-faced man said.

"One is the painter?" he said, waving the drawing of the angel.

"That is so. The other is an Englishman."

"Ha, I was just thinking about the English. Do I need an Italian translator?"

"The painter speaks English."

Stalin made a show of puffing his cheeks then blowing out hard. "So it is time to go to work."

Caravaggio entered with Simon. Yagoda trailed at a distance. Stalin rose to greet them. "Gentlemen, welcome to Marksburg. I am Stalin."

Caravaggio bowed politely and was about to introduce himself when Stalin interrupted, telling him he knew who he was and how much he admired his work. "Too much religion in your paintings but I liked them anyway. I was raised to be priest and was five years in Greek Orthodox seminary but later in life, I reject religion. There was no religion in my Russia and there is no religion here so I feel at home. A joke. Your painting that is my favorite is David holding head of Goliath. No religion. Simply power."

"I liked this painting also," Caravaggio said. "Maybe I'll do it again."

"And who is this English person?" Stalin asked. "And why is he fighting on side of Italian people?"

"I am Simon Wright, your excellency. I was a humble boilermaker in life. I fell in with Giuseppe Garibaldi because I admired him."

"I could use good boilermaker," Stalin said. "I like these steam cars very much. Germans have them. We have these in Russia too, you know, but they go kaput a lot. Why you admire Garibaldi?"

"He speaks about a better way forward, a more humane Hell. I suppose I like that."

Stalin sat down and bade them to do so too. Yagoda remained standing in the shadows. "A better Hell with him in charge, I suppose," Stalin said.

"I don't think it's about that," Simon said.

"Believe me, boilermaker, it is always about that. Tell me, gentlemen. You are my enemies. You destroyed many of my army with your excellent cannon. What is purpose of you coming here?"

Caravaggio answered. "King Giuseppe sent us to arrange a meeting with you. He is on his way but we could travel faster with these machines."

"On his way from where?" Stalin asked. Yagoda had told him but he wanted to hear it from the horse's mouth.

"Iberia."

"Which you have told Yagoda he has also conquered," Stalin said.

"Not by war," Simon said. "By alliance."

"This is amusing. You call it alliance. Pedro was destroyed. I call it coup d'état."

Caravaggio splayed his hands and shrugged. "Whatever it may be called, it is done."

"So Garibaldi in such a short time rises from obscure nobleman to king of Italia, king of Francia, and king of Iberia. I think is remarkable."

"And you, your excellency, are now tsar of Russia and king of Germania," Caravaggio said.

"Yes, but I was ruler in life. This man was, well, I will be polite and not say more."

"I was not there in his time," Caravaggio said defensively, "but I understand he was also a great man in life."

Stalin laughed. "Let us not compare size of our sexual organs. Tell me what is deal you propose."

Simon had been mulling the best way to put it but he forgot his little speech and blurted, "We want to make a deal for the children."

Stalin shouted in Russian, "Yagoda, did you know this?"

The colonel stepped into the light and swallowed hard. "It is the first they have spoken of this."

Stalin looked furious. He froze Simon with his steely gaze and said, "How you know about children?"

"The French learned about them," Simon said, his mouth suddenly dry.

"Why you want children?"

"We don't want them. Their mother does."

"You have their mother?" Stalin asked, his voice rising.

"We do. She misses them very much."

"Then tell this live woman to come to Stalin. She can stay here with children. Problem solved."

"It is not so easy," Caravaggio said. "This woman and other live people who are with us, they wish to return to their homes on Earth. They need soon to go to Britannia. This is where they can make it to home. I do not have the understanding to tell you how this is possible but they say it is possible and I believe them."

Stalin fidgeted with his moustache. "So, you wish me to give up children who I like very much. What do you offer in return?"

Simon played his cards. "Blast furnaces and very large steam boilers. We will give them to you."

Stalin's droopy eyes opened wide. "Who has these things? You, boiler man?"

"We don't have them. We have the means to build them. Caravaggio will show you."

The artist reached into his blousy shirt prompting Yagoda to pull a pistol, but Caravaggio didn't have a weapon. He had several sheets of printed paper.

"These are front pages of two books," Caravaggio said. "Books that living people brought with them to Hell. We have these books."

There had been discord within the Italian camp concerning the strategy. Some felt it was an enormous mistake to enable Stalin's powerful war machine by giving him access to the technology. Doing so, they argued would condemn them to eventual defeat and oppression. And without the books, they would not have the ability to use the technology for good, to make Hell a better place. Others felt they owed it to the Earthers to trade them for Arabel's children. It was Garibaldi who had the idea that broke the impasse.

"Why don't we make copies?" he had said. "If we have to give Stalin the originals we will also have the technology. It is my belief that in Italia, Francia, and Iberia we can find enough iron forgers and boilermakers like Simon together with builders and other qualified men and women who hail from modern eras to beat the Russians and Germans even if they have the books too. We can be first."

Before leaving Iberia they had searched the palace for parchment, paper, pens, and ink and during their search they also recovered Pedro's book on explosives. The Earthers were pressed into service and anyone in the Italian army literate enough to copy words were put into wagons, each with a page or two cut from the books. Inside the bumpy wagons they made their copies. When Caravaggio returned from his foray into Marksburg Castle he would quickly copy the diagrams and illustrations. In the fullness of time they could have a scribe make unified copies from all the scraps but a piecemeal effort would do for now.

Stalin examined the pages Caravaggio handed him, called over young Nikita and told him to find Pasha for his opinion.

"I must show my technical experts," Stalin said grandly.

Caravaggio and Simon agreed.

"You have whole books?" Stalin asked.

"Yes, if we have a deal, we will bring the books when we return," Simon said.

"So you propose to exchange these books for the children?" Stalin asked.

"That's right," Simon said, "the children and the living woman who is with them."

Simon held the carrot; Caravaggio showed the stick. "This exchange should be very simple and it would be the best way. However, you should know there is another more difficult way. King Giuseppe comes here in peace or he comes in war. He has a very large army. Many Italians, French, and now Iberians. He also has special weapons that he used to easily defeat the Moors who were threatening Burgos. We must get the children the easy way or the difficult way."

Stalin rose abruptly and said, "You will wait." He summoned Yagoda and the two men retired to an adjoining chamber.

"So, my enemy comes and threatens me in my own house," Stalin seethed.

"I am sure they would prefer an exchange," Yagoda said. "They probably do not wish to appear weak, so they threaten war. It is a common tactic."

"Yes, but I do not like being on the receiving end of threats," Stalin said. "What do you think about these special weapons he mentioned? Do you think he means the singing cannon?"

"Perhaps."

"How many have we made in the German forges?"

"There were eight at last count but two of them exploded during their tests and one of them is useless with cracks."

"And how many do they have?"

"We do not know."

"Can't you get a spy into their camp?"

"We will redouble our efforts," Yagoda said.

The door opened and Pasha entered with the book pages.

"What do you think, Pasha?" Stalin asked. "Would these books be of use to us?"

Pasha was lightheaded from rushing up and down the castle's steep stairways. Speaking Russian seemed too difficult in his state and he displeased the tsar by asking in English. "Please, first tell me," Pasha said.

"Nikita told me other living persons carried these here. Did they come from Dartford too?"

"I did not ask," Stalin answered in Russian. "I want to know if books are useful."

"Yes, I expect so. Quite useful. They're from the early twentieth century, a time when the industrial revolution was in full swing and everything depended on innovations in iron production and steam power. We are more medieval than modern. You know this. If these books offer a practical guide to achieving these technologies we could leapfrog into a different era, one with machines, electricity …"

"And far better weapons," Yagoda said.

Pasha sighed, "Yes, I suppose that too. But listen, I would need to see the full texts to know just how useful these books are. They would have to be very clear and prescriptive. There are so few competent technical people about."

"You are competent," Stalin said. "You are brilliant."

"Well thank you for that but …"

"I know, I know, you know nothing about weapons."

"More importantly, I know nothing about making steel or making steam boilers."

"Have a drink, Pasha," Stalin said. "You look so pale. I will tell our visitors that we will meet with them and see if we like whole books."

"They're still here?"

"In the next room."

Pasha grew excited. "I'd like to talk with them, if you don't mind. I want to learn more about the live people who brought the books. I want to know if they came from Dartford and I want to know who they are."

30

With Ian at work, Giles bucked up his courage and ventured out for the first time since he came to Eaton Mews. After shaking off the paranoia that everyone who passed was looking at him, he got more comfortable and almost enjoyed being out in the sunshine. His task at hand, however, proved somewhat difficult. He didn't want to stay out long but finding a shop that sold pre-paid mobile phones in a high-end neighborhood like Belgravia was a challenge. He had to walk a mile down the King's Road to find an O2 store.

When Giles got back to the flat he cut the phone out of its plastic and charged it up. When it had enough juice he punched in a number for a man named Dan Wiggins. It hadn't taken advanced sleuthing skills to find him. His name had been in the paper. He was on LinkedIn. His current position was listed.

Giles reached the bank's switchboard and asked for Dan Wiggins in the IT group.

"Hello, Wiggins here."

"Mr. Wiggins, this is Giles Farmer. I'm a reporter. I wonder if I could speak with you about your wife, Tracy?"

There was silence on the line until, "I don't wish to speak with you."

"Please don't hang up, Mr. Wiggins. I think I know what happened to your wife."

"What happened to her is that she's dead."

"Why do you say that? That hasn't been reported."

"I wouldn't know what's been reported. I stopped reading the news or watching TV. All I know is they gave me her ashes. I couldn't even see her because of the contamination. And they told me not to speak with people like you, so if you'll …"

"No wait. It wasn't what they're saying. It wasn't bioterrorism. It was something else. And despite what they told you, she may not be dead."

"What did you say?"

"She may not be dead."

"Fuck you."

The line went dead.

Giles took notes on the call and opened up the laptop computer Ian had given him. It was one of Ian's old ones, a fairly ancient model which Ian had found at the bottom of a closet. Giles methodically removed any software that could connect the computer to the Internet so that it was only good for word processing. It was on this snoop-proof computer that he'd begun working on a definitive article on recent events at the MAAC in Dartford, South Ockendon, and Iver, weaving together all the threads into a troubling exposé of sorts. Even he would have to admit that it wasn't really an exposé since he had no proof for what he was claiming. It was more like an educated guess, a cohesive explanation that assembled multiple, seemingly disconnected facts into a narrative that had an internal logic to it. It wasn't proof of what he was asserting but it was the kind of piece that could force those in the government to disclose the truth. He'd be labeled a kook, a conspiracy theorist. He'd be officially ridiculed but none of that mattered, and anyway, he was used to that. The important thing was that he'd be vindicated. He'd said all along that the MAAC was potentially risky. He was sure he'd been right. It was just that he'd had no idea of the kind of risk that would materialize.

He typed.

When I reached Dan Wiggins on the phone, the father of two told me something that had not been reported upon publicly, namely that he had been told by officials that his wife, Tracy Wiggins, had died from her alleged exposure to an undisclosed bioterror agent. He has been given her ashes. I believe this is part and parcel of the larger government cover-up.

He worked on his piece non-stop for the rest of the day. Ian came home late that night after a business dinner but the two didn't even see each other. Giles woke up alone in the house and started working again. He finished the final polish before lunch.

He entered another number on his burner phone. It was for *The Guardian* newspaper.

"Derek Hannaford."

"Hello, Mr. Hannaford, this is Giles Farmer calling. I write a blog called *Bad Collisions.*"

"Oh yeah, I've seen it."

"You have?"

"On the fringe, wouldn't you say?"

"Well, I don't know, actually. Look, the reason I'm calling is that I have very real evidence of a government conspiracy to cover up a mishap at the MAAC in Dartford by inventing a bioterror story to explain what happened at South Ockendon."

"And what do you think happened?"

"I don't want to say over the phone."

"Look, I'm fairly busy at the moment."

"Dan Wiggins, the husband of one of the South Ockendon victims, has been given what he's been told are the ashes of his wife, Tracy, and was instructed not to speak publicly about it."

The reporter instantly sounded more engaged. "How do you know this? It's the first I'm hearing about it."

"I know because he told me."

"Giles, can I quote you on this?"

"No you can't."

"Then why did you call me?"

"I want to show you an article I've written. I'd like *The Guardian* to publish it."

"Why don't you email it here and I'll have a look."

"I can't do that. One of the security services bugged my flat and remotely deleted files on my computer. I'm calling you on a pre-paid phone. I'm hiding out. It may seem paranoid to you but it's very real to me."

"Then what do you suggest?"

"Meet me tomorrow at seven outside the Covent Garden Marks and Spencer. I'll give you the article then."

"All very cloak and dagger."

"Sorry."

There was a pause. "All right. How will I recognize you?"

"I'll find you from your photo in the paper."

Giles felt buoyant for the first time in days. He plugged the computer into Ian's printer and watched the pages of his article fly out.

Trotter's assistant informed him one of his analysts had come by to see him.

"Send her in."

The young woman said, "I thought you would wish to hear this right away."

She opened her laptop and played an audio file that he listened to expressionless until he heard a part that made him smile.

"I can't do that. One of the security services bugged my flat and remotely deleted files on my computer. I'm calling you on a pre-paid phone. I'm hiding out. It may seem paranoid to you but it's very real to me."

When it was finished, Trotter said, "Didn't I tell you that monitoring the newspapers might be productive?"

"You did, sir."

"And didn't I further say that if Farmer did try to contact one of them it would most likely be *The Guardian*?"

"Right again, sir."

"Thank you. That will be all."

When she had left, Trotter called one of his people in the operations directorate. "Mark, Anthony Trotter here. I'd like you to come see me right away. There's a special thing I need for tomorrow night. In London. That's right. Completely off-the-books."

Giles was stationary in a sea of pedestrian traffic on the Gloucester Road in South Kensington. He waited outside the English language school where his mate, Lenny Moore, worked as the bursar. Giles knew Lenny well enough. He wouldn't linger at the office. When five o'clock came around he'd be out the door and he was.

Lenny was away from the college so quickly Giles had to jog after him and call his name.

Lenny turned and looked more than a little surprised. "What are you doing here?"

"I wanted to talk to you."

"Ever heard of an invention called a telephone?"

"I couldn't risk it. They probably know we're friends from our call logs. They'll be monitoring your calls."

"Who's monitoring my calls? What are you going on about?"

"It's about my work. A lot's happened since I saw you. Can we talk somewhere? I'll buy the beer."

"You'll buy?"

"Well, I am a little tight actually."

The pub was crowded but they found a small table. Seated together they almost looked like brothers, both very slender, both with big, unruly hair. Giles gave a full accounting of what had happened and when he talked about fleeing his flat after finding a camera in a light fixture, Lenny began looking over Giles's shoulder at the people in the bar. He was not a skeptic. He generally believed Giles on the conspiracy front.

"Are you sure no one's following you?" Lenny asked.

"We're good. I'm completely off the grid."

"So what are you going to do?"

"I'm going to keep lying low. I'm staying with a school friend—you don't know him. He thinks I'm off my rocker but he's not making any moves to evict me. The only thing that's going to make it safe for me is to get my story out someplace credible."

"What about your blog?"

"I said credible."

"Good point."

"The thing is, I've got an appointment to meet the science editor for *The Guardian* tomorrow night at Covent Garden."

"That's good, right?"

"Yeah, it's good. But I'm a bit worried he might tell someone who tells someone, if you know what I mean. That's why I'd like you to meet him."

"Me? What would I have to say to him?"

"Nothing. You'd just give him this." He handed over a sealed envelope.

"Is that your story?"

"No, it says where I'm really going to meet him. Not far, on the Strand. He'll go walking there and I'll follow to see if anyone is tailing him. That's all you've got to do. Give him the envelope."

"How will I know him?"

Giles gave him *The Guardian* folded to the science pages. Derek Hannaford's photo was circled.

"When?" Lenny asked.

"Tomorrow at seven. Outside the Marks and Spencer."

Lenny groaned. "But Giles, the footie's on the tele tomorrow night."

"It'll be quick. You'll be home in time. Please."

Lenny put the envelope and the paper into his messenger bag and passed Giles some money to buy them another round.

It was a warm evening and the streets around Covent Garden were packed. Giles arrived on foot at six-fifty and found a good vantage spot at the Sunglass Hut across the street that was open till eight. No one bothered him while he tried on glasses and peered at the entrance to the Marks and

Spencer.

"Good man," he mumbled, when he saw Lenny arrive at the Marks just before seven and start to nervously study the faces of passing men.

The reporter was late but only by five minutes. He stood there checking his mobile but Lenny, only ten feet away didn't seem to notice him.

"Come on, Lenny, come on," Giles whispered. "What do I have to do, lead you by the nose?"

Finally, it clicked. Giles saw Lenny spot the reporter then check the newspaper photo.

Lenny approached him and started to talk.

A woman on the street screamed.

Giles dropped a pair of sunglasses on the floor.

Lenny and the reporter were down, bleeding from head wounds.

There had been no shots. No sounds at all other than those of a busy London street.

Giles couldn't move.

A store clerk asked what had happened and ran to the window to see.

Giles saw two men in suits run up to the fallen bodies and kneel beside them. One of the men shouted for someone to call 999 then both men were gone.

The clerk said, "Oh my God! There's blood. I think they're dead."

Giles willed his legs to work. His first step crushed the sunglasses. His next step took him to the door. Before he knew it he was running. People, cars, everything was a blur, and he kept on running until his lungs felt like they were going to catch on fire.

31

The morning was like all mornings, oppressively gray and dull. Predatory hawks circled ominously over the Marksburg Castle and the great river.

Their steam car flew a white flag and they were allowed to come within yards of the outermost gate of the castle before being waved out.

Emily began to visibly shake as she walked through the gate. John put his arm around her waist and whispered an encouragement. He knew what she'd been through inside these thick, dank walls.

Brian and Trevor were just behind them, protectively flanking Arabel and staring down the grim-faced Russians and Germans who lined their route staring back.

In the main bailey where she had seen men impaled on Himmler's frame, a severe man with close-set eyes approached wearing the coarse uniform of the Russian army. He stiffened at the sight of five live people.

"I am Colonel Yagoda." His English was rudimentary and he used it sparingly. "You will follow me."

Emily knew the room where they were taken, the great room where she had first met Barbarossa. It was different now, appearing less cavernous with the addition of more furniture and the removal of the German king's long banqueting table. The new owner had redecorated.

Chairs were set around a threadbare woven rug off to the side of the large hearth. Thick candles on tall iron poles supplemented the light from the fire. Yagoda directed them to sit.

Brian nudged Trevor. "I don't like the look of this."

Soldiers entered, enough of them to line the walls of the room. It was a theatrical display of power and unity. Green uniforms of the Russians, alternated with blue uniforms of the Germans.

"We're in the lion's den," Trevor said.

Arabel had been working hard to keep herself together but her defenses began to crumble. When the tears came she covered her eyes with her hand. Emily reached over and took her other hand.

John didn't wait for the last soldier to fall into place. He told Yagoda their agreement was for the children to be seen first.

"You have books?" Yagoda asked.

They had been searched. Yagoda would have been told but he played along. "We have them."

"Children will come."

Arabel began to hyperventilate and Emily got up and knelt beside her, rubbing her shoulders and trying to soothe her with whispered words.

The wait seemed interminable and then, they were there.

Arabel slowly stood.

Sam began running across the expanse of the room, his hands in the air, shouting, "Mummy!"

Delia told Belle that it was okay to follow. The little girl refused to drop Delia's hand so they walked at a measured pace.

Arabel dropped to her knees on the rug to be Sam's height and to Emily, the boy's collision into her arms evoked the collision of protons that had precipitated all of this.

Belle pointed and said, "Look, Auntie Delia, Auntie Emily is here too."

Emily left Arabel's side and went over to Belle, sweeping her off her feet and kissing her soft face.

"You must be Delia," Emily said.

"And you must be Emily."

"Thank you. Thank you from the bottom of my heart."

"They're dear little children," Delia said. "Thank God they're back with their mother."

John joined them and Yagoda seemed annoyed that everyone was moving about as they pleased.

"Come, let's go see mummy," Emily said to Belle.

Delia gave John a hug. "And you must be John Camp."

"You're hugging the right guy. Brian and Trev, come over here."

Delia kissed each of them. "All of you are my knights in shining armor," she said dabbing at her tears.

"Have you been treated well?" John asked.

"As well as expected in a place like this," she answered. "They're all gaga over the children and that means kid gloves. Especially Stalin. They seem to turn him into a regular Uncle Joe. I'm so pleased you managed to find Arabel. I was desperately worried. Was she in Spain?"

"Yeah," Trevor answered. "We had quite the time."

"You're the one I know nothing about," Delia told Brian. "Are you with the government?"

"Only if you count working for the BBC," he said with a laugh. "Your license fees in action."

"Wait a minute. I recognize you," she said. "You're Brian Kilmeade, the ancient weapons man on the tele."

"The weapons are ancient, my dear, not me."

"Well thank you all," she said. "You've put yourself in grave danger to rescue us. In my heart I knew you'd try but during the long dark nights my head wasn't so sure. Can you get us out of here?"

"We're going to try," John said.

"How?" she asked.

"We're going to make a trade."

"Us for what?"

"Books."

She gave a smile of instant comprehension. "Will they go for it?" she asked.

"Our negotiators met with them and they think so."

"And if they don't? They're not nice people, you know."

"We're backed up by an army of Italians, French, and Spanish a few clicks from here."

"Clicks," she happily repeated. "I do love a military man."

Arabel was clutching both children to her breast, asking them the wonderfully mundane questions she'd been thinking about non-stop. Had they been ill? Were they eating? Did they miss their mummy?

Yagoda halted all the conversations by clapping his hands together.

"Stop now," he commanded. "Children have been seen. Now they must go."

"No!" Arabel shouted, making Sam jump and Belle cry.

Yagoda spoke in Russian and some of the soldiers responded by approaching Arabel.

Trevor made a move to intervene but John warned him off. "Let's play this out. We can't take on all of them."

A soldier put his hand on Sam and Arabel responded by slapping and punching at the man.

"Emily, you've got to control her," John said.

She agreed and told her sister that once they did the deal, everyone could leave together. "You knew this would be hard. We talked about it."

"I can't let them go," Arabel sobbed.

"I'll take care of them," Delia said. "Don't worry, dear, they'll be fine and hopefully you'll be reunited in no time."

Arabel ripped herself away from her sister and said to Yagoda, "I want to go with them."

Trevor began trying to talk her down.

"No, Trevor," she said. "I'm sorry but I've got to stay with them."

Yagoda immediately agreed. "You can go with."

Arabel told her people, "I don't want to leave you but I can't leave them. Just get all of us out of here. Please." She held out her hands for Sam and Belle to grab. "Come on children, show me where you've been sleeping."

Arabel followed Delia to the door and just as she was about to disappear she turned and gave them all a brave smile.

"You sit now," Yagoda instructed. "Pasha comes to look at books."

Pasha.

Caravaggio and Simon had told them about this enigmatic Englishman who had asked questions about them—who were they, were they from Dartford, what were their names? They hadn't understood many of his questions and couldn't remember them in any detail. But something about this Pasha had stuck in Emily's mind and she'd conflated him with the image of the man she had briefly glimpsed that day in the German camp when Stalin had come to meet Barbarossa. Were they one and the same? She'd almost asked Caravaggio to make her a sketch of Pasha but he was pressed into service to make copies of the diagrams in the books. Throughout a largely sleepless night she wouldn't allow herself to go that one step further.

Pasha entered through the same door that Arabel had departed.

He walked straight toward her, ignoring everyone else.

"Emily." It passed from his lips like a combination of a name and a sob.

"Paul," she said. "It *is* you."

"You know him?" John said.

"He's my old boss, John. This is Paul Loomis."

She went to him and they embraced. He cried so mightily it was as if he had held the tears in for these past seven years and now the damn had burst.

"Who is he?" Trevor whispered to John.

"He was in charge of MAAC before Henry Quint."

"The one who offed himself after he shotgunned his wife and another bloke?"

"That's the one."

"Fuck me."

Yagoda was once again impatient. He shouted at Pasha that the tsar was waiting.

Pasha pulled away but with their hands still touching she said, "It *was* you at Barbarossa's camp."

He looked confused. "You were there?"

"Yes."

"I thought your friends said you'd just come two weeks ago?"

"Seventeen days. But I was here before. I came back."

"Why in heavens did you do that?"

"For the children and my sister. Didn't you know I was related to them? Didn't Delia tell you?"

"I wasn't allowed to see them. Stalin restricted access. I only found out about you yesterday from your friends. I didn't sleep a wink last night."

Yagoda shouted again but they ignored him.

"How did you get to be with Stalin?" she asked.

"It's a blur, really. I died in Sidcup. Some sweepers, as they call them, picked me up and delivered me to a man named Solomon ..."

"Wisdom," she said. "That awful man."

"Ah, you've met. He sold me to the highest bidder who happened to be the Russian ambassador, and after a harrowing journey, I was deposited in Stalin's imperial palace in Moscow. He calls me Pasha, so I suppose Paul is gone but Pasha soldiers on."

Yagoda was physically pulling them apart now and Pasha was manhandled into a chair.

"Show him books," Yagoda demanded.

They all sat down and John removed the two books from his pack. When he gave them to Pasha he introduced himself.

"Heard a lot about you. I came to the MAAC after you were gone. I'm the head of security. Trevor Jones is my deputy and this gent is Brian Kilmeade who you might remember from his TV show on medieval weaponry."

"So nice to meet you all," Pasha said. "I'm afraid I didn't watch much television." He took the books and sat back down but before looking at them he said to Emily, "I really must know what happened. Did something go wrong with the Hercules project?"

"Very wrong. Your successor, Henry Quint ..."

"*He* got the job?"

"Unfortunately yes. Quint exceeded the limits of Hercules I and went straight to Hercules II parameters."

"Thirty TeV?"

"Yes, thirty."

"And you produced strangelets," Loomis said. It wasn't a question; it was a statement.

"We did. And gravitons."

"Christ! And the combination …"

"The books, please!" Yagoda shouted.

"We need to close the inter-dimensional hole," Emily said. "We don't know how to do it."

"Now, Pasha!" Yagoda exploded.

"I'm sorry," Loomis said. "I'd better look at them."

Emily watched the man who now called himself Pasha, running his fingers over the books reverentially before opening the cover. His face softened. Perhaps he was remembering sitting in his cozy study in Sidcup on a Saturday night with a good book and a glass of whiskey. To read he held the book quite far from his face. He used to require reading glasses but here he seemed to have none. She remembered sitting in his office at MAAC doing what she was doing now—watching him read one of her reports and waiting for his comments the way a child waits for a parent's approval. And when that approval came, gently laced with some sage comments and suggestions, she used to be truly happy, floating from his office on a cushion of air.

"Sorry about the loose pages," John said.

Loomis began examining them.

John leaned in and whispered something light to cut the tension. He wondered whether the blast furnace book had made the bestseller list in 1917. Loomis smiled.

He got to the last page and turned his attention to the book on steam boilers. That one got the same methodical treatment.

Half an hour passed. Trevor was getting increasingly agitated. He kept looking over at the doorway where Arabel had disappeared.

Loomis closed the cover and rubbed his weary eyes.

Yagoda stopped his annoying pacing. "Well?" he demanded.

"Look," Loomis said in English. "As is abundantly clear, I know little about these seminal technologies. However, I would say that these books provide practical details on large-scale industrial production techniques. I believe one could adhere to the texts and make large furnaces and steam boilers. That is not to say that a process of trial and error would be needed to reduce the engineering to practice, but the books are enabling. I haven't been here very long, but I haven't met a single nineteenth- or twentieth-century engineer. Unlike me, these people probably led virtuous lives."

"Paul, you made one mistake," Emily said, her lips quivering and eyes filling with tears. "You were the most virtuous man I ever knew."

His smile lasted but a second. "Let me tell you what I did, Emily. I came home early after a meeting was canceled. I found Jane in bed—in our bed with our next-door neighbor, a smarmy fellow, a chartered accountant who talked about golf incessantly, a man I tolerated at best. But he was fit and robust and laughed a lot and I was, well, the man I was. She was naked, on top of him, moaning with pleasure. I had never heard her moan like that. They didn't see me and I slipped out. I instantly became a different person. I didn't recognize myself, even my thoughts. Everything seemed automatic. I went to the downstairs closet where I kept my father's shotgun. I loaded both barrels and put two more shells in my pocket. I climbed the stairs. They were finished and lying side-by-side. I didn't say anything. I didn't give them time to say anything or cover themselves. I fired at close range and quickly turned away from the result. I reloaded and put the barrel in my mouth and reached for the trigger. An instant later I was intact, in a pleasant meadow looking up at a featureless sky. I was here. Any virtue I may have possessed was erased by my act."

"Oh, Paul," she said.

"Paul is gone, Emily. I'm Pasha now, a beast who works for other beasts."

John had noticed that Yagoda had left the room after Pasha's pronouncement on the merits of the books. Now he was back with another man who, although before John's time, was instantly recognizable—the small powerful figure of Joseph Stalin.

"So, Pasha, the books are good?" Stalin said in English.

Loomis looked at him with terribly sad eyes. "Yes, they are useful, I would say. Very useful."

"These books," Stalin asked. "Only copies."

John answered with a lie. "They're the only ones."

"Good, good," Stalin said.

John spoke up, "Then we have a deal."

"And who are you?" Stalin asked.

"I'm John Camp. I'm a soldier."

"American soldier," Stalin said cheerfully. "I had many American friends. I wonder how many are in Hell in America. One day, maybe with these books I will build fast ships to go to America and see how it is. Maybe I see cowboys and Indians." He laughed heartily in anticipation of his next sentence. "Maybe I see Roosevelt." He pointed at Emily. "Who are you?"

"Emily Loughty. Sam and Belle are my nephew and niece."

"That is nice. Big happy family. What do you do?"

"I'm a scientist, like Paul."

"Very nice! I like scientists." He turned his gaze on Trevor and Brian. "And you two?"

"I'm a soldier too. And a policeman," Trevor said.

Brian said, "I can't believe I'm talking to Joseph Stalin. Unreal. I work in television and the movies."

"We have no movies here. Maybe one day, eh?"

John stepped into the conversation. "Do we have a deal?"

"A deal, a deal ..." Stalin pondered. "Tell me, where is Garibaldi?" Stalin asked.

"What does that have to do with a deal?" John asked.

"He comes into my country with a big army and you ask me what this has to do with deal?" Stalin fumed.

"He's not far," John said. "He's waiting with that big army for us to return with the children."

"He likes children?" Stalin asked. "I like children too. They are precious to me. The books are very nice but I need better deal."

John saw Emily's hateful stare.

"Oh yeah," John asked. "How much better?"

"You bring me Garibaldi's head and we have deal."

John stood up. "That's not going to happen."

The soldiers were finely attuned to Stalin's gestures. At a slight, upward movement of his head they drew weapons, swords and pistols, and began moving from the walls in a tightening noose.

"John?" Trevor said, testing his fists.

"Don't," John said. "You're making a big mistake," John told Stalin. "This is a good deal. These books can change everything. We go home with our people, no one gets hurt."

"You think I care if people get hurt?" Stalin said. "When life was precious thing I liquidated millions to achieve goals for Russia. Here nothing is precious except for children."

"For Christ's sake," Loomis yelled. "Take the bloody deal and let these people leave." He chose one of the slowly advancing soldiers and blocked his path, a symbolic but useless gesture.

"Take him away!" Yagoda shouted, and two soldiers grabbed him by the arms and began pulling him to the door.

"Leave him alone!" Emily shouted.

Loomis called to her as he was about to be dragged through the doorway. "Emily, I know how to plug the hole."

"How, Paul? How?" she screamed, but he was gone.

Brian and Trevor were braced for contact. "What do you want us to do, guv?" Trevor asked.

"Stand down," John said. "We can't win this. We tried, we failed."

They let themselves be taken.

"If we're not back by tomorrow afternoon, Garibaldi is going to attack," John said, his arms pulled behind his back.

"Castle is strong," Stalin said.

"It won't hold up to his weapons."

"We have these weapons too." He made the whistling noise of a singing cannon. "I give you until morning to agree to bring me Italian's head." He stood before Emily and because of his height had to look up at her. "Then I torture this woman to see if it change your mind."

"You're a fucking bastard," John seethed.

"This is Hell, Mr. Camp. Here we are all fucking bastards."

32

It wasn't a prison cell but it wasn't a comfortable guest room either. The locked room was in the castle tower, several floors below the breezy chamber where Emily had been kept during her last confinement at Marksburg. This room was outfitted with the basics. Straw mattresses on the stone floor, a basin of drinking water, and a slop bucket in one corner. The men turned their backs when Emily had to use it.

The single window was too small to wiggle out of even if they had the time to dislodge the bar. As the sky darkened so too did the room and without candles it would be pitch dark soon. They sat with their backs against the cool stone walls.

"This sucks," Trevor said. It was a minor variant to what he'd been saying for hours and John was getting irritated.

"Yes, Trev, of course it sucks. We know it sucks. That makes us all grade A suckers. What else were we supposed to do? Pound the castle with cannon fire and rockets with the kids inside?"

"We had to try the non-violent way first," Emily said. "We tried and failed."

"Don't mind me," Trevor said. "I don't like being locked up and I especially don't like Arabel getting split from us."

"Giuseppe and the others will get us out," Emily said without much conviction.

"When the Italians attack this tower is going to get smacked hard,"

Brian said. "It's the easiest target and a direct hit'll bring a few thousand tons of stonework down on our noggins."

"God, I hope Arabel and the children aren't here," Emily said.

"So, you got a plan worked out, bossman?" Brian asked John.

"The only thing I can think of is raising a racket in here, making them think that one of us is sick or that two of us are brawling, anything to get the guards to come inside. Then we overpower them, etcetera."

"Oldest trick in the book," Brian said.

"Probability of success?" Emily asked.

"Not high," John said. "But what else do we have?"

"You can agree to Stalin's terms," Emily said.

"And take out Giuseppe?" John asked. "Are you really suggesting that?"

"No, of course not. But it gets you out of here. One of us gets out which is better than none of us."

"Oh, please," John protested.

"You could tell Garibaldi not to hit this tower," Trevor said. "You could give him the layout of the place. That'll be helpful when he storms it."

"Zip it guys," John said. "I'm not leaving you." He said it to everyone but he was looking at Emily.

"Then send Emily," Trevor said. "Or one of us."

"I'll think about it," John said.

The last traces of light disappeared.

The room was dark and silent. They had stopped talking. The others could tell Brian was dozing by his incipient snorts. One after another they fell asleep until deep into the long night John was the only one awake.

He had his arm around Emily. Her head was heavy on his shoulder. Although his limb had fallen asleep nothing was going to make him move it and disturb her.

Until—

There were two dull cracks outside their door followed by a sharp cry then a third crack.

Trevor awoke and started to say something but John shushed him. Brian woke up with a "What?" Emily's head lifted from John's shoulder.

They all stood up, squinting into the blackness.

There was a sound of a key in the lock.

John whispered that he would take one side of the door, Trevor the other, Brian the middle ground. He pushed Emily down to the mattress and told her to stay low.

The fumbling continued. John felt along the wall until he was sure he was to the right of the door.

The lock caught and the door swung open.

The light of a brightly burning torch momentarily blinded him.

A huge figure filled the doorway illuminated by candlelight from the hall.

Trevor pounced first, just as Emily recognized the great bald head with its scraggly fringe and shouted, "No! He's a friend!"

Trevor was already on the ground, having been swatted away by the giant of a man.

John recognized him too from Himmler's caravan.

"Andreas!" Emily said, rushing to hug him. "Dear Andreas."

"You thought about Andreas?" the eunuch asked in German.

She fell into German to answer. "Of course I did."

"You remembered me?"

"Yes! I remembered you."

"Did you go to your home?" he asked.

"I did."

"Why did you come back?"

"I had to save the children."

"I saw them," he said. "I wanted to play with them but the Russians would not let me. I do not like the Russians."

John was outside the room, surveying the damage. Three Russian soldiers were collapsed on the floor near a stout, bloody axe handle. John commandeered their pistols and swords and distributed them to Trevor and Brian but Emily begged off.

"Andreas," she said in German. "Do you know where the children are being kept?"

"In King Frederick's palace. No, it is not his palace any more. Silly Andreas. Joseph is the king. They are in a chamber two floors above the great banqueting hall."

"Can you take us there?"

"It will be difficult. There will be soldiers."

"We have to try."

Emily told the others what she had learned and Trevor asked John, "How do you want to play it, guv?"

"We're going to have to go right into the lion's den," he said. "Our best hope is that the lion's asleep."

They ran into trouble right away but they knew it was coming. Andreas told Emily that two guards were patrolling the entrance to the tower. They had seen the eunuch enter so with Emily's instructions, John sent Andreas out first to banter with the guards using the two Russian words he knew— *da* and *nyet*, over and over. When they were distracted by his antics, John, Trevor, and Brian made fast, silent work of them then dragged their unconscious bodies behind a wagon. They crossed the outer bailey easily and John peeked through the gate that led to the main bailey and the palace.

The bailey looked deserted except for some tethered horses that must have caught his scent for they began to whinny. He heard some Russian voices coming from across the courtyard but the torches illuminating the bailey didn't cast their light far enough to make them out.

He decided to send Trevor and Brian to the left. He and Emily would go right. They'd hug the walls and creep around the perimeter until they flanked the palace guards. Andreas would slowly march right down the middle of the bailey.

"Can you tell him to act drunk?" John asked Emily.

"He always acts a bit drunk," she said.

"Have him exaggerate."

She had him kneel down so she could whisper the instructions in his ear and then kissed his cheek for encouragement.

"Andreas will act drunk now," the huge man said happily.

He wasn't going to win any awards for his performance. He weaved and sang and overplayed the part and most importantly, he moved too fast, prompting them to navigate the perimeter at a run. In the darkness Brian tripped up on a bucket but Andreas's awful singing drowned out the clatter.

The six soldiers guarding the palace entrance were hardened Russian troops, part of Stalin's elite guard. They were not the sorts to be distracted by an oaf like Andreas.

When he got within twenty feet, one of them came forward to challenge him, lowering his pike and growling in Russian.

"Da, nyet, da, nyet," Andreas said waving his arms and hopping on one foot.

Three more guards came forward to assist their comrade and two held back, drawing their swords just in case.

"When I say go," John whispered to Emily, "you do not go. You stay."

The pike man ordered Andreas to halt and when Andreas didn't, he made an aggressive move forward preparing to spear him.

"Go!" John said, loud enough for Brian and Trevor to hear but not so loud as to wake the palace.

There wasn't an attack plan. John saw Brian going for one of the men by the door so he went for the other one. Swords clashed and the three soldiers near the pike man turned back toward the door. Trevor fell upon them, swinging his sword wildly and catching a non-dominant arm with a lucky blow. The man grunted and kept fighting.

The pike man made the mistake of turning his back to Andreas. With one giant step, the eunuch enveloped the man in his arms, lifted him off his feet, and crashed him down to the ground. A boot to the face did the rest. Andreas picked up the man's pike the wrong way around but rather than switch the polarity, he gripped the pole above the steel and used the blunt end as a long club, showering the nearest men with blows.

Brian drew first blood with a sword thrust to a belly and quickly turned to help Trevor who was up against a skillful opponent. John's adversary was also a highly accomplished and strong swordsman who matched him stroke for stroke and drove him back on his heels. The soldier kept coming, taunting him in Russian and though John couldn't understand what he was saying, it got his blood boiling which only made him fight harder. He ducked under a looping slash and came out of his crouch to deliver a left fist to the man's bearded face, followed by a knee to the groin and a right-handed sword chop to the back of his neck. The blade must have shocked the spinal chord because the man went down, paralyzed.

John looked up in time to see Brian knocking the sword out of one man's hand allowing Trevor to fight him in a style he preferred—he dropped his own sword and engaged in a punch-up, pummeling the man with fists to the face and gut. Brian kept going with his sword and cleaved his last opponent's face. Andreas seemed to finally figure out he wasn't using the business end of the pike. With a backward thrust, he skewered the last man through the chest.

Emily emerged from the shadows and they began to drag the mumbling and groaning bodies to the darkness of the perimeter wall. Standing on either side of the now unguarded palace door were two longbows and full quivers.

"These'll come in handy," Brian said, grabbing them and stashing them out of the torchlight.

The only light inside the great hall came from the dying embers in the hearth but it was just enough to show the outlines of tables and chairs.

"Which way?" Emily asked Andreas.

He began to lead them across the hall to a rear corridor lit by torches spaced every thirty or forty feet. At the end of the corridor a door led to a pitch-black staircase. John took down one of the torches and moved to the front, just behind Andreas who clomped up the stairs, pausing on the first landing to let them know that this was where King Joseph slept.

On the next landing they heard loud snores. John handed the torch to Brian and poked his head around the corner. By the light of one wall torch, he saw a single guard on a chair midway down the hall, his head bowed, snoring into his lap.

"Ask him if it's the room about halfway down the hall?" John told Emily.

Andreas said yes.

"One man," John whispered to Trevor and Brian. "I'll take him."

"No, me," Trevor said.

John gave him a single nod to the affirmative and stepped aside.

Trevor sized up the situation and decided not to crawl or tiptoe. He merely walked at a fairly normal and leisurely pace until he was standing over the guard who at the last moment awoke and gave him an unfocused, bleary look before getting a fist to the temple.

The door was secured from the outside with a heavy bolt which Trevor slid open as quietly as he could.

John signaled for the others to follow him as Trevor disappeared into the room. At the door, John lifted the limp guard back onto the chair. They all went inside and shut the door behind them.

Delia woke first and sat up in her bed.

She was about to scream when Trevor rushed forward and clamped a hand over her mouth.

"It's us," he said.

Brian held the torch high. Arabel awoke with a start. Emily wrapped her up in her arms. The children were in their own bed, sleeping through the intrusion.

Arabel pulled away from Emily and stood before Trevor. "I knew you'd come," she said, stepping into his outstretched arms.

"Come on," John said. "Everyone needs to get dressed on the double."

"Can I touch the children?" Andreas asked Emily.

"Of course you can. Let's just wake them gently first so they won't be afraid."

"Come on, darlings," Arabel said over their heads. "Wake up so we can have an adventure."

Dressing Belle was like dressing a rag doll but Sam hopped to it and got very excited very quickly when he saw the swords.

"Who's he?" he asked, pointing at Andreas.

"He's a friend of Auntie Emily," Emily said. "He wants to shake your hand. Would you like to shake his?"

Emily instructed Andreas how to shake hands and the giant extended his huge paw and squeezed down so delicately that he would not have broken an egg.

"Her too?" Andreas asked.

"You may pat her head," Emily said.

He did so and broke out a smile that showed his nut-brown teeth.

"I like children," he said.

"I'm sure they would like to play with you, Andreas, but we really must get them to safety," she said. "We have to leave the castle."

"Tell him we need a horse and wagon, better yet a covered wagon," John said. "Even if we found the car it would take too long to charge and it would make a racket."

Arabel carried Belle and Delia toted Sam though he was wiggly and said he wanted to walk on his own and carry a sword. They retraced their steps down the stairs and through the great hall. John and Brian took the lead and exited into the bailey. It was deserted. The only signs of their struggle were puddles of blood on the courtyard stones. Brian retrieved the bows and quivers and he and John shouldered them on their free arms.

Emily ran up next to John. "We need to find Paul Loomis," she said.

"We have no idea where he is," John said.

"He said he knew how to fix this. We've got to get him."

"Listen, Emily," he said in a low voice the others couldn't hear. "Our odds of getting out of here are slim. Our odds of getting out of here by wandering around this castle and looking for one man are zero."

"But …"

"Think about the children. We need a wagon."

She nodded and went to Andreas. "Which way to a wagon?" she whispered.

"The stables are down there," he said, turning off down an alleyway. Trevor had the torch now and he made sure everyone could safely navigate the passageway between a palace wall and the outer perimeter wall.

There were low-pitched noises ahead, animal-like grunting noises that suddenly stopped.

Brian slipped the bow off his arm and nocked an arrow.

There were whispers in German. Andreas heard his name and responded with his own whisper. Two figures stepped away from the alley wall, a rotund man and a skinny woman, both naked from the waist down.

"Why aren't they wearing trousers?" Sam asked.

The man smiled at Andreas and waved.

"Who are they?" Emily asked.

"They are my friends," Andreas said. "They were fucking."

"I see," Emily said. "Can we trust them not to say they saw us?"

"They will not say anything. They hate the Russians too."

"It's okay," Emily told the others while Andreas went to have a word. "He says they won't talk."

"That's going to put me off shagging for life," Brian said.

The stables were at the other end of the alley. The horses stirred and shifted in their stalls when they entered. John and Trevor went looking for a wagon and Brian went to inspect the horses and tack.

The operation took longer than anyone would have liked because by the time they had hitched two horses to an enclosed wooden caravan the sky was beginning to lighten.

With the children bundled inside with Delia, Emily, and Arabel, Andreas led the horses by their reins. Brian walked beside him, scanning the dark road, his fingers on the bowstring. John had the point, sword and pistol at the ready, and Trevor trailed behind, protecting their rear.

The road ran parallel to the outer castle wall and led to the drawbridge gate. John knew the next steps would be difficult. The massive drawbridge would need to be lowered. There would be soldiers.

With the gatehouse in sight, John signaled for Andreas to stop leading the horses. Delia got out to hold the reins and Emily took Trevor's place, watching the rear.

John, Brian, Andreas, and Trevor crept forward. They had to pass by the main barracks filled with hundreds of sleeping German and Russian soldiers spread out on cots over six packed floors. Past the barracks was the gatehouse. They snuck a glance into the gatehouse windows. The room was candlelit. A few soldiers were playing dice; others were dozing around the table, heads in arms. Andreas pointed and pantomimed moving a drawbridge windlass back and forth. They would have to get through these men before reaching the drawbridge.

"No easy way," Brian whispered.

"Hard and fast," John said.

He and Brian nocked arrows and readied their bows. On John's signal, Trevor pulled the gatehouse door wide open and got out of the way.

Two arrows sliced through the air and caught two of the dice players in their chests. Brian adeptly re-nocked and fired again and while he was nocking his third arrow, Trevor, John, and Andreas piled into the room. John and Trevor used swords while Andreas just used his giant hands to knock heads together. Most of the gatehouse men were dozy and drunk. They didn't fight like elite soldiers. They went down without much of a fight, succumbing to sword thrusts and Brian's arrows.

Brian entered and had a look around at the gatehouse mechanicals. He had devoted an entire episode on his TV show to drawbridges and medieval castle defense and he quickly got the lay of the land. He identified the windlass that controlled the lifting mechanism of the inner portcullis and began winching up the heavy iron grate.

He called out to the others. "Those two windlasses over there do the drawbridge. Those chains go to lifting drums overhead and the counterweights drop through these trapdoors. Trevor, you and Andreas can start in. That windlass over there'll lift the outer portcullis."

"I'll get the wagon," John said, leaving the gatehouse.

The women were overjoyed to see him return. He took the reins from Delia and had everyone climb back in then slowly and as quietly as he could, led the horses past the dark barracks.

The inner portcullis, a giant iron grate, was now fully lifted, allowing the wagon to roll underneath it into a vaulted tunnel. John could partially see into the gatehouse through a narrow observation slit. Andreas's big shoulders were pumping one of the windlasses forward and back. He could hear the heavy chains turning on the overhead wheels and see the lightening

GLENN COOPER

sky of early dawn starting to appear as the massive drawbridge lowered. Once the bridge was down, the outer portcullis, a matching grate to the inner one, would have to be raised.

Inside the gatehouse, none of them noticed one of the gatehouse men head banged by Andreas, emerging from his stupor and crawling out the door. From there he picked himself up and stumbled toward the barracks.

"Almost there," Brian told Trevor, "keep working it." The ratcheting was harder work for Trevor than Andreas who hadn't even broken a sweat. Brian gave John a thumbs-up through the observation slit and John climbed up to the driver's bench on the wagon when the drawbridge clunked into place.

The air filled with shouts from the barracks as the alarm was raised and passed from cot to cot and floor to floor.

"Get the kids down low," John called out to the women in the wagon. He gripped the reins tightly but he was staring at a huge iron grate blocking the way.

Andreas grabbed the windlass for the outer portcullis and shouted at Trevor and Brian, "Eile, eile, gehen!"

They got the message and ran out the gatehouse to the waiting wagon.

Brian jumped in the back of the caravan and took up a firing position with his longbow that also served to put a body between the attackers and the women and children. Trevor climbed up beside John on the driver's bench.

The grate began to lift.

"They're coming!" Brian shouted.

Trevor shouted at the portcullis. "Come on!"

Brian let an arrow fly and told Delia to keep feeding him with more.

John watched the grate rise inch by inch. Judging by Brian's exhortations from the rear, there wasn't going to be enough time for it to fully lift. The moment he thought he had the minimal clearance he snapped the reins and shouted at the horses. The wagon lurched forward.

The top of the caravan scraped loudly on the portcullis spikes.

A mass of soldiers was swarming toward the rolling wagon. Emily lifted

380

her head up from Sam's squirming body and glanced out the back.

Andreas appeared running toward the wagon, just in front of the closest soldiers.

"Andreas is coming," she shouted. "Slow down!"

"We can't," Brian shouted, trying to get an arrow off around the hulking man's frame. "For Christ's sake, keep going!"

Brian saw an arrow sail past the wagon and he swore. Then another one whizzed overhead. Then the pursuing archers went for an easier target.

Andreas suddenly stopped running.

Arrows pierced his back.

He turned around and more pierced his chest. He tried to run toward the wagon but he couldn't. He dropped to his knees.

"No!" Emily cried.

Andreas's eyes locked with hers.

The wagon was accelerating and the distance between them was increasing.

Andreas managed one last shout to her, "Please remember Andreas!" and then he fell forward and was trampled by the swarm.

"I will," Emily whispered, her eyes glistening.

John had no choice but to let the horses do a full gallop on the winding road spiraling down the mountainside.

Inside the wagon everyone thrashed from side to side and Belle began to cry.

"Are they coming?" John asked Trevor.

Trevor cocked his pistol and partially stood to see over the top of the wagon. Dawn was breaking and he had a clear view uphill. The coast was clear. They'd left the soldiers behind. "We're okay." Then he saw a horse and rider, then another. "We're not okay."

He fired his pistol and the nearest rider fell.

"Take mine," John shouted, passing his pistol up.

Trevor fired again. The second horse reared and threw its man.

Trevor sat back down.

In the gunmetal gray of dawn John saw the Rhine's murky waters and in the distance the wooden bridge that led to the Italian camp on the west bank.

Horse hooves dug into the packed-down dirt road. A sharp turn was coming and he shouted for everyone to brace. The wagon swayed so hard he was afraid they were going to tip but they kept going, cheating gravity.

The road straightened and Trevor had another look behind but Brian who was also monitoring the rear beat him to the punch.

"They've mobilized the cavalry," he shouted. "They're coming!"

John snapped the reins again and exhorted the horses to go flat out.

They were down at sea level now, running parallel to the river. The bridge was looming.

Brian kept up the spotter chatter from the rear. "They're gaining on us!" Then, "There's something going on up on the ramparts. It's a bloody cannon."

John had to slow the horses to take the turn onto the bridge and when he'd made it he drove them back to a gallop. The wagon wheels whirred loudly on the rough wooden planks.

"Tell Brian to fire his pistol into the air," John shouted. "I want to let the Italians know we're coming."

Trevor rapped on the front of the wagon and in a shout passed the order along.

"I left the bloody thing back at the gatehouse!" Brian yelled.

Boom.

The percussion was followed by a whistling sound that John knew all too well.

His cursing was drowned out by a shell from the Russian singing cannon exploding hundreds of yards in front of them to the west of the Rhine.

Arabel screamed and threw herself over Belle.

Brian saw the barrel of the cannon disappear with recoil. Then it came back into view. "They're reloading!" he shouted.

The only one who seemed unafraid was Sam who cheerfully parroted the boom and whistle.

"They'll hold their range and wait for us to drive into it!" John shouted to Trevor.

"Take us into the fields when we're across," Trevor said. "We've got to avoid straight lines."

Once across the bridge the verges were too steep and wooded to get off the road. The horses galloped closer and closer to the point of impact of the last round.

"I can't get off the road!" John shouted.

He saw a tree on fire fifty yards on.

The impact point.

A second round well timed would blow them to pieces. He thought about pulling up and stopping the wagon but Brian shouted that the Russian cavalry was approaching the bridge.

If John were up on the ramparts, he'd be touching the fire hole of the cannon in about five seconds.

Boom.

John saw a flash coming from a thicket ahead followed by an unmistakable whistle.

Garibaldi.

The cannonball impacted the pale castle walls midway between the ground and the ramparts but it was enough to send the Russian artillerymen into a defensive posture.

The wagon sped past the impact point.

Ahead was a sight almost as wonderful as the cannon flash. A cavalry division composed of Italians, French, and Italians were galloping toward them and when they were nose-to-nose, they parted and streamed in single file to the right and the left of the wagon, galloping to engage the Russians.

Trevor let out some joyous shouts as they passed the soldiers who raised their swords and whooped back.

"Beautiful!" Trevor shouted. "Fucking beautiful!"

"Are we going to be all right?" Emily shouted.

"For now we are," John shouted back, then more quietly, "For now."

The main concentration of German troops and the remaining divisions of the Russian army were bivouacked in a vast encampment to the east of Castle Marksburg. Stalin had been awoken and told of the escape. In a fury he sent a rider to mobilize the combined army and that army was now breaking camp.

"Get my boots!" Stalin commanded Nikita. "And where is Yagoda?"

"He has been summoned."

Yagoda arrived, tucking the last of his shirt into his pants, looking dazed from his rude awakening and the after-effects of too much wine.

"How did this happen?" Stalin growled.

The rat faced colonel said he didn't know but would find out and destroy the responsible men.

"Let us start with the man who was ultimately responsible," Stalin said, drawing his fancy pistol and without hesitation shooting Yagoda between his closely spaced eyes.

Stalin pulled his high boots over his trousers.

"Let's go, little Nikita," he said. "We are going to have a war, a very big war."

33

"How're you doing this fine morning?" Christine asked.

She had just removed the blonde woman's ropes that tethered her to the toilet during the nights. Christine brandished a kitchen knife to discourage an escape attempt.

They had made things as comfortable as possible considering the tight space. There were duvets and pillows on the floor. There was water from the sink. There was a toilet, of course. She was provided with three meals a day and snacks if she kept her mouth shut and didn't raise Cain. But they didn't let her have any booze, not a drop, and predictably, she'd spent most of the week in withdrawal—not body-writhing, skin-crawling withdrawal, but it hadn't been pretty or easy.

The fight had gone out of her. She was calm and collected this morning and asked an appropriate question. "I've lost track. Is Roger back at school?"

"He goes back Monday. This is Saturday," Christine said, laying down a plate of eggs and toast.

"Can I see him today?"

"I don't think he should see his mother tied to a toilet."

"He knows I'm in here."

"How could he not? All the ranting and raving you went through."

"I was sick."

"Tell me about it."

"What did you tell him?"

"That his mum was sick with a tummy problem and needed to use the loo a lot. We told him we were nurses."

"He believed you?"

"I think so. He's a lovely boy."

"I know that."

"He doesn't deserve the way you treat him."

She didn't say anything.

"Do you even remember how you treat him when you're drunk?" Christine asked, her arms sternly folded.

She teared up. "I've had a hard time."

"I know hard times. Molly knows hard times. You don't know hard times."

"Ted doesn't ..."

"I don't want to hear it again. Ted doesn't pay his child support. He left you for a chippy. The council's cutting your benefits. Shut up. You've got a lovely son, a nice house, you're safe, well fed, able bodied. You don't know what bad is."

She rolled her eyes. "In Hell?"

Christine hadn't been keen to tell her but Molly, in a fit of pique responded to her "poor me" blubbering by telling her everything. The woman hadn't believed a thing and Christine had left it at that.

"Yeah, in Hell. I don't give a toss whether you believe me. But here's the thing. I don't know if you've ever crossed the line enough to punch your ticket there, luv, but child abusers, child molesters and the like, well in Hell they get treated much like child abusers in prison if they're stupid enough to talk about it. But in Hell it's forever. We've got you sobered up. Stay that way and take care of that lovely little boy. If you don't we'll be waiting for you on the other side."

"You sound like you're leaving."

"We're going today."

"Thank God. Will you leave me untied?"

"No, but I'll leave the knots loose enough that you'll be able to get out in a few hours. And don't call out to Roger to do it for you. It'll traumatize him. You're sober and sensible enough to understand that."

"Where are you going?"

"So you can tell the police?"

"I'm just curious."

"We're going to see my mum. I never got to say goodbye to her."

In the lounge, Roger was doing a jigsaw puzzle. Molly was on the sofa eating biscuits.

Christine got down on the floor. "I made you sandwiches," she said.

"I'm not hungry."

"Not for now, for later. You'll find them on the kitchen table under foil."

"You'll get them for me later?" he asked.

"I would, my love, but Auntie Molly and I have to leave now."

The boy looked up sharply. "But I don't want you to go."

"I know. We don't want to go either, but it's time."

"Is mummy still in the loo?"

"She is but she's almost all better. She'll come out to see you before you know it."

"But don't go in there," Molly said. "Even if she asks you. Remember what I said about ladies and their privacy?"

Roger nodded. "Will you come back?"

"No, we won't be coming back, sweetheart," Christine said, "but I hope you remember the lovely week we had together."

His lower lip quivered.

"Now don't cry," Christine said. "You're a big boy and big boys don't cry. Now give me a big goodbye hug."

With the small body in her grasp, Christine choked back tears. She peeled his arms off her and Molly moved in for hers.

Closing the door behind them, Molly started to speak but Christine was fighting her emotions and just said, "Please don't say anything, all right?"

The cottage in Stoke Newington resembled a garbage tip. The rovers had sucked the house dry of food and drink, discarding everything that couldn't be eaten. In the lounge, kitchen, and bedrooms they had tipped over most of the furnishings in varying states of drunkenness and combativeness. And like locusts that had consumed all a piece of land had to offer, it was time to move on. Christine's sister had the good fortune of not yet returning from her holiday in Cornwall but when she did she probably was not going to be overjoyed.

In Hell, Talley was unquestionably their leader. On Earth, Hathaway had progressively co-opted his authority. His knowledge of modernity placed him in a position that even Talley's reptilian brain could recognize was essential for their survival. Yet that didn't prevent Talley from asserting his dominance, especially when loaded with alcohol. One particularly ugly physical confrontation had left both men bloody and chairs destroyed.

That morning, Hathaway had awoken first and unable to find anything to eat beyond a packet of frozen piecrust dough, he righted an overturned wing chair and stewed.

Hate was his friend. It had kept him company every day in Hell and every day back on Earth. Revenge was aspirational. He put it on a higher plane than satisfying his basic biological needs. Rix, Murphy, and their wives were his raison d'etre. He had hated them enough to kill them but that wasn't enough. When he found them in Hell they were sitting pretty, at least by the standards of most Heller bastards. Rix had Christine. Murphy had Molly. Forever. They needed a good crashing. They needed to be in rotting rooms. He realized he would have a yawning void in his desperate existence once he'd destroyed them but destroy them he would.

It hadn't been easy. Their village of Ockendon had enough fit men to be capable of defending itself from rovers. Other villages were easier pickings. What a rush it had been finding the women alone in the woods that day. After a day of raping, at night he would have rolled their heads into the village like bowling balls. Now he regretted not crashing them as soon as they got to Earth. But the whole experience had been too jumbled and confusing. He wouldn't make the mistake again.

His hate lived somewhere on the border of rational thought. The logic went something like this: he'd been forced to kill the four of them because they were going to turn themselves into the police. Mellors had ordered the hit. Clean up the mess, Lucas, Mellors had said. Clean it up or we'll all be in the soup. He was in Hell because he had killed them. Yes, the kidnapped girl had died but he hadn't been there when it happened, had he? No one knew what kind of celestial judge condemned you to Hell but maybe he wouldn't have gotten tagged with her death. How did he know? So it was them, Rix and Murphy, Christine and Molly, who were responsible for landing him in Hell.

Talley shuffled in looking bilious. "Give me something to drink."

"There's nothing left."

"Fuck there isn't."

"Have a look if you don't believe me."

Talley opened the liquor cabinet and found one bottle. "What's this then?" he said triumphantly.

"It's Margarita mix. No liquor in there."

"Don't believe you."

"Try it then."

Talley had mastered twist tops and soon had a swig in his mouth that he expelled all over the room.

"Told you so," Hathaway said. "There's no food left either. It's time for us to move along."

"To find the molls?"

"Yeah, to find the molls."

Christine's eyes began to well up as soon as she crossed from Eye to Hoxne on the Eye Road. There were a couple of new bungalows and houses nestled in the trees, but the entrance to the village was unchanged from her memories. The cottages, the hedgerows, the old pipe works, all of them stood where they had permanently resided in her mind's eye.

"Well?" Molly asked.

"It's the same."

She drove the Mini over the little bridge that traversed the River Dove. The Hoxne Swan came into sight. Her first pub. She'd played under the tables in the public bar as a small girl and had her first real drinks there at fourteen with impunity—sickly sweet vodkas and lime. She'd been married in the church on Green Street, had her reception under a tent in the Swan garden and she and Colin had spent their wedding night in The Angel Hotel in Bury St. Edmunds.

Her hands began to shake on the wheel when she saw the red phone box outside the post office and general store.

"What?" Molly asked.

"It's just up there."

There were a few people talking outside the store. She drove slowly past and at her mother's trellised cottage, her mouth was almost too dry to get the words out. "That one."

"It's pretty," Molly said.

She didn't want to park a stolen car out in the open on Low Street so she drove around and left it on the little-traveled Church Hill. They spritzed themselves with cologne and walked down the small public way connecting the two streets.

"You knock," she told Molly. "The shock could kill her. I'll wait outside. Be gentle, all right?"

"I know what to do, luv."

Molly knocked then knocked again. After a long wait a frail and stooped white-haired woman answered, leaning hard on a cane.

"Oh, hello," the woman said. "Are you from the council?"

"No, luv, I'm not."

"I see. The girl who helps out on weekends called in sick this morning so I thought the council had sent someone else."

"Oh dear, didn't you have any lunch then?" Molly asked.

"I was just going to have some corn flakes and perhaps cut some fruit into it."

"Well then, I'm Molly. I'm not with the council but I'd be happy to sort out something a bit more substantial for you. Would you like me to do that?"

"That would be very nice," the old woman said. "Molly, did you say? But you're not from the council."

"No but I know how to fix a nice lunch."

Christine hadn't been able to catch a glimpse of her mother but she heard her voice. It was shakier but still very much hers. When Molly disappeared inside Christine walked up and down the street, remembering who used to live in each cottage.

"Hey."

She turned around. Molly was at the door motioning her to come.

"What did you tell her?"

"That there was someone I wanted her to meet. She's a bit confused, just so you know, but she's very dear."

Christine stepped inside as one might enter a holy site, walking slowly and reverentially, taking everything familiar. Entering the kitchen her mother's back was to her. Molly had heated a tin of ravioli.

"This is the woman I wanted you to see," Molly said.

Her mother turned and blinked in confusion. "Hello."

"Hello," Christine whispered.

"And what's your name, dear?"

She came around the table. "Don't you recognize me?"

The old woman studied her face and seemed to be troubled in an unfocused way. "I'm sorry, I …"

"It's me, mum. Don't be scared. It's your Christine."

Hathaway began driving at sundown. Their bellies were empty. All of them were accustomed to hunger but their time on Earth had already made them soft. Food was easy to come by here and Youngblood and Chambers in particular were whining for grub.

"We're not stopping," Hathaway said. "It's too dangerous. We'll eat when we get there."

"What kind of grub?" Youngblood asked.

"Hot grub," Hathaway said. Then he smiled. "And maybe some cannie food if we're lucky."

He had one of Gavin West's maps. Asking Talley to navigate was like asking a donkey for help so he kept the map on his lap and peeked at it from time to time. He felt safer once he had turned off the A140. Fewer headlights, fewer passing cars. Dark B roads.

Molly had helped Christine put her mother to bed. The traumas of the day hadn't killed her, as Christine had worried, but they had exhausted her.

At first her mother had simply ignored her. She had returned to her plate of ravioli and had slowly finished it before saying, "My Christine is dead."

They had steered her into the tiny sitting room and deposited her in her TV chair.

"Can't you see, mum?" Christine had said. "Can't you see it's me?"

Forced to study her face, the old woman became agitated and had said, "Am I dead?"

"No mum, you're not dead."

"Then how am I with my daughter?"

"I came back to see you."

"That doesn't happen."

"It happened this time."

"She died, you died, such a long time ago." The old lady screwed up her face in confusion. "You did some bad things."

"I know I did. I am so sorry for what I did. I never got to say goodbye to you."

"You look like Christine."

"That's because I am Christine. Will you forgive me, mum?"

"Of course I forgive you. I'm your mother. Are you sure I'm not dead?"

"You're alive mum. It's me who's dead."

"Is she dead too?"

"Yes, Molly's dead too."

"She made me ravioli. My girl couldn't come today."

Christine closed her mother's door and joined Molly downstairs in the sitting room. The only alcohol in the house was sherry that she poured into two glasses.

"I don't think she's all there," Molly said.

Christine drank hers in one go. "Sometimes I was thinking I was getting through to her, that she was, you know, believing me, then the next minute she's off on a cloud."

"They get that way sometimes."

"This was a mistake. We should leave in the morning," Christine said.

"And go where?"

"I don't know. Somewhere, anywhere. I don't even care if we get nicked. I'm tired of running."

The back door crashed open showering the kitchen with wood and glass.

Before they could even get out of their seats, Hathaway was standing over them, the other rovers behind him.

"This is too bloody perfect," he said. "Too bloody perfect."

Ben's mobile rang. It was one of the only nights since the crisis began that he'd simply walked away from the job for a few hours and taken his wife to a restaurant. One night out wasn't going to repair his marriage but it was a positive step. The MAAC restart was in nine days. Hopefully, that would be the end of it. Nine days until normalcy. Nine days until he could once again give himself over to the comparatively welcome realm of domestic terrorism.

His wife looked livid when he glanced at his phone.

"Really, Ben, you promised."

He didn't recognize the number. "I'm sorry. I'll just check to see if it's urgent."

"Not at the table," she said. "People are looking."

He rose while answering and headed for the entrance.

"Ben Wellington."

"Yes, Mr. Wellington, this is Constable Kent from the Suffolk Constabulary."

"Yes, constable."

"I've done what you asked. I've kept an eye on Mrs. Hardwick's cottage. I hope it's all right to call at this hour."

"Quite all right. How can I help you?"

"I was passing by in my private vehicle when I saw some men getting out of a car at her address."

"How long ago was this?"

"No more than a minute."

"Did they go inside?"

"I couldn't say. I passed by and drove on to place the call."

"How many men?"

"Four. Would you like me to intervene?"

Ben said no so loudly the maître de looked up angrily. "Do not intervene. Please keep the property under surveillance from a very safe distance. Do not call in your colleagues. I will be there within one hour. If there are any further developments call me immediately."

He rushed back to the table, threw down a handful of bills and met his wife's furious gaze with a sorrowful shake of his head.

"I'm sorry. You'll have to take a cab home. I promise I'll make it up to you."

The waiter arrived with the entrees.

"Please don't bother," she said.

Youngblood came bounding down the stairs. "There's an old woman in a bed, that's all."

"You leave her alone," Christine said, shaking with rage.

"Not much meat on her," Youngblood said, heading to the kitchen. "But some."

"Want to know how we found you?" Hathaway asked.

"Not particularly," Christine said.

"Your Gavin told us. Right before we crashed him."

The women looked at each other, too scared to ask about the fate of Christine's son, Gareth.

"Just him?" Christine managed to ask.

"Who else did you expect?" Hathaway asked. "Did we miss one of your dearies?"

"There's no one else," Christine said.

"Yes there is. Your sister. We waited for her for a week but she never came home. Lucky lady."

"You've got a hard-on for me don't you, you piece of shit?" Christine said.

Hathaway rubbed his crotch. "You don't know the half of it."

"Let's start the raping," Chambers said.

"There's time for that," Talley said, asserting control. "We want grub and strong drink."

"If there's no cooked grub," Youngblood said, "I say we cannie the old woman."

"Let us go to the kitchen," Molly said. "We'll cook."

Talley grunted his approval. Molly's knees almost buckled when she stood. Christine saw the fear in her eyes and reached out to steady her.

"Watch them," Talley told Chambers. "What about the drink?"

"There's only this bit of sherry," Christine said.

Talley chugged the bottle dry and started to open cupboards looking for more.

"There was a pub just down the road," Hathaway said. He looked at the mantelpiece clock. It was eleven. He mumbled that he had no idea when pubs closed anymore but that they'd do better waiting until the place cleared out.

"We'll go after we have grub," Talley said. "Then we'll get drunk, then we'll do our raping."

"That's why you're the bossman, Talley," Hathaway said. "Always there with a plan."

Talley, failing to appreciate the sarcasm, seemed pleased at the compliment.

The Security Service helicopter picked up Ben from Thames House in Millbank and flew to Dartford. Rix and Murphy were waiting with their minders near the MAAC tennis court.

The Gazelle made a touch and go landing and Rix and Murphy belted in.

"What's going on?" Rix asked. "They wouldn't tell us shit."

"We may have them," Ben said.

"Where?" Murphy asked.

"Hoxne. The local constable saw four men at the cottage. I told him to stand down."

"If it's them you saved the chap's life," Rix said. "Just four men?"

"Yes, why do you ask?"

"In case they pulled in hostages," Rix answered quickly.

"I see. I know the house has nothing to do with Hathaway," Ben said.

"Do you now?" Rix said.

"The elderly woman who lives there is a Mrs. Hardcastle. She's Christine's mother."

"How long have you known?"

"I found out when we returned from Hoxne. It wasn't hard to find out."

"So why didn't you say anything?"

"I didn't see the point. Better for you to think you had one on me."

"You're a fucker, you know that?" Rix said.

"So I've been told. As recently as tonight."

Rix pointed at the two MI5 officers with Ben. "Just you lot?"

"And you."

"You deputizing us?" Murphy laughed.

"Something like that."

"Are you armed?" Rix asked.

"I'm not. They are. We'll put down in the same field as before."

"Thirty minutes to touchdown," the pilot announced.

Murphy whispered into Rix's ear. "Do you think our gals are there?"

"I hope not, Murph, I bloody hope not."

"You watch them," Talley told Youngblood. "We'll be back with drink. And don't start the raping till we've returned."

Youngblood stuffed more sliced bread in his mouth and pointed a kitchen knife at Molly and Christine. "Don't you try nothing with me or I'll crash you good."

Hathaway, Talley, and Chambers walked down Low Street toward the Swan. The village was dark and quiet. They passed a car parked nose-out in a small driveway and failed to notice a man ducking down in the driver's seat.

Constable Kent waited until they were gone and quietly got out. He let them get some distance on him then followed until they disappeared around the back of the pub.

He called Ben's mobile but got voice mail. After leaving a brief message he resumed his pursuit.

The landlord of the Swan was the last one in the pub, doing his final cleanup. He'd locked the front door but not the rear and when he saw Hathaway come in he said, "We're closed, mate."

Hathaway kept coming, followed by the two others.

"Did you not hear me? We're closed."

"Yeah, but we're thirsty," Hathaway said.

The landlord, a young, fit fellow didn't seem much intimidated. He had an old cricket bat behind the bar and showed it. "You'd best be out of here or I'll call the police."

"What do you think you're going to do with that?" Hathaway said with a toothy grin.

"Look, gents, this is a nice quiet village pub. I don't court trouble but I don't shy from it either." The rovers sidled up to the bar, close enough for the publican to smell them. "What's with you anyway?" he asked.

"We've come a very long way to drink at your establishment," Hathaway said, admiring the hearth and the beams. "Very old worldsy. Now are you going to serve us or are we going to have to serve ourselves?"

Something caught the eye of the landlord. A face at the front window of the pub.

Constable Kent signaled with his hand that he was coming around to the rear.

The young man raised the bat defensively but in the blink of an eye, Talley and Chambers vaulted the bar and were on him, biting, gouging, punching.

"You, stop!" Kent shouted, coming around from the lounge bar. "Police."

Hathaway had been admiring the killing going on and looked up. "You're the police, old man?" he asked. "Come on in, have a drink with us. It's your last orders, mate."

The landing lights floodlit the dark field. The helicopter put down and with torches in hand, the MI5 team and the Hellers ran toward Low Street. Ben's voicemail chirped and he saw it was from the policeman. He listened to the message on the run and told everyone to stop.

"The pub," he said. "They went to the pub."

They crept to the window by the front door and one of the agents looked in. The lights were on. The man swore and drew his gun.

"One man down," he whispered. "Blood everywhere."

"Watch the front," Ben said to him. "We'll go in the back."

The second armed officer led the way into the rear door. Constable Kent was on the floor in the public bar, mutilated beyond recognition. Ben swallowed hard and checked his revulsion as he retrieved Kent's wallet and identity card.

"Rover work," Rix said.

"There's another bloke behind the bar," Murphy said. "Barman possibly."

Ben instructed them to open the front door to the other agent and told them to search the premises.

"They won't be here," Rix said. "They'll have loaded up with booze and gone back to their new nest."

The men ran up Low Street and crept toward the front windows of the trellised cottage. Crouched in the flowerbeds, Ben pointed at Rix to look inside.

The curtains were closed but there was a small gap between them.

He saw men's legs walking past. Then he saw a hand resting on the arm of a chair. A woman's hand. He changed his position slightly to see more. He made out a few wisps of hair and an ear.

Christine.

Murphy saw his expression change as fear and anger set in.

Rix frog stepped away from the window and motioned for the others to follow him a few yards away.

"Our girls are there," he said to Murphy.

Ben asked, "Your wives?"

"Yes."

"Did you see both of them?" Murphy asked.

"Just Christine."

"As this is a hostage situation, perhaps we'd better call for reinforcements," Ben said.

"No time for that," Murphy said. "They'll get boozed-up fast then very bad things'll happen."

"We've got to go in now, and we've got to go in hard," Rix said. "You lads have got to go in shooting to kill."

"We don't operate that way," Ben said. "Regardless of the circumstances, we will take these men into custody lawfully and use lethal force only if absolutely necessary."

"And I thought you were a smart bloke," Rix said. "Believe me, it'll be necessary."

Ben sent one of his men to the rear with Murphy and told them to await his verbal signal.

Ben, Rix, and the other armed agent made for the front door.

Ben took some deep breaths while the agent gingerly tested the doorknob. It turned. Ben nodded at him and shouted, "Go!" at the top of his lungs.

The front room was so small that upon entry they were in the thick of it with the rovers and the women with little room to maneuver. When Murphy and the other agent pressed in from the kitchen it was almost impossible to move.

Christine's eyes met Rix's for the briefest moment before the melee began and Molly shouted, "Colin!"

Ben was the first to go down with a whiskey bottle to the head. One of the MI5 men made the snap decision that lethal force was indeed on the table but before he could fire his weapon, Youngblood clamped down on his neck with his teeth and ripped out a hunk of flesh along with his jugular. The other agent had better luck and got off a pointblank shot into Chambers' head before Talley stabbed him under his ribs with an upwards killing thrust.

Talley turned to Murphy with a grotesque smile and said, "Come on, then. I'll cannie you and rape your woman and then I'll cannie her."

With the pent-up rage of thirty years in Hell, Murphy launched himself at Talley.

Hathaway grabbed Christine by the hair and pulled her out of her chair into a chokehold.

"Come on, Jason," he taunted. "I want you to be watching me break her fucking neck."

"No, *you* come on, Lucas," Rix said, his chest heaving. "Be man enough to take me on. Winner gets Christine. What do you say?"

Youngblood's mouth was red. Primed with violence he wanted more and he turned his attention to Rix whom he swatted in the face with the back of his fist.

Rix took the blow and after an impotent glance toward Christine, he furiously engaged Youngblood, fighting like rovers fight with hands, feet, and teeth.

Hathaway seemed to enjoy watching the fighting but suddenly he yelped and turned around. Molly had picked up one of the rover's kitchen knives and buried it in his flank. Hathaway let go of Christine, sneered at Molly and punched her in the jaw.

"Molly!" Murphy yelled. He and Talley had bloodied but when he saw his wife motionless on the ground, he went into orbit. He landed a hard punch to Talley's Adam's apple and when he began to cough and choke, Murphy kneed him in the groin then hit him again in the neck even harder. Talley's face went blue and he fell to his knees, choking to death.

Youngblood outweighed Rix by forty pounds and was getting the better of him. A crushing blow to the top of his head put Rix on the floor beside a stirring Ben. The whiskey bottle that knocked Ben out was lying there. Rix took it and swung it hard, breaking it against Youngblood's knee.

Youngblood screamed in pain and doubled over giving Rix the target he wanted. With an uppercut, he shoved the broken bottle into Youngblood's belly and he kept thrusting and twisting it until the rover's shirt was soaked with blood. He didn't stop until Youngblood crashed to the floor, lifeless.

Murphy saw an opening and dragged Molly away from the fray to the kitchen.

Rix wheeled around at the sound of Christine's cry.

Hathaway had the knife Molly had used on him and had Christine back in a chokehold.

"Lucas, don't!" Rix cried.

"Now you're going to see this knife in her brain!" Hathaway shouted.

He raised his knife arm high to bring it down.

There was an explosion.

Hathaway's nose was gone replaced by an angry red cavity. He fell backwards against the blood-splattered wall.

Rix looked down at Ben. He was lying on his side, his arms extended, holding a dead agent's gun.

"Bloody good shot," Rix said, helping him up.

Christine was in his arms in a tick.

"We didn't know you were over here," she sobbed.

"Yeah, but we knew you were," he said, kissing her.

"Who's he?"

"This is Ben Wellington," Rix said. "He's a Pooh-Bah with MI5. It seems our lot is too much for ordinary coppers."

Ben felt his bloody scalp and said woozily, "Pleased to meet you, Christine. We've been looking for you." He surveyed the carnage at his feet. "Christ."

"There's your lawful arrest," Rix said. He called into the kitchen. "Murph, how's Molly?"

"She's coming around."

Christine looked at Rix. He told her to go to Molly.

Ben sat down and removed the magazine from the pistol and unchambered the live round. "Thank you," he said. "They would have killed me too."

"I'm sorry you've lost men," Rix said. "What now?"

"Now? Let me think. I'd better get a cleanup squad up here immediately. We'll need a cover story. God, so much to do. Let's get back to the chopper. We'll have the medics meet us in Dartford."

"You're going to lock us up again?"

"Yes, but you'll be with your wives." He felt his head again and mumbled, "Which is where I should be. With mine."

Christine climbed the stairs alone. Her mother was asleep, oblivious to everything that had occurred. She bent over and kissed her on the forehead.

"Good-bye, mum," she said. "Please remember your little girl, all right?"

Downstairs, her cheeks wet with tears, she asked Ben if he was certain things would get sorted.

"I just talked with my people. A large crew is already on the way. By the time her carer arrives in the morning no one will be the wiser and she'll have new carpet. The mess in the pub's another problem entirely but we'll sort something out there too. Christ, I've got to find out about my pair's next of kin."

The five of them left through the back door and made their way through the village and the fields to the waiting helicopter, Murphy holding onto Molly, Rix, arm around Christine, and Ben at the rear, giving a phone debriefing to an MI5 incident group which was assembling at Thames House.

The women climbed into the Gazelle first. Ben wobbled a bit, dizzy from his concussion. Rix stepped up and helped him in then reached into the cab to buckle his belt.

Ben looked at him curiously.

"Sorry, mate. We've got some unfinished business," Rix said. "Take care of our girls."

And with that, he and Murphy disappeared into the night.

Ben tried to unbuckle himself but he realized he was too ill to give chase.

He sighed heavily and asked the women, "Did they tell you they were going to do this?"

They nodded.

"Did they say where they were going?"

"We haven't got a clue," Christine said. "But they'll come back to us. I know they will."

It was so dark they couldn't see their hands in front of their faces.

"Is anyone there?" It was Youngblood's voice, not five feet away.

"Fuck, is that you, Youngblood?" Hathaway said.

"Yeah, it's me."

There was another voice. "Crashed us good."

"Talley," Hathaway laughed.

"Where are we?" Talley asked.

They heard trees rustling and an owl calling in the distance.

"Near a wood," Youngblood said.

"Back in Hell, are we?" Talley said.

"Where else?" Hathaway said, picking himself off the grass. "Can't believe I died a second time. Bloody marvelous. Fucking Colin and Jason. It's all tied between us. I killed them once, they killed me once."

"We had a time, didn't we?" Talley said, getting up. "Plenty of good grub, good drink."

"Not much raping though," Youngblood said.

"I reckon we're a good old ways from Ockendon," Hathaway said. "We ought to find our way back."

"Why?" Talley said. "Rovers can make do most anywhere. There's bound to be a village we can plunder."

"I'd rather be back in Ockendon in case Jason and Colin and their molls wind up there again," Hathaway said. "Tie needs to be broken."

Their eyes were becoming accustomed to the dark. They were in a clearing. There was indeed a wood nearby. A louder rustling confused them because there wasn't much wind.

The rustling became a stampede of feet.

Then yells, yells they recognized.

Rover yells.

And before they could run, curved rover knives tore through their flesh.

In the morning, there would be nothing more than a pile of bloody bones with shreds hanging off them and in the woods, a party of rovers would be sleeping with bellies full of cannie-food.

34

Garibaldi called it a strategic retreat.

Stalin's combined armies dwarfed his own. His Italian, French, and Iberian contingents made for a formidable fighting force but they only numbered several divisions, not a full army. Antonio had taken a thousand men to Rome and most of the Iberian army remained in Burgos with Queen Mécia. He needed the main French army and they were in Paris.

When John and his group made it to the Italian camp there had been scant time for greetings. Garibaldi had wanted to lay eyes on the children, of course, and he had defied his arthritic knees by dropping to the ground and playing with them for a while before addressing the raging battle.

Simon had made a beeline to the wagon and had helped Alice down, the two of them exchanging tender words.

While Garibaldi conferred with John and others on tactics, the Italians broke camp and prepared for a three hundred mile flight across the heart of Francia.

Garibaldi had stood over his map table and had said, "Five hundred brave men will impede Stalin's advance with guerrilla tactics and give our main force enough time to make it back to Paris. Hopefully Forneau has been able to keep the peace in our absence and hold the alliance together."

"Any news on Antonio?" John had asked.

Garibaldi had been unable to get the words out and it was left to Caravaggio to say it. "We had a messenger. The news is bad. Caterina

Sforza betrayed us to King Alexander. The Macedonians have Roma and Napoli. Antonio is destroyed."

"I'm sorry, Giuseppe," John had said. "He was a good man. Christ, you've got a lot on your plate."

"The first thing on this plate of mine is to help you fine people and these children get home," Garibaldi had said. "Children should not and must not be subjected to our terrible world."

Now after four days of hard travel Paris was within reach, only a day off. Time was of the essence. John began marking his countdown of days with exclamation points instead of lines. There were only seven days until the MAAC restart and they were still a long way from Dartford.

The rations were poor and the children had become listless. Along the way, Garibaldi reluctantly confiscated food from villages and towns. It was not the way to start his new reign of compassion but he had little choice. At least the people had not been subjected to torture and rape, the standard practice of foraging soldiers.

Messengers had been shuttling back and forth between the retreating column and the guerrilla vanguard and the reports were puzzling. Fighting along the front had dwindled and was sporadic at most. And almost all the wounded enemy soldiers they encountered were Germans, not Russians.

The consensus in the Italian camp was that Stalin had decided to wait to press his attack, perhaps to recruit more German forces from Barbarossa's far-flung dukedoms, perhaps to await more men to arrive from Russian territories.

Whatever the explanation they breathed a collective sigh of relief the next morning when they entered the sprawling, walled city of Paris. Forneau and a large faction of loyal French nobles greeted the returning army with banners and flags. Forneau had indeed kept the alliance together.

There was little time for preparation and little time for goodbyes. The Earthers couldn't afford to spend the night resting in Paris. Garibaldi had a hundred fresh troops mustered to take them the next leg. Bread, cheese, and dried meat were collected from the royal kitchens. Rested horses were exchanged for worn-out ones.

"Tell me where you intend to make your crossing?" Garibaldi asked the assembled Earthers.

John was about to say Calais, a beach he knew from past crossings, but Brian answered first. "Bulogne-sur-Mer," he said. "That would be the best."

"Why there?" John asked.

"I know those waters from my sailing days," he said. "It's a good beach, not the least rocky, nice straight shot to Dover and from there into the Thames estuary."

"I'm all right with that," John said.

"How will you find a ship?" Garibaldi asked. "Guy, are there any French vessels in those parts?"

Forneau shook his head. "Robespierre was not a proponent of a vigorous navy. The Duke of Bretagne commands a small fleet of galleons at Brest but he is hardly in our sphere of influence. We have no ships at Bulogne-sur-Mer but there are many fishermen. We will give you silver to buy your way across."

"Well, I guess this is goodbye again," John said reaching for Garibaldi's hand. "Your accomplishments have multiplied but so have your challenges. I wish there was more I could do."

"You have done much. Fare thee well. Get Emily back home. Get Arabel and her sweet children back home. Get all these fine men and women back home."

Earthers and Hellers exchanged hugs and handshakes. Trevor was cradling one child in each arm and Garibaldi patted both heads at once. When it was Emily's turn with Caravaggio he kissed her on both cheeks and handed her a rolled paper.

"It pained me greatly to make this but I thought you would like it," he said with a sly smile.

She unrolled the paper; it was a heroic portrait of John driving a steam car, his jaw resolute.

She kissed him again. "I do love it."

A voice piped up from the circle. "I'm not going with you."

It was Alice. Simon had her hand.

"What are you saying?" Tracy asked.

"I'm saying I'm staying here," Alice said, "with this good man. I've come a very long way to a very bad place to find the man I love. I can take the coward's way out and leave him behind or I can be courageous for once in my life and stay with him and join his cause."

Martin said, "Alice, you must know that you will age and Simon will not. You will die one day and Simon will live on."

"Thank you, Martin. You're a wonderful doctor and a good man. I have no reason to doubt you. But back home I will grow old and I will die too with only my cats for company." She sniffed back some tears. "God I will miss my cats, but I will miss little else."

"I will try my best to find you a cat," Simon said.

She tenderly touched his arm. "Who knows," Alice said, "maybe one day I'll even be able to ply my trade as an electrician here."

"We will be honored to have you join our ranks," Garibaldi said.

"Last chance to change your mind," John said.

"My mind is set," Alice replied.

Stalin was not a heavy drinker in life and death had not changed his habits. As his caravan bounced along on the bad road he held his small glass of wine with an extended arm to prevent spilling any on his uniform. General Kutuzov sat on the opposite bench trying to fill his own glass for the umpteenth time. Stalin watched the burgundy stain spreading on the old fellow's knee with contempt.

"So, comrade, you disapprove of my tactics?" the tsar said.

"Not disapprove, nothing as strong as that. I merely wonder whether it is ever wise to break a single mighty force into two smaller forces."

"Technically this is what I have done but eight in ten men are with us, two in ten with the other group. Pasha, what do you think?"

Loomis was on a smaller bench at the rear of the caravan. "I am not a military man," he replied.

Stalin clucked at him, "You are not a military man, you are not a weapons man, what kind of a man are you then?"

"I am a broken man."

"Such a maudlin soul," Stalin said. "You must have Russian blood."

"Let us drink to Russian blood." This came from the newly promoted chief of secret police, Vladimir Bushenkov, another man who served Stalin in life. He was blind in one eye from a drunken fight and wore a leather patch to hide the disfigurement.

"No, let us drink to our Pasha," Stalin said, raising his glass. "He informed us that they would take the children back to Britannia in hopes of returning to their own time and place." Stalin suddenly and explosively raised his voice. "I want these children back. I want all these people back. The children give me pleasure. The others are useful. This Emily can work with you, Pasha, scientist-to-scientist. John Camp is a good soldier, I think. And this Trevor Jones too. This Brian fellow, they say he is a movie star! I want all of them to work for me. I will not punish them for escaping but I will crush this Garibaldi thug, that's for sure."

"I hope we don't catch them," Loomis said.

Bushenkov reacted with fury and perhaps to demonstrate his bona fides for his new position he drew his pistol.

"Sit, sit, Vladimir," Stalin said, "Put your gun away. In my day, I would have had a man shot for saying this but Pasha can get away with treason, can't you, Pasha? In the past I could liquidate a scientist and have a hundred more to take his place. Not here. So go ahead, be maudlin, be a traitor, more power to you. We will continue north through the friendly low countries and we will outflank them. They will have to cross the channel and it will be done from friendly soil in Francia, somewhere between Calais and Bulogne-sur-Mer. I am sure of this. On Earth and in Hell, this is where the English invade France and where France invades England. And we, my drunk general and my maudlin scientist, we will be there waiting for them."

35

Trotter was angry with everyone but himself.

The headline in *The Guardian* was: Assassination.

Why had their science editor, Derek Hannaford, and a bursar from an English language college named Lenny Moore been gunned down by long-range sniper fire in central London? Why were the men meeting? There had been nothing in Hannaford's diary, no known connections between the two of them. The police had no leads other than to suggest that the murders were not amateur jobs. There had been no robbery, no known history of threats. Both men had spotless criminal records.

Trotter had his off-the-books operations man, Mark Germaine, across the desk from him. He had the envelope his team had snatched from Lenny Moore's pocket. The note inside was from Giles Farmer to Hannaford: *Sorry to muck you about but feel safer if you would go to Bow Street in front of the Opera House. Just in case they listened to our phone call. Giles Farmer*

"So he got the better of you with some schoolboy tradecraft," Trotter said.

"Apparently," Germaine said.

"And you took out this Moore person by error."

"He looks remarkably similar to Farmer. You've seen the pictures. Through a scope at night from a rooftop two hundred yards away, well, I can't fault my lads too much."

"Can't you? Here's what I can't do, Mark. I can't get the DG to squash

410

the Met's investigation because I can't tell him about the op."

"The police will come up empty. Our lads used non-traceable 9mm ammo and Russian VKS sniper gear. The three CCTV cameras covering their points of entry and egress were, how shall I say, conveniently offline that night. We're blameless."

"That's not the correct word, Mark. We are not blameless, but hopefully, for your sake, we will not be found out."

"My sake?"

"I'm too valuable. Things going on."

"What was behind the op? If my balls are in the ringer I should know why."

"It's above your pay grade. Know your place. The only way to make things right with me is to get the correct man next time."

"Where is Farmer?"

Trotter stood, signaling the end of the dressing-down. "Unfortunately, I have no idea."

Giles had been drinking. Heavily.

He had always been fond of beer in a laddish sort of way, but for a solid week he had been anaesthetizing himself by means of Ian Strindberg's abundant liquor cabinet. Conveniently, he found out that he was a quiet and mournful drunk. He kept to his guest bedroom and made no noise, broke no furniture or object d'arts. Ian was too busy at work and too non-empathic to intervene beyond asking, the few times their paths crossed, "All right, mate? Sure there isn't anything I can do?"

Giles felt adrift and increasingly desperate. One of the bullets had been meant for him. He should be the one dead and buried, not Lenny Moore. In his boozy fog he wondered what non-existence felt like. He didn't pay heed to notions of the afterlife but he'd never considered himself an atheist either. Not even an agnostic. He had simply never thought about death and its aftermath on a personal level before. Did the lights just go out? Did one have any sense of non-being?

People were disappearing. Emily Loughty was missing. Eight people from South Ockendon were missing. Tracy Wiggins's husband had been told she was dead but the story behind it, her remains returned in an urn, all of it smelled rotten. People were disappearing and at the same time unknown people were appearing. Two intruders at the Iver North waterworks that were too special to be handled by the police. Multiple intruders on a quiet estate in South Ockendon, tagged as bio-terrorists, yet there were no arrests or cogent updates about the investigation. Three points on a map: Dartford, South Ockendon, Iver. Connect the dots and all of them ran over the great MAAC oval.

What happens when you die, Giles thought?

If there's an afterlife, where is it?

Does it exist on a spiritual plane?

What if it wasn't spiritual; what if it was tangible?

He began to cry. Goddamn MAAC. Goddamn it! What secrets were so devastating that the government was willing to kill to protect them? What Pandora's box had MAAC opened?

He looked at the bottle of gin and then Ian's laptop, unopened since the murders. Both were on his bedside table. His hand wavered between the two.

He knew what he had to do.

He reached for the computer.

To cover their tracks Rix and Murphy stole three cars the night of the Hoxne massacre, one after another. They drove south without much purpose until daybreak when they found themselves on the outskirts of Reading. Then they wandered another hour before Murphy spotted a sign for an Internet café, then treaded water for another hour waiting for it to open. Christine had passed Rix some money before they parted and they used it to buy access from a suspicious clerk who sniffed at them then showed them how to log onto the Internet from one of the booths.

"Never done this before?" the clerk asked, curious about their utter lack of savvy.

"Does it look like we have, sunshine?" Murphy said.

Five minutes later they were done.

"You've got fifty-five minutes left," the clerk said, looking up from his magazine.

"Yeah?" Murphy said. "What's our refund then?"

"No refunds for unused time."

"Tell the bloke who owns the Internet that he's a scumbag," Murphy said.

Rix knew the way. He'd been to Poole for bucket and spade holidays when he was a boy and Lyme Regis wasn't much farther down the coast. In three hours they were there.

Crawling down Broad Street, rubbernecking for street signs, they came to the Rock Point Inn. Beyond, the sea was tranquil and shimmering in the midday sunshine.

"Wouldn't half like a pie and a pint," Murphy said.

"No way, Murph," Rix said. "Let's get done what needs doing. I'm going to ask that lad."

He opened the window and asked a boy if he knew where Kingsway was. The boy pointed the way and soon they were driving down a street lined with white and pastel semi-detached houses.

"There it is," Murphy said, pointing at the number on a mailbox.

"My heart's beating out of my chest," Rix said, pulling to the curb.

"It's hate that's goosing it along, not nerves," Murphy said.

Rix went to the front door of a pale yellow house, took a big breath, and worked the knocker.

He heard a television playing and a man calling out, "Yeah, yeah, hang on."

The door opened. He had to be in his mid-eighties but he looked good for his age, robust and beefy with a ruddy complexion from baking in sun and marinating in booze. His hair was pure white but he still had all of it and it was parted the same way that Rix had remembered.

"Hello Jack," Rix said. "Remember me?"

The man looked at him blankly for a moment.

Then his face contorted in horror.

He fled from the door, heading toward the back of the house, saying to himself, "It can't be, it can't be."

He reached the door to the back garden and flung it open.

Murphy was standing there, blocking his way.

The man's ruddy complexion turned the color of the nice cream door and he fainted dead away.

36

The tension was making everyone mute.

The South Ockendon eight had dwindled to four. They rode together in one of the covered wagons. The absence of Alice was weighing on all of them, especially Tracy who had come to rely on her strength. Charlie had forced himself to pick up some of the slack by playing the clown but his heart wasn't in it. By the first night of their journey he dropped the act and became sullen. Martin and Tony sat across from them, exchanging worried looks.

The best road from Paris to the coast was also the most dangerous one. John had put everyone on rover alert. He had tempered his warnings with the reassurance that their protectors, a hundred Italian soldiers chosen by Garibaldi, were capable of dealing with threats from all manner of predators roaming the countryside. But all of them knew that an attack could still happen. They also knew time was running short. They had five days to get to Dartford and it would take almost two more days to get to Bulogne-sur-Mer. That left three days to make the crossing and they didn't even know if they could find safe passage across the channel. John had considered taking steam cars to shave a day or more from their timeline but without armed soldiers keeping pace, the women and children would be far too vulnerable.

At their last brief rest stop in a glade, Martin had told Tony, "I just want to tell you, I've made a decision."

"About what?" Martin had replied.

"If we don't make it back in time, if the whole MAAC thing doesn't come off as advertised—basically if we're stuck here, then I don't want to carry on. The thought of being trapped here is beyond impossible."

"I don't want you talking like that."

"I'm sorry, but I have to. You're a doctor. You're also my rock. I don't think I'll be able to do it myself so I want you to do it for me."

Martin's stoicism had cracked a bit and he hid his wet eyes with a hand. "Would you please stop!"

"Just tell me you'll help me," Martin had begged.

Martin lowered his hand and showed his red eyes. "I will help you and then I'll do it too."

The rest of the Earthers were in the other covered wagon. The children slept on the floor at their feet and the six adults took the hard benches.

"Look at those angels," Delia said, adjusting their blanket. "Dreaming peacefully without a care in the world."

"Sam wants a sword just like Trevor's," Arabel said.

Trevor was chuffed. "Did he really say that?"

"He did. This morning."

"What did you tell him?" Emily asked.

"That he was too young."

"Good," Emily said.

"I'll buy him a plastic one when we get home," Trevor said.

Arabel's mood turned. "If we get stuck here, he'll have to learn to use a real one."

"Don't even think that," Emily said.

Arabel asked, "What are our chances of getting home? Tell me please while the children are asleep. I want the truth."

Enough eyes fell upon John that he felt obliged to answer. "We've overcome a lot of obstacles to get as far as we've gotten. If we get a few lucky breaks we'll make it."

"Seems to me the biggest problem is finding a boat," Trevor said.

Brian had been quiet for hours but he piped up, "Bound to be one. Boats and the sea go together like tea and milk."

"God, I'd love a cuppa," Delia said. "And a plate of jam-filled biscuits. And … Oh, I'll shut up. No more talk of delectables, but if we get back I'm never going to complain about the canteen at work again."

Yet once triggered, the ever present food conversation took wing. They traded favorites and revised their first- thing-I'm-going-to-eat list.

Emily stopped the flight of fancy with a non sequitor that had been weighing on her. "Paul said he knew how to fix this."

"There's a lot of smart people working on the problem back home," John said. "Didn't you say they were the best minds?"

"They are and I hope they have an answer," Emily said. "I only know that I don't have one and I've done little else than work through thought experiments. Paul was *the* expert in strangelets. Not in MAAC, not in the UK, but in the world. No one had his depth of theoretical knowledge. It's a tragedy I didn't have a chance to talk with him."

The wagon stopped abruptly, waking the children.

John quickly sidestepped them on his way out. Trevor and Brian followed, gathering weapons just in case.

"Want a bow?" Brian asked.

"I've been getting on pretty well with a sword lately," Trevor said.

"Whatever works, mate," Brian said. "Whatever works."

In the other wagon, Charlie hopped out too and ran toward John's group.

The wagon driver pointed to the halted column twenty yards ahead. He spoke no English and by way of explanation offered an exaggerated palms-up shrug.

The captain of the Italians, one of Garibaldi's trusted underlings rode back to the wagon. It was dusk and the woods lining the narrow road seemed to press against their column.

"What's the matter?" John asked, sword in hand.

"One of my men saw torchlight in the woods," the captain said in impeccable English. He had been an officer in Mussolini's army and had studied classics before joining the fascists. Garibaldi admired him for his experience and erudition. "In case of trouble I did not want you to be off

417

guard."

Brian squinted into the woods and nocked an arrow.

"Thanks," John said. "I think we shouldn't stop. We should go all night if your men can take it."

"My men are strong. We will keep riding. The woods are dangerous. There has been talk of how you say, grandi gruppi of these beasts."

"Sorry, I don't understand."

"These beasts, these rovers, have found that they cannot steal food and people from towns and cities if they roam only in small groups. So, they have learned to cooperate and form big groups. This is a great danger, I think."

A soldier let out a horrific scream from the rear of the column and others shouted in Italian, "To arms! To arms! Rovers!"

The rovers attacked from both sides, pouring out of the woods, brandishing their long, curved knives. Every portion of the Italian column was being attacked simultaneously.

John hacked at the nearest rover and put him down, then fended off another three. Yelling curses in French, a rover slashed the belly of the captain's horse, spilling its guts. The captain went down, his right leg caught under the dying beast. Pinned, the nearest rover made quick work of him, stabbing him repeatedly in the chest.

Up and down the line, the battle raged. Steel clanged on steel, fists thudded onto skulls, musket balls and pistol shot slammed into flesh. There were nearly as many rovers as soldiers but the rovers had the advantage because they were fearless and savage and denizens of the night.

At close range, most of Brian's arrows found their mark. When he exhausted his supply he drew his sword and fell in with Trevor. They protected each other's backs, hacking and thrusting at the ragged, foul-smelling men.

John kept trying to fight his way back to Emily's wagon but for every rover he destroyed, another attacked.

In the wagon Delia and Arabel clutched the terrified children and pulled them to the front. Emily took one of the swords lying on the floor and pushed Martin and Tony aside.

"Where are you going?" Arabel shouted.

"To fight!"

"Don't!"

Emily didn't listen. She jumped out the back and saw a rover straddling an Italian, about to plunge his knife. She swung her sword down onto the top of his skull and cleaved it.

The soldier smiled at her, said, "Grazie, signora," and sprang back into action.

Another rover came at her. She used her favorite Krav Maga move of deflecting his raised knife arm with an inside-out lateral forearm deflection, ready to counterattack with her sword but he was too strong and the knife kept coming.

She felt a spray of blood on her face.

The rover's knife was gone and his hand too.

John finished the man off with an upwards thrust to his chin.

There wasn't time to say anything. There were more rovers coming but John stayed planted by Emily's side.

Inside the other wagon Martin, Tony, Tracy, and Charlie huddled in fear, listening to the horrible sounds of fighting.

"What should we do?" Tracy cried.

"We have to stay here," Tony said. "They're rovers. We'll be slaughtered."

Charlie was muttering to himself and the monologue got louder.

"What are you saying?" Martin said.

"Rovers killed my brothers," he said slowly, moving to the wagon flaps. "Rovers killed my father. Rovers killed my grandfather. I am going to kill them."

"For God's sake, sit down, Charlie," Martin said.

"I'm not afraid anymore. I was afraid but now I'm not."

He took one of the swords and then he was out the back.

The three of them looked at each other in shock. All they could do was listen to the awful sounds. Cries in Italian and French, then a shout from

Brian and a reply from Trevor.

The wagon flap parted again.

"Charlie," Tracy said.

But it wasn't Charlie. It was a rover, his fetid breath instantly fouling the interior.

The rover locked eyes on Tracy and opened his toothless mouth exposing a brown tongue. He crawled fully in. Less than six feet separated them.

Tracy tried to scream but nothing came out.

But Tony did scream.

It wasn't a scream of terror but of rage.

He hurled himself at the rover who was off guard, his mind probably set on raping.

Tony head-butted the man's skull and the rover grunted in pain. Somehow his knife came to be in Tony's fist. He pounded it into the man's torso over and over. The only thing he had ever pounded so hard was bread dough.

He heard Martin talking to him.

"You can stop, Tony. You can stop. You've finished him."

Tony did stop. He dropped the bloody knife and began to sob.

Martin held him and said, "That was the bravest thing I've ever seen."

Writhing, agonal bodies of rovers and soldiers lined the road. John, Emily, Trevor, and Brian were finding fewer and fewer rovers to fight and then, the remaining attackers slithering back into the night and it was over.

The Italians let out an exhausted victory call. Emily sat on the ground, too fatigued to speak.

"You're a tiger," John said, between pants. "I'd take you into battle every day of the week."

"The children," she gasped, trying to rise.

He helped her up and got to the wagon the same time as Trevor and opened the back. Arabel and Delia cried out in relief. The children were safe.

The fifty or so remaining soldiers tended to their wounded. The ones that could be saved were bandaged. The ones too far gone were bundled, groaning and hideously writhing, into the supply wagons for deposit somewhere more dignified than the side of the road to be carved and eaten by the rover stragglers.

John assembled the Earthers. The wagon drivers were destroyed. They would consolidate into one wagon. John and Brian would drive.

Suddenly Tracy asked, "Where's Charlie?"

They searched frantically. Two rovers were on their bellies, shirtless and groaning away, their flanks a bloody mess. They were lying on top of something. John pulled them aside.

"Doc!" John shouted.

Martin examined Charlie's lifeless body then pulled the lids down over his staring eyes.

"Poor, poor Charlie," Tracy cried.

"Come on," John said, softly. "We've got to go."

"We've got to bury him properly," Tony said with conviction. "We can't let those bastards have him."

John sighed and agreed.

He didn't say what he was thinking.

If we don't hurry we'll be digging more graves.

They couldn't see it but they heard it.

The early morning fog was so heavy the only way they knew they had arrived at the coast was the sound of the breaking waves.

John and Brian had driven the wagon virtually non-stop for a day and a half since the rover battle. One last dangerous night in the French countryside had now yielded to a murky dawn.

The two men had been pushed to the limit, refusing to let Trevor come up to relieve them. They wanted him with the others in the wagon in case of another attack. Pressed together, the others intermittently dozed on each other's shoulders and tried their best to keep the restless children amused.

Now they had arrived, closer to their goal but still far away.

John pulled back on the reins. "I'm scared to go any further," he said. "We could be heading to a cliff."

Brian agreed. "Pea soup."

They climbed down and went to the back to help the others out. The soldiers dismounted and collapsed to the ground.

"You look like shit," Emily said, holding onto John.

He kissed her. "You say the nicest things."

Brian started walking away and John asked him where he was going.

"Small matter of a boat," Brian said. "Just a quick rekkie."

There was nothing they could do until the fog lifted so they sat in a circle and divided up the remaining food and water.

John took out his pad and drew a short, thick exclamation point.

Three days.

The sun never shone on this world but it was there, behind a permanent blanket of clouds. As the rising sun warmed the ground the fog over the land faded first.

John thought he heard something and stood.

"What?" Trevor said.

"I don't know," John said, looking around.

"Is it Brian?"

"I don't think so."

The fog lightened.

"Jesus," John said.

They all stood.

Sam tugged at his mother's dress. "Mummy, why are there so many horses?"

Stretching to the east, some two hundred yards away, was a continuous line of horses, hundreds upon hundreds of them and a thousand soldiers or more with dozens of caravans and wagons, an army materializing from the miasma.

The Italian soldiers, too fatigued to reach for their weapons, could only point weakly and lament their fate.

A single rider approached at no more than a trot, as if by coming slowly, he might magnify his authority.

Standing beside his caravan, Stalin handed over his spyglass and said, "You see, Pasha? I told you we would find them."

Loomis adjusted the focus and found Emily standing among the Earthers. His tears puddled the image and he gave the telescope back.

"Tears of joy?" Stalin asked, laughing.

"You won't hurt her or any of them, will you?" Loomis asked.

"If they remain good and loyal subjects, why would I hurt them? Same goes for you, Pasha. Remember that, please."

The one-eyed rider stopped a few feet away and dismounted, holding his reins with his left hand, his right hand resting on the pommel of his scabbarded sword.

"I am Vladimir Bushenkov," he said. "You will hand over your weapons and come with me. The tsar wishes your company again."

John turned to Emily. "We almost made it," he said. "We came damned close."

"Is Paul, I mean, Pasha here?" Emily asked Bushenkov.

"He is here."

"At least I'll find out how to beat the strangelets," she told John. "If we ever get back, I'll know how to do it."

Behind them they heard Tracy's thin, tired voice calling out, "Excuse me. Are those supposed to be there?"

John and Emily turned their backs on Bushenkov and faced the sea.

Dozens of black lines appeared through the blanching fog, bobbing up and down. A sail was visible, then more and more of them.

Martin and Tony were shouting now for everyone to look this way and that.

To the north and the south of the Russian line, masses of men appeared from the thinning fog.

Thousands of men.

A light cannon fired off a warning. A shell crashed inland over the Russian line.

Bushenkov's prominent Adam's apple rose and fell in a gulp and he swore in Russian.

"Miss me?" It was Brian calling to them, approaching from the beach accompanied by a squad of standard bearers.

News of the flanking armies spread through the Russian cavalry ranks. Men shouted, seeking their orders.

Stalin howled in rage. "Who are they? Who are these bastards? Garibaldi is in Paris. He can't be here."

The word came down.

Iberians.

There was more cannon fire. This time the shells landed closer to the Russians. A low, throaty roar swelled up from thousands of Iberian lungs and the Russians began breaking ranks and fleeing inland.

Stalin refused to budge until General Kutuzov appeared at his side and pulled him into his caravan.

Loomis began to run toward the sea but Stalin ordered his personal guard to bring him back and when they did he kicked and screamed at them to let him go before he was forcibly thrown into the caravan. Its horses were whipped into a gallop and the caravan joined the retreat soon fading from view.

Bushenkov had remained in place, seemingly caught between the devil of the Iberians and the deep blue sea of Stalin's rage. John got into his face and said, "Get the fuck out of here. We've got a ship to catch."

The secret policeman's chin quivered. Without uttering a word he mounted his horse and galloped away.

Behind Brian, a larger phalanx of Iberians appeared on the beach. The fog was now so transparent that the full majesty of the Iberian armada was visible at anchor along with dozens of beached longboats.

Finely dressed soldiers parted to reveal Queen Mécia in their midst, walking up from the sand, her leather boots wet from the surf, steadying herself on the arm of her man, Guomez.

John and Trevor greeted Brian with weary bear hugs.

"You knew they'd be here, didn't you?" John said.

"Put it this way," Brian grinned. "I was hopeful."

Trevor shook his head and grinned. "Once a sly dog, always a sly dog."

The queen smiled and nodded to Brian but went straight for the children. Delia picked Sam off his feet and Arabel lifted Belle so Mécia didn't have to stoop.

"What a miracle," she said, Guomez translating. "The most colorful and fragrant flowers, her majesty can ever recall seeing. She is most happy she could come to the rescue of the children, indeed all of these living persons. She wishes you well and hopes you are able to return to your own land."

"Come on then," Brian said, his voice choking. "You'd better be off. The wind's a bugger so the crossing won't be a quickie."

"You're not coming with us, are you?" Trevor said.

"I'm not."

Trevor got angry, "For fuck's sake, Brian, you ..."

Brian shushed him. "Look, mate. I made a deal. As magnanimous as she's sounding, she's a tough old bird. She wouldn't help unless I agreed to stay. I swear she's a bloody clone of my first wife."

"We can try to reason with her," John said.

"It's not her you'd need to reason with," Brian said. "It's me. Alice did it and so can I. Look, people," he said to all of them, "I always thought I was born a few hundred years too late. I've always been happiest pretending to be a medieval soldier, prancing about like a twit in period pieces. The last month, with this adventure we've been on, I'll say this: in the land of all these dead bastards I've never felt more alive. Now all of you, bugger off home. I've got to negotiate my new title. I was thinking Prince Brian the Lionhearted. Got a ring to it, don't you think? And one last thing, Trev. Come here."

Trevor came over to him, trying to hold his emotions in check.

Brian leaned in and whispered, "You did good, mate. Best damned student I ever had."

37

Mellors regained consciousness tied to a living room chair.

When his glassy eyes focused on Murphy and Rix seated across from him he pulled against his ropes. He looked like he was about to scream.

"Shhh," Murphy said. "Anything louder than a whimper, Jack, and I'll cut your tongue out."

"This isn't possible," Mellors said.

"That what you think?" Rix said. "A long, illustrious career as a detective, rising to the exalted rank of detective chief super, and that's the best you can come up with. This isn't possible."

"Am I dead?"

"Not yet," Murphy said. "But surely the lion's share of your scumbag life's behind you, wouldn't you say, guv?"

"You're dead," Mellors said. "Both of you are dead."

"Bingo!" Rix said. "You finally got one right."

"You've been dead for thirty years."

"Right again," Murphy said.

"You're young. Like you were. What are you, ghosts?"

"Now you've lost your way again," Rix said. "We're not ghosts. We're flesh and blood just like you. Well, maybe we don't smell quite as fresh. Here have a snort." He leaned forward and passed his forearm under Mellor's nose.

Mellors grimaced, his eyes widening.

"So how old are you?" Rix asked.

Mellors didn't answer.

"I'll say you're eighty-five, eighty-six," Murphy said. "What do you reckon, Jason? Probably retired eight to ten years after we kicked it. A good twenty years of retirement. Nice fat super's pension supplementing all the filthy lucre he made off with during his years of wickedness. Lovely seaside house. Probably flush with mateys in the local bar. But I don't see a woman's touch. All alone, Jack? Wife leave you, did she?"

"Cancer," Mellors said.

"The tragedy of it," Murphy said.

"Fuck you!" Mellors shouted.

Murphy got up and punched him in the face. "I said, shhh, didn't I? One more bit of noise and you will regret it."

Mellors spit blood onto the carpet.

"It's really difficult to get that out of a nice beige pile," Murphy said, "though I have to say, that hasn't been one of our principal concerns these past three decades."

"Tell me what's going on," Mellors said. "Tell me how you're here when you were killed. I was at your bloody funerals. Tell me how you haven't aged a day."

"Tell you what," Rix said. "Let's take a little stroll down memory lane. Let's relive a little episode in our lives that you probably haven't bothered to even think about since 1985. After we've had that stroll, we'll tell you everything, explain all the mysteries of the universe, bring you well into the fold."

Jack Mellors pushed his way through the crowded pub to the farthest table in the back, close enough to the gents to smell the urinal cakes whenever someone opened the door. The big man with silver temples folded himself into a chair and put his pint onto a beer mat.

"Sorry I'm late," he said.

"No problem, guv," Murphy said.

"You're wrong about that," Mellors said. "You lads have a big fucking problem."

"Now hang on, Jack," Rix said.

"Don't fucking Jack me," Mellors said. "I'm your fucking DCS. My friends call me Jack. You don't."

"I was going to say that this problem is best described as our problem," Rix said.

"Oh, no, my son," Mellors said. "Don't you try that one on. I'm your fucking superior. When we're on the straight and narrow, I'm your superior." He lowered his voice and looked around. "When we're engaged in certain nefarious activities, I'm also your superior. You're bent cops. I'm your bent chief super. Got it?"

"The package was light, guv," Murphy said. "I hope you don't think we were skimming."

Mellors gulped at his beer. "It's hardly called skimming when you've come up almost two kilos short," he said. "That's not a skim, that's a fat load."

"Look, fault us for not weighing the case or whatever," Rix said, "but they insisted on doing the exchange at King's Cross, out in the open. They've never shorted us before."

"Well, you're well short now, aren't you? You're short twenty-five thousand pounds fucking sterling. And you're going to make good on it or I will unleash our little snarling friend on you. Actually, I'll unleash Nicky onto you and onto your ladies. Nicky, once unleashed, will look for pounds and pounds of flesh, know what I mean?"

"Leave our wives out of this," Rix said, seething.

Mellors leaned back in his chair. "Relax, lads. I know you don't have that kind of ready dosh. I've got a way for you to make it quick and easy and get yourself square with me and Nicky."

"How?" Murphy asked.

"There's a nice simple job in Knightsbridge. Rich banker fuck. You'll take something from him. He'll gladly pay you fifty grand for its return. Nicky gets his twenty-five, I get ten since I'm your superior and all, and you get five each. Everyone wins."

"What is it we take?" Rix said.

"His little girl."

"I won't do a kidnapping," Rix said.

"Oh you'll do it, sunshine. Just picture your wives missing all those pounds of flesh. Shit, get them to help. Ladies are just the ticket when you're snatching a kid."

"There's five grand not accounted for," Murphy suddenly said.

"Eh?"

"The split on the fifty grand. There's an extra five."

"Oh yeah, excellent maths skills," Mellors said. "You're going to have to take one of Nicky's boys with you. He'll be getting five as well. You know Lucas, don't you?"

"Yeah, we know Lucas Hathaway," Rix said.

Mellors asked for a glass of water.

Murphy got one from the kitchen and held it to his bloody lip while he drank.

"Did you know that little Jessica Stevenson had asthma?" Rix asked. "Bad asthma."

"Of course not," Mellors said.

"We as good as killed her as if we'd put a knife through her heart," Rix said.

"Things happen," Mellors said. "You've got to think fast, not panic. You still could have gotten the ransom. It all would've been square. But what did you too do? You folded like a cheap suitcase."

"We couldn't live with what we did," Murphy said.

Rix stood and began pacing. "We were going to turn ourselves in, do the time, whatever it took to try to make things right. We were going to do that but Lucas must have called you and you must have told him to do us. Admit it, Jack. You had us taken out."

"Did you think I was going to go down for your fuck-ups? You must be joking. Yeah, I had Hathaway do you and then I made sure armed police were onto him straight away. I whistled past the graveyard that night and here I am. Eighty-five years old, healthy as a horse, still shagging every so often and with a happy bank manager as one of my drinking mates. And where have you two fuck-ups been all these years?"

"Us?" Rix said. "We've been in the place where you're going."

Ben hadn't left Dartford in days. He felt as much of a prisoner as the Hellers in their locked cells. He had spent so much time interviewing Molly and Christine that he joked he almost knew them better than his own unhappy wife.

He had long since appropriated John Camp's office as his own and he was there, reviewing interview tapes, trying to find a clue to the possible whereabouts of Murphy and Rix. He cued the video file where he had the women talking about the night of the kidnapping of Jessica Stevenson. His gut instinct told him that untangling this tale of woe would lead him to the men. There wasn't much time. The MAAC restart was coming.

One of Ben's agents called the office phone.

"Yes, I'm at a terminal," Ben said.

"Quick, punch up the South Ockendon live feeds," the agent said.

As he did so he said, "There hasn't been any activity there for almost a month."

"Camera six. Hurry."

He clicked on the correct icon and Murphy and Rix came into view looking directly into the camera from the same house on the estate where they'd first appeared.

"Did you reach Ben Wellington?" Murphy said into the camera.

"I'm here," Ben said.

"Did you miss us?" Murphy asked.

"Desperately. Why are you there?"

"Because we want you to take us to our girls," Rix said.

"Stay put. I'll have someone there shortly."

"That's all right," Rix said. "No hurry. We've got a last bit of business to do."

He disappeared from view and came back, dragging a chair. A large, white-haired old man was tied to it.

"Jason, who is that?" Ben said, his voice rising.

"This is the bastard that's responsible for us and our girls going to Hell, Ben. Not that we're not responsible, but DCS Jack Mellors is Hellbound too. We wanted to make sure that when he arrives we'd be able to find him. When you send us back we're going to return to our little shithole of a village in Ockendon. And when we get there we're going to find Jack Mellors and we're going to put him in the worst rotting room in Hell."

Murphy held a knife to Mellor's throat.

"Don't do it!" Ben shouted.

Murphy ignored him.

38

The Iberian ship heaved and rolled on the giant swells. John and the Earthers could have had several small cabins to themselves but they wanted to stay together, so the captain gave them his own generous cabin to occupy as a group. The captain, Jose Manuel Ignacius, knew these waters so well he could have navigated without sight. On Earth he had been at the helm of one of the Duke of Medina Sidonia's invasion vessels in 1588 when Phillip II went up against Elizabeth I and tried to turn England Catholic again. The Spanish Armada was defeated then but Ignacius survived to die years later in a tavern brawl. In Hell, he had been pressed into service on the high seas over and over, most recently when he experienced defeat at the hands of Henry's fleet. John neglected to tell him that his singing cannon were instrumental in the Iberian's demise that day. That would have been like him telling a New York City taxi driver that he might have killed his cousin in Afghanistan.

The ship, El Tiburón, accompanied by a dozen Iberian warships, plowed into the storm-churned waves. In the captain's stern cabin, the exhausted party of ten wanted to sleep but most of them couldn't because of galloping nausea.

"Isn't there anything we can do?" Delia asked Martin.

Martin could hardly answer through his own retching. "No. Nothing. Just. Endure."

Only the children and John were able to sleep.

Arabel and Trevor sat beside them on the captain's bed, a bucket at the ready for themselves.

"Thank God they're out like lights," Arabel said.

"Angels," Tracy said, stifling a gag from the captain's armchair.

Emily was next to John on the cabin floor, propped against a starboard wall, his head on her shoulder. "Let's hope they stay asleep for most of the crossing," she said. "Like this one. I don't know how he can sleep through this."

The 40mm grenades pounded the farmhouse.

Explosion after explosion tore apart the mud-brick walls. John had to flip up his night-vision goggles to endure the flashes. He moved to his left to check on Tannenbaum but he knew what he'd find. T-baum's head was half gone. He swore a few times and refocused. There'd be time for a more human reaction later.

"Cease fire! Cease fire!" he radioed.

The desert became quiet again.

John lowered his goggles and radioed, "We're going in, both squads. Stay sharp."

He gave a hand signal to his men and they began slowly moving forward, closing on the wrecked farmhouse. Pockets of flames glowed green through his optics.

His headset crackled with the voice of a Black Hawk pilot. "Major Camp, this is your ride home. We're about three clicks out. We saw your fireworks. Awaiting instructions."

"Hit the LZ in five mikes. We've just got to clean up our mess. One KIA. Repeat one KIA."

"Roger that. Five mikes."

They reached the collapsed perimeter wall. Bodies of two Taliban snipers lay among the rubble.

"Mike, you ready to make entry?" John radioed.

"I'm at what's left of the back door."

"All right," John said. "Counting from three, two, one, go."

The Green Berets flooded in.

There was rubble and debris everywhere in large heaps and small piles. John saw some legs sticking out and an arm with part of a disembodied shoulder against an intact portion of wall.

Then a man's voice coming from the corner. In good English he called out, "Help me, please! Hostage. Hostage. American interpreter. Don't shoot!"

Mike Entwistle was closest.

"Careful," John said, moving in.

"Haji with plastic ties on his hands," Mike said.

"Please help me. Guys, I am interpreter for American soldiers. Taliban took me. I am injured. I can't feel my legs."

John stepped over a mangled body and a mound of collapsed ceiling.

He was ten feet away.

Mike had a switchblade in his hand about to cut off the man's plastic cuffs.

John yelled, "Mike, don't!"

Giles looked at the clock in the guest bedroom.

It was 4 a.m.

He'd been up straight through the night finishing and polishing his magnum opus, his get out of jail free article, as he'd taken to calling it. For how else was he going to be able to protect himself from whoever had killed Benny and Derek Hannaford? Putting his article out there was going to insulate him from harm. He poured everything he knew and everything he suspected into it. There'd be no reason to eliminate him without making the story even bigger. Certainly he wished he'd had more than a deductive case. He wished he'd had more data, more interviews but the time had come to go public. The article was titled: *The Mystery of the Massive Anglo-American Collider: Have We Opened a Nasty Door to Another Dimension?* He had re-installed the software onto Ian's computer to allow it to connect with WiFi and now his finger was literally hovering over the keyboard. The list of addressees included almost every broadsheet and tabloid newspaper, including *The Guardian* which was still grinding away on the bizarre murder of their science editor.

He hit send.

It had been the first night Ben had slept at home in a week and he had come to regret it. He'd be spending the next night in Dartford in preparation for the MAAC restart the following morning and depending on what transpired he might not be home again for a while. His wife had been in no mood to play nice and had pointedly decided to retire for the night, slamming the bedroom door while he was fielding a call from MAAC. It seemed the Heller Alfred had punched a guard and had to be Tasered.

After reading a bedtime story to his girls he crept to his bedroom where his wife was either asleep or pretending to be—it didn't matter which. Soon he had fallen asleep with his arms folded in anger.

His mobile phone went off on full volume and his wife reacted furiously. He slithered out his side and answered.

Trotter was on the line. It was 4:30 in the morning.

"What's going on?" Ben asked moving to the hall.

"A negative development. Very negative. I've sent you an email with the file. It seems a science blogger named Giles Farmer has connected a series of dots and come to a more-or-less correct conclusion on what's been happening."

Ben was outside the girls' room. He peeked in while Trotter was talking. By the glow of a night-light they looked achingly beautiful.

"I see. Can we contain it?" Ben asked.

"No we can't. It's gone out to every newspaper in the country."

"Jesus, that is bad."

"Yes, quite. Look, I'm on my way into the office. You ought to head to Dartford, control the situation there. There's likely to be a press melee before long. I've got a long list of people to get to, high and low, but I wanted you to be among the first. Look, Wellington, I know it's not a popular view, but I think this article should cause us to cancel the restart. We should mothball the collider now. Any further problems and we won't be able to contain the story."

"Above my pay grade, Tony."

"Understood. Just looking for all the support I can get."

John woke in the dark. He felt for Emily but she wasn't next to him. By the light of a single candle in a hurricane glass he saw the sleeping figures of all of his people camped out around the cabin. Emily was beside Arabel. Trevor had given his spot to her and taken the floor, next to Martin and Tony.

He had no idea how long he'd been out but judging by the pressure on his bladder it had been a long time.

Outside the cabin was the captain's privy and he spent a while standing there, the ship gently rolling beneath him.

He came back to the cabin.

"Hi."

Emily stirred and came to him.

"It's calm," John said.

"Thank God. The storm broke a few hours ago. We can all finally sleep."

"Sorry to wake you."

"Don't be. How are you so immune to sea sickness?"

He kissed her. "Just am. How long was I out?"

"Almost a full day."

"Christ! About what time is it?"

"I'd be guessing. One? Two?"

"This is it then."

"This is it."

"Where are we?"

"I saw land off to that side before it got dark."

"Portside is England. I'm going to find the captain."

"Okay."

"If it's two we've got eight hours to get to Dartford."

"I know," she said.

Captain Ignacius was high on the stern, looking down on the helmsman on the deck below.

He waved John up and greeted him in English. "Did you have a good rest, my friend?" He was a handsome, middle-aged man with long hair tied with a ribbon.

"Too good. I've lost my bearings," John said.

"We are almost at the estuary. Southend will be somewhere off the starboard bow."

"What time is it?"

"It is time the wind increased, my friend," Ignacius said, pointing at the slack sails. "We're dead calm. First too much wind, now not enough. I am aware of your appointment. I no longer pray but perhaps you should."

Heath bragged he could see as well in the dark as the light, and though it was one of his typical exaggerations, there was some truth to it. His night vision was hyper-acute, a trait that served a rover well.

He remembered his youth and how, as a shepherd, he was the one designated to find a lost lamb in the blackness of a moonless night. He remembered when he was a young man, a runaway from the farm to seventeenth-century London, how he was the member of the gang who had the easiest time tracking a mark along the dark and foggy banks of the Thames and sneaking up for a bashing. And now in Hell, his nocturnal prowess had served him very well indeed for two and a half centuries. He reckoned he was the strongest, smartest rover he'd ever encountered and he traded on his reputation by expanding his territory.

Heath had grown tired of limiting his raids to the small hamlets and villages that lacked enough men to band together and fight back. He had dreams of amassing a huge band of rovers, hundreds of scum to terrorize entire towns like Crawley and Guildford. But why stop there? Why not dream even bigger and take on the crown itself? Why not take London one day? After all, he had plenty of time. All he had to do was keep from getting crashed on a raid or by one of his own.

Tonight, running through the forest, his lungs full of damp night air, he was feeling good. A week before he'd raided the camp of a large rival band of rovers, scum who'd been competing with his lot for a long time. First he personally crashed the band's chief taking his head right off his shoulders, "right easy," as he put it, and then he held it high during his little speech to the other members of the rival gang.

"You lot fall in with me and you won't get crashed. You know who I am. I'm Heath, the one who can see in the dark. I've got big plans. Are you in, or are you out like Cock Robin here?"

He stopped at the edge of the woods and whistled like a bird, halting the eighty rovers behind him.

Eighty!

Most scum he'd ever led by far.

Biggest band of rovers he'd ever heard of.

Across the meadow was the village of Leatherhead. It wasn't a very large village but it was big enough to have a nighttime guard, some with muskets the story went. There was talk of good grub and barrels of beer. There was even talk of some molls who still had their looks. Leatherhead was big enough that he'd given it a miss until now.

But with eighty scum, tonight he was taking Leatherhead. Tonight he was going to do some serious crashing and raping.

Dawn came to Dartford.

In their cottage Dirk and Duck automatically awoke to the first light filtering through the gaps in their shutters.

It wasn't cold but Dirk always liked a bit of a fire, for the coziness, he'd say.

His head was aching from too much beer the night before. He'd kept his promise to John Camp and brewed up a barrel but it had been sitting there calling his name. Two weeks ago he began sampling it and a week ago he began drinking it in earnest. There was still enough for Camp but not enough for the entire village. When Duck's back was turned he unplugged the barrel and tipped some beer into his mug and added a few splashes of water. Best headache cure around, he reckoned, chugging it down.

He and Duck heard it the same time and ran to open a shutter.

They both poked their heads out and looked up the road toward the direction of the noise.

"Would you look at that, Dirk?" Duck said. "I think we're fucked."

The Earthers were on the deck of El Tiburón giving the Iberian sailors a spectacle. The sailors knew they had a special cargo and now they were marveling how special it was.

The winds had freshened, whether through prayer or luck, and they had entered the estuary at dawn.

John had been trying to visualize a clock in his head since first light. Two hours later he announced, "It's about eight o'clock. Two hours to go."

The river was narrowing, the estuary receding to the east. John was looking for the hairpin turn that would herald their near arrival.

Captain Ignacius joined them at the bow.

"Will you know the location?" the captain asked.

"I've made this trip before," John said.

The captain nodded then looked upriver and said, "Ha! Will you look at that?"

There was a small fishing boat ahead with two men casting nets. At the sight of twelve Iberian warships approaching, the fishermen capsized the boat and began to swim ashore.

"I wish I had another two hundred ships," Ignacius said. "We caught the English sleeping on this day. With a full armada, we could have been planting the Iberian flag in London." Then he found something else amusing, little Belle following the gulls with her eyes. "Do you like these birds, my dear child?" he asked.

"Yes! Look at the birdies, mummy!" Belle said, waving the hand Arabel wasn't holding.

"They're seagulls, darling," Arabel said.

"I like them too," Sam declared. "We're following them, aren't we? Why are we following them, Trevor?"

Trevor gently squeezed the little boy's hand and said, "'Cause that's the way home."

"There!" John said, pointing. The river was making a turn to the north.

"Yes, that's it," Emily agreed.

"You sure?" Trevor asked.

John nodded. "A jog to the north, a jog to the south, Dartford will be along the first straightaway."

"Thank God," Tony said, "but if you ask me we're cutting it too damn close."

"I can't believe I'm actually going to see my kids soon," Tracy sobbed.

"We're not home free yet," John said. "Captain, anything you can do to get your longboat ready to deploy, that would be helpful."

"Very good, Señor. I will make the boat ready."

Emily came to John's side and whispered, "Do you really think we can make it?"

He sported a very tired smile. "Seems to me we're going to have to row like hell and run like hell if we're going to get our asses out of Hell."

39

Trotter had been right about the press scrum.

The day before the MAAC restart satellite trucks began arriving at Dartford shortly after Giles Farmer's article appeared online. Stuart Binford, the MAAC press officer had been authorized to say only two words, "No comment" and he had said them hundreds of times that day.

A series of emergency meetings involving British and American officials had been hastily convened and during one of them Trotter had put forward his position that the Farmer piece had tilted the balance toward canceling the restart. But Leroy Bitterman and others had shot him down. Beyond doing the right thing by the brave men and women who had risked their lives to bring back the innocents, Bitterman had argued that Matthew Coppens' newly improved software algorithm would shut down the collider within a few nanoseconds of the materialization of the returnees, or for that matter, their non-materialization once full 30 TeV power was achieved. That, he had said, would further mitigate propagation of strangelet-graviton fields. Even though their panel of distinguished scientists had failed to produce a workable plan to sever the dimensional connection, they had nonetheless agreed that limiting the duration of high-energy collisions to the absolute minimum was clearly in order.

When the discussion had moved on, Trotter had leaned over and whispered to Ben, "Thank you very much for speaking out on behalf of my proposal," to which Ben had responded with nothing more than a weary, cheek-puffing sigh.

Trotter had been called into an early afternoon meeting at Downing Street to appear before the Cobra emergency response committee. The prime minister had decided that in light of the Giles Farmer revelations he had no choice but to widen the need-to-know circle to include the cabinet security committee. An incredulous group of government officials who had expected the government to rubbish the ridiculous assertions they'd read over morning coffee, had listened to the PM, Trotter, and energy secretary Smithwick tell them that Farmer had gotten things pretty much spot on.

During the course of the Cobra meeting the BBC had gone live to Lewisham where Giles Farmer had been spotted returning to his flat and had consented to an on-air interview.

The PM had directed the sound to be turned up and Trotter, while watching the young man haltingly but convincingly articulate his conspiracy theories had broken a pencil under the table.

"Perhaps Mr. Trotter might tell us whether MI5 or MI6 had anything to do with the deaths of this Mr. Moore and Mr. Hannaford," the home secretary had asked when the TV was muted.

"To the best of my knowledge, neither agency had any involvement whatsoever," Trotter had said, but he had thought, need to know, need to know, none of you have the need to know.

At dawn on the restart day, the sky over London was pink and promising.

Even at this early hour the temporary control room in the MAAC recreation center was loaded with technicians. By 8:30 the observers arrived. Leroy Bitterman took his place beside Karen Smithwick. George Lawrence, Ben's boss at MI5, had shared a car from London with the FBI director, Campbell Bates and they sauntered in together. Trotter arrived on his own and found his seat without acknowledging Bitterman or any of the others. He was tired. He'd spent most of the night huddling with Mark Germaine, his operation's man, trying to figure out if Giles Farmer might still be eliminated without fanning the flames of the conspiracy he'd painted. Henry Quint also cut a lonely figure. It pained him to be sidelined and he'd been wondering guiltily whether he'd be happy or sad if Emily Loughty never returned. The only one who was willing to associate with him was Stuart Binford, who pulled up a chair at the rear of the hall, but Quint didn't care to reciprocate.

Matthew Coppens was in operational control. He worked through the start-up checklist with David Laurent. Around the huge MAAC underground oval twenty-five thousand magnets were cooling to 1.7K. Matthew looked at the schematics on the giant screen to see if any magnets were failing to cool properly. Blue was the color he wanted to see and all around the map of Greater London, blue dots lit the map like a necklace of sapphires.

By nine a.m. breakfast was collected from the detention cells. Murphy and Rix had been allowed to share cells with their wives.

"Last good food," Rix said, scraping his toast into the last of the egg yolk on his plate.

"Last coffee," Christine said. "I don't want to go back."

"Could be worse," he said, patting her on the knee. "We've still got each other."

Next door, Murphy was enjoying his post prandial teeth brushing. "When I was alive," he said. "I never paid any mind to the marvels of toothpaste. Now it's one of my favorite things. I'm going to miss it."

"Oh yeah?" Molly said. "Don't fancy using a leaf anymore?"

He rinsed his mouth. "What if their bollocks machine doesn't work and we have to stay here?" he asked.

"Then you get to brush your teeth to your heart's content."

"You know what I mean."

She went to the sink and took his hand. "Then I suppose we'll be locked up somewhere—not together, mind you—until we grow old and die and then we'll wind up back you know where."

"In that case I hope their bollocks machine works," Murphy said, looking at her reflection in the mirror.

Ben came to the detention level and slid open the Plexiglas windows on each cell door to announce that everyone would be taken down to the transport room in thirty minutes. The men from Iver, imbecilic as always, stared blankly, as if Ben had made an announcement to a couple of hamsters. Alfred and his Heller mates swore and made their usual ruckus. Mitchum, the rover, had recovered from his bullet wound well enough to be eating solid food for the last week and he protested that he didn't want to go anywhere. But Murphy, Rix, and their spouses greeted Ben warmly, as one might a friend and colleague.

Rix put his face next to the window and said, "You were square with us, Ben. Sorry we had to muck you about."

Ben nodded by way of accepting the apology. "You were, no you *are,* a good copper, Jason. However, I wish you hadn't killed Jack Mellors."

"That's because you're not an evil bastard, Ben. You're one of the cowboys who always wore a white hat. Take care of yourself and don't do anything in your life that lands you on my patch."

The sky over Dartford was about as bright as John had ever seen it in Hell, a monochromatic whitish-gray that modestly constricted his pupils. Try as he might to keep that image of a ticking clock in his mind, he had lost track of it during their transfer from the galleon to a longboat and during their passage to the south shore of the Thames. They were somewhere in the fourth hour since the dawn but he was unsure how much time they had until 10 a.m.

Now, with the Iberian ships coming about and sailing toward the estuary, they were on dry land and they were running. John had Sam in his arms and Trevor had Belle.

John looked over his shoulder. Delia wasn't keeping up.

"Help her!" John shouted and Martin and Tony fell back and each took one of her hands.

"There it is!" Emily shouted when the thatched roofs of the village came into view across the meadow. "We're almost there."

Ben led the security procession from the detention level down to the old subterranean MAAC control room which they had begun calling the transfer room. All the Hellers were shackled and dressed in cotton jumpsuits to spare them the indignity of nakedness on the other side, which according to Molly was a nice touch. Because the young rover, Mitchum, worried Murphy and Rix the most, his wrists and ankles were also bound with natural hemp so that they could deal with him safely if and when they transferred.

In the well of the control room they were chained to iron loops bolted to the floor. Thirty feet below their feet, the giant synchrotron was nearly at full power. Eleven Hellers stood there, sizing each other up, Murphy and Rix trying to keep things light for their ladies.

No one at MAAC had any idea whether John and Emily and Trevor and Brian had been able to find Delia and Arabel, Sam and Belle, the Ockendon eight. No one knew if anyone had managed to get back to Dartford for the exchange. No one knew what would happen if an attempt was made to exchange eleven Hellers for sixteen people. Would five of their own be left behind in Hell? Leroy Bitterman had grown fond of saying at high-level government briefings, "Politicians seem to think that saying the following is anathema but scientists embrace it: ladies and gentlemen, *I don't know what's going to happen.*"

Ben stood before the Hellers and looking only at Rix, Murphy, Christine, and Molly, he said, "Fifteen minutes to go. Godspeed."

The control room was locked and the guards were withdrawn from the level.

Ben chose not to join the dignitaries and technicians in the recreation center control room. He wanted to be alone with his thoughts. He walked through the MAAC lobby, the windows and doors frosted to keep out the prying telescopic lenses of the media camped outside the perimeter fence. Ben had grown comfortable with John's security office. He went there and with a sense of detachment that matched his mood, he watched both the control room and the transfer room on closed-circuit monitors and wondered if he could ever be as close to his wife as Murphy and Rix were to theirs.

The muddy road outside Dirk and Duck's cottage was deserted. A few wisps of white smoke puffed from their chimney.

All of the Earthers, save the children, were bilious and gasping from the stress of the day and the exertion of the run through the meadows. Tony said he was going to throw up and Martin patted his back. Delia could no longer stand. She dropped to the road and sat cross-legged with her head in her hands. Tracy sat beside Delia and held her. Arabel took Belle from Trevor and Emily took Sam.

"This the spot, guv?" Trevor asked, between pants.

John caught his breath to say, "This is it. I hope to God we're not too late."

"We're not too late," Emily gasped.

"How do you know?" John asked.

"I just don't think we are. Sorry, not very scientific."

John called over to the cottage. "Hey Dirk, it's John Camp. Where's my beer?"

The cottage door opened.

Every door up and down the road opened.

English soldiers with muskets poured out, lining both sides of the lane.

John told his people not to move.

"So close," Delia panted. "We were so close."

A large man dressed in finery appeared in Dirk's door, a mug in his hand. "Here is your beer, John Camp," King Henry said, "and I am drinking it!"

When Henry stepped into the road others followed. Cromwell was there, looking pensive. Solomon Wisdom glanced fearfully at John and gave the impression that were it not for all these armed soldiers, he would be nowhere near the place. Dirk and Duck, awed by the presence of their monarch, still looked sad their friends had walked into a trap.

John pointed threateningly at Wisdom and said, "Last time I show you mercy, Solomon. Last time."

"You burned my house," Wisdom shouted. "You stole my silver and gold. Did you think I wouldn't find a way to get even?"

"You have no idea what I'm going to do to you one day," John shouted, causing Wisdom to retreat behind some soldiers.

Cromwell called out, "Throw all your weapons down, if you please."

John told his people to empty their belts. A small pile of swords, knives and pistols were dropped into the mud.

Henry stepped forward.

"Who is that?" Delia asked.

John said, "Delia and Arabel, meet King Henry."

"Tell me," Henry demanded, "what became of Queen Matilda?"

Delia asked for help to stand and Martin lent an arm. Tracy rose too.

"I'm afraid she didn't make it out of Strasbourg in one piece," John said.

"A pity," Henry said. "After so many years I felt a modicum of fondness for her. But these, these marvels will wipe away my lamentations. Behold these children! I do wish to have all you persons to reside at my court, and yes, good physician, my leg is much improved thanks to your medicinal tea," he said with a nod toward Martin. "But the true reason I am come here is these children! More precious than jewels, more precious than gold! Now come one and all. We will return to Hampton Palace. Guards, take them!"

"Sixty seconds to full power," Matthew announced. "Seventeen TeV, eighteen, nineteen …"

There were too many faces for Ben to watch at one time. He chose two: Leroy Bitterman who was biting his lip and Jason Rix who was smiling at his wife.

"No, wait!" John shouted. "You don't want to frighten them, do you, Your Majesty. Why don't you take the boy? You can hold him. His name is Sam. You always wanted a son, didn't you? Almost everything you did in life, all those wives, all those murders, you did them to have a son."

Henry wiped at his cheek and looked at the moisture on his finger, as if remembering something long forgotten.

"John, what are you doing?" Emily said.

He didn't answer. He kept addressing the king. "You only had one son. Do you remember how happy you were when Edward was born? He was only ten when you died. You only had him for ten short years. This boy, Sam, can be yours for much longer. Would you like to hold him?"

Arabel said, "No," but Emily fell in with John. "It's okay, Arabel. Don't worry."

Henry began to walk through the mud.

"Your Majesty, please," Cromwell said.

"Hold him up, Emily," John said.

"John, are you sure?"

"Do you trust me?" he asked her.

She held Sam, wriggling, by the armpits and straightened her arms out.

Henry reached for the boy. In one fluid motion John bent to retrieve a knife from his boot and stepped forward to wrap an arm around the king's neck.

He pressed the knife to Henry's jugular and shouted at the soldiers to stay back. "One move! One move from any of you and I will spill his blood."

"Fifteen seconds," Matthew said, "twenty-five TeV, twenty-six …"

"Do as he says," Henry cried. "Do not advance."

"That's good," John said, squeezing his neck harder. "And you don't move either. I don't want to hurt you, I really don't but I will."

Emily clutched Sam back to her chest.

"What now?" Trevor asked.

"We wait and pray," John said.

All eyes in the control room were on the countdown clock. Protons were hurtling around the great London oval at the speed of light and colliding with one another releasing tiny bursts of almost unimaginable energy.

Matthew saw his instruments climb past 29 TeV and he filled his lungs to shout, "Full power!"

As Ben was watching Bitterman's tense face, he thought at first the power had failed to the cameras or the monitor.

Bitterman's face was gone.

Everyone was gone.

The control room was empty.

All the chairs, all the terminals, everything was there, but no people.

An automated voice was blaring, "Power-down protocol initiated, power-down protocol complete."

Ben was blinking in shock at the blank screen when motion on the transfer room screen caught his attention.

He jumped up and ran through the MAAC lobby toward the elevators, screaming at his agents there to follow him.

The elevator ride down to the transfer room level seemed to take forever and with every long second, Ben felt the pressure building inside his head.

He ran to the locked doors and ordered them opened.

There was hugging and there were tears and there were two restless children running about with abandon.

Trevor let go of Arabel and called to Ben, "Never any doubt, mate, never a moment's doubt."

In something akin to a trance, Ben hugged Delia, performed a headcount and said, "Not all of you made it."

"We lost some people," John said. "But we picked up one gentleman."

Ben stared into the face of a large, regally dressed man looking around

449

the room in befuddlement.

"Ben Wellington, I'd like you to meet King Henry the Eighth. Your Majesty, this man serves the queen of England, Elizabeth the Second."

Ben couldn't speak.

"Where are my men?" Henry mumbled. "Where is Cromwell? Where is Dartford?"

"We'll explain everything," John said. "I'm sorry I had to manhandle you."

"Are we really home?" Tony asked, blinking through his tears. Martin put his arm around him.

"We are," Emily assured him. "We're really home. Ben, did they power-down all right? Were there any problems? I need to speak with Matthew and my team."

"I think there was a problem," Ben said weakly.

"What kind of problem, Ben?" she asked, her voice constricted with fear.

"They're gone. They're all gone."

They rode the elevators up, Henry blanching at the feeling of acceleration.

Emily was pumping Ben for more information but he had none. As the elevator slowed she asked him, "Did our experts come up with a solution?"

"I was told they came up empty," he said.

As soon as the elevator doors opened Ben's mobile went off. The signal had been blocked below ground.

Henry's mouth went slack as he looked around the glass and steel lobby.

John and Emily watched Ben's face with alarm as he took his call. It was the face of someone being put through a wringer.

"Slow down," Ben said. "For Christ's sake, please slow down. All right. Yes, I know you can't reach the DG or Trotter or Smithwick. I see. Where? Yes? Good lord. All right, listen up. Call Downing Street and call the MOD. I need to address the Cobra committee immediately. Get a helicopter over to Dartford to take us into London. And notify Buckingham Palace that they need to have the Queen on stand-by to meet someone important."

He pocketed the phone.

"John, Emily, Trevor," Ben said, pulling them aside. "I appreciate you must have gone through more than I'll ever know, but I need you to come with me to London. Everyone else will be run through medical checks in the infirmary and we'll have to keep them in quarantine until we get our stories straight. Our visitor, well, we'll have to figure out what to do with him too."

"What were you just told?" John asked.

"It's chaos out there. There are a very large number of men, Hellers, by the sound of them, violently assaulting people in Leatherhead. An entire class of boys has disappeared from a boarding school near Sevenoaks, and there's some kind of major disturbance ongoing at a shopping center in Upminster."

John put his arm around Emily and the two of them sat down on a lobby sofa.

"You okay?" he asked.

"No, are you?"

"Not really," he said. "Are you up for this?"

"What choice do we have?" she asked.

He tried to smile. "I'd say none. At least we got your sister and the kids back."

"Thank God for that. But here's the rub, John." She tried to keep going but she began to weep. He comforted her as best he could and she was able to finish her awful thought. "I think the one person who knows how to fix this horrible mess is still in Hell. We're going to have to go back and find Paul Loomis."

Read on for an excerpt from **Down: Floodgate**, *book three in the* **Down** *trilogy.*

Excerpt
Down: Floodgate

1

Half the boys were standing ankle-deep in muddy pond water. The other five were a few feet away on boggy land. None of them said a word until Harry Shipley, the youngest by almost a year, a boy prone to panic attacks in the best of circumstances, began to blubber. He was the only thirteen-year-old, officially too young for the form, but academically too advanced to have been held back.

"Not now, Harry," Angus ordered, searching the bleak landscape for anything familiar. "Not a good time."

Angus Slaine was head boy of the Year Tens at Belmeade School. He was tall for his age, devilishly handsome with an angular face and longish blonde hair. Glynn Bond, his best friend, was the first to slosh out of the water. Angus followed and Glynn offered a hand.

"What the fuck?" Glynn said. He was a muscular boy with a solid wrestler's body and a low center of gravity.

Angus removed his loafers and emptied them. "Is that a question or a statement?" he asked of Glynn.

"I want to know what's happening," Glynn said, emptying his own shoes.

Boris Magnusson's mouth was stupidly open. "We all do," he said.

Harry was pulling at his loose woolen trousers that had slipped halfway down his backside. Between sobs he announced that his belt buckle was missing.

"Shut up, Harry," Angus snapped. "I won't say it again. Would you three stop looking like wankers and get out of the water?"

The boys obeyed and joined the others on the soft grass. There, the lot of them tried to make sense of what had just occurred. They had gone back to their dormitory to change out of their PE kits into school uniforms for maths class. It was their first GCSE year and although exams were a year away the pressure was mounting, particularly for the weaker students. It was Belmeade practice and part of the mystique of the elite boarding school to push the boys to sit the exams at the end of Year Eleven. Boris and Nigel Mountjoy were struggling academically and it had fallen to Angus to try to sort them out. The answer had been staring at him in the form of Harry's pimply, rodentine face. Annoying Harry. The maths whizz. The one they called Shitley, the boy every pupil wanted to punch. Angus made a tacit deal: Harry would tutor Nigel and Boris in exchange for his protection, and the arrangement had stuck. They were about to leave their dormitory with five minutes to spare, more than enough time to cross the green, run up the stairs, and find their desks in Mr. Van Ness's classroom, when, in an instant, they were in a clearing surrounded by woods, half in and half out of a scummy pond.

Danny Leung asked the others if their uniforms were as messed up as his. He was the ultimate outsider who had worked himself into a position of respect by dint of his mad footballing skills. His father was the cultural attaché at the Chinese embassy. When Danny enrolled at Belmeade as a junior boy, Angus's father had made the casual remark at the supper table that Mr. Leung was probably a spy and Angus had duly reported the gem to his mates. Danny was henceforward, Red Danny.

"It's more than my belt buckle. My zipper's gone, my buttons are gone, my tie's gone missing."

The other boys had the same wardrobe problems.

Craig Rotenberg asked if all of them had eaten porridge for breakfast.

"What kind of stupid question is that?" Glynn asked.

"It's not stupid," Craig said. "Maybe we were drugged. Maybe we were knocked out and taken out of school."

"I didn't have porridge," Nigel said.

"Me neither," Danny said. "I hate porridge."

"It doesn't mean we weren't drugged," Craig said.

"Natural materials." They all looked at Harry who repeated it more emphatically. "Natural materials."

"What are you going on about, you git?" Nate Blanchard asked angrily.

"Our shirts and socks and underwear are cotton," Harry said, sniffing back his tears. "Our blazers and trousers are wool. Our shoes are leather. All the metal bits, the plastic buttons, the polyester ties, that's what's gone missing."

"Who the hell cares about our clothes?" Boris yelled. "Our entire bloody school's gone missing!"

"We'll need to have a look-about," Angus said, sweeping his arm at the encircling woods. "There's bound to be someone around."

"How're we supposed to keep our trousers up?" Boris asked.

Kevin Pickles was a lad who had long compensated for his short stature with a rapier wit. Making other boys laugh was a damned sight better than being called gherkin. He had wandered away from the group and was now calling to them from tall grass halfway around the pond.

"How much will you give me to keep your willies from showing?"

"What did you find?" Danny called back.

Kevin held two fishing poles high over his head and ran back to join the others. Angus inspected them and declared them to be rubbish. They were hardly more than long, whittled branches with lengths of crude line tied to the ends. The barbed hooks, complete with writhing worms, were carved from bone.

"Let me see one," Glynn said, taking a rod and inspecting the line. "What's this made of? It's not nylon."

Stuart Cobham was the fisherman of the group. He snatched the rod from Glynn's hand, passed the line through his pinched fingers and said, "I think it's gut."

"Gross." That from Andrew Pender, a pale, willowy boy who counted on Harry to be the principal recipient of derision.

Stuart tested the strength of the line and declared it perfectly adequate for its proposed task.

"We don't have anything to cut it," Nigel said.

"Sure we do," Stuart said, putting the line in his mouth. He bit down and used his lower teeth as a saw until it cut through. In several minutes they each had several inches of line to cinch up their belts and some of the boys secured flapping shirts too.

Angus was aware that everyone was waiting for him to choose a direction of travel. He looked around for inspiration. The sky was a featureless pale shade of gray. The woods surrounding them looked more black than green. There was a light breeze carrying a hint of a bad odor.

"That way," Angus said.

No one asked him to justify his decision. They followed him through the meadow in a loose scrum. Glynn drew alongside him.

"There's got to be an explanation," Glynn said.

"Maybe we're being punked," Angus replied. "Maybe it's a TV program."

"I don't see any cameras," Glynn said.

Harry was crying again.

"Do you want me to shut him up?" Glynn asked.

Angus didn't answer. He was pointing at something on the ground. "Look at that," Angus said.

Stuart was employing one of the fishing rods as a walking stick. He used it to part the grass where Angus was pointing. "I think it's blood," he said.

"I think you're right," Angus agreed. "There's more over there. There's a trail of it. I think it goes into the woods."

"We should be careful," Glynn said. "We need weapons."

"What do you think's going to happen?" Boris asked in a mocking tone. "Are you scared a polar bear's going to pop out like in *Lost*?"

"Try not to be a complete prick, Boris," Angus said. "Everyone stay sharp. If we are being punked and filmed our reactions will be on YouTube until the day we die. You'll never, ever get laid if every girl on the planet sees that you're pathetic wankers."

The meadow grasses gave way to a trampled-down path through a thicket of brambles. Just beyond lay a dense forest. Walking through the thicket along the path, Glynn's jumper caught on thorns. He pulled away and left a small patch of Belmeade blue behind with a bit of gold embroidery, part of the S in School. Once inside the wood, the canopy blotted out much of the thin daylight. Tall pine trees creaked in the breeze. The forest floor was a carpet of needles, ferns, and large, flat mushrooms. Angus lost the blood trail but found it again with dots of crimson on a creamy expanse of fungus.

The boys were walking in silence. Even Harry was quiet but his prominent Adam's apple bobbed up and down with each wooly-mouthed swallow.

Angus stopped and turned to signal the boys to stop too.

They all heard it. A low moan.

Danny picked up a thick stick and some of the others followed suit. Ahead was a naturally fallen tree, its massive trunk and roots lying on the ground.

Here's where the sixth-form boys are going to get us, Angus thought. They'll be springing up, filming us with their mobile phones and having a good old laugh at our expense. Don't let them make us look foolish.

He took a deep breath, walked up to the tree trunk and slowly leaned over it.

"Shit!"

The other boys recoiled at his cry but Glynn, suspecting a ruse, clapped Angus on the back and looked over himself.

"Jesus."

A gaunt young man was looking up at them with pleading eyes. "Help me."

"What is it?" Nigel called out from the rear.

"He's hurt," Glynn said. "He's hurt bad."

The other boys slowly came forward, almost too scared to look. They lined up on their side of the tree and forced themselves to look over. Kevin was too short and had to hike himself onto the log.

"We should help him," Stuart said.

Angus found the courage to speak to the young man. "What happened to you?"

"Rovers," he rasped. "Gut-stabbed."

"You're stabbed?" Glynn said.

The man took his hands off his abdomen. His intestines were visible through the gaping wound.

Several of the boys dropped back a few feet. Harry threw up.

"We need to get you help," Angus said. "Which way is help?"

"Are they still about?" the man panted.

"Who?"

"The rovers."

"I don't know what you're talking about. We didn't see anyone else."

The man said, "At least I won't be eaten."

"Did he just say eaten?" Danny asked Craig.

Angus began to climb over the log. When Glynn asked what he was doing he replied, "Let's just see if this whole thing's staged. He's probably trying to frighten us with a sack of sheep guts."

Glynn followed and the two boys kneeled at the man's side.

"Christ, it's real," Angus said, when the man moved his hands away. He turned his head and gagged at the man's rank odor. "It's fucking real. What the hell is going on?"

"You got any water, friend?" the man asked.

"No but we can try to bring you some from the pond," Glynn said.

"I haven't seen you before. Which village do you hail from?"

"We're at Belmeade School," Angus said. "Well we were."

"You're too young."

"Too young for what?" Stuart said from the other side of the log.

"Did you see my mate?" the man said. "When the rovers come we hoofed it. They got me but I hope my mate got free."

Danny noticed something off to the right. A patch of dark blue on the forest floor.

While the boys were debating how they were going to bring water to the man they heard Danny calling. "Guys, I think you need to come here."

There was a blue cap lying next to a man's head. The rest of the body was several feet away on bloodstained pine needles.

Transfixed by the horror, the boys looked into the head's staring eyes and then those eyes blinked and the dry lips moved.

Most of them screamed.

They ran back to the gut-stabbed young man.

"Your friend's dead!" Angus shouted.

"He's not dead."

"Tell us where we are and what's going on," Angus demanded. "We won't help you unless you tell us."

"You don't know?"

"We have no idea, all right?" Glynn yelled at the top of his lungs.

"You must be new 'uns," the man rasped. He managed a short painful laugh. "Well let me be the first to welcome you to your new home. Welcome to Hell."

Find out what happens next in **Down: Floodgate**, *available now!*

Interested in reading other books by Glenn Cooper?

Try the following titles:

- The Down trilogy -
Down: Pinhole
Down: Floodgate

- Stand alone books -
The Tenth Chamber
The Resurrection Maker
The Devil Will Come
Near Death

- The Library of the Dead trilogy -
The Library of the Dead
The Book of Souls
The Keepers of the Library